The Broken Earth

To Mary & Martha —
sisters in crime

Joel Terry May

The
Broken
Earth

America's Journey Home

JOEL TERRY MAY

ARCHWAY
PUBLISHING

Archway Publishing books may be ordered through booksellers or by contacting:

Archway Publishing
1663 Liberty Drive
Bloomington, IN 47403
www.archwaypublishing.com
1 (888) 242-5904

Because of the dynamic nature of the Internet, any web addresses or
links contained in this book may have changed since publication and
may no longer be valid. The views expressed in this work are solely those
of the author and do not necessarily reflect the views of the publisher,
and the publisher hereby disclaims any responsibility for them.

Any people depicted in stock imagery provided by Getty Images are
models, and such images are being used for illustrative purposes only.
Certain stock imagery © Getty Images.

ISBN: 978-1-4808-7648-4 (sc)
ISBN: 978-1-4808-7649-1 (e)

Library of Congress Control Number: 2019903746

Print information available on the last page.

Archway Publishing rev. date: 5/24/2019

After the war that destroyed the fabric of America, soldiers, slaves and the rest of the country must find its way again. Where do the slaves go when they are placed on the road of freedom, and how do they survive without the means necessary? What does the vanquished soldier find when he struggles to return to a southland destroyed and defeated? How does citizenry right the ship of state? These are the questions these characters must face in their journey home.

CHAPTER 1

Appomattox

THE BRIGHT RAYS OF HOPE BEAT BACK THE gloom of night, pushing darkness into its hiding places, while mockingbirds, blue jays and the mourning dove with its gentle coos competed for their audiences. The rays of sunlight were beginning to break through the blanket of fog that floated over the alluvial creek bottom. The Creator's handiwork was on full display for all to witness. Every mighty brushstroke made known in each beautiful tree, each wildflower, each wispy cloud above in the bright blue sky and the meandering of every stream that flowed through the green meadows afoot. All things were coming alive with the new dawn. The morning sun rose to illuminate a new day and the deeds of man.

The peace that cloaked the countryside this fine morning followed a day of battle, where the depths of Hell were dredged up to corrupt the serenity of every heart, of every young man placed there. These were the days that Satan himself ran with liberty and unbridled zeal throughout the embattled land of the young nation. And he would not relinquish his hold until the Creator's anger caused the mountains to tumble down upon the injustice that led a sovereign nation on a path of doom.

The Almighty's anger was yet to be assuaged because there was a long road to recovery, whose ruts ran like deep wounds being cleansed with blood overflowing. The souls of forgotten soldiers, whose bleached white bones lay on the hillsides and along the roadways, cried out for *honor*. Souls of slaves and their grandchildren yet to be born cried out for *justice*, and the souls of the broken called out for *mercy*.

John, in his dream state, thought he heard the sound of men

hammering lumber together while building something like a barn or a house; however, it was the sound of a huge black crow pecking at his head with its long narrow beak trying to dislodge a ragged piece of flesh from his temple. His eyes popped open and he got his first glimpse of the bird driving its narrow beak into his skull, determined to tear away the bloody flap of skin. Yelling at the bird did not get it to leave, but it continued to tug at him. John started to flop like a fish pulled from the water and thrown onto the bank. His arms were pinned down. He was stacked, like cordwood, with the bodies of dead soldiers on the battlefield waiting to be buried that morning. He succeeded in getting loose from his predicament and the crow flew away.

He stood up and looked down at his battered body, almost naked, except for the tattered pair of long underwear. He reeked of death. He started running as fast as he could across the battlefield, dodging dead horses and dead soldiers, falling into holes created by mortar blast and climbing back out, screaming all the way until he reached the creek beside the tree line.

"Looks like that soldier is in a hurry to get away," commented another soldier on burial detail.

"He just missed a quick trip to *Hell*. I wish all of them would get up and run off so we could sit in the shade and sip on that jug of corn whiskey you found," said the other.

John, half stumbling, jumped into the creek and submerged himself for an extended time hoping to cleanse himself of the putrid smell of decaying flesh. Catching his breath, he dragged his trembling body to a sandbar and sat there gathering his thoughts. Was this a terrible dream or was he awake?

He sat there waiting for his heartbeat to slow down and his body to stop shaking. Inside his head a voice spoke, "*It is not your time, go home now, and find your purpose.*" Was he still dreaming, or was he having a nightmare?

He sat in the water for a very long time pondering what his next move should be while minnows and tadpoles swam between his legs. Sand started to collect where he sat in the fast moving stream, and began to cover his legs. And then he heard another voice, but this voice was coming from the outside of his head this time.

"Hey friend, after your baptism is complete come up the creek bank and share a cup of coffee with me!" the voice said.

John stood up, still fairly groggy in his thinking, turned around and looked at the man. It was a Union soldier, an officer at that. John wasn't sure if he should fight him or drink his coffee. He looked at himself, soaking wet, mostly naked and half dazed. He really wasn't dressed for battle. Once he considered his situation, he felt the gentlemanly thing to do was accept his offer of coffee.

"A hand up this slippery bank would be much appreciated," John requested, extending his hand.

He began to assess the man's camp quickly upon releasing his hand and regaining his footing on solid ground again. He saw two horses ground hitched in a grassy patch busily cropping grass, and a dead man propped against an oak tree, in a seated position with his pants down around his ankles. The dead man was not a soldier as his eastern attire would indicate.

"I would like to thank you for your hospitality," John commented, accepting a cup of coffee. "I think it most gracious of you to treat your prisoner in such a way. I just hope I don't end up in that man's predicament."

"Sir, you are not my prisoner," the Yankee told him. "You obviously are not aware that Robert E. Lee has accepted Ulysses S. Grant's gracious terms of surrender. The war is over and you can go home now."

"Let me explain that poor man's circumstances. I came upon him at dusk as I was searching for a place to make camp. I heard him scream and came quickly to find him bitten by a rattler. I killed the snake and assessed his situation, which appeared to be grave."

"I told him he was bitten by a rattlesnake and he said, *"Rattlesnake my ass."* I confirmed that was exactly where he was bitten. He thought he had squatted on a broken stick or was caught by a sawbrier because of the sharpness of the sting. I told him his time was short since the snake had bitten him in a place that I could not administer aid. The venom worked quickly and I gathered all the information I could to relay to his employer, and his family."

"I made him as comfortable as possible and waited with him as he passed. He was very upset that he lived through the war just to die by snakebite. I would appreciate your help with the burial. You might want to search his gear for some clothes. I hope you did not have some perverted notions about this scene upon first appearances."

"Of course not, it was just a little peculiar, and I believe I have seen it all in this crazy war. I can't believe this madness is over and I am still alive. My name is John Fairfax Bernard, and I hail from New Orleans, Louisiana. It is a pleasure to make your acquaintance," said John.

"Let me introduce myself. I am Sean Matthew O'Brien, from Jackson, Mississippi. Folks just call me Matt."

John looked at him with surprise, "So you deserted your country and fought on the Yankee's side!"

"No, I fought for my country and you fought for the deserters, mister!" Matt responded.

"Before you start judging me," Matthew declared, "and calling me a traitor you better hear me out. I had an appointment to West Point by recommendation of Joseph Davis, elder brother to Jefferson Davis. His family was dear friends with my family. That was before the Confederacy came about."

"Upon graduation I was fortunate enough to be assigned to our nation's capitol, where I met Abraham Lincoln. I worked at the President's requests and it is my privilege to serve him in the capacity of personal attaché. As an emissary I relay messages from the President to his commanders in the field. I also communicate with the Confederate command when necessary. I am not required to spy and I don't. My family does not hold with slavery and neither do I."

"And furthermore, this war was inevitable; the institution of slavery had no place in a nation that holds freedom as one of its basic tenets. However, war could have been avoided, but our Southern Senators and Congressmen were driven by the demands of the wealthy planters that put them in office. They saw it as their sworn duty to secede from the Union. We may have lost an entire generation because of it."

"I hope we can be civil and maybe I can help you find your way home, if it is your desire to travel south," eloquently stated Matt.

"*Boy*, Matt! You sure can talk up a storm. I am beyond judging someone. I only joined because the Yankees invaded the South. I am through fighting this war. I will leave that to the cowards who stayed home and made big speeches. I just want to get back there as soon as possible. I will look over that dead man's belongings and see what things I can use. I am feeling a little naked standing here in my long-johns. What about his horse?" John tentatively asked.

"You can have his horse and the rest of his things. He had a nice saddle and saddlebags, and a new repeating rifle too. He doesn't need any of that stuff now. I just want some help getting him into the ground before the sun heats up and he starts getting ripe," reasoned Matt.

Looking over the valise lying in the bushes, John found a rather large wardrobe. "Did you see this leather suitcase of his," asked John, "it has some fancy duds, writing materials, pictures, paper money, gold, razor and fine smelling soap. He was some fancy."

Matt chuckled. "No, I did not see that, but, you surely could use that soap. It is now the spoils of war. His untimely death is your gain. Please bathe before you dress in those nice clothes."

Matt shared some bacon, cold biscuits and hot coffee with John. He had a letter in his hand intended for General Grant from President Lincoln. He was contemplating the route he would take to deliver the letter.

"Are you returning to your unit this morning, or will you be interested in going with me to the signing of the armistice," he asked John politely.

John looked at him very seriously and said, "I don't know what I will do. Do they put us in prison or do they tell us to go home, I mean just like that, like nothing has happened?"

"Only those accused of war crimes will go to prison," Matt assured him.

"I have an odd feeling about that letter in your hand. The man that wrote it is in some sort of danger!" John declared to Matt.

"You took a hard blow to your head. There is a letter from the President; although, you could be right because he has been in danger ever since he took office," Matt reflected.

"Yes my head is hurting something bad," John remarked, while placing the palm of his hand against his bloody forehead.

"If I'm not mistaken, you will be asked to swear allegiance to the constitution and promise not to bear arms against the United States again, and then lay down your arms and go home. Since you have no uniform and no weapons that were used in battle, except your newly acquired things, I believe you will be good to go; however, you can go with me to the formal surrender and stand with your brothers in arms, if you wish," Matt reassured him.

John helped the Yankee bury the dead man in a shallow grave. Then he mounted his newly acquired horse, freshly bathed and finely dressed, and wearing the handsome boots taken from the dead man. He knew the man would never again fully appreciate them as he could. He crossed back over the creek in the direction of the battlefield littered with the dead carcasses of mules, horses, oxen and soldiers. He carefully maneuvered to reach a group of soldiers sitting around a small campfire drinking coffee given to them by their Yankee counterparts after the fighting ceased.

John rode up next to the group and politely asked, "Can you tell me the whereabouts of *Company C*? I have to rejoin them."

"Fellow I don't know who you are, but this war is over, we have been defeated; furthermore, what's left of Lee and this man's army has been scattered to hell!" said the haggardly looking, and beaten down Rebel soldier.

"We are just asking ourselves how the hell we are gonna find our way back home, with nothin' but this here donated Yankee coffee and nothing to eat. Here we sit, like some pack of mangy dogs, and you saunter up on that fine horseflesh, wearing those fine clothes. We were just thinking how that there horse will help a mite in solving our dilemma" stated the surly soldier. With that said he slowly lifted himself off the ground and started in John's direction.

"What you think about that mister?" he said with laughter and indignation.

"I think you might have another think coming," boldly stated John, as he pulled out his newly acquired revolver. "I am a soldier, just like you, and I was fortunate enough to climb down from that burial pile this morning and walk over to those woods over yonder and find myself a dead man. You go find your *own salvation* or step up and swallow some of this here lead I am about to donate on your behalf."

There was a long pause and the soldier stepped back while reconsidering the situation. "I guess I have no takers! Good day!" He pointed his horse in the direction of the nearest known town, *Appomattox Courthouse.*

Forlorn and dejected, John rode his bay like they had known each other for years. It was an exceptional animal, not your old crowbait that was evident at war's end. He pondered his next move, not having a sense of direction and still weak from battle. John passed groups of soldiers all hump shouldered and downtrodden. He looked into each of their faces, sad as they were, hoping to find someone that bore the slightest bit of familiarity to him.

"Hey, Thomas Smith, is that you!" called John from his horse with an elation that even surprised him.

"Yeah, I am Thomas Smith, who are you?" he replied.

"It's me, *John ... John Bernard!* Don't you recognize me?" he said to his old friend.

"John, last I seen of you they were stacking you on a pile with them other stiffs. I thought you was dead and now you stand before me in a new suit-of-clothes, on some fine horse, what's doing friend," half smiled Thomas.

"What the hell! Did you die and Saint Peter sent you back in them fine duds?"

"No, I ain't dead you nut, but they thought I was, with this wound to my forehead," explained John. "I woke up on that pile of rotten, smelly, dead Rebs and I decided to run down to the creek to take a bath."

A group of fellow soldiers were starting to gather around to hear this story.

"Well, you see, there was this Yankee sittin' on the creek bank, and he offered me some coffee. I am some suspicious and confused, so I just took him up on it. He told me, the war was over and I decided I did not have to kill him. Then I seen this here dead man propped up against the tree with his britches down around his ankles. I was again unsure of what to do next. He explained the man had been bitten on the butt, when he was doing his business, by a rattlesnake. So that is how I came about these clothes, this horse and the rig that goes with it."

"Well, that sounds like a farfetched story to me, but likely true. Can you really believe it?" Thomas asked. "This war is finally over, and we are still alive and going home to our families; if they are still there," stated his friend with a long exhale of wind demonstrating his doubt of his last remark.

"We are going to the signing of the truce. They're going to make us swear allegiance and give up our guns. I hate to see them take General Lee's sword. You might get to keep your gun since you ain't dressed like no soldier. Do you want to go with us?"

"Yeah, I'll go with you, what else have I got to do on this historical occasion! It ain't like I made other plans," so aptly put by the young man striding into the beginning of a new life with an uncertain future.

They made their way down the road in the direction everyone else was going. The way was lined with straggling soldiers weary with battle fatigue. Together they marched into a larger gather where Yankees and Rebels stood around talking to each other like old friends at a church social expecting dinner on the grounds. It was a beautiful day with high floating clouds in a sea of blue sky. It was a surreal event, and hard to imagine with everything that had taken place over the last five years.

The war had finally come to an end and soldiers, along with their families, and millions of freed slaves would begin the journey of forging a new nation. It would be a colossal attempt to repair the fabric of a nation that had been rent beyond repair.

CHAPTER 2

"HEY! THOMAS, HAVE YOU GOT THAT SACK OF personal effects I asked you to hang onto if I died?" asked John, as he rode his horse beside the trudging soldier.

"Yeah, I still have it. What is so special about it?" queried Thomas, "I never understood why you ask me to keep-up with it, because, you never told me what to do with it if you died."

"I didn't plan on dying, but just in case I did, I didn't want to lose it. That's why! Carson Walker, our friend from Charleston gave me a book, some kind of journal, he kept about the war. He was doggedly insistent that it find its way home to his sister and mom. He put a lot of stock in that book. He went on about the value of the written word to those that lived after the author had spent his life. He always held up the Bible as an example and said without it we would be just wandering through life with no perception of right and wrong! I always thought more people were killed in the name of *religion* than anything else," John commented.

Confederate soldiers strolled around and ate heartily of the food provided so graciously by the Union army. Those witnessing the gathering of armies would think it a family reunion; likewise, it would have been hard to establish what enmity could have existed between these men to cause them to fight each other, much less actually kill one another. It was commonly stated among soldiers that this was a *rich man's war and a poor man's battle.*

It did not seem possible that the madness of war: the battles, the deaths, the mutilations of the human body, the scarring of the American landscape, the destruction of farm and families, the burning of cities and towns and the total and complete upheaval of the societal structure of a nation, could come to a screeching halt with the meeting of two men, a few kind words and the simple stroke of the pen. It must be true that the pen is mightier than the sword. *Unbelievable!* Absolutely unbelievable!

A silence fell upon the gathering soldiers, as three horsemen meandered through the group. The silence was so complete, and so precisely orchestrated, one would have thought a heavenly conductor had set his baton. Two soldiers led the way for a single rider sitting gallantly atop the regal beast commonly referred to as Traveler, the commander's chosen mount, his close and cherished companion. It was the General himself, Robert E. Lee! Not a single man spoke, not even a whisper, as they watched events unfold. They knew they were privileged to witness history. On April 9, 1865, in the parlor of Wilmer McLean, Generals Grant and Lee met to discuss terms for surrender. It was a mutually agreed upon site.

McLean was no stranger to the ravages of war. It was upon his farm that the battle of First Bull Run occurred in Manassas, Virginia; afterwards, he sold that farm and moved away to avoid the horrors of war, so he thought! That was the start of the war and now it was the end of the rebellion, as Northerners viewed it.

It was Lee that arrived first, followed shortly by General Grant. Grant's aides assembled outside the home until which time they were summoned to convene in the living room of McLean's home.

It was Grant that spoke first, "I met you once before, General Lee, while we were serving in Mexico, when you came over from General Scott's headquarters to visit Garland's brigade, to which I then belonged. I have always remembered your appearance, and I think I should have recognized you anywhere."

"Yes," replied Lee, "I know I met you on that occasion and I have often thought of it and tried to recollect how you looked, but I have never been able to recall a *single feature*." The old soldier, sixteen years Grant's senior, addressed his counterpart with the utmost sincerity.

They exchanged pleasantries and finally discussed the terms of surrender. Grant, with great respect and admiration, told Lee that his soldiers must take an oath to never take up arms against the United

States again, and they had to surrender their weapons. He made the allowance that officers could retain their side arms, swords, personal baggage and their horses. Soldiers had to give up their horses and mules. Lee had informed Grant that the infantry and cavalry had furnished their own mounts. Grant then amended the terms to allow the cavalry and infantry retention of their horses.

At some point General Lee found himself in a locked stare with Colonel Ely S. Parker, an aide to Grant. Parker was a member of the Seneca tribe of New York. He was writing the final draft of the surrender terms. It was said he had the better handwriting of those present. Lee offered his hand to Parker and Parker responded in kind.

"I am glad there is one true American present here today!" stated Lee to Parker.

At which, Parker replied, *"We are all Americans here!"*

At the conclusion of formalities, Lee bowed to the attendants and followed by his aid, Colonel Marshall, left the McLean house. A soldier delivered his horse, Traveler, to him. Once mounted, he turned to face General Grant, removed his hat and with it saluted the General. General Grant removed his hat and did likewise. The war was finally over, with the exception of some remote outposts.

General Lee made a somber trip back to his army to relay the news. He told them how proud he was of them for their courage and sacrifice and bid them a safe trip home and a good life to follow. Every man to himself turned in somber reflection and took the first step on a long journey home.

Matthew O'Brien had gathered his belongings and proceeded to leave the McLean house. He spoke to General Grant and his entourage, standing on the porch. "I do believe you executed your assignment with the utmost civility and respect in regards to your defeated counterparts. The Commander in Chief could not have performed any more admirably in your stead," so stated Matt.

"It was not my intention to continue the suffering any more than had already been. I have no enmity with my fellow countrymen. We have all suffered enough. Let the dead bury the dead. Fare thee well,

Captain O'Brien. Have a safe journey, and may our paths cross again someday, in better times I hope."

With that said the General turned to the departing Confederate soldiers. He came to attention and saluted the men as they laid down their weapons and walked away in single file. The Union soldiers did likewise, and there was no humiliation afforded the defeated army as they began their long journey home.

There was some disturbance at the point of gather between a man dressed in non-military clothing and a Union soldier. "I will not give up my guns. These were never used in battle I tell you," said John to the soldier.

"But all you *Rebs* have to give up your guns! It's the orders," said the Yank.

"I think I can help you sir," said Matthew, the young Captain, as he moved his horse up beside the two men. "This man has recently joined the ranks of civilian in aid to the recently formed *Commission on Southern Rehabilitation and Repatriation,* and he will be required to retain his firearms and his mount. Will that be sufficient sir?" asked Matthew.

"Well, certainly sir! I was not aware of his circumstances," replied the Private.

Matt motioned for John to move away from the other soldiers to the side so they could speak privately. "I hope I wasn't overstepping my boundaries by volunteering your services for our homeland's reconstruction process Mr. Bernard. It will take many young men with the right attitude and determination to guide and protect the South in her recovery while there are so many that only want to profit from her weakened state. Do I have your commitment sir?"

"Well, I guess so. I seem to be as a fallen leaf on a fast moving stream these days, just looking for somewhere to attach myself. I don't rightfully have my bearing yet. Just this morning, I woke up in burial detail," pondered John.

"And I might add, on the wrong end of that detail!" stated Matt with a smile.

"Then what are we to do now? Where do we go and when do we leave?" asked John

"We need to go to Washington to see Mr. Lincoln. He has a new assignment for us and we need to get acquainted before he gives us the details. We will also need to get provisioned. I think we will pass through Richmond on our way to the nations' capital. Are there any more questions that need addressing John? If there are none at the moment we need to get moving."

"Wait, do you have any openings in that *Commission* for another former soldier, that's looking for *reassignment?*" inquired a tattered Rebel soldier walking from behind.

"To whom do I have the privilege of speaking?" replied Matthew.

"My name is Thomas Smith of the southwest Georgia clan of Smiths. I served alongside Mr. Bernard here with the former army of Northern Virginia. I will be honored to offer my skills as a woodsman, a scout and a *true Southern gentleman.* And, I am also considered a crack shot with all firearms, of which I do not possess at the present; unfortunately, it seems they have been confiscated by Mr. Lincoln," spoken so eloquently by Thomas. He stepped back and waited for a response.

"There just might be an opening. What do you say Mr. Bernard, do we take this rabble with us on our assignment? Can he be trusted to live up to his personal endorsement, or was he overstated?" asked Matt, with a wink unbeknownst to Thomas.

"I think we should take him on with conditions. He must first demonstrate he is capable before we fully commit. We haven't acquired a *pack mule* yet and he looks sturdy of build." They both laughed.

"Follow me Thomas. We need to make a visit to the quartermaster to acquire some gear and a mount for you. We can't have you parading through Washington in that Rebel uniform. They might think we lost the war and are being invaded. They may shoot you on sight. Plus, you could use some cleaning up in the nearest available creek," smiled Matt.

"I ain't wearing no Yankee uniform. They can just shoot me before I do that!" protested Thomas.

They were able to secure a horse for Thomas. Matt had significant authority within the military by way of a letter signed by the President and Grant. He could literally move mountains to get things done with the President's seal.

There was no civilian clothing to be had; that came courtesy of John's acquired wardrobe, but all the necessary gear to outfit Thomas was obtained. They were able to acquire a pack mule and pack. Many things were hard to come by during the war.

They made their way to Washington through Richmond. The streets were littered with the rubble of burned out buildings and destroyed warehouses. People were milling about trying to regain a sense of order after a war that was as close to *hell on earth* as one could possibly be. Some were literally picking up their lives, brick by brick, salvaging any usable remnant left behind after the conquering army passed through. Men would hardly turn their heads as they passed, but women stared at them as if they were evil incarnate. John and Thomas wanted badly to explain that they were not Union, but they pushed on.

They were used to seeing the destruction that resulted from battle. They were battle hardened and had grown accustomed to having death all around them. It was something that they knew from sight, sound, smell and touch. Death and destruction were the canvas and media of war. It was a picture painted much too often for them. It would live with them for the rest of their lives, during waking and sleeping moments, forever, no matter how they wished it wasn't so.

What was it that allowed a man to fight on when others around him perished, day-in and day-out? No one knows, but it had to be special to a man's character to push himself, and, those around him to fight on in the face of imminent doom.

The three men stopped to watch two children, a boy and a girl, digging a woman from beneath the bricks and mortar of a fallen building. The children stopped, stood up and turned in their direction. It became obvious it was their mother they were trying to uncover. John stepped down from his horse and went over to the woman and started to uncover her. He could see that she was face down. The boy, who looked to be ten years old, picked up a stone and hit him in the arm with it. John kept digging. Thomas and Matt got down too, and proceeded to help.

They uncovered the woman. John lifted her, and began to walk down the street carrying her in his arms. The others followed. Matt approached two men with a mule drawn wagon. He asked if they would convey the woman's body and the children to the proper place for her internment. They agreed. Matt offered them money for their troubles. They would not take it, nor did the children when offered. Their hurt and pride would not allow them to accept charity. The three men continued on in silence.

They had been traveling hard and needed to make camp soon. "Let's try a café somewhere for a hot meal, if we can find one," Matt suggested. They found one open at the northern part of town and decided to give it a try.

John was the first one to go inside. "Are you open for business?" he inquired as he stuck his head inside.

"Yes, we have some offerings, come on in," said an older gentleman.

John entered, followed by Thomas and Matt. They sat at a table in the corner. It did not matter where they sat since there were no other patrons.

"We are mighty hungry," added Thomas. "We can eat almost anything, except possum."

The café owner looked sternly at them and said, "It hasn't been our policy to serve Yankees, but that's about to change, as is everything else now that the South done lost the War. I've got beans and pork with a side of cornbread, maybe a slice of cobbler, 'iffin you're lucky."

"That will be fine with us," said Matt, "and they are not *Yankees*. They are confederate soldiers just recently hired to help us rebuild that which has been destroyed. They had to be changed into some better clothes because the lice and fleas had taken up residence in their uniforms and refused to be evicted from them. Maybe we can all become Americans again with the passing of time."

They ate well that night and finished it off with some hot coffee and cobbler. It so happened that the café owner also had some dry goods for sale. They purchased some denim jeans and shirts and undergarments for men. Thomas got himself a new pair of boots as did John. They both got themselves a new corncob pipe and some smoking tobacco. They were feeling mighty splendid. John paid for the purchases with money taken from the dead man.

"All we need now is a mattress to sleep on. I haven't slept in a bed in years," said Thomas, quite pleased with himself.

"I think we will push on to find us a camp site northeast of town tonight," explained Matt. "We have a ways to go tomorrow and we need to get an early start. Let's gather up our things and move out." They got their purchases and the extra food the café owner's wife prepared for them.

John bumped Thomas on the shoulder as they were tying down their things on their horses, "Watch those men next to that hardware store across the street, I don't like their looks. I believe we will see them again, very soon."

"Me too," said Thomas.

A suitable site for camp was located in a gap with a fast moving stream. There was plenty of water for them and their horses. There was also a small clearing close by. They unsaddled the horses and hobbled them so they could graze. It was not cold and they did not need to cook, but they built a decent size fire. Then they made it look like they were sleeping with blankets laid over pine straw away from the fire. They quickly posted themselves back of camp in the edge of the woods. It wasn't long before they heard the sound of horses not far off. They waited in the dark for the bandits to make their move.

They made too much noise to be highwaymen. When all was settled someone let out a scream and they began firing at the pretend men in the blankets. That was the sign for Matt, John and Thomas to cut down on the muzzle flashes. The attackers were bunched together, unfortunately, making them an easier target. It was over as quickly as it had begun. Thomas was the first to move around the camp when no further sounds were heard. He tossed a piece of wood onto the fire and there was no movement. He walked to the other side of camp and stepped into the woods. He found three dead men and one gutshot.

"Looks like we got 'em all but one; he's not long for this world though, been gutshot *allrightee!*" said Thomas.

The others came out and inspected the dead. They walked over to the wounded man. "It appears you dirty bushwhackers done picked the wrong group to hit, *feller!*" commented John to the ailing confederate. "Y'all are probably just some filthy renegades at that. Do you have anything to say for yourself?"

"I'm hurt something terrible, mister. We didn't mean anything bad; it was that Amos Ballard that threatened to kill us if we didn't do what he told us. We ain't renegades, just hungry Rebs wanting something to eat. We thought you was Yankees. Can't you help me, have you got some whiskey? Oh, I want my mama!" cried the young man.

John spoke, "We ain't Yankees and we ain't got no whiskey! You best be making your peace. I will shovel dirt over you and say a few words, but I will leave your partners for the buzzards."

With that said John pulled his pistol, shucked all but one bullet and dropped it beside the young man. They walked away and waited. They heard the pistol fire. The young man suffered no more.

"I could use some coffee, how about you fellows?" asked Matt.

He shut up and squatted down beside the others. Someone was leading some horses in the bushes. They each drew their guns except John who left his with the dying bandit. Into the firelight walked a boy leading two horses.

"I figured they didn't need them anymore and they shouldn't be left to starve," said the boy that they saw earlier trying to dig his mother from under the rubble.

"Well! Are you going to make that coffee or what?"

"Who the hell are you, and don't you know you could have gotten killed out there, son?" asked Thomas.

"My name is Samuel Ambrose Martin, we met today in Richmond. We buried my mom and I left my sister with my aunt Mildred. You looked like tinhorns, the way you was dressed, and I thought I better look after you. You might have gotten yourself killed if I didn't hit that one man with the rock and make him scream out," declared the kid.

"I wondered why someone yelled first," said Matt, "but that does not explain why you are here."

"You don't think I was staying with my *Aunt Mildred*, do you?" Samuel declared. "I've got two horses; I'll sell one and do some sight-seeing. *Now, who's fixin' that coffee?*"

CHAPTER 3

BIRDS WERE SINGING AT FULL THROTTLE, AND horses snorting, wanting a drink of water. Samuel had a fire going and coffee boiling while Matt had fried some bacon to go with the biscuits the café owner's wife had packed for them. Matt intended to reach Washington as soon as possible and would have to drive hard to get there as planned.

"Rise and shine gentlemen, the horses need oats and water. No beauty rest around here," said Matt with a chuckle. Samuel thought that was funny and laughed out loud.

Thomas rolled over, jumped up, and grabbed Samuel while running off to the creek. He jumped in a deeper spot and they both went beneath the water, completely.

"*Wahl*, what was that for? Have you gone loco?" cried Samuel.

"I thought you needed something funnier to laugh about, and a bath," said Thomas with a smile. "Throw me some of that sweet smelling, fancy soap you've got there John." John got up, got his soap and tossed it to Thomas. They were all laughing now, except Samuel.

John went to the dead men and searched them for identification. He found no information to establish their identities and found very little of value.

The horses looked like farm horses that were probably stolen from a farmer and under what circumstances he did not want to ponder. The saddles were old but reliable.

He found a name inscribed inside one set of saddlebags. It stated, *"Property of James W. Fontaine."* He turned the bag over and found a hidden compartment sewn inconspicuously. He opened it and found *$1463.00* hidden there. The dead men were unaware of the hiding place. With the help of the others he moved the bodies to a ditch.

Together they were able to cave in the sides enough to cover the bodies. No words were said over the bodies, at least nothing favorable.

After they gathered their horses and prepared to break camp, John told them about the saddlebags and its contents. "I think we should inquire on our way to Washington about this Mr. Fontaine. It would be the right thing to do to return the horses and money if at all possible. There was only one gun that was worth keeping. I put it in the saddlebags with the holster."

They started out early before the sun had fully heated things up. It was a beautiful day and riding went smoothly. They met some civilians, probably farmers, heading into Fredericksburg. They inquired of them if they had any knowledge of a James W. Fontaine. One man said that might be the Fontaine that raised sheep for wool in a valley just north of Fredericksburg. He wasn't sure, but it would be advisable to check with the postmaster in town. They traveled on with intentions of reaching town before dark.

Before nightfall, they reached the outskirts of Fredericksburg. John thought it better that he find them a place for the night and a stable for the horses. Matt agreed. John went off in search of a suitable place. He located a farmhouse where a lady had upstairs rooms to rent. She could stable their horses and provide a meal as well. He went out to the place they agreed to meet and got them to follow.

Once they arrived at the farmhouse the lady's son met them and took their horses to the barn. Samuel went with him to help. Together they removed the saddles and put them in the tack room. They laid out hay and oats for them to eat while they curried them.

Samuel asked, "Where is your father?"

"He is dead, killed by a *Yankee bullet* here in town December 13, 1862. He wasn't even fighting, just walking across the street and got hit in the head by a stray bullet!" recalled the boy.

"My name is Michael, what is yours?"

"My name is Samuel," he said as he extended his hand. "My father was killed in the war also. My mother was killed yesterday when a cannonball hit the building where she was buying some flour. She was buried that afternoon and then I left."

"I am sorry to hear that. Who are the men traveling with you?" Michael asked.

"One is a Union captain, and the other two are Rebel soldiers. They are real nice to me, and they are going to Washington to visit President Lincoln. They are going to help the South rebuild. That is all I know about them for now," insisted Samuel.

They noticed the young lady became uneasy when she saw a Union officer in her house. "Ma'am, I can leave if my presence is offensive to you. I will find another place to stay for the night," Matt politely stated.

"No, that will not be necessary. I must admit I was taken aback when I saw your uniform. I heard the war is over, but I still have a fear of soldiers, more Yankee than Rebel. It will take me years to start trusting again. Are you soldiers also?" she asked of John and Thomas.

"Yes, we are Confederate soldiers, I mean former. We are going to Washington to help Matthew here on a mission to reconstruct the South. Your hospitality will be appreciated greatly, and we can pay for all that you so graciously offer," said John politely.

"I will have some food prepared shortly gentlemen. You will find a well outside and soap in the pan to wash up before I have dinner ready. Please excuse me while I finish my work," she said as she moved back into her kitchen.

"Everyone, come to the table, supper is ready," Emily smiled. "Who wants to say grace?"

Startling even himself, Thomas blurted out "I do, I haven't had the chance to say grace since I left South Georgia."

"Fine!" says Emily.

"Dear Lord, you may not remember me, or my voice, but I come to you humbly giving thanks for these precious folks and the victuals they share with us. I also want to thank you for watching over me and carrying me safely through this war. I pray your forgiveness and mercy on me and all like me as we travel home again to start our lives anew. I pray for the

protection of this family too. Lead us and guide us. In His precious name we pray, Jesus Lord, Amen."

"Now that was truly a sweet blessing," commented Matthew, "will you please pass those peas my way, Thomas?"

After a nourishing dinner and coffee, they relaxed and talked outside on the porch while Thomas played some pleasant tunes on his harmonica. Mrs. Landis, Emily, told them about her husband, Walter, and his untimely death.

"He was a spiritual person, not necessarily religious though. He could see The Creator in everything. He had a reverence for all God's creatures, big and small. Somehow, I think he knew his time was nigh, and he could feel it too! He found joy in hard work and seeing a job well done. He instilled that in Michael. He taught him some very good values to live by. I think I could sense a special closeness to the Lord in his prayers, as if they knew a secret amongst themselves. We often prayed together. He always said that God will provide for all of our needs. He was right! I am sorry to go on so in front of you men. I know you have seen enough of death and personal loss to fill many lifetimes."

"Matthew spoke, "I believe I can speak for all of us here. We do appreciate your candor and your sacrifice. We have been far from a woman's voice and her spirit all these many days, months and years that have separated us from home. The gentle spirit of the female and the family's love have been the larger cost of this war to the soldier. Trust me when I say, you are a respite for a weary soul."

They found their way to sleep and were awaken to the smell of fresh coffee and bacon frying in the skillet. *"I think I must have died and gone to heaven!"* shouted Thomas.

"If you wake me like that again," angrily blasted John, "I will *send you there* myself."

They helped Mrs. Landis clean up after breakfast, and thanked her for the hospitality. Matthew handed her a twenty dollar gold piece for services rendered. She refused because it was more than expected. He reassured her it that they received far more than expected. She graciously accepted payment.

"We must find the postmaster and inquire about Mr. Fontaine, can you point us in the direction of your local post office Mrs. Landis?" asked John.

"Yes I can. You say you are looking for a Mr. Fontaine," Emily said with a puzzled look.

"Yes we are, *Mr. James W. Fontaine*. Do you know him, Mrs. Landis?" John asked somewhat surprised.

"I did. He was my brother-in-law, my sister's husband. They found him and my nephew, his son, dead at the crossing, coming back from Richmond less than a week ago. They went to collect on the wool that was taken to market and were on their way back. We buried them several days ago. Their horses were never found," announced Emily with sadness.

"Would you recognize the horses if you saw them ma'am?" asked John.

"I certainly would!" she replied.

"Samuel, you and Michael bring those two horses out here in the daylight!" John commanded them.

"Mama, they are Uncle James' horses. I couldn't be sure in the night and I did not want to say anything if I wasn't certain," shouted Michael with great emotion. There was no doubt in Emily's mind. They were his horses alright.

"Yes, they are James' horses! How did you get them? Did you find the men that killed them?" Emily cried with tears streaming down her cheeks.

"We were attacked by the men responsible for their deaths. We can only assume that, since they are dead now themselves. We would like to return them to your sister ourselves, if it isn't too far off the beaten path. We are due in Washington soon. Would you be so kind to direct us?" John asked politely.

"Michael, hitch up the wagon. We are going too. They are on the way to Washington in Stafford. I will be ready before you can saddle your horses," she said.

CHAPTER 4

THEY MADE GOOD TIME ALONG THE ROAD that morning. The men followed behind the wagon with Mrs. Landis and Michael at the reins. They had to pace themselves just to keep up with the wagon. The time passed quickly as they found themselves driving down a tree lined road to a farmhouse in a quaint valley with lush, green fields dotted with white sheep along the hillsides.

"Mama, mama, come quickly!" shouted a young girl running towards the house. Her ponytails and skirt bottom were flopping to-and-fro as she nearly fell on her way up the porch steps, holding the front of her skirt with both hands.

"What is it child?" her mother asked in desperation.

"Mama, Aunt Emily and Michael are coming, and some men are with her and they have daddy's horses!" She said as tears flowed down her face.

Pauline Fontaine stood on the porch bracing herself as her sister and nephew swung the horses and wagon almost sideways to a stop, throwing dirt skyward. "*Pauline, Pauline they found James' killers and retrieved the horses*. I just found out this morning. They stayed with me last night and asked where they could get information about James! I couldn't wait to tell you. I know this does not bring James back, but ...," Emily stopped talking when she saw Pauline fall to the ground.

John was the first to reach the widow as she crumpled to the ground. He slid his arm beneath her shoulders as she was supported halfway by the porch steps.

Samuel saw the well beside the porch and hurriedly grabbed the bucket and dipper. He set them next to Pauline and John, and placed the dipper full of water beside her lips.

John wet his scarf and wiped her face. She started to mumble something. Samuel turned the dipper so water could reach her mouth. Slowly, she regained her composure and stood up to greet the entourage, with John's help.

"I am sorry we disturbed you so. We struggled just to keep up with Mrs. Landis. We had an encounter two nights ago with some rogue bandits, once soldiers, and discovered upon their demise that they were in false possession of someone else's horses. I am sorry for the loss of your husband and son. I found a hidden compartment where your husband hid his money in his saddlebags. It may be of little consolation, but it is yours," said John as he handed her the envelope.

Mrs. Fontaine placed the envelope inside a pocket on the right side of her dress. She dusted herself off from the fall, stopped and stood rigidly as she gazed into the face of Samuel. All were watching her as she took a full measure of him. She regained her poise and asked him his name.

"My name is Samuel Ambrose Martin!" stated like a soldier standing at attention.

"My name is Pauline, Pauline Eliza Fontaine. My maiden name was Martin. You look like a cousin I used to play with when I was a little girl. His name was William T. Martin; we just called him *Willie T.*"

"My father's name was William T. Martin," he said sadly. "He died in the war."

"Well, I am very sorry for your loss Samuel. Where is your mom?" Pauline asked.

"We buried her two days ago. She was killed when a cannonball hit the building she was in. She was buying flour to bake my sister a cake for her ninth birthday. My sister is staying with my Aunt Mildred now," he said.

It was all anyone could do to avoid crying. There was not a dry eye amongst them.

Again, Pauline had to find her inner strength to compose herself. She was overcome with sadness for Samuel's situation.

"You look so much like little Jamie, my son. I thought he had returned from the dead when you rode up on his horse. I believe that is why I fainted. He had blond hair and green eyes. James, myself and Elizabeth, my daughter, each have brown hair. He was your height and about your age I guess. He was ten. How old are you?" she asked.

"I am ten and will be eleven in October," he said.

"Do you have a dog, ma'am?"

"Yes, we have Lady. She is out in the fields protecting the sheep. She will be home later and I will introduce her to you. Forgive my manners. Won't you all come inside? Elizabeth can serve some of that sweet tea she makes with molasses and that spring water from beneath the trees. That well has the coldest water around. It comes from an artesian spring."

Pauline ushered everyone inside. She graciously seated everyone, and asked Emily to prepare something to eat while she went to her bedroom to freshen up. She could not believe the rush of emotion that had overcome her. She was overwhelmed with the resemblance of Samuel to her son. She knew at that moment that he was a godsend and she would have to convince him to stay with her.

She got up and went through the kitchen, out the backdoor, onto the back porch. She looked out the back and saw Michael and Samuel playing with Lady beneath the oaks. Samuel was on his knees and had his arms around her neck hugging her. Michael was laughing and Lady was just wagging her tail with delight. She loved him just as she loved Jamie. Pauline grabbed her apron and wiped the tears away again.

Emily stepped out the kitchen door just then and hugged Pauline to her breast. "I know! He has to stay," Emily suggested.

They were all refreshed after they ate a meal of fresh mutton roast placed between slices of freshly baked bread, topped with a tomato and bell pepper sauce Pauline had canned the previous summer. They washed it down with Elizabeth's sweet molasses tea. Matthew thanked the ladies for their hospitality and reminded the others that they had to travel further before they rested. John and Thomas went out to gather the horses and pack mule. Matthew met them in the yard beneath the tree.

Everyone had gathered around to see them off when Matthew

spoke up. "There seems to be a problem. We have miscalculated the number of mounts and riders. There are only three horses and four riders. It looks like someone will have to stay back. Do I have any suggestions?"

"I have room if someone needs to stay over," suggested Mrs. Fontaine.

"I think Samuel is without a mount since he was only caring for the Fontaine's horses," said John thinking out loud.

"Wahl, it looks like I am the odd man out, doesn't it," said Samuel. "I guess I will have to stay over and work long enough to buy myself a horse. I'll have to catch up with you fellers later on down the road. You do need a man around the house Mrs. Fontaine, to do those manly chores. Do you fellers think you will get by without me to watch over you?"

"Yeah, I think so Samuel," spouted Thomas. "Don't forget to take the soap with you next time you jump in the creek."

They all laughed, even Samuel this time. Lady, the collie, was standing beside him and she wagged her tail to indicate she understood the humor as well.

"Samuel, we would be honored to have you stay with us," chimed in Mrs. Fontaine. "Wouldn't we Elizabeth?"

"Yes we would. I can show you all the good fishin' holes too!" exclaimed Elizabeth.

"Well, that settles it. Samuel stays and we've got to go. Thank you all for your hospitality," said John.

And they all said their goodbyes. Thomas looked back as they rode away and they were still waving goodbye. He waved again and turned to wipe the tears from his cheeks.

CHAPTER 5

Washington D.C.

WASHINGTON WAS A CITY ON THE MOVE. THERE was the hustle and bustle of horse drawn streetcars, carriages and all sorts of humanity, going every which of way. The movement of Union troops was evident everywhere you looked. It was 6:00 p.m. on Tuesday, April 11, 1865. Matthew suggested they stay at the *National Hotel* on Pennsylvania Avenue, where they could prepare for an audience with the President.

"I would like to stop at a café on the way. We can clean up once we get checked into the hotel," Matthew informed the others. "I think we all could use a bath. We will need to be fitted for a new suit of clothes. It will be quite an occasion for us; though, I have seen him often and believe this will be a time of jubilation for him. He has suffered much with the tragedies of war. Are you men the least bit hungry?"

"I believe I could eat a *mule*, if it was cooked just right," Thomas shouted with renewed enthusiasm.

"I would prefer something a little more conventional and a lot more pleasant to my taste buds, if you really want to know," replied John.

"Well, I know this little restaurant on a side street that suits my taste," says Matthew. "It has always served good food."

After making arrangements for their livestock at the livery, they walked on down the street.

The sign read *Mildred's Home Cooking Café.* "This must be the place; looks like my kind of place," says Thomas.

They entered the café to be greeted by a jolly lady as round as she was tall, "Come in gentlemen, have a seat. I've got what you want, if you've come to eat. My name is Mildred, what will it be?"

"What's *special* today, Mildred?" asked Matthew. "I meant to say with the exception of you."

"*Sweetheart*, your mama raised you right! I've got the usual fare, pot roast with gravy and all the trimmings: carrots, potatoes and onions. I just baked some apple pies to finish that off. All you can eat and all you can afford!" She let out a belly laugh with that said.

"We will take a round of that," replied Matthew, "and start with some coffee, if you have any fresh."

They all were completely satisfied with their meal and the dessert. It had been a long ride and they were truly tired. They made their way to the hotel after recovering their personal belongings from the livery. The lobby was a palatial setting compared to the outdoor living the soldiers had grown accustom to over the years. Matthew stepped up to the desk and signed for him and his guests.

"That will be $2.50 per room per night in advance, sir," said the clerk. "And we do have facilities to wash before you sleep, I might suggest."

"Are you sure we can afford to stay here?" John whispered in Matthew's ear.

Matthew reached in his saddlebag and retrieved a leather case. He removed a letter from the case, unfolded it and presented it to the clerk. The clerk quickly noticed the Presidential seal. He read the endorsement and saw it was signed by none other than Abraham Lincoln himself.

"Will that be sufficient for the expenses during our brief visit to your fine city; or, will you need anything else?"

"No ... No sir! Your credentials are sufficient, sir!" He handed three sets of keys to the men. "Your room numbers are 225, 226 and 227; you will be right down the hall from the *famous actor, Mr. John Wilkes Booth*. Enjoy your visit gentlemen, and if you need anything, just ask!"

The pale looking clerk wiped a long strand of black hair across his bald head with his shaky right hand.

"The rooms are up that staircase to your right, gentlemen. He took a seat on a stool as quickly as they left his desk.

After putting their things away, they agreed to meet in the lobby. The desk clerk indicated an all night bath house and barbershop was on the next block down, one block over. John was the first in the lobby and he looked around at the opulence that surrounded him. He was truly amazed. There was still a war being fought and people were walking around enjoying the good life while young men were dying, daily. John was a man of average height, lean with wide shoulders. It was obvious that he had missed many meals, evidenced by his gaunt features. He had a three day beard and could use a haircut. He had dark hair and brown eyes with a serious look about them. You could tell he meant business when he gave you that straight on look. He was still wearing the revolver and holster he acquired just a few days ago.

A shorter man walked through the lobby, very well dressed, in a black suit and starched white shirt, finished with black bowtie and polished patent leather shoes. He stopped in mid-step as he saw John standing there, like a gunfighter looking for an advantage before a shootout. John turned around to find the man only steps away, staring at him.

"Can I help you mister?" asked John.

"No, I am fine. You look like one of those western dudes; all you need is a cowboy hat. My name is Booth, John W. I am an actor, currently playing at Ford's theatre in the play, *My American Cousin*. I hope I haven't offended you," stated the gentleman.

"No you haven't. My name is Bernard, John F. The pleasure is mine." John reached out to offer his hand. Mr. Booth responded in kind. John was a little disturbed by the less than firm handshake and something else. He got a sense of impending doom associated with this man's persona. Something was not right about him.

"I was just recently released from service with the Confederate army and am here on personal business. I'm originally from New Orleans, but I have never seen play acting, sir. I hear you are an actor of notoriety."

"I've been around. My father is an actor, so is my brother. I have never been to your fair city, New Orleans, a jewel of the South," said Mr. Booth with an air of respect and regret.

"Maybe your craft will take you there someday, Mr. Booth," John stated encouragingly.

"No, I think not, Mr. Bernard. My time is limited, and I truly regret that there are many places I will not get to visit. I will leave so much unfinished business. I want to thank you for your service to our beloved Confederacy. Our cause is not completely lost. Good evening sir." He turned and walked through the front door, into the night.

Shortly thereafter, Thomas and Matthew came down to the lobby. "Fancy! Less than a week ago we were sleeping in a briar patch, scratching fleas," smiled Thomas. "What do you think John?"

"I think there is something wrong with that actor, John Booth. I just met him and I got a weird feeling when we shook hands, kind of spooky. I just don't know what it is. He also talked like he was not going to be around very long. Very strange," commented John.

"Yeah, this place is fancy, *too fancy.*"

They left the hotel, walked down the street, had a real tub bath, got a haircut and a shave.

"You two fellows look presentable," stated Matthew. "I thought there might be *real human beings* beneath all the dirt and hair, now I know there are. Tomorrow we will get fitted for suits, so we will be presentable before Mr. Lincoln."

They walked around and took in the sights. They commented on just how strange it felt not to be on the battlefield. The sheer presence of so much quiet was almost overwhelming. The peace would take years to absorb after nerve-shattering battle conditions, day-in and day-out. Would they ever be normal again? That was truly the question!

When they arrived back at the hotel the desk clerk flagged them down. "I have something for you gentlemen. It was dropped off after you left."

He handed Matthew an envelope. Matthew opened it and removed the contents. There were three tickets for the play, *My American Cousin*, at the Ford Theatre for Friday, April 14th. There was also a note that read: "Mr. Bernard, just a small token of my appreciation. I understand you are accompanied by two friends. I hope you will be able to attend. I believe it will be a performance *you will truly not forget.*" Signed: Yours truly, John W. Booth.

They retired to their respective rooms and found sleep nipping at their heels. John fell into a deep dream-state early in the morning. He dreamed his maternal grandmother was calling him to come home. She was of the Cherokee people, from the mountains of North Carolina. Her English name was Isabella, but her people called her *Shadow Talker.* He envisioned her standing beneath the gigantic arms of a huge live oak, her long hair blowing in the wind.

Her voice was musical like a clear mountain stream, rolling over the boulders of time. The cadence was that of a tribal song, passed down through the ages. *"Come home, come home--- where your thoughts will soar on a starry night, where your spirit will cry out for truth, where your heart will love with the innocence of a child, and your soul will seek wisdom and understanding."* Then he heard a gunshot, and he sat straight up in bed! His heart was racing; otherwise, he was fine. It was just a dream, he thought, or was it?

He could not go back to sleep; so, he just got out of bed, washed his face and got dressed. It was still early and he did not want to wake the others. He remembered the large dining hall off from the lobby and decided to see if he could get something to eat. He found light traffic there so early in the morning.

A waiter approached as he seated himself, "May I get you something, sir?" he asked.

"Yes, I would like a cup of coffee and a piece of pie if you have any," John said with a smile.

The waiter responded with a nod of his head and quickly walked away.

John looked around to get a sense of his surroundings. He recognized the back of Mr. Wilkes' head as he was having a conversation with three men and a woman. They were on the far side of the hall and paid him no mind.

John could not shake the dream he had. He was trying to recall each of the elements to the best of his ability. The waiter placed a cup on the table and filled it with hot coffee. He placed a slice of blackberry cobbler beside the coffee.

John felt his grandmother's word still stinging him like a hard rain hitting the bare skin. The vision of her standing under the live oak was etched in his mind, and he felt her voice pulling him closer. He was in a trance and almost jumped out of his seat when someone touched him on the shoulder.

"Pardon me, I didn't mean to startle you, sir. I could not sleep and thought you might like some company. My name is Madelyn Cooper," spoke the beautiful young brunette, as she seated herself beside John.

She motioned to the waiter for another cup. "It must be the change in the weather that affected me so; my mind is so cloudy these days. I sometimes don't know just where I am," she said dragging her accent a little too syrupy.

"Ma'am, I know I might appear to be slow, but isn't it customary for most women to remove their make up before they go to bed?" John inquired.

"Well, mercy me, isn't that odd!" she smiled at him.

"Yes, so is your phony Southern accent. I do believe you should scoot over here closer to me if you plan to reconnoiter that table across the room. You would look more natural at this angle, and more like you are with me," he said with a crooked smile.

"I guess I appear to be a rank amateur, Mister …?"

"John Bernard, My pleasure to meet you Miss Cooper. Polish will come with experience. I am a former soldier hoping to learn new skills myself."

"I believe you are suspicious of that group. Am I correct?" John pried in a pleasant manner.

"If you must know, I am shadowing that woman, Mary Surratt. It is the first time they have met in public, together. I have seen her with the others, but not with the man with his back to us. He dresses much better than the other men. They look more like rogues. I may be out of line, being candid with you John, but I have to trust you. You are very alert to your surroundings and I am just getting my feet wet, so to speak. Training is at a premium these days and most of it is on the job sort."

She looked John square in the face and asked, "You wouldn't expose me to them would you?"

The group got up from the table and was heading directly at them, with Mr. Booth in the lead. John turned and pulled Miss Cooper to him and placed a strong, determined and convincing kiss on her lips. He held her long enough for them to pass their table and had to push her backwards to separate the two.

Mr. Booth smiled as they passed and said, "Isn't it the way with spring, all things turn to love!"

"What ... What was that all about Mr. Bernard?" she asked as she struggled to get her breath. "Aren't you being a little forward?"

"No ma'am, that was on the job training. That man you did not recognize was Mr. John Wilkes Booth, the actor. He would recognize me and I wanted to look inconspicuous, that's all!" John smiled heartily, "You performed like a natural. I believe you will be just fine with a little practice." He laughed at himself.

"Oh, you do!" She bent in his direction and kissed him harder and longer, then, she slapped him. "That's for not being a Southern gentleman, and asking before you take advantage of a lady's good nature, Mr. Bernard. Good night!"

CHAPTER 6

THE SUN WAS UP. IT WAS A BEAUTIFUL SPRING day and a rooster down the street was crowing at his finest. He thought it his duty to boast about his prominence and popularity throughout the barnyard, in this case just a backyard, in the nation's capital. The lobby was filled with people checking in and checking out. The dining hall was also starting to fill with hungry folks just waking to a new day. Matthew spotted John, and pulled Thomas along as he stumbled to catch up.

"Good morning all," John greeted with the most chipper voice, "hope everyone enjoyed a good night's rest, coffee anyone?"

"I'll have coffee, eggs, toast and that rooster's neck for breakfast. I think he started crowing at three o'clock this morning," proclaimed Thomas with a foul temperament, as he rubbed his eyes.

"The same for me," Matthew told the waiter standing next to him, "but, substitute sausage for *the rooster neck*, please. We looked for you in your room. Have you eaten already, John?"

"Yes, I have eaten. I could not sleep after a dream woke me early this morning. I came down, not wanting to wake you. A very interesting thing happened while I drank my coffee. I met a young lady that was following another woman. The lady sat down with me while the woman and three men met in the dining hall having some sort of rendezvous. It seems as though she was doing detective work, and I am not sure for whom. The odd thing was that one of the men was Mr. Booth, the actor. This town sure has some peculiarities, if I say so myself."

"These are peculiar times, they are! You will be surprised to know your new responsibilities will rely on your heightened skills of subterfuge and detective work. You are going to work for your Mr. Lincoln sniffing out crime and graft at all levels of society and government. Your background will aid you in your new endeavors," stated Matt.

"Just what did he say?" asked Thomas, scratching his head.

"I think we are going to start spying on folks," answered John.

"Let me explain it better. Mr. Lincoln knows there will be carpetbaggers and scallywags waiting to pounce on the Southern people in their weakened state once this war is finally over. There will be Northerners and Southerners as well, looking to get wealthy at the disadvantage of others during the rebuilding years. He will need truly devoted and patriotic men working together to inform him of the malfeasance and corruption that occurs; you will have to be proactive at times. I mean to say you will place yourselves in harm's way at times to complete your duties."

Matt paused, "Have I got the right men for the job?"

Thomas rolled his eyes. "My head is spinning, but, I want to do the right thing. I am tired of fighting and would like for people to do right by one another. I am willing to learn this new job. Yes I am. Tell Mr. Lincoln to sign me up!"

"You tell him *yourself*!" Matthew moved his arms while the waiter delivered his plate. "I have to go to the city telegraph office to inform him we are in town. He will respond with a time for us to meet. I normally just go into his office without invitation, but, seeing I am bringing new men inside to begin a new phase of the operation it is appropriate to make formal requests of his time. He is a busy man and I have the ultimate respect for him and his office. What is your response John?"

"You needn't ask, but, since you have. When we met I was wallowing in a creek, half naked. I heard a voice in my head telling me it wasn't my time to die; so, I felt I was given another chance at life. I am no longer a Rebel soldier, but I am an American citizen. I don't think it accidental that I lived through this war nor do I think our meeting was accidental. I feel especially privileged to have this opportunity to serve the President, my country and my beloved homeland. It is exciting to learn something new. I wish to apply all my experience and skills as a citizen soldier."

"You once said I had a lot to say," Matthew chuckled. "You sound just like a damned, *slick-tongue politician* stumping for re-election."

Thomas leaned back and slapped his knee, "Don't he though!" He almost fell completely backwards in his chair until John caught him. Then they all laughed.

After breakfast, they went down to the city telegraph office with Matthew. He sent his telegram to the President requesting an audience. They went from there down to the men's clothiers. They got fitted with the proper attire at the haberdashery. That was something new for Thomas and John. They felt somewhat violated at moments, but survived the whole affair with Matthew's encouragement.

As the day flew by they started getting hungry again. It seemed fascinating to them how they were starving as soldiers, lucky to have one meal a day and now they were getting accustomed to eating three meals a day, and expecting it too.

They decided to step inside *Constantine's Tavern and Diner*. The place was clean with a fancy bar the entire length of the establishment. They seated themselves and were greeted by a buxom waitress named Hilda. "We are serving a special today: sausage, sauerkraut, potato salad and baked beans"

"What else do you have?" asked Thomas.

"More of that," she said.

"Alrightee then, that's what we will have," Thomas replied.

Just as they were finishing their meals and the mugs of beer they were drinking, they noticed two big fellows standing at the bar, looking over at them.

"We whipped them lousy, Southern hillbillies, and now they come in here to eat and drink, like they own the damn place. We should throw the swine out on their ears. What do you think, Lester?"

"I think you need to take a whiff of yourself and see who the pig really is," spouted off Thomas.

Thomas was no giant of a man, but he was country-strong and

never backed down from a fight. He had no backup in him at all, folks often commented. Others said he got his fire and temper from his strawberry-red hair; whatever the source, he could hold his own in a fight.

"Now, Thomas, this is where we will begin training. You will have to learn not to fall victim to provocation of your lesser. They will always try to provoke you with their imbecilic antics," softly spoke Matthew.

Lester turned around and looked straight at Matthew, "What kind of lily laced talk is that, you Southern trash?"

"See Thomas, this man's mother let her children run wild and they were raised by barnyard critters. That explains the foul odor you smell when he opens his mouth," Matthew verbally prodded the man.

Lester lunged at Matthew to grab him with his extended left hand. Matthew stood up and with his left hand swung the thick beer mug head level at Lester's expense. Lester's nose was flattened and teeth went flying. Blood was splattered onto his buddy standing a step behind him. As Lester slumped to the floor, his partner stepped forward. John had anticipated as much and tripped the man, while guiding his head with his hand placed behind it to land squarely on the edge of the oaken table. He also slumped to the floor. Matthew paid Hilda for the meal, as his friends stepped outside.

"I think I am beginning to understand," Thomas quipped.

CHAPTER 7

AFTER BREAKFAST, THE THREE MEN WENT over to the tailor to pick up their new suits. They were stopped at the desk in the lobby, where the clerk handed Matthew a telegram from the President's office. The day was beautiful, with bright blue skies, and the cherry trees around the capitol grounds were in full bloom. They were anxious to learn of the contents in the telegram. Matthew pointed them up Pennsylvania Avenue, in the direction of the White House, where a favorite bench sat beneath budding trees.

"It says we are to meet the President promptly at 9:30 A.M. Friday, April 14th, in his office. We will also meet with the Secretary of the Treasury, Mr. Hugh McCulloch."

"He will briefly lay out plans for the new Secret Service Department, whose mission is to search out and eradicate any and all counterfeiting operations. I find this very exciting, don't you men?"

They all agreed and each felt very fortunate to be part of something so challenging and essential for the nation's welfare; however, they hadn't a clue what to expect next.

"How's about we all take a ride out of town, into the countryside?" Matthew suggested, as he was in an extraordinarily good mood this fine day, and had time to kill. "I believe it would be safe to venture out, but still smart to bring our weapons in case highwaymen lurk about. There are those still holding out and will be for some time. The peace may be harder and longer to win than the war."

"Or lose it!" Thomas chimed in with his usual exuberance. "I would like to ride some and stretch my legs in the hills a little. I am still somewhat edgy from battle fatigue and jumpy from being in town. Don't get me wrong; sleeping on a feather bed and eatin' regular don't hurt my feelings none, but I may feel my nerves calm down a mite bit if I could breathe some good country air."

For Thomas, talking was as natural as a hen pecking corn, folks liked to say. He was good at easing the mood for those around him.

The hostler brought their horses out into the center of the livery for ease of saddling. He told them they were fed well and curried twice a day. He took pride in his work, for which they tipped him an additional one dollar coin. He smiled from ear-to-ear.

The livery owner strolled in and Matthew discussed the possibility of trading the horses that he and Thomas rode, with other horses of like quality. They needed to travel south and he explained that horses wearing the U.S. brand would not be endearing to Southerners. The man could appreciate their predicament.

He tried to steer them to a couple of older nags but Matthew quickly diverted his sight to some more attractive horses in a pen, to the rear of the stables. The livery owner said he could not see such a trade being in his best interest. Matthew reached in and produced the letter of procurement signed by U.S. Grant, the General of Supreme Command and Abraham Lincoln, President of the United States.

"We will take the bay and the roan and sell our horses to someone else as we leave town, if that is more satisfactory to you," Matthew commented as he motioned for the boy to bring them up for closer inspection.

The rotund older man began to shake and had trouble getting words to form. "I ... I believe those would be better horses, best suited for your needs; now that I look at it from your perspective mister! I would be proud to take those two horses in an even trade, and even throw in replacement saddle blankets, saddles and bridles for those U.S. branded ones for an additional sum, say of $250.00 each."

"Maybe, we should just take the horses and look for our own tack," Matthew smiled at the others as he spoke. Even the boy understood the levity.

"Now ... now, maybe I was being a *little hasty* about them other things; we will see what we can dig up," the old man pushed for a favorable edge.

"How about we pick out what we want!" was Matthew's reply.

"Alright, you win!" the old man threw up his hands in defeat.

About thirty minutes later they were traveling along a country road with two beautiful horses, new saddle blankets, saddles and bridles. They had the boy rub extra oil on the new saddles to help with the break-in.

They were still laughing at the livery owner left crying that they were thieves. They all knew he had profited more than his fair share during the war. It still amazed the two ex-confederates what a difference a week made in their lives. They rode down in a meadow to a fast moving stream that ran through a stand of hardwoods. They got down and stretched their legs as the horses eased up to the stream to partake of the good water. The men also stretched out to drink some, too.

"Now, that is some good tasting water; think I'll have some more," John said as he pulled his canteen from his horse to fill with the cold water.

"I think I will call my mare, *Belle*. I've been waiting for her to tell me her name. She just whispered in my ear as I brushed by her. Belle it is! Thank you my precious traveling companion." The horse pricked up her ears when he spoke her name, as if that had always been her name. John gently stroked her head, and a bond existed from thereon.

They observed a man on a horse as he eased down a hillside, across the stream. He did likewise and dismounted, so his horse could also drink.

"It's a fine day gentlemen!" he greeted them. "I thought my horse was tired of standing around all day and would like a stroll in the countryside." The man was a tall, handsome fellow, with dark black hair and strong features.

"If you men are not familiar with the lay of the land, I would like to tell you about the fare down the road. There is a tavern just a few miles down the road that serves a decent meal for a traveler."

"That sounds like an invite to me," Thomas was quick to add. "I think my stomach has caved in."

"I am beginning to think there is no bottom to that pit, you call a stomach," laughed Matthew.

"I believe you are beginning to know him well, my friend," smiled John. "Join us when you cross over the creek and we will ride together."

"My name is Jacob Hewitt. My father hailed from North Carolina, of the Cherokee Nation. Up ahead is Surratt's Tavern, which sits in a settlement more commonly, referred to as *Surrattsville*. It seems the old man loved the whiskey and built himself a tavern. It, along with his other half-hearted ventures, was left to his widow and children. An older couple manages the place for the widow who lives in town in her boardinghouse. The wife serves a decent meal."

"My horse's name is Stonewall, as she can be cantankerous at times; and, my dog's name is Blue."

"Is your dog invisible?" John pondered with a stroke of his chin, simulating deep thought.

"No, he will make his presence known when he trusts you. He is very cautious. He has saved my life more than a few times," proudly proclaimed Jacob.

They arrived at a two story tavern in a small settlement. There was a hotel, a gristmill, a sawmill, and several other buildings scattered about. They dismounted and tied their horses to a hitch rail; surveying their surroundings before entering a strange place, they walked into the tavern, one after the other. The room was dark, with very little light stealing through the shuttered windows. A shorter lady, with a pleasant demeanor greeted them and offered them the day's special, pot-roast with potatoes and onions, with a pan of cornbread on the side. They accepted and looked around at the other patrons, as their eyes adjusted to the low light.

John noticed the young lady he had met the previous morning, sitting in the corner, alone. He told the others and they looked in her direction. She pretended not to know.

Matthew suggested she may be working and it served her purpose not to be recognized. That did not discourage John. He walked over to her table and introduced himself. "Excuse me young lady for interrupting your privacy, but I noticed your horse may have a stone in its left front hoof; it seemed to be very uncomfortable as I walked by. If that is your buggy parked in front."

"Thank you, kind sir, I shall have a look at it now if you would be so kind to assist me," said the attractive young lady as she scooted back her chair, cleared the wrinkle from her dress, and proceeded outside.

Once outside she turned to John and said, "I am on duty at the present and watching for Mrs. Surratt, as we think she has selected this location as a rendezvous spot for meeting other Southern sympathizers, to plan who knows what event they have conspired. I will contact you later today if you wish. Aren't you staying at The National Hotel?"

He indicated yes with a nod while pretending to look at her horse's left front leg. "Thank you so much sir for remedying that nuisance from my horses' hoof," she politely commented as they reentered the tavern.

They enjoyed the delicious meal prepared by the woman of the tavern. It was a time for the men to get better acquainted as they relaxed. John and Thomas lit up their pipes as did Jacob when they offered tobacco. It was still out of character for the soldiers to be so comfortable and they felt awkward in this setting.

Jacob explained that he did not take with slavery and could not bear arms against his native South; therefore, he sat out the war and traveled westward to the territories, more precisely Oklahoma, where the Cherokees had been relocated along with all of the other Eastern tribes during the Indian Removal Act, instituted by Andrew Jackson. He revealed to them that he worked as a Federal Marshall and had police privileges within the Cherokee Nation.

He was in Washington speaking with dignitaries on behalf of the Cherokee Council. His duties were completed and he considered traveling south as the war was coming to a close.

"We will be on the move in several days, heading due south. If you want to tag along you are welcome. There are still some confederate forces that have yet to succumb. Jefferson Davis is said to be on the run, but they will find him soon. I am sure we will encounter many soldiers returning home and they will be hungry and tired and a dangerous sort. The freed slaves may be on the move, or they may stay put. That will make for a messy situation. It is anybody's guess how this whole mess will turn out in the end," were Matthew's sentiments.

"We are lodging at *The National Hotel*."

"I will be sure to contact you, if I decide to tag along," commented Jacob as he turned to watch the woman entering the tavern.

They all took notice, with the exception of Miss Cooper, who appeared to be searching for something in her handbag. The woman walked up to the tavern keeper and spoke quietly to him, to which he went behind the bar and got something concealed within a quilt. It could be some guns that were inside the quilt; whatever it was, it was obvious she was displeased he produced the items. She spoke a little louder to him and walked out the front door. The man promptly went out the backdoor with the concealed items. A short time later the man returned and outside a horse and buggy could be heard pulling away in a hurry.

Miss Cooper paid the tavern keeper for her partially eaten meal and walked to the door. She turned at the door and spoke to them, "Good day, gentlemen!" and was quickly on her way.

"What do you say we mosey back into town and find a saloon to wet our whistle?" Thomas said hoping to find someone with similar desires. No one spoke up. "Looks like I will have to go it alone if I have no takers. It must be a church night!"

"We will go with you for your protection," John said, "trouble seems to follow you. Let's get on back. I don't want to miss the Cooper girl if she comes a calling. I am interested in what she has discovered on her outing today. I feel something big is about to happen."

They left the tavern and made their way back into Washington. Jacob tagged along.

CHAPTER 8

THE THREE MEN AGREED THAT TAKING SOME
time to relax before dinner was a good idea. Matthew went next door
to John's room and found him going through the personal items that
Thomas had saved for him.

"What do you have there, John?" Matthew inquired of him as he
was sorting out things from a canvas bag rigged with a drawstring.

"Oh, they are just a few things that have sentimental value to me.
I have a crucifix made from walnut that my grandpa carved for me. He
said it would protect me and I should keep it close at all times. It gives
me comfort and I hold it when I pray; but that is hard to do when both
hands are squeezing a gun and people are shooting at you. Those are
the times when I pray more fervently than ever."

"I also have a picture of my family. It includes my parents, grandparents, brothers and sisters and I keep it in a leather pouch. A traveling
photographer sat up business in town and dad traded out a basket of
fresh shrimp for some tintypes. Dad ended up cooking them since the
man had no idea how to go about preparing shrimp or any seafood for
that matter. He was from Cleveland."

"This here is my *gris-gris* bag. It contains things I hold important
to my family and my connection to them. There is salt, an arrowhead,
a kernel of corn, and a pebble from my favorite stream signifying water,
a lock of my mother's hair, and ashes from home symbolic of fire and
most important of all is the breath of my grandmother which is life.
There are *seven* ingredients here, which is a *holy number.*"

"I also carry this small Bible in my pouch as well. I was told that an
angel placed it on my nightstand as a gift when I was injured as a child."

"What is that other book you have there?" Matthew questioned as he picked up a letter bound book with the name, *Carson Walker* inscribed on the front cover.

"That's a personal journal of a friend that died in Cedarville, a place in the Shenandoah Valley; I think it was August of last year. His name is Carson Walker. He asked me to get it to his mom and sister, if he didn't make it home."

"He caught a Yankee bullet in the heart. He just finished a cup of coffee when Union cavalry came out of nowhere. He always said he'd rather go quickly than waste away as many of us did." Scratching his head, John asked, "If you are interested in it, look it over. I've not had the time or heart to take it up myself."

Matthew picked up the journal, opened it and leafed through a few pages and stopped. He wasn't certain if reading another man's journal, especially a dead man, was violating something sacred. He paused and decided to go forward. It was written as a letter to home. It read:

19 February, 1862
Dear Mom and Elizabeth,
Today started as any other day. The little animals all seemed in harmony with their surroundings: birds singing and squirrels playing chase. That was before all hell broke loose. I know the horrors of war but today was one of the worse. The bombs were deafening. It was like lighting striking beside our heads, over and over again! Time was going in slow motion, like a bad dream when you are running and you can't get anywhere. When the fighting was over I looked over to my friend Billy Johnson. I commented that was a close one. He said, "Too close." I looked closer and I could see where his right arm used to be. I tried to tie it off, but there was nothing to tie off. I applied my bandanna to stop the bleeding, but, it was no use. He asked me to hold him until it was over. I held him in my arms like a mother holds an injured child. He did not cry, not once. I couldn't stop crying. I watched as his lifeblood flowed out of him unable to do anything but hold him. I swear he was smiling, and he was looking out beyond as if he saw someone walking closer from a great distance. The strangest thing happened next. He called out to his mother, "I'm coming mom, please hold my hand

until I get to the other side." He reached with his right shoulder as if his arm was still attached. I could not stop shaking for two days. I helped bury him under a chestnut tree. I mailed a letter to his family, praising him in battle and told them how he was a good boy, every day. I believe he told me his mother died while giving birth to him. He had a father and sister. I wondered how he knew his mother. They lived down the road from his grandparents in the mountains of Tennessee. Mom, you were all I could think about after he died. I am thankful to have such a good and decent mother. I have always loved you. Good Lord, I pray you let me get home to see my family once again. Give Dad my best.

Forever,

Your loving son and brother,

Carson.

Matthew closed the book and sat in a chair against the wall. He was silent for a while as he looked out the second floor window. When he spoke his voice broke, "I believe this is very personal and very poignant. I would like to read further if that's fine with you. And, I would like to help deliver this to his family. This is quite revealing and heartfelt. It is a treasure that should be passed down. I wish I could have known this soldier."

John smiled, "*You did!* There were thousands of boys just like him that laid down their lives for the man next to them. They did not die for any stinking cause. They marched through Hell, ate bad food, slept in the cold, the rain and the snow. They fought mosquitoes, chiggers, dysentery and Yankee soldiers. They asked for very little and got even less. They had hearts straight from the good Lord's bosom. They buried their comrades and stood to fight another day, each time it was asked of them. The fields and streams ran red with the blood of heroes that will never breathe another breath again, on this good earth. They will run as little boys again into their mother's arms forever laughing, knowing they fought the good fight. They ran the good race. Yes Matthew, *you knew many* like him."

There was a long silence between them until Thomas opened the door and shouted out, "Is anyone hungry?"

They enjoyed a fine dinner in the dining hall and the evening went peacefully.

During the night John was restless. He had another early morning dream. There were people milling about with laughter and jubilance but he was very anxious. He could not contain himself, his body was trembling, and he knew he had to act but there was no movement coming forth. It was as if his body had been paralyzed. *A blast went off!* He jumped from his bed onto the hotel floor. It took him some time to get his bearings. What may have been seconds seemed like minutes. He splashed his face with water, straightened himself, got dressed and went downstairs. This time, he was not alone. He found Thomas, Matthew, Jacob and Miss Cooper all seated at a table, drinking coffee.

"I had a bad dream, and could not sleep. What your excuses for being here so early?"

"We were restless as well," stated Thomas, "and we found Jacob and Miss Cooper here in the dining hall. Sit, it's time to eat. Have a cup of coffee."

"Call me Madelyn," she smiled. "Matthew explained that we all seem to be working on the same team, just different missions. I explained to them prior to your arrival that we have suspicions that there may be some espionage in the planning that involves your acquaintance, Mr. Booth. I understand you have tickets to the play tonight. I just got notice that the President will attend also. That information has not been circulated to the public, but it will be given to the Ford Theatre management as customary precaution. So, I ask if you would keep an eye out for any peculiarly odd behavior tonight. Mr. Booth will be preoccupied, as he is in the play."

"We certainly will, Madelyn," Matthew replied, "and we may have occasional contact with you in the future with our mission as well, professionally speaking that is."

Madelyn excused herself because it had been a long evening and she needed some rest to continue on.

"Well, you gentlemen do live an exciting life, right in the midst of things!" Jacob ordered breakfast and further explained he would like nothing better than to tag along on their journey south. "I have some friends that I would like to see in Mississippi. They live in the Jackson area."

"Wonderful!" Matthew explained, "My family lives there as well. There is strength in numbers. We will have a stronger entourage."

"I never know if you are complimenting someone or just calling us a bunch of bumbling jackasses," Thomas pondered while scratching his head. They all laughed.

The three gentlemen dressed in their new suits with shiny black shoes and walked to the Capitol. They arrived early for good measure. Promptly at nine o'clock they were ushered into the oval office where President Lincoln welcomed them with a handshake. He called each of them by name as he welcomed them. Thomas could not speak as he was awestruck. He just shook his head yes and no in response. The others looked at him and could not believe their friend was suddenly mute. They almost laughed out loud at him, but decided better to not laugh. He also introduced Hugh McCullough, Secretary of the Treasury.

"We have a lot to speak about, but, I have a Cabinet meeting with General Grant in attendance at 9:30 A.M. So I will be brief and concise in our purpose for meeting this morning. You have been chosen by Mr. O'Brien to be the first agents of the *Secret Service*, a branch of the Treasury Department. Counterfeiting has usurped America's power and authority before and during the war, in the North and the South. Because you are native to the South you will be especially valuable as coverts. Mr. Bernard, your familiarity with Louisiana, and moreover *New Orleans*, will prove even more useful. We believe a group is establishing a base of operation there as we speak. New Orleans is the largest city in the South and fourth largest in the United States."

Mr. Lincoln walked to the window and looked out over the Capital lawn. He paused briefly while gathering his thoughts. He spun around with his arms still locked behind his back, lifted his head as it was focused about his feet. He looked Matthew square in the face, "Sir, I am promoting you to the position of *Major* in the U.S. Army, but, you will not be able to display your insignia because your first assignment will require you to be *disguised as a civilian*. Just hang your new uniform in the closet for a while." He shook Matthew's hand as he was all smiles.

"Now, can I trust you men to follow and execute all of the orders of your Chief in Command, Mr. McCullough, to the best of your ability?" The President was silent, waiting on a response.

"Yes sir," was the reply from each of them. Thomas must have repeated himself at least three times, as he had to be told by John to release the President's hand. Then they laughed.

The President thanked them and wished them well in their efforts to help reunite the nation. He informed them they would receive further details and instructions directly from Mr. McCullough.

Before they parted, John wanted to say something to the President. "Mr. Lincoln, I have a bad feeling about something; I've been having some bad dreams lately. I don't know how to say it, but ..." John paused.

Abraham Lincoln, the President, looked directly into John's eyes, laid his right hand on John's left shoulder, and said, "Don't worry, I had a dream too, this very morning. *I was walking through the White House and people were crying. I saw a casket there and I asked who it was. They said the President was dead.* It was startling; however, many fine men have died fighting for a worthy cause, and I am also willing to lay down my life as well. Just maybe," he paused again and with a deep breath said, "it will suffice to bring healing to our nation, which can use all it can get. I thank you John for your concern." That was all he had to say as they were ushered from his office. A strong foreboding rested on John's heart.

CHAPTER 9

THERE ARE DAYS THAT A PERSON REMEMBERS
for the rest of his life: every detail, every sight, every sound, every
emotion and even the faintest of smells will be a reminder of how they
felt on those special days, years and years hence. Today would be one
of those days for Matthew, John and Thomas, and many others as well.

Later, after meeting with the President, they met with McCullough,
Secretary of the Treasury. He laid out plans for the new service and
guidelines for operations and communications. He presented them
with credentials and new shiny badges that identified them as agents of
the government. The badges were numbered: 1, 2, and 3, *the first agents
of The Secret Service of the United States Government*. He insisted they
keep them concealed for their protection.

After reviewing how they would travel and operate as undercover
operatives in the South, they were given funds and told how to reach
his office for any purpose or need that might arise. In the event it was
necessary to reach the Secretary, they should refer to him as *The Eagle*
in future communications. His staff would know to whom it referred.
He wished them Godspeed, and bid them farewell.

They went back to their rooms, changed into casual attire, and
went out to a predetermined boarding house to meet with Jacob, and
dine. As they entered the boarding house a lady ushered them into a
large dining room occupied by a long table with a bench to each side.
Thomas was the first to recognize Jacob near one end, but did not speak
to him as he noticed Jacob's attention was focused on a particular conversation between two men nearby. Moreover, he pretended to have no
recognition of him. He whispered to the others before they spoke out.

They found a place at the other end of the table opposite Jacob. The
men ate their meals with minimal conversation, taking notice of each

participant at the table. Most of the diners gave little cause for attention; however, the two men near Jacob looked suspicious. They were young, rough sorts, with shifty eyes always combing the room. Once the new agents finished eating, they paid the lady and left the boarding house. They found a nearby park where children were feeding the ducks on the pond. Soon they were joined by Jacob.

"Hello gentlemen. How did your presidential meeting go this morning?" he asked, while searching for a stone to skim across the pond.

"It went well; the President was in a fine mood this morning. We got our appointments and should be ready to push on in the morning."

"It appears you have been doing some detective business yourself," Matthew stated, as he rose from the bench to greet Jacob with a handshake. "You would make a worthy addition to our team!"

"Well, it went like this. I sat down to eat and the two men next to me went silent. They looked my way and I held up my right hand and said, *how!* Then one smiled to the other and said, just a dumb Injun, and went back to their conversation. I gathered they have some plans which had to be accelerated due to unforeseen events. I did hear them mention the names Johnson and Stanton. I don't know what significance this may have, but, if we can see Miss Cooper this evening we may want to pass it on to her. And thanks for not recognizing me; that was essential to my disguise."

Jacob skipped the stone across the water and turned to them, "I will be ready to leave after breakfast tomorrow as well. I am ready to see new country and old country, again."

"By the way," John spoke up, while rising from the park bench, "I think those were the two men seated with Mr. Booth and the woman Madelyn was shadowing the morning we met. This may truly interest her."

He selected a stone and skipped it on the pond. Cutting eyes towards Jacob with a friendly grin, he said, *"Now, that's how it's done!"*

The men whiled away the afternoon walking around the Capital, taking in the sights and observing the movement of people, military and civilian. Afterwards, they went to their rooms to rest and prepare for the evening. Neither Thomas, nor John had ever attended a play before. Matthew picked up the journals of Carson Walker and sat on his bed, leaning against the headboard. He opened to a journal and began to read:

4 March, 1862

We know what we have been told and led to believe; that is, we are fighting to defend our Southern culture, the sanctity of our agrarian ways, gentlemanly manners and the nobility of our Southern ladies. When I witness death and destruction every day, this hell that we call war, I must ask myself if this is the penalty of enslaving another race of people. There is a fundamental flaw in the thought process that sends young men to systematically slaughter each other, just to prop up cheap labor. Is minimizing labor costs that important to the rich? My heart has witnessed more than God intended my soul to see. How many must die before we realize the errors of our ways? Our leaders have failed us. This should have never happened! Who is man enough to admit he was wrong? When is enough, enough? God save us from the error of our ways!

Matthew had to cease reading. He had not been directly involved in battle, but he witnessed it all. He clearly grasped the passion. He had been called for a higher purpose. He had no desire to fight against his Southern kinsmen, nor did he want to rebel against the U.S. He, like many others from his generation, knew slavery's time was over. He knew that one day his leadership would be called upon when the North and South were reunited. He had a shared vision with Abraham Lincoln. He knew within himself that he was a man of destiny. Matthew had conviction of the soul and a tenderness of spirit. Carson's journals had a tremendous effect on him. He could feel the richness and sincerity of the soldier's perspective throughout his writing.

———※———

Matthew gathered his friends in the lobby having made contact with Madelyn Cooper. Thomas brought Jacob to the hotel so she could hear firsthand, the exact words of the conspirators.

"I will get someone assigned to Secretary of War Stanton, and Vice President Johnson. I am sure that is whom they intended; although, who really knows their intentions."

Madelyn stared out ahead while placing her right hand on her mouth and chin, "Those being the same men we, John and I, saw with Mary Surratt gives credibility to the notion she is somehow involved in some plan or conspiracy associated with the Confederacy. Confederate sympathizers have been witnessed at her boarding house. We found, through an associate planted in the boardinghouse, that the suspected guns in the blanket were merely sticks meant to look like guns to throw us off. Your information is greatly appreciated. Please contact me again if there is anything else to report." She left them standing in the lobby.

After dinner, the three men caught a carriage to Ford's Theatre for the long anticipated play. Thomas and John did not know what to expect, this being their first time to attend such an event. It was a cultural event beyond their realm of experience. They were dazzled by the opulence of high society. Men were dressed like heads of state and women dressed like they were entertaining the Queen of England. Thomas felt like a fish out of water. He just followed John, and John followed Matthew's lead. They were given seats on the front row to the right of the stage. They watched the play and pretended to be entertained. This kind of playacting was too far from the reality they had come to know. It was not to their taste at all.

As they watched the play John began to feel something odd about his surroundings. He felt a chill and it quickly turned frigid, causing stiffness in his joints. He could not move his arms or legs. He looked around at the others and noticed nothing unusual about them.

Suddenly *a dark shadow* moved before his eyes from the left of the stage towards the right. His attention was quickly drawn upwards in the direction of the President. At that precise moment he saw the peacefulness that rested upon Mr. Lincoln's face and heard a gunshot blast. The President slumped forward out of sight. There was a struggle in the President's box.

Someone within the theatre screamed, *"The President has been shot!"*

A man jumped from the President's box directly onto the stage. It was John Wilkes Booth, the actor. Booth yelled out, *"The tyrant is dead!"* and limped out the back exit of the theatre.

John could not move. He was paralyzed just like in his dream. He was horrified! This wasn't a dream and he could not wake up to find everything alright. He just sat there with his mouth wide open and he could not close his eyes. What was happening around him? Why had he been foretold of this terrible event and why was he prevented from taking action? John could not grasp the circumstances around him. Events from the last week were overwhelming his senses. He could not understand for the life of him the revelations that were coming without invitation. The dreams, the visions and events were extraordinary.

He recalled the day he sat in the creek and was informed he had been spared because there was more for him to do. His grandmother also advised him to go home. What was this gift he had been given? Or was it a curse? He was frightened. He was brought to the reality of the moment by Thomas gripping his arms and shaking him violently.

"Wake up! Wake up John! The President has been shot! We must catch his killer." Thomas was screaming at John, who was slowly coming out of a fog. *"What happened to you? You look like you've seen a ghost. Are you in some kind of trance?"*

John could not speak. It was as if he had been struck dumb and lost use of his faculties for the moment. Then he jumped up, pushed Thomas aside and ran out of the theatre. Once he was in the street he looked in both directions until he spotted a church steeple to his right. He ran with abandon, like he was in a dream. He pulled on the door, but it was locked. He pounded on the door, but no one answered.

He looked south of where he stood and saw a larger church. It was a Catholic church and there was a light coming from inside. He quickly bolted in that direction. He pulled at the huge door and it opened. He ran inside to find a little old lady kneeling at the altar and the priest lighting a candle on the landing above and to the right of her. He ran to the front and moved into the second pew.

He fell to his knees and made the sign of the cross. He looked directly at the crucifix placed in the center, high up. He wept as he saw the crucified Christ hanging from the cross. He took in every detail: the blood running down Christ's side, the nails in his hands and feet, the crown of thorns on his head with blood flowing from it also.

He looked up remorsefully at Jesus' head resting on his chest. *"Oh Father, what have I done to bring on your wrath? What must I do to appease you? Forgive me for all my failures, my sins and my shortcomings! Oh, Jesus! Did I bring this horrible thing upon our President?"*

"Please! My heart hurts so badly, I can't even imagine so much pain. What must I do to overcome this agony? Please help me! Please oh Lord, I beg of you!" John fell on his face and sobbed.

Then he heard an angelic voice, *"Do not worry John. Abraham is with me now. He is home again."* These words came as clear as if someone stood in front of him.

John saw a vision as he lifted himself from the floor. He saw Abraham walking high above with heavenly hosts escorting him on each side. John's fear dissipated. Peacefulness settled over him, enveloping his whole being. He felt a sense of serenity that all things would be well.

John methodically made the sign of the cross and said, *"Thank you Jesus,"* and left the church to find his friends again.

The whole theatre was in pandemonium. People rushed to the President's aid. Several doctors in the theatre were quickly on the scene. In short order they had moved President Lincoln from the theatre across the street into a boarding house. A doctor removed the bullet and a blood clot from the President's head. Abraham Lincoln was stretched out upon a bed too short for his tall body, rendering him diagonal across the mattress. People came in and people left. They kept Mrs. Lincoln from her husband until he passed. It was 7:22 A.M when a doctor pronounced him dead.

Secretary of War Charles Stanton spoke, *"He belongs to the ages now!"*

Matthew and his friends gathered in the street with many others, waiting for answers to their questions. No one was really ready for the truth. Word quickly got out that someone made an attempt on the Secretary of State's life too. It was a failed attempt, only wounding him.

Secretary of War, Stanton, issued a reward of one-hundred thousand dollars for the arrest of John Wilkes Booth for the murder of the President.

Thomas was overwhelmed with emotion and like Matthew, was in a state of shock. "There is nothing for us to do!" Matthew put his arm around Thomas' shoulder. "Let's go down to the hotel. What do you say, Thomas?" They made their way to the hotel, silence prevailed.

They sat for an extended time, pondering the events, before anyone spoke. Finally, Thomas spoke with a low voice, as a man who'd lost a dear friend.

"I only met him today and I can't believe the hurt my heart feels for him. I fought in Chancellorsville with Stonewall Jackson and it took a hold to me when he died some days later; but, this is something that surely takes my breath from me. I just can't believe it happened so quickly. He was shaking my hand just this morning and now ..."

"He was not only the President, but he was a friend and a mentor to me!" Matthew stopped, gathering his thoughts and his breath. "He was a symbol of what was good in man and America as well. We have lost more than a man. The South has lost their best friend. He was our Northern Star, our guiding light. Booth wanted to be a hero. Instead, he will be forever known as a fool and a villain." He daubed at his eyes to catch the tears with a handkerchief.

"He knew his time was nigh. He told me just maybe it was meant to be!" John looked up at the ceiling, "That's what he said. He wasn't afraid, because he saw it in a dream. I admire and respect him for his courage and conviction. He stood up to the world and told us the time had come to end the scourge of slavery, popular or not, he did it!"

"And, do you know something, he was right! It should never have been and it was well past the time for it to end! And you are also right, Matthew. He would have been the perfect man to guide us in our nation's recovery; but, now that chance is lost because of Booth's foolish actions. I saw him. Abe Lincoln is in the loving arms of our Lord. I saw the angels leading him home! He is finally at peace!" John spoke his mind.

They moved to the dining hall for breakfast, having foregone sleep. They were seated, drinking coffee, when Jacob walked in, followed by Madelyn.

"The President is dead! He has succumbed. I was there when he breathed his last breath. I will never forget our friendship," said Jacob.

"Did you really know him?" Thomas asked with surprise.

"Yes!" Jacob replied. "I met him when I was five and my father pulled his wagon out of a mud hole up to its axle. He said that oxen could never best his fine dray horses, but father put our oxen to work and they pulled that load of corn out of the mud in a single try. I believe he knew they would. He was a fine man and not a truer friend could be found. There will never be another like him."

Madelyn wept. "The army has taken up the pursuit of Booth, and all of the government's resources will be afforded in the efforts to round up all of his co-conspirators. I want to thank you gentlemen for your assistance to me, but it appears we failed to stop the one event, unthinkable above all, that could have happened. There are no bounds to evil men and their desires to destroy all that is good among us. Well, I must go now and I hope we cross paths again." She turned and walked from the room with a heavy heart.

CHAPTER 10

MATTHEW, THOMAS AND JOHN SETTLED UP
with the stable owner and rode over to the general mercantile to load
up their purchases. They loaded the pack mule with provisions for their
journey south and ammunition for their new gun purchases. Thomas
and Matthew each got a new Henry repeating rifle like John had.

It felt strange to be leaving town just as the announcement of the
President's death was settling upon everyone. There was a quiet and
emptiness about the place, not just on these three men. People were
openly weeping everywhere they turned.

The desk clerk was crying as they left. He was having great dif-
ficulty grasping the fact that the assailant was none other than the
famous actor, John Wilkes Booth, for which he so proudly proclaimed
as a resident of his fine hotel.

A little girl in the mercantile asked her mother why they killed the
President. She wanted to know was Mr. Lincoln a bad man. The woman
told the child he was a good man, but she could not give an answer to
why he was killed. She did not know either.

The boy that worked at the stable could not lift his head when they
tipped him for the care he gave their horses. He simply stated thanks
and goodbye as he turned to retreat to the rear of the stables.

"I will be glad when this day is over!" proclaimed Thomas. "This
almost feels like a nightmare that I should be waking up from mighty
quickly. Hey, there comes Jacob!"

Jacob came down the street on his mare Stonewall, leading a fully
packed horse, followed by his hound. "This is Blue. You finally have his
approval. He was doubtful at first, but finally agreed to travel with us.
What direction do you plan to take on this odyssey of yours?"

Matthew drew near the others and delivered the planned course of travel. "I believe we will travel due south to Charleston, and from there west on to Jackson, and south to New Orleans on our final leg. Does that suit your fancy, Jacob?"

"That sounds mighty pleasing to me. I think I may have to pass on Charleston because I left an angry, young lady my last visit there. I do look forward to cooling my heels in the Mississippi River in New Orleans. I will have myself another cup of strong French coffee and some more of those delicious pecan pralines they make down there. What are we waiting on? The whole darn swamp will have dried up before we cross the Pontchartrain," laughed Jacob, as he put his horse in a trot.

"If we make Stafford by dinner we can check on Samuel," Thomas thought out loud. "I bet he has really settled in with Mrs. Fontaine by now. She is a real lady, that one! Maybe, I might come back and help her raise those sheep one day. And she knows her way around the kitchen for sure."

"Now there is your *true motivation* my dear friend. You will not pass on a hot meal," laughed John.

They traveled well that day. The horses seemed anxious to be on the road. It would take some time for the horses and the men to get use to each other; however, the road appeared to be a welcomed change for man and beast. Traveling together would provide the men time to grow accustomed to each other's ways and personalities.

The awareness of peace after the bitterness of war was a concept that would take more than a proclamation of words to penetrate the fragile soldier's consciousness. It would be years, maybe decades, before the country could find level footing again. With a civil war it might take generations to overcome the ugliness that prevailed, notwithstanding the deep divides between the freed slaves and their captors.

Pausing at midday to rest the horses and stretch their legs, Thomas went across the creek to relieve himself. "Don't get snake bit my friend. Look around carefully. I don't want to be digging a hole for you," yelled John with a chuckle.

While watering the horses, they heard a pistol shot and ducked down to get their bearings on its direction. Had Thomas seen a snake or was someone shooting at him? Jacob motioned for them to stay down. He crossed the creek to reach the other side as he pulled a large knife from its sheath. He slowly pushed through the bushes as another shot rang out. He got down on his stomach as he proceeded further into the brush. Then Thomas walked up with a turkey in one hand and a confederate sword in the other.

"What are you doing in the dirt, Jacob?" Thomas asked as he stepped over him and crossed the creek.

"This gobbler walked out in front of me as I was squatting down and I shot him. I had my gun in my hand while I was watching for rattlesnakes. When I was walking back I saw this here Johnnie Reb leaning against a hickory tree with his sword at arm's length pointing directly at me! Of course he was only a skeleton dressed in rags and a Yank was dead at his feet. I shot him too, mostly out of fright. I hope I didn't scare you all. We can give this to Mrs. Fontaine in trade for another meal," Thomas smiled at his thoughtfulness.

"And you can bury those soldiers before we go, since you were kind enough to shoot and rob the dead!" Jacob inserted with frustration.

It was getting late in the day when they topped the hill and could see sheep in the valley and smoke coming from the chimney of the Fontaine house. They approached the house cautiously since they saw horses in front and a man posted nearby.

Jacob laid back and circled around behind the place and dismounted his horse in a thicket of oaks with a row of cedars across the front. He tied his horse and pack horse so they could crop grass while he was away. He used his stealth as he exchanged his boots for a pair of moccasins stored in his saddlebags.

His approach was undetected as he made his way to the back of the house. He looked through the screen door to find the lady and her daughter tied to their chairs at the dining room table. They were scared. The daughter was crying as the mother tried to look strong for her. The woman's dressed was torn, partially exposing her breast. Her face was red and blood trickled down from her lip.

He also saw the boy lying in the kitchen next to the stove with blood on his head. It looked like he had been struck with a piece of stove wood. He caught the boy's eye as he looked closer. The boy was alive and playing possum. He made a sign to him to keep silent and the boy winked to acknowledge his command.

Matthew was the first to speak as they approached the house. "Hello the house! We are passing through and would like to water the horses if that is alright with you."

Slowly Matthew dismounted as John and Thomas held their positions. They had the straps off their pistols, but did not let on like there was any suspicion. The man posted outside did not speak, but a man walked out the front door and looked at them.

"What do you men want?" barked the man wearing a Confederate uniform, as he stepped off the porch. He looked to be the person-in-charge.

"Just wanting some water for our horses, if you please," Matthew stated again as he looked around and counted four horses.

"Get your water and git out of here! Don't need no trash crossing our property, you hear me?" the man yelled.

"Yes sir, you do have a mite pretty place here I must say; and I bet your missus must be proud her man done come home a hero to take over the affairs," Matthew prodded some to get a reaction.

"What do you know about my missus, you Yankee trash?" the man turned and walked back towards the house as he spoke. Another man, this one wearing a Yankee uniform, walked out onto the porch and they stood side-by-side.

A fourth man stepped out the back door with his pistol drawn, only to get the large steel blade of Jacob's knife thrust right into the middle of his sternum, piercing his heart. His eyes blinked once as he was lowered to the ground. Jacob removed his knife and wiped the blood on the back of the man's shirt.

He made his way through the house with Samuel behind him. Samuel untied Pauline and Elizabeth and directed them into the bedroom per Jacob's instructions.

Thomas and John had moved their horses apart to add some separation in the event of gunplay. That was inevitable. Just as the dust was settling from the shuffle of the horses' hooves, Jacob came through the screen door with a war whoop as he drove his knife into the man standing in front of the door. He did not open the door, but went right through it screen and all, driving it onto the man. They both landed on the porch with Jacob in the better position.

That was all the heads-up they needed to pull their guns and blow the two villains straight to hell, where they belonged. It happened so fast Matthew had just barely cleared leather before the men toppled to the ground. The man that was on the porch laid across the swing with a bullet through the forehead, while the other man fell in the dirt with two bullets an inch apart through his heart.

"Why did you waste an extra bullet on that one, John?" Thomas asked.

"I just wanted to make a point, that's all," John replied with a smile. "Don't mess with my friends!"

Jacob got up, removed his knife, wiped it on the dead man, and put it in his sheath. He flung the broken screen door off the porch and dragged the dead man to stack him with the one John shot. "Clean up your mess Thomas! Do you want the ladies to walk out here and have to view this?"

About that time Samuel walked out with a shotgun. "It was a good thing you fellers came along when you did. I was about to take care of this by myself." They laughed.

Pauline came through the door holding Elizabeth to her side. She had changed her dress and pulled her hair back into a bun. "Thank God you came along when you did! Clean up and I will prepare dinner."

"I got us a turkey, Miss Pauline," Thomas proclaimed like a little boy who was proud of himself.

"Just put him in the pan and we will cook him tomorrow," she smiled back at him as a mother would to confirm approval.

They ate dinner after introductions were made and the men repaired the door and removed the dead men to the barn. They would have to bury them tomorrow. It had been an eventful day. Pauline and Samuel explained how the men came up to ask for food and pounced on them. They hit Samuel across the head with the stove wood and thought him dead.

Poor Elizabeth was still visibly shaken by the ordeal. She hadn't spoken a word. It was too traumatic for her to absorb as quickly as Samuel or her mother. Her mother was very aware of her continued fear. She would have Elizabeth sleep with her as long as it took to get through this. She wasn't over the loss of her father and brother yet, and this just compounded the issues.

The men offered to sleep outside in the barn, but Mrs. Fontaine would not hear of it.

The next morning the rooster crowed and Samuel had the fire going in the stove. Pauline had bacon frying and coffee on the table. Everyone was up and washed and sitting at the table, even Lady the dog was in her new favorite place, next to Samuel. Elizabeth was smiling as she sat next to Jacob. Everyone noticed the partiality she had for him that morning. She must have felt some security in his presence. Pauline pretended not to notice.

Matthew sipped his coffee with tremendous delight, "Boy, this is great tasting coffee! Miss Pauline, you always set the best table for us. I hope you know we will have to tie Thomas to the horse to get him to leave here."

"Nobody is making him leave!" Pauline laughed.

"Yes they are. He has signed on to work for the U.S. Government, and he has a job to do."

"Don't I get a say around here?"

"I think your words were, "I can out shoot any man around and I will make a good scout for the United States Government.""

"Yeah, I did sort of shoot off my mouth a bit," Thomas squirmed, "but I can make my way back when we are done, can't I?"

"That will be up to the lady of the house. There is a long road to travel before you ever cross that bridge my friend. Now eat your breakfast!"

It was bittersweet to leave these dear people. There was such a warm feeling. And the depth of adoration among them was something rarely found.

Thomas presented Samuel with the Confederate sword he had found and Jacob presented Elizabeth with a Cherokee necklace made by his grandmother.

He said it had special power and the Great Spirit would guard and protect her as long as she lived. It would also form a bond between them in this life and the hereafter. She smiled boldly as she ran and jumped into his arms. She hugged him so hard, and tears flowed down his cheeks as he held her tight. As they left they all felt something special had just occurred in their lives. Jacob felt a spiritual bond with these folks like those found in the Cherokee circles he had known.

Leading the dead men's horses with their bodies draped over them they rode to a point five miles north of Fredericksburg looking for a place to bury them. Matthew suggested they throw them in a gulley and cover them with leaves and brush. Thomas suggested burning the bodies, but John said they didn't have the time. They did shovel some dirt over them to hold down the stench. No one had words to say over the bodies except, good riddance.

The only livery stable in town was willing and able to buy the Rebs' horses and saddles. All other liveries were closed, burned or just out of business. It paid to be compliant with the Union army. Matthew made arrangements for the proceeds to be delivered to Mrs. Fontaine.

Making excellent time they rode into Richmond with enough time to eat, feed the horses and ride on past town in search of a place to camp. They saw Robert E. Lee riding Traveler to his temporary home in the Richmond countryside. His beautiful mansion, Arlington was no longer his home. The United States Government had taken possession of it, and would establish a national cemetery on it grounds; even to include its extensive gardens. Outside of town the men set up camp for the night.

CHAPTER 11

THE ROADS WERE HEAVILY TRAVELED BY
former Confederate soldiers trying to get home from the war. They were
weak from battle, malnourished, poorly clothed and had long distances
to travel to reach home with hopes of finding family and renewing a
life that was forever altered. There were also many that had suffered the
loss of limbs and used homemade crutches to walk hundreds of miles.
Those leaving prison camps were weak from squalid conditions, and
had even lesser odds of returning home successfully.

There was the consideration of recently freed slaves that left lives of
internment to seek out a better life. They were told freedom meant to
leave the plantations with the tattered clothes on their backs and nothing else. They were given very little assistance. They scavenged anything
they could find to live on; even eating the bark off trees just to stay alive.
Some left for other plantations with a reputation for better treatment.
Many stayed on where they were and worked for shares, and were often
cheated. Others were not told of their freedom until years after the war
was over. Some were even killed by the slaveholders because they did
not plan on giving up their property without compensation. These were
dangerous times and the roads were not safe to travel. The life of any
man, black or white was in a constant state of danger.

Matthew advised John and Thomas that as they moved south to be
on guard constantly because they were targets for highwaymen, soldiers
and anyone looking to improve their lot. By having horses, guns, a pack
mule and supplies made them subject to attack day or night. It would
be better for them to camp or bed down in more protected places like
towns or farms where they could conceal their livestock. It was recommended to keep firearms ready at all times.

Their clothing was that of any common man: boots, denim and

work shirts. They tried not to stand out, but any man not wearing a soldier's uniform was considered suspicious, and they were wearing new clothes too. People would wonder by what means they had acquired new clothes at war's end.

Matthew informed them their story would be they hired on to work for the railroad, and were just a survey crew sent forward to assess the conditions of track and stations and to report back what material and labor were necessary to restore them to operating condition. This should suffice in deflecting any unnecessary attention from themselves; although, these were troubled times indeed.

Thomas built a small fire beside the creek in the center of the clearing they chose to use for camp. After stripping the horses and hobbling them in a patch of grass nearby, he made a pot of coffee. "How does a cup of hot coffee sound?"

John replied, "Didn't you *just* eat?"

"Yes, but I like a cup of coffee when I smoke!" He took out his corncob pipe and prepared to light it.

"Stop!" Jacob insisted.

"What? Do you see a snake?" Thomas said as he jumped backwards.

"No, I just want to give you something before you light those *hillbilly* pipes." Jacob went to his packs and brought out several pipes made of briar. "Here, take this Thomas. Matthew, you and John can have one too."

"These are very nice Jacob, they look like Petersons. Where did you get them?" Matthew inquired.

"They were a gift from the *Washington Bureau of Indian Affairs*. You know how they are always giving gifts to us Injuns, things like beads for Manhattan. Well, since we smoke peace pipes they thought it appropriate to give us some white man's pipes. So, here you are! Smoke them and enjoy. A gift from Uncle Sam," Jacob smiled.

Thomas scratched his head, "Do I know your *Uncle Sam?*"

"That's just an expression, meaning the government!" John explained.

"You'll have to help me, I guess that is a little too complicated for me," Thomas admitted.

"When we reach North Carolina I will branch off west to the mountains. I have friends and relatives to see in the Cherokee Nation. I can pick up your trail in Jackson, Mississippi. Do you plan to tarry in Charleston?" Jacob asked as he reached down to get the coffee pot from the stone where it sat.

"Not long, maybe a few days. John has something to deliver to a fallen soldier's family. It should be brief, unless we meet up with some of your old sweethearts while in town," Matthew smiled.

"If you do, it would be most beneficial for everyone concerned if you did not mention my name. I left in haste my last visit. I would also recommend you get off the main roads and travel some of the old trading routes the Indians used. The old *Natchez Trace* is still a good road. It would take you away from the dark element of which you spoke earlier. You have to be leery of just about everyone these days. I will miss the excitement that comes so naturally to you, but maybe it will be safer for me to part company, for a while." They laughed at his assessment of them.

John drank his coffee as Thomas stretched out, placing his head on his pack and crossing his legs. "Tell us something about that country you plan to travel; it is in the mountains, is it not?" John posed his question to Jacob as they peered into the night sky now bright with the majesty of stars popping out everywhere.

"Well, where do I start? It is a beautiful garden, a heavenly spot in the western edge of the state that runs down into Tennessee. They call it the *Smoky Mountains*, at least the white folk do, because its peaks often rest above the clouds. It is spiritual to my people. A remnant of the Cherokee people hid out in those mountains during the great Indian Removal to Oklahoma. We call that forced march west, the *Trail of Tears*. Those that stayed behind in North Carolina are called the *Eastern Band of the Cherokee Nation*; even though, they have not been recognized as such, by the government or the Cherokee Nation."

"When I say the mountains are spiritual to my people, it is to say they find harmony in nature there. Not only do they walk with the spirits that forever roam the hills, but they seek balance in what the Creator has given. They take full responsibility to care for Mother Earth while getting all their needs from her."

"The Cherokees once called the greater part of the eastern half of this land their home. But the mountains hold special meaning to them. There is a reverence that can be felt when you travel the mountains and drink from the mighty streams that cascade down the mountainsides. The trees are great within themselves, and many of the stands of timbers are virgin to the white man's axe. The Great Spirit can be found in many animals. The black bear is just one of them. No one owns the mountains; we are only visitors here."

Jacob's dog Blue came out of the darkness and lay down beside him as he drank his coffee.

"I appreciate your reference to the spirit of the *Smoky Mountains*," John replied as he reached over and placed a broken limb on the fire causing a spray of sparks to fly into the night sky.

"My maternal grandmother hailed from those mountains. She is also of the Cherokee nation. Her maiden name was Isabella Morningstar. She was called *Shadow Talker* by her people. She saw the spirit in all things: the bayou, the Spanish moss, flowers, trees, birds and every kind of animal, and even the food the earth provides us. Her spirit was never bound by this world."

"She often spoke of the mountains of her youth. She said they were the source of her education. As she walked in the woodlands and breathed in the fresh mountain air, knowledge was imparted upon her. Nature was her classroom, defining her inner spirit, searing a brand on her soul. Her vision ran deeper than sight."

"She used to say that everything has its own spirit; even the stones spoke to her. I have read in the Bible that *the very stones will rise up and proclaim His name, Him being Jesus,* the *redeemer.* She had a reverence for everything: the sky, the moon, and the stars. She could even hear music in the wind."

"I never knew anyone like her. She speaks to me even now, in my dreams. I believe she is guiding me. And, she has bestowed upon me a small part of her gift. It is becoming more of a responsibility to understand it and learn how to use it," John explained.

"I know her people. They speak of your grandmother with reverence still," Jacob said. "It is said that she was an *enlightened one*, a gift passed down by the ancients. She gave them prophecy that is still making itself known today and probably will be for generations to come. She was a true visionary!"

"What a small world it is. You and I are truly brothers! I am glad we made this connection. You are fortunate if she has passed some of her gifts on to you. It does come with a great responsibility. Indeed it does!" spoke Jacob.

"You may be the reason I was drawn to this small gathering," Jacob surmised. "Something spoke to me that morning we met, in a dream. I was encouraged to ride south of town for what I thought was just to clear my head, but I see now there was something more at work. I have felt an extraordinary spirit come upon me, a spirit of exceptional strength and courage, as I travel with you on your journey. It feels like I have a responsibility to protect and guide you. It is truly an odd feeling. I can't say I've ever felt anything like it before."

"This is all very stimulating! I must say this conversation has overwhelmed our friend Thomas," Matthew declared. They looked over at Thomas lying a short distance from the fire, with his eyes closed and mouth wide open, snoring up a storm. Their laughter did not wake him nor did it phase Blue, Jacob's dog sleeping next to Thomas.

Before sunrise Thomas had a fire going, coffee brewing and bacon frying in the pan. He fried some eggs too. Chicken eggs were a rare commodity during the war years. It was just as hard to travel with them as it was to acquire them. If Thomas's upbringing on the farm did anything for him it was to cultivate an appetite that was never ending. That made his foraging for food and constant thought of his next meal one of his greatest assets to his friends.

Jacob jumped from his sleep at the sound of Blue baying a short distance from the camp. He slid on his boots, grabbed his pistol as

Matthew and John did likewise. Thomas did not divert his attention from making breakfast. Jacob ran through the woods, dodging trees while branches slapped him across the chest and about the face. He followed the sound of the barking dog. He came upon the dog across the creek under some trees, where the sand had been deposited for many years at the wide bend in the creek. The dog was standing next to a hollow log about thirty feet in length and its opening about four feet in diameter. Matthew and John quickly arrived where Jacob stood, dripping wet from crossing the creek.

"What do you think, Jacob?" Matthew asked as he drew to one end of the hollow log and John approached the other. "Could it be a coon or a bear in there that needs to be smoked out?"

"I don't think so, raccoons usually run up a tree to escape and a bear wouldn't run from a dog. I believe there is a man. It makes sense how Blue is barking. He barks differently under different circumstances. Let's just shoot into the log and see what happens," Jacob posed to the others.

"*No! Don't shoot!* We is coming out! Please, please, don't kill us, we are not bad!" Quickly, from both ends of the log appeared a set of legs. One set belonged to a small slave boy and the other to a young white boy. They both stood up and walked to front and center of Jacob. They were both wearing tattered clothing and both stood shaking as the black child spoke.

"We mean no harm. We are afraid of Massa Sam; he done herded all us colored folks into the barn and was gonna set fire to it. I just got through a hole only I could squeeze out of and ran down to Tommy's house for help. We borrowed Massa's mule and rode for help. It done too late to save them!" the child cried. "We uns done seen the fire as we ran away, and it lit up the night sky somethin' fierce, sho nuf did!" The two boys stood there, as sobs racked their bodies and they found no comfort from the men.

About that time Thomas arrived and grabbed the boys by their arms and began to lead them towards the camp. "Don't you fellows understand them? They are tired and scared, and hungry too."

He led them into the camp, seating them next to the fire. He fed
them, and comforted them, as he got them to tell more of their story
to him.

While the men drank their coffee, John led the boys' mule into
camp. "I think we need to check out the boys' story. Don't you men
agree?"

They saddled their horses and the boys led the way. They ascertained
the black child's name was George and the other boy was Tommy.

Tommy belonged to a widow lady that lived on a piece of ground
once farmed by her husband before the war. It took everything they
could manage for his mother and sister and him to scrape out a living
from the tiny farm. Soldiers took their one milk cow and killed their
hogs and chickens as they saw fit, whenever they passed their way.

George was a skinny slave boy belonging to Sam Bolling. He lived
on a tobacco plantation nearby.

When they arrived at the plantation manor they could still see the
smoldering remains of the huge horse barn off to the side. They hurried
down the lane between rows of white fences where a small herd of fancy
horses once played, but now very few remained. Horses were cropping
the lush spring grass near the old oak trees. The beautiful carriages
had been removed from the barn so they would not be destroyed. That
would have been a foolish waste of valuable property. There were two
colored men digging a grave in a family plot, in a grove of trees.

George's mother came running and screaming as the men approached with the boys leading the way on the mule. She was hysterical
to see her son was alive. She thought he had surely died when the barn
was burned. George slid off the mule to meet her halfway. He was just
as amazed as she. He thought surely they all would have perished in
the fire.

A woman sat on the ground, rocking back and forth, with her legs
beneath her. She held the hand of her dead husband as she cried over
him. She wailed, emitting horrendous outburst, setting the nerves of
all present on edge. There was no comforting her.

Matthew approached a young lady sitting on the front porch. John could discern just how the events played out without being told.

"Ma'am, my name is Matthew; may I be of help in your time of need?"

"My name is Sarah, and I am afraid there is nothing you can do. But thanks for offering. The troubles are over, and now it is time for healing and moving forward." She stood up, smoothed out her dress and placed the rifle she held against the large, white pillar that supported the front of the beautiful home.

"Let me describe what has happened here over the last twelve hours."

"You don't owe us an explanation Miss Sarah," Matthew offered.

"Yes I do! Please allow me to explain the events as they played out. My father fell into a fit of rage and decided his slaves would not be taken from him. He felt they were his property and nobody could care for them as he could. I know that seems to be somewhat contradictory, but, he was raised with them and saw it as his birthright to watch over them and protect them. He could not comprehend setting them free to wander through this world without someone to guide them and protect them; so, he felt he must end it here, once and for all. He could not reason otherwise."

"He killed the overseer with a shovel because he would not obey his wishes. That was not a great loss in itself. Mother could not stop him from setting the barn ablaze with all of the people inside. I tried, but he would not listen. It had gone too far at that point. I threatened to shoot him and he turned on me like a rabid animal. You see, I had no other choice! I had to kill him to save the slaves. What else could I do? He has not been himself since brother was killed at Antietam. I let them out as quickly as I could. No one perished." She mustered all of her remaining energy to walk over and embrace George. She believed he was lost in the fire, as did the rest of them.

Sarah gathered everyone together in the yard. She directed some of the men to put the overseer in the pine box and deliver him to his widow. They were told to inform her that he was killed as was her father while trying to save the barn, and nothing more.

Arrangements were made for her father to be dressed in his Sunday's best for burial in the family cemetery. Mrs. Bolling was taken upstairs where she was administered a sedative and fell fast asleep.

Sarah acted quickly and concisely while she was under a rush of adrenaline. She knew decisions had to be made, and there was no time to waste, before her authority to control the situation was lost. She had to seize the moment.

She told George's mom, Nellie, to get several women ready to cook. "Get three of those hams from the hidden root cellar beneath the corncrib, a basket of sweet potatoes, a big pot of pinto beans, and enough cornbread for all to eat. These men are going to join us for a celebration! A celebration of life! Make enough apple pies to go around. Have Uncle Willie brew plenty of his famously strong coffee. Several of you men place boards over sawhorses for tables."

The plantation was busy with folks hurrying about with various tasks. Mr. Bolling was interred in rapid fashion, with Preacher Roberson saying words over the deceased. Things were happening so quickly no one was quite sure how to react when Miss Sarah gathered them all together that afternoon.

"Everyone, come close together so I do not have to repeat myself. I am tired and know you all are, as well, but I have something very important to tell everyone, and I am glad we have visitors here to witness this special occasion."

Sarah paused a moment. Taking a deep breath and letting it out slowly, she leaned her head skyward before she spoke again.

"Today, I lost my father, someone I dearly loved. He loved me very much, too. He loved each of you, and that may sound odd since he held you in bondage. Unfortunately, his death was necessary to save y'all today."

Sarah had to pause again to compose herself.

"He is no longer your master. You are free! The war is over and you are free just like I am free. You are free to roam the countryside as you wish; however, where would you go, how would you survive? That was my father's concern that you would not be able to fend for yourselves. Many former slaves have been set free and told to get out, and don't come back, just like that!"

"My brother is dead, father is no longer with us, and my mother does not have the capacity to make decisions concerning this place; so, here I am, alone, to put things in order."

"I propose a deed to forty acres for each family here. And, you will have a home built on your land with resources from the plantation. All I ask of you is help to farm the land. We will share the profits from what we produce. You will have whatever you produce from your plot for your own gain. You do not have to stay on here, but I doubt you will find an offer such as this, anywhere."

"This is a new day and I hope you will stay on as partners, with me. Together, we can forge something better. There are those of my generation that saw change coming. And there were those that wanted things to stay the same. Take your time and discuss this offer amongst yourselves as we enjoy this time of celebration. I believe father is with us in spirit, and would be pleased to find us all here, as one extended family. Silas, will you lead us in a blessing of this food?"

"Yes, I certainly will, Miss Sarah!" said the former slave Silas, with an air of elation and joy. "Let us all bow our heads, and give thanks. I know the Good Lord is right here amongst us as we mourn the loss of Massa Sam, but I also knows He extends good things to us all in the midst of bad occasions. Mr. Lincoln done seen fit that we are no longer slaves to be lorded over like dim- witted children, and it cost him his life, along with untold thousands of dem white folks, on both sides of the fight. We have so many blessings this day, and the biggest may be the overflowing of kindness from Miss Sarah. Lord, let us be thankful for all things; and, I pray you direct our path as we enter the *Promised Land*, Amen!"

Everyone gathered to share in the feast that was prepared in short notice. Tommy, accompanied by his mother and sister, came across the meadow to join them, per Sarah's instructions. Sarah greeted them graciously and directed them to share with them.

Matthew was very awed by Sarah. He admired her for her stamina, and courage, especially so close to the death of her father. He also noted her moral fortitude to plot a course of action so bold and forward thinking. Changing the status of slaves from property, to property owners, made sense morally, and showed great business sense. She was an extraordinary person, indeed!

He felt a kindred spirit. It was not Matthew's desire to participate in the slaughter of fellow countrymen, or the downfall of his beloved Southern homeland; nor was it his way to perpetuate the status quo either.

He was a strong man, broad shouldered, and on the tall side for his time. But his real strength came from within. It came from a source of inspiration of the friends and acquaintances his parents kept. They were teachers, and associated with people that upheld like values in their home, and about their travels. They always encouraged Matthew, and his siblings, to use their heads when all around them were losing theirs. People, who knew Matthew, understood why he avoided the urge to fight. His strength was never questioned.

It was his deep-seated sense of justice that drew him towards Sarah. He felt she was a true pillar of strength and character, especially in a time when the nation had lost its moral compass.

Matthew's parents weren't advocates of slavery, nor did they condemn those that were. It was confusing for him and his siblings not knowing where his parents stood on the issue. They always taught *Christian values,* and the proper respect of others, per the constructs of the *Golden Rule.*

He was always puzzled when he heard hushed voices late at night. It sounded like his parents speaking to slaves, followed by great commotion that would end with his parents retreating back to bed as if nothing had happened there. His parents never spoke of it and never recanted any activities that happened in the night. Neither did he ask them about those nights.

It finally came together in his mind, on the day of his departure to West Point, just what his parents were doing. It was early morning when a group of patrollers came to the house and asked his father and mother if they saw one of Mr. Wallace's runaway slaves called Big Jim come this way. He ran away with his wife and three children in tow. His tracks were lost about a mile away at the edge of the swamp. It just seemed natural for them to pass by this way, stated the leader of the patrollers. His parents could not have seemed more surprised than the slaveholder himself how they could have escaped and just disappeared into the landscape. That night Matthew had clearly heard and watched his mother and father as they aided the escaping family of slaves with provisions and instructions to the next place where they would be assisted. It was then that he knew and realized just what a sacrifice and danger his parents had put them in, being an origination point in the *Underground Railroad*. They did not want anyone, including their children, to know their sentiments about slavery; because it might reveal their contributions to freeing slaves and have them arrested, and maybe even put to death for their actions. Their love of their fellow man was so strong and their hatred for slavery that they were willing to sacrifice everything. That was love! Even after the war, their participation in the Underground Railroad had to remain a secret just to protect them from angry folks that would retaliate and cause them bodily harm, or worse.

Matthew alluded to their activities later on that day as he boarded the train in Jackson for the Academy. He smiled after hugging his brother and sister, along with his parents, and said, "This will be a much safer train ride than the one Big Jim's family is taking. Don't you agree, Mom and Dad?" He smiled as he waved from the train window; however, his parents stood in complete shock on the platform at the station. They were bewildered at what they thought was a complete secret to everyone.

Everyone enjoyed the food and the festive atmosphere. Sarah made it her duty to become better acquainted with Matthew and his fellow travelers. He told her about his background and work for the President and discussed their new job as surveyors, destined for New Orleans.

Her interest was piqued by the knowledge of their destination. She abruptly stopped talking to Matthew and sent one of the little girls from the table to get Evangeline. Evangeline arrived at the table, standing next to Sarah. She was a slender young woman with light skin, and very pretty too. She could pass as Sarah's sister if you looked closed enough.

"Did you want me Miss Sarah?" Evangeline asked in a very soft and pleasant voice.

"Yes, Evangeline, these men are on a journey to *New Orleans!* Was it not your wish to travel there, someday?" She asked in an elevated voice, with a hint of excitement and anticipation.

"Why, yes it certainly is! You know my mother was sold to a plantation owner in Louisiana. She told me the last time I was with her to stop my crying. She said she had a dream that a young man, name of John, would lead me home to her after we got our freedom! All I gots to know is *which one is John*, and will he lead me there." Evangeline was almost in a state of euphoria.

Sarah looked at the men and explained. "Evangeline has lost her father here today, as well. My father sold her mother to a man in Louisiana. Her mother, Frances, is also a beautiful woman and my mother could not tolerate it any longer to have her on our plantation after Evangeline was about five years old. She finally realized who her father was, and would not have that woman anywhere on this property. Just to spite my father, and punish Frances, she had mother and child separated. She could see the resemblance in Evangeline and my father. Could you find it in yourselves to allow her to accompany you on your journey south?"

Matthew looked at his companions, and looked back at the ladies. "We have already experienced danger in our travel thus far and cannot assure her safety as we travel farther south. Would she be willing to risk dangerous conditions?"

"*Mister*," Evangeline quickly replied, "I will risk anything to find my mother once again. You cannot understand how it feels to be ripped from your mother's arm as they dragged her off, and not knowing if you will ever see her again! I will fight to protect you men from any danger that might befall us. So, don't you worry about me! I will go, and I will pay you for the privilege, any way you want. I am now a *free woman*. I will follow you all the way, hiding in the shadows, if you won't let me travel with you. Will you let me go with you, please?"

"It looks like we have another traveling companion, men! We start out about sunrise, after coffee that is. That handsome, dark haired fellow over there is John. He must be the one your mother spoke of from her dream. I have seen him baptize himself, but I haven't seen him eating locusts and honey, yet. The two other men are Jacob and Thomas. Thomas is our dinner bell, so to speak. He doesn't let us miss dinner time. Jacob and his dog, Blue, have proven invaluable to our safety several times so far. Blue will introduce himself when he is more comfortable around you. He is slow to warm to new friends."

The next morning Sarah and Evangeline called the men to eat breakfast in the manor. Evangeline was dressed in riding clothes that Sarah had given her and carried a carpetbag filled with other things she was given. She had her hair tied up in a bun. She was very attractive with her new appearance, no longer looking like a former slave. Mrs. Bolling was still upstairs and did not come down to meet them.

Sarah walked up to Evangeline and held her arms out to embrace her. They came together in a hug of genuine, heartfelt sincerity.

Sarah spoke, "We played together as children, now I can truly call you my sister; because you are, and I am free to say it! Freedom can come to us all, if we approach each other with love. You will always have a home here, if you want it. Please try to let all the bad you've felt here fade away with time. Father's death can be a new beginning for many. Don't miss out on the blessings, my sweet and loving sister. I will miss you."

Evangeline mounted the beautiful horse Sarah had saddled for her. Saddlebags and a sleeping roll were placed behind the saddle. This was the same horse Mr. Bolling prized so, and had hidden in the swamp, to prevent the Yankees from stealing it. What a coincidence that she would be riding it off to freedom. This could be the last time for her to see this place and the people she loved and trusted so much. She said her goodbyes to everyone.

Silas gave her a cross carved from a cedar branch. "Let this be your North Star to guide you on your way. That way, you will never be lost, baby girl."

As she turned to walk her horse away there came a sudden urge to stop. She jumped off the horse and ran to her Uncle John, the big man standing beneath an old oak tree. He caught her in his arms and held her tight, and she threw her arms around his neck. They both had tears running down their faces as they shared their goodbyes in private. Evangeline told him she would return once she had found her mother, his sister. But he could not speak. He just stood there with tears rolling down his cheeks.

Into the morning sun they rode, waving goodbye, and not looking back. The future was ahead of them, far greater than even their imagination could conceive. Evangeline knocked the dust from her shoes as she galloped down the lane, beneath rows of trees, and the fences that hung in disrepair.

CHAPTER 12

THE COUNTRYSIDE FAVORED THE TRAVELERS.
They made their camp in a clearing, beside a fast moving stream. The
next morning Thomas was up before everyone and had coffee boiling.
John got up, slid on his boots and poured a cup of coffee. He squatted
beside the fire and wished Evangeline a good morning as she walked
over and sat beside him. She sat cross-legged with her dress covering
her knees.

"Did you have the dream, Mr. John?" she asked quietly.

"What dream was that, Evangeline?"

"Did you have a dream that Miss Sarah and the plantation were in
danger; and, she was calling for help?"

John jumped straight up from the ground, "Yes, I did! I thought
it was a nightmare. It happened just before daylight, and I could not
return to sleep. Renegades were torturing some of your people and
Sarah was screaming for help! How did you know that?"

"Cause I dreamed it too, and it was as real as you standing there!
She was calling for Matt!"

Matthew rolled out of his bedroll as he was just waking and could
vaguely make out the conversation. "What did you say about a dream?"

"We both had a dream about renegades attacking Sarah and the
people on the plantation; and she was calling for help," John explained
briefly.

"Thomas, are you ready to ride?" Matthew asked.

Before Thomas could reply, Jacob came from the field where the
horses were hobbled, leading his and Matthew's horse. "Get your guns
Matt, your horse is ready!"

"How did you know, Jacob?" Matthew asked

"I saw an owl in the camp before dawn. I took it as a warning of

impending danger; so, I just wanted some horses ready to travel, if
necessary. Get your boots on!"

"Keep an eye out; we will be back as soon as possible!" Matt said
as he mounted his horse.

Thomas said, "We may slip into the village up ahead and grab
some provisions."

"Just be careful!"

"Enough said, be on your way, and *Godspeed!*" John replied.

Jacob and Matthew sped away in a gallop as time was of the essence, if they wished to avert a perceived danger, based on corroborating
dreams.

Meanwhile, John agreed that they should go into the village of
Franklin and pick up a few things, since they had an extra person with
them. The three riders were side-by-side with Evangeline in the middle.
She rode well for someone of limited experience. It was obvious this
was not her first ride. John looked in her direction and saw a beautiful
young woman full of pride, as she rode erect in the saddle, her chin up
and body balanced, with the cadence of the horse's canter.

Thomas looked in her direction and gave John a nod. It was as
two big brothers were keeping a watchful eye on their beloved little
sister. These were two brave and commendable young men, much like
thousands the war had produced. Many of these fine men were lost to
battle, disease and other various maladies before the war's end.

Although, there was almost as many not so desirable sorts that
survived the war, and took their toll on unsuspecting and undeserving
citizens along the way. These malcontents would operate for many
years after the war, robbing, killing and destroying everything they
could for their own selfish gain. The war opened the door for scalawags
to plunder the crippled South. It was as if the Devil himself was un-
leashed, and many of the culprits were Southerners themselves. It was
hard to unwind the actions of some that experienced the unrestrained
audacity of war. Once a dog has tasted blood it can't return to its old
nature. Nobody is able to let down their guard and feel safe while evil
goes unchallenged.

They approached the small town of Franklin, in southern Virginia, and walked their horses up to the general mercantile. Dismounting, they went inside to look around. There was not a lot to be had: some canned goods, homespun clothing, few medicines, an old saddle and some tack, several farm implements, an empty gun case and miscellaneous items. There wasn't much left after the war to purchase. An old slab of wood was laid across two barrels to make a crude bar along the right side of the small building. Three men were propped along the bar drinking from a jug of homemade corn-whiskey. Thomas walked up to the store keeper and asked if he had any coffee, smoking tobacco and a tin of salve.

"I've got some salve and tobacky, but no coffee mister," he replied. He looked kind of nervous like, glancing at the men along the bar, and back to Thomas.

"Well, I'll take what you got," Thomas commented as he watched the men and made note of John's position.

"That's a mighty fine looking slave girl you've got there mister. Would you be interested in tradin' fer somethin'?" said the biggest and nastiest looking varmint posted at the bar.

"She ain't no slave and not for trade either!" Thomas retaliated emphatically.

"Well, let me restate myself. What will you take for your *whore?*" the man slurred. "Cause I am gonna take her anyway you look at it!"

A woman ran from the building dragging her son, hoping to escape the apparent danger.

Thomas looked down at the ground for a brief moment and looked up at the men sitting at the bar. "Boys today would be a sorry day to die, and that kind of talk will only serve to get you killed." He knew that laying down the law wasn't going to be enough to sway them from action.

As quickly as the man stood up and pulled his gun Thomas pulled his bowie knife, and threw it. It landed where he aimed, right in the center of the man's throat. The man dropped his gun and grabbed for his throat, all the while falling backwards, upsetting the board across the barrels.

The second man anticipating trouble pulled his gun and swung it around at Thomas. John had already drawn his gun and fired. He shot the man in the belly, just above his belt buckle, a wound meant to cause a slow and painful death.

The third man fell backwards with his hands high above his head, upsetting the board laid across the barrels, "Don't shoot! I am *not* with them. Please don't shoot!"

The gut shot man was crying and shouting at John. "You've done kilt me, and it hurts mighty bad! What do you plan to do now, mister? Either give me some whiskey or finish me off?"

John asked him, "Are you a soldier?"

The man blurted out "No! What does that matter?"

"That means you are gonna die a slow and painful death mister. And it doesn't make sense to waste whiskey, good or bad, on a dead man! You should have chosen your friends more wisely. I have no pity for trash that stayed home and let good men go off and fight for them, and die in battle."

Thomas paid the storekeeper, gathered his purchases, and walked with John and Evangeline towards the door.

"Use whatever those lowlifes left behind to cover the expense of putting them in the ground," he said.

As they approached the plantation they slowed their pace; Jacob separated and worked his way around back and sought high ground. Screams could be heard ahead of them. Matt slowed his horse to a walk as he traveled down the lane towards the plantation. He tried to appear casual as he approached the main house.

He saw Evangeline's uncle, Big John, tied to a tree, shirt ripped from his back, and blood streaming from the cuts left by lashes of a whip. He estimated there were at least ten men, maybe a dozen. Several black women encircled Miss Sarah, who was lying on the ground, disheveled and bleeding from her lips and nose; they were in a posture of protection.

"Pardon my interruption, gentlemen. I am on my way south and I'm looking for a little hospitality for me and my horse. Could you spare some grain for him and a bite for me?" Matthew inquired.

"Do we look like a welcoming party mister?" shouted the man in the center appearing to be in charge.

"Why does a man with a Southern accent wear that Yankee hat?" another man posed.

"Well, fellows, it is like this! I joined the U.S. Army before the war broke out because of scum like you!" Matthew expected the worse after his commentary.

"Well, let's just give this no-account a good whippin' to go with his smart mouth! What do you think about that?" The man pulled his gun and pointed at Matthew.

"*Wahl*, I reckon you are just a sorry bunch of *marauders* that don't know when to stop, especially when you are surrounded and about to shake hands with the devil," he said with undeniable confidence.

The man with the gun looked from side to side, and turned to face Matthew, "*Bull . . .*"

That was the last word he ever spoke, because before he could complete his thought a bullet travelled through his skull, exploding it like a watermelon rolling off the barn roof. He dropped like a sack of corn. Jacob had positioned himself atop the house, behind the left front chimney on the north side. He shot when he felt to wait any longer would certainly mean the death of Matthew.

At the very next moment another blast, from a shotgun on the other side of the house, lifted a man standing in the buckboard and flung him to the ground like a ragdoll. The shotgun nearly tore the man in half.

Men came from every imaginable place: the slave quarters, the henhouse, the blacksmith shop and even the outhouse. They let out a scream that sounded like a Rebel-yell as they came down on the remaining marauders. The rogues did not have time to react due to the swiftness of the attack. The black men were armed with pitchforks, hoes, shovels, hatchets and even broken tree limbs. Even Old Blue, Jacob's trusted dog, got in the fight. The battle was over in several short minutes. There were thirteen dead men lying on the ground, all white, and not a single man from the plantation was hurt, except Big John, who still hung from the tree. The women even got a few kicks and punches in after the worst was over.

Old Silas came out to the scene, holding the shotgun in the crook of his arm. "I's knew where it was hid and I's didn't think Miss Sarah would mind if'n I borrowed it. I never shot a gun before and it kicks like a mule. It sure was a sweet thing, and I's like the way it bites too. It nearly bit that man into two pieces."

"I didn't know who had that shotgun, but I sure was glad you came along when you did!" Matthew grinned. Everyone laughed at his remark.

He walked over to the tree and cut the ropes that bound Big John's hands. John fell to his knees and slowly got up again while removing the ropes off his wrists. Matthew removed his shirt and walked up to John and draped it over his shoulders.

John turned to face Matthew, with tears running down his face, and said "Thank you sir." And they both walked over to Sarah. Big John reached down and scooped her up in his large arms and walked towards the house with two women close behind.

Sarah asked John to wait just a moment. She motioned for him to turn facing Matthew. She looked into Matt's eyes and after a brief pause, she said, "I don't know what brought you back, but thank God you came!"

"Didn't you call for me? That was what I was told by Evangeline!" Matt looked deeply into her eyes in response.

"I think I did, I must have," she said, as Big John turned to carry her into the house.

CHAPTER 13

MATTHEW AND JACOB STAYED OVER AND SLEPT in the house per Sarah's insistence. The next morning Mrs. Bolling greeted them after they washed up, and came down to the dining room for coffee. Uncle Silas had told them that she wanted to meet before Sarah came down for breakfast. The cook, Matilda, brought them coffee as Mrs. Bolling thanked them for all they had done in the last few days.

"The war has brought out the worst in people and the best. I never imagined things would have turned out as they have. I believe God has *a specific plan* for *everyone that seeks His will,*" explained Mrs. Bolling, "and it is for us to figure out *just what His plan is.* I have to find the courage to carry on without my husband."

"Sarah will be my shining example of strength. She is very young, but she is strong and capable. She has a vision of how things should be. With her strength this place will prosper and someday be a better place than it was before the war. I want to extend an open invitation to you all to visit as long and often as you wish."

Jacob responded, "Often times the *Great Spirit* causes fire upon the Earth for cleansing. Like the phoenix we return stronger. Sarah has been endowed with tremendous strength. We are honored to be your guests."

Matthew could see glimpses of Sarah's strengths in her mother. He felt a strong bond with her just by being in her presence. He and Jacob stood up when Sarah came down the stairs towards the dining room.

"Good morning everyone!" she said as she smiled and seated herself. "I must admit that I am exhausted. The last two days have almost taken the very life from me. How are you today mother? I hope you have enjoyed our guests." Sarah was very concerned for your mother's state of mind after having lost her husband just two days earlier, and under the extraordinary set of circumstances.

"I am surprisingly well, considering. Your friends are most pleasant and kind. I regret that I am a bit weak and somewhat weary. Please excuse my absence gentlemen as I go to my room for a little rest." The men rose as Mrs. Bolling left the room.

Sarah spoke, "I don't understand how you knew we were in danger yesterday. What prompted you?"

Matthew replied, "John and Evangeline both had a dream that you were in danger. They said you were calling my name, and Jacob had a premonition as well."

"That could tie in to *the curse*," she said, almost as if she was talking to herself alone.

That comment caused Matthew to search his mind for some faint memory about a curse. He remembered a journal by Carson Walker that mentioned a curse that could somehow affect a girl named Sarah, and their future. He hoped to carry her away from everything associated with it, and start their lives anew; that was if he had lived beyond the war, which he didn't.

"Sarah, do you by any chance know someone by the name of *Carson Walker*?"

"Yes!" she said somewhat startled. "He and I were engaged to be married, but he was killed in battle. How do you know him?"

"I didn't know him, but John did and that is why we are to going to Charleston before New Orleans. He gave John a journal to deliver to his sister and mother in the event of his death. I read about a curse which he referred to in relation to someone named Sarah. He hoped to take her away to avoid the curse. Would that Sarah be you?"

"Yes it would be me!" Sarah stood up and walked to the window for a brief time before responding further.

"I guess now would be a good time to explain. I knew Carson from our time spent in Charleston. We have a townhouse there. Father was born in Charleston. He loved going to the city to escape the rigors of the plantation. He and mother enjoyed the social life at various times of the year there. He said that the sea air was good for us. Carson and his family were dear friends of ours.

He was the most kind and gentle soul I think I have ever known. We practically grew up together, like brother and sister. His thoughts were often very profound. It is still very difficult to believe he is gone. I would never have imagined him being the sort to go to war. He was a very gentle spirit."

Sarah shifted her position to face them now. "It was in Charleston that our connection to the curse began. Father purchased a young slave girl while on vacation with mother. She could only be sold as a package deal with her older brother. He saw her at the slave auction and just had to have her. Mother was pregnant with me at the time and did not accompany him that day."

"The story goes like this. The woman's name was *Frances*. Frances' mother was the mistress of *Jean Lafitte*, the pirate or privateer; whichever title you prefer, still the same. Her name was *Marguerite*, a French mulatto, originally from Saint-Domingue, on the Island of Hispaniola. She had a two-year-old son. He kept them aboard one of his ships off Galveston. He took her to New Orleans when he had to flee the U.S. Navy in Galveston and leave his operations behind."

"When in New Orleans she discovered Jean was married and there were other mistresses kept in different apartments throughout New Orleans. Mr. Lafitte was a very popular man. This did not sit well with Marguerite and she sought retribution. She, a very jealous woman, went to a *voodoo priestess* and requested a curse be placed on Jean Lafitte. The voodoo priestess did not want to perform this curse initially because Lafitte was a well liked character in New Orleans. He had helped Andrew Jackson defeat the British at *Chalmette,* which turns out to be in exchange for some kind of pardon from the Governor of Louisiana for his piracy. Anyway, she regretfully decided to continue in spite of her initial hesitation. *A curse was placed on Jean Lafitte, and his offspring.* Lafitte sold Marguerite and her son into slavery at the auction block in New Orleans when he found out about the curse. Three years later he was killed off the coast of Cuba and buried at sea. His son from his marriage died at the age of twelve from yellow fever. *Marguerite was pregnant with Frances, Jean Lafitte's child, when she was sold.* Neither one knew at the time."

"So, it appears that my father was cursed indirectly by sleeping with Frances and being Evangeline's father. Men working on the plantation told me that he was never rational again after she was born. I couldn't say because I was just an infant. I think the toll of having to hide the fact that Evangeline was his daughter, and her having to live as a slave with the others was too much for him emotionally. He loved them both very much. Later, he sold Frances to appease Mother, and that tore him apart inside, as did the pain it caused Evangeline."

"The man that received the whipping is Frances' older brother, John. He would not divulge any information the marauders sought. I told them there was *no gold hidden here* or at least none that I knew of, but they believed otherwise; however, John spoke not a word, even if he knew of any gold."

"There you have it. *That was the curse Carson wished to protect me from when we were married.* It remains to be seen if it has been extended to Evangeline. I must say, she does have special gifts." Sarah sat down at the table after she recounted this story.

Jacob and Matthew had no reply after hearing the story told by Sarah. They had been through a great deal since the assassination of Abraham Lincoln and everything else that followed. Anything seemed possible and nothing would surprise them. Matthew felt very strongly there would be a future connection with Sarah. She was more substantive than other females he had met.

After breakfast they advised the men of the plantation to dispose of the bodies in the gulley and keep their guns, ammunitions and anything they could use, but not to keep any clothing or articles that might bring suspicion to them.

"Do not let any harm come to yourselves. Be alert to any strangers that arrive at the plantation. You are in charge of the protection of Miss Sarah and your families. I will give her contact information to reach me from Washington if the need arises." Matthew embraced Sarah as did Jacob.

Silas spoke before they mounted their horses. "Sir, thank you for everything you have done for us. You have been our guardian angel. *And don't worry about those men;* what the hogs would not eat we ground up with corn and fed the chickens. There is no trace of those bad men left on this good earth."

With a casual canter they were on their way to rejoin the others back at camp. The birds sang a beautiful melody as they passed down the lane on such a lovely, spring day. Seemingly, without a care in the world, the two men and their beautiful horses chewed up the miles and traveled down the road with a deeper friendship and another shared moment of valor between them.

CHAPTER 14

EVANGELINE HAD A FIRE STARTED, COFFEE IN the pot, and just began to place fish in the skillet to fry when Thomas' eyes popped open to realize someone had risen before him. It wasn't daylight yet. He pulled on his pants and boots and walked over to the fire. He wanted to appear as if he had been awake for some time. He was not about to let her know that he was startled or upset that she had beaten him to rise. Not only had she started a fire and began to cook, but she had caught fish from the stream next to camp before all of that was done. She had caught and cleaned the fish, and was now cooking them even while Thomas slept. This was possibly more than his manhood, and pride could stand. He walked over to the coffee pot and filled his cup. He placed the pot back on a large stone next to the fire and walked over to see what was in the skillet.

"Where did you get them fish, and who eats fish for breakfast?" he asked with a certain air of indignity.

"Well," she said kind of mocking his South Georgia accent, "I brought my skillet over to the creek and began to sing a sweet little Negro spiritual and they rose up and began to dance on the water. They followed me up the creek bank and I sang them into the pan. They did not tell me that they could not be eaten before any certain time. So I just cooks 'em! Don't you eat fish Mr. Thomas?"

"Don't you go getting smart with me young lady?" My name is just plain Thomas, no mister! And I think you should be ashamed of yourself, telling such a tall tale. I just thought it odd you got up so early to do all of that. That's what I meant!"

"Mr. Thomas, I mean Thomas, I am used to getting up early and preparing food. I hope you haven't forgotten that I was just a slave until a short time ago. I am surprised that you get up early and fix your own morning meal. Don't your women folk cook for you?"

Thomas walked over and squatted next to the fire, across from Evangeline. "I am not much older than you. I left home at sixteen to join the army. I must be about twenty years old now. I ain't ever been married and we have to fix our own food in the camp since there are no women folk to care for us."

"We were poor coming up. Most white folks don't have much. We got by, just like the Negroes, making do with what we had. We had money only when we sold the cotton crop. My ma and pa got by. We children did our part and I felt like it would help them if they had one less mouth to feed. So I left home in the middle of the night while everyone was asleep."

"I never really knew why we was a fightin', just had it to do. I mostly know'd that the Yankees had invaded the South. I never took to slavin' myself, didn't think it would be pleasing to the Lord. I didn't mean anything bad. Just was surprised to see you awake so early. I forget that you did not grow up cared for as some have been. And you can forget that slave stuff from now on. You are free and that is not how I look at you. I see a beautiful young lady with a future as bright as the sun!" He started to turn red in the cheeks and hoped she could not see him blush in the predawn firelight.

Thomas and Evangeline sat quietly as she prepared their breakfast. They listened to the birds as they declared the dawn of another day. The sunrise was exceptionally pretty that morning and there was a light fog across the camp that quickly burned off. The smell of hot coffee was enticing. John got up, stretched, and walked over to the creek to wash the sleep from his eyes. He put his pants on over his long underwear quickly after remembering there was a woman in camp. He had not lived among women folk in a very long time, not that he minded. The smell of the burning hickory, mixed with coffee and fish frying in the pan overwhelmed his sense of smell so early in the morning. He filled his cup and sat next to the fire.

"*Fish*! Where did they come from?" he asked puzzled, while scratching his head.

"Evangeline sang them into the pan! What do you think?" Thomas answered quickly.

"Don't be a smarty with me so early in the morning. You must have slept on a rock to wake up so vile!"

"He is still mad because that is what I told him when he asked the same question earlier. How are you, Mr. John?"

"I am doing well, Evangeline, nice of you to ask. And you can call me John if you prefer. We are on an equal basis and I hope we will become friends over time. I hope the others will return with good news sometime later today. I have been very worried about them."

"I don't think we need to worry about them. My Uncle John assured me in a dream last night that all is well. Great spirits are watching over Jacob. He is a *special* one."

Evangeline was startled at how much she was speaking and how much she had opened up to these men who were yet strangers. She felt close to them; no longer were there barriers like she had always felt among other white people. These men were different, or maybe she was different now. Maybe she was beginning to understand what it truly meant to be free. Maybe there was something to this freedom notion. It felt good! She just hoped it would last, even if it was just with certain people. She knew her life was changing and she looked forward to finding her mother and discovering what their lives could be.

"I hope I haven't spoken out of place."

"Not at all! I am not certain I understand this gift I have been given. It is all very new to me. Some may think it strange to be talking about dreams and spirit beings like they are real people. I am becoming more at ease with things I do not understand. Thomas and I have seen so much death in the past few years that nothing surprises me anymore. So much evil abounds. My grandmother was very spiritual and she must have passed it on to me. Maybe it has been given for me to lead you home as you have said, and that is all I need to know," John said. "I will give it my best shot."

"All I know is if you two keep talking those fish are going to walk back into that creek. Let's eat!" Thomas spouted off.

They ate the fish and Thomas helped Evangeline clean up after breakfast. They did not have anything in particular to do but wait for the others to return. Evangeline walked down the creek to clean up while Thomas and John sat back and smoked their pipes. They watched over her as brothers would watch over a sister. They were aware that danger existed everywhere and would protect her at all cost.

She was a beautiful young woman. Her skin was very light and her hair very dark and wavy. She kept her hair in a bun. She let if down to wash it with the same bar of soap she used to bathe. The men turned themselves away from her as she entered the deeper pool and demanded some privacy.

John nudged Thomas as he saw three men walking down the road about a hundred yards back around the curve. "Better get my gun when you get yours. I will keep an eye out. Tell Evangeline we have company. They may not be friendly."

John and Thomas stood around the rock lined fire pit as the men approached.

"Hello the camp," one of the men called out. "Can you spare some coffee?"

"Come on in, pour yourself a cup."

"We are traveling south, going home, and our luck has been terrible. We have been living off rabbits. Can you spare some grub?" asked the older of the men.

"We are soldiers like you," stated John. "We were fortunate enough to be hired by the railroad to go south and perform land surveys for new lines; otherwise we would be flat broke. We can spare some jerked meat and canned peaches but little else until we shoot something ourselves."

The three men filled their tin cups and drank the hot coffee. As they sat around the ashes of the breakfast fire Evangeline walked up. Two of the men stood up and the third did not rise. They removed their hats and recognized a lady present. It was not lost on Thomas or John that the third was not as gentlemanly as the others.

"I guess you were not raised in the South, mister!" John looked at the man with contempt. "We were taught to show respect for a lady."

"I don't see a lady. I see a slave girl, whose mama liked the old master too much. Could be someone's whore herself!"

Without a thought Thomas leaped the distance that separated the two and kicked the man in the head. The man rolled over and came to his feet. He pulled a knife and spread his legs and arms for battle. Thomas was just as quick to pull his Bowie. John grabbed his rifle and showed the men he had no intentions for them to interfere.

Evangeline screamed and indicated this was not necessary, but it did not suffice to stop something already set in motion.

They parried with the big knives and words were spoken, but not words of peace. The man nicked Thomas' left forearm, tore his sleeve and brought blood to the surface. There were many attempts to get at each other's midsection and the area of combat grew ever wider. They fought near the pack mule and got it riled up. It started to bray and kick. Thomas moved to his right causing the other man to move to his left. That placed him dangerously close to the mule. The mule kicked with his rear legs hitting the man squarely in the back. The man lost the grip on his knife as he was thrust forward and fell face down on the up-wardly positioned knife. It lodged deep inside his stomach, piercing his heart. Thomas grabbed him and quickly turned him over on his back. It was too late. The fight went out of him as did the light from his eyes.

The man spoke and his final words were, *"I didn't mean you no harm … this damn war … oh Jesus help me …"* and he died.

"Mister, he wasn't no bad man! I don't know what got into him. He was the type to give the shirt off his back to someone. It just wasn't like him. It was like some evil spirit took over. I just never saw anything like it." The man sat down and cried.

"He was my oldest brother. He made it through the war and all that hell, to die like this. How will I tell my folks?"

Thomas walked over to the boy and sat beside him for a while. John and the other man took turns digging a grave for the fallen comrade beneath the tree near the stream. They buried the man and piled rocks high to stop wild animals from digging him up later. Thomas had a Bible in his saddlebags. He got it out and read from Psalms: "The Lord is my shepherd, I shall not want; He maketh me to lie down in green pastures: He leadeth me beside the still waters ..." He could not continue. He choked up. John finished it from memory.

They provisioned the two remaining men as much as they felt appropriate. The tattered soldiers moved onward with troubled hearts, shallow hopes and donated supplies.

CHAPTER 15

MATTHEW AND JACOB RODE INTO CAMP LATER
that same day and found Thomas and John fishing along the creek
bank. Evangeline was placing dough in the Dutch oven to have bread
with the fish she anticipated the men catching. It has been a long day
and the men were tired and satisfied to reach the camp and find it in
good order, and their friends safe.

"Hello! I see you two have been taking the time off to relax and
enjoy yourselves, while Jacob and I took care of dangerous business,"
Matthew smiled with his lighthearted comments.

"Stick those poles in the dirt and come over to the fire that I might
share the news with you."

Thomas and John did likewise and made their way over beside the
fire. Jacob was more observant as he tied his horse in the tall grass to
feed. It did not escape him that a fresh grave was off to his left that
wasn't there when he left camp earlier.

Matthew reported the events of the battle back at the plantation.
He told them that the marauders were under the impression that there
was gold hidden there and thought by beating Big John, the woman
would give up the location. Sarah said she would have told them if she
knew of any, but she did not.

"*Did he tell them?*" blurted Evangeline.

"No," Matt replied, "did he know something Sarah and the others
did not know?"

"*Yes, John knows, but not Sarah!*" Evangeline stopped what she was
doing and turned to walk back to a log and sat down on it.

"Massa Bolling, I mean Mr. Bolling, my father, told John and me
about the gold and had John help him buried it. You see he knew his
property would go to his wife and daughter, Sarah. But he wanted John

and me to have something to start life with, after the war that is. He told me that he loved me and that I was his daughter too. He knew Uncle John and I would help the other slave families get on their feet. He did not realize the depth of Sarah's love and wisdom in dealing with the needs of the slaves. He had amassed a great fortune and planned well. He left Mrs. Bolling with plenty of property and had gold deposited in Northern banks for them to have after the war. He was a very smart man and had a big heart also."

"He was broken hearted after the war's end and feared his large extended family would be broken up and scattered with the wind. He, like many slaveholders, did not realize that these were human beings; not property like a horse or dog that needed someone to care for them."

"Now I have this burden on me that I must decide what to do. John is my uncle and he will not do anything without involving me. After I find my mother, if she is still alive, we will resolve this matter as best we can."

Matt spoke to everyone, "We will get an early start in the morning. I think after Franklin we will go to Elizabeth City where we can look for a paddle wheeler to take us down to Charleston to conduct our business and move on. From what I understand, the greater portion of Charleston was burned by accident in 1861 and Sherman caused no damage when he visited. He felt there wasn't much left to destroy that they hadn't destroyed themselves."

John spoke for the first time since the others returned. "I think we better skirt Franklin. Thomas and I may have worn out our welcome there. We left a couple of dead men there that wanted to take Evangeline. They were some bitter men and they wanted to take it out on anybody. We were in the right, but, that doesn't matter much now. There may be others that want to settle something if we passed through again. It would be best to leave it alone."

Jacob cleared his throat. "It appears to me that you have been doing more in camp than just fishing. I don't remember that grave in the high grass before we left. What happened there?"

"No!" Thomas spoke. "We had some Rebs traveling through and

one decided to make the same mistake and throw insults at Evangeline
and we began to fighting with knives. He fell on his knife after the
mule kicked him in the back. He spoke his regrets before he passed.
He left a very sad little brother behind with the task of explaining his
death to their folks."""

And Evangeline is a better catcher of fish than we are, but we will
catch enough soon," John commented.

"You better get started quickly because old Blue is eating what
you had on that stringer!" Jacob laughed as Thomas started running
towards Blue to get what fish he hadn't eaten yet. They all laughed.

Later on about dusk, after eating the tasty fish and bread that
Evangeline cooked, they settled around the fire to smoke their pipes
and discuss their plans. Jacob indicated he would start in the direction
of the mountains tomorrow and after business there leave for Jackson,
Mississippi. His intentions were to rejoin the group at Jackson and
travel south with them to New Orleans. He warned them to be vigilant,
but realize that traveling with a former slave girl would pose problems,
no matter how light skinned she was. There were too many attitudes
deeply imbedded in generations that would not be changed overnight.
They could not retaliate every time an ill word was spoken.

He explained he was often approached by ill words because of the
color of his skin. Being of Indian ancestry was not held in high esteem
by many. He learned to overlook it and found he was the better man
for it. He preferred to judge men by their character and hoped they
would do the same.

"I do not believe people hate me because I am *Cherokee,* but that
they hate because that is their disposition. *Hate comes from fear, fear
comes from the unknown, and it is often passed down to the next generation.* Just maybe they have many things that they feel are wrong or
unfair in their lives and I become a focal point to place their anger;
whatever the reasons I have learned not to make their anger my problem," Jacob related.

Evangeline explained she was not offended as much as Thomas and
John, because the spoken word did not harm her like the physical and

emotional abuse she had witnessed and experienced as a slave in her former life. They all agreed to take a more measured approach when possible for her sake. Times were strange, the nation was in transition and many people were on the move and found their old value systems were crumbling.

Even John and Thomas found themselves going through a major rethinking of their attitudes and how they should act and move in the old circles from which they came. It would be odd and challenging as they approached their friends and families traveling back into the Deep South again. How would they react to people talking down the former slaves, especially Evangeline; and how could they explain their reformation and working for the U.S. Government after fighting for the South against the Union for four years? These truly were strange times and just how it would play out would remain to be seen by all concerned.

The camp was alive with activity as the sun rose on another beautiful spring day. Evangeline and Thomas had breakfast cooked and hot coffee for all. Jacob's dog, Blue was eager to travel. It seemed he was listening in on the plans and wanted fast action from Jacob this morning.

Jacob watered his horse and packhorse, and filled his canteen for travel. After saddling his livestock, he drew everyone close.

"My heart is heavy as I leave this group. I have grown to feel a brotherly connection. I bid you farewell and pray safety for you on your travels. I look forward to our reunion later this month in Jackson. I hope you travel with care and find the road to your liking. Good bye all!"

The group of travelers broke camp and traveled southeast in the direction of Elizabeth City. It was there that Matthew had plans to secure passage on a sternwheeler to Charleston.

Along the way they encountered a large encampment of former slaves, or freedmen as they were beginning to be called. It appeared President Lincoln's idea of a *Freedmen's Bureau* was coming to fruition. He had started legislation to establish an organization which would fund and facilitate the distribution of abandoned lands to the newly freed slaves and to oversee transactions, disputes, contracts, wages and overall coordination of freedmen with their transition to lives as free and independent people. This organization was underfunded and undermanned; however, it was instrumental in establishing some sense of order and justice in a changing world. It also established schools to educate the Negroes and schools of higher learning, colleges to be more precise. It aided in the establishment of religion and the growth of churches for that purpose. There were great hopes of improvement for their lives, but everyone knew it would not come easily.

Evangeline talked to some people she had met earlier near her former home. They said they could help locate her mother through this *Freedmen's Bureau*. She thanked them, but it was her conviction that she was going in the right direction with the help of friends.

After arriving in Elizabeth City, Matthew found a freighter at dock. It was a confederate sternwheeler taken from its owner on the St. Johns River in Florida and converted into a troop transport. He approached *The Darlington* and wished to board but was told he couldn't by a soldier standing guard. This prompted him to request a visit with the soldier's commanding officer, which he was also denied. Glancing back at his friends, Matt turned and with a hard right fist knocked the soldier to the ground. Other soldiers came to his rescue as Matthew held his arms in the air to indicate no resistance, "Take me to your commanding officer!"

Once in the presence of a sergeant, Matthew requested to speak to his highest commissioned officer and insisted that it would not get him in trouble. The sergeant was convinced. Matt was delivered to Captain Wilson on the ship's upper deck. Once Matthew presented his credentials as an active Major in the U.S. Army and explained he was assigned onto a highly sensitive mission the Captain expressed his regrets and extended his ship's services to them. The ship was to pass through Charleston and it would not be a burden for his party and their horses to board.

Once on board, Matthew instructed John and Thomas on how to conduct themselves. He wanted them to separate themselves during most of their stay on the boat and to be observant and listen intently to conversations as they meandered through the crowd. Their mission, their job, had begun and it may be possible to gain valuable information while traveling in the company of others from this point forward.

He also spoke to Evangeline and requested she attach herself to John in a subservient manner. She understood exactly what he meant and did not have any ill feelings about his intentions. Matt noted how she had enough knowledge of the white folk's mannerisms to successfully make the transition from servant to white and back, conversationally when needed. This measure of cloaking was to avoid attention while on the boat. He wanted their passage to arouse as little attention as possible.

They left the docks of Elizabeth City about the noon hour and traveled out into the Albemarle Sound. There was tremendous activity along the waterways. It would take some time, but commerce would steadily increase now that the war was over. Businessmen wanted to make money; that had always been their aim. Opportunists would move in and take advantage of the South's weakened state as quickly and long as possible. Crooks of all denominations from the North and South would ply their trade on the unsuspecting victims.

It was a beautiful day and the view of the open water and the many seabirds circling overhead thrilled Thomas and Evangeline. They pushed out beyond the Outer Banks, the barrier island that protected the sound, and were full speed southward towards their destination.

They all appeared lighthearted as a group, but individually they each were in deep contemplation of their recent past. Each wondered about the future and how their aspirations could be achieved.

John and Thomas felt a great burden lifted from them just by knowing that they had survived death on the battlefields. They also carried the *soldiers' burden* that follows war when so many fellow soldiers did not survive and they were fortunate enough to carry on. They wished this war had never happened. The feeling of *survivor's guilt* would never leave them as long as they lived. The memories of fallen soldiers and of those that died from disease as well would haunt them while awake and asleep. They would never escape it; however, they must forge ahead and explore the possibilities of life after the war.

Evangeline conversely gave thanks to God for allowing this war to bring an end to the institution of slavery. She intended to embrace each new day; she wanted to experience a normal life as a young and free woman of color.

Matthew was given a note by one of the sergeants as they passed on the outer walkway of the boat. He opened it and found an invitation to dine with the Captain and the boat's pilot that evening in the Captain's quarters. After speaking with John about the invitation, Matthew made his way to the Captain's quarters. He was ushered into the tight, but ample accommodations.

"Mr. Ballistae is our host tonight, Major O'Brien. He is sympathetic to our cause and I trust him to keep our conversations in confidence. He watches the coming and goings of many people and knows things that occur on the waterfront that can escape the ordinary man. I haven't told him anything about you, but he knew without a word that you were traveling clandestine. He is very perceptive and your method of boarding was not overlooked." Captain Wilson leaned back in his chair and deferred to Mr. Ballistae.

"Major O'Brien, I don't know the nature of your mission; however, I believe I know someone that may be of interest to you. He moves from North to South very frequently, and always seems to have great financial means; however, I have yet to hear of his occupation or his benefactors. That, in and of itself, may not be enough to arouse suspicion but on one of his journeys south he left a satchel behind. It was brought to my attention by an orderly. So I thought I would return it the next time he travelled with me. I inspected the satchel and found it filled with money. He never came to me about it, and I never brought it up. Here is the satchel Major O'Brien. This man tends to gamble in a card game here and there, but he isn't what I would call a true gambler. He calls himself Simon Bartlett, and he just happens to be on this trip going to Charleston. I believe he is now calling New Orleans his home. I hope this can be of help to you," politely stated the white-haired gentleman.

"Thank you very much for your information. This may be the connection I was looking for." Matt opened the satchel and pulled out a neatly arranged stack of bills. He took one bill out of the stack and turned it around, flipped it over again and held it close to the oil lamp at the center of the table. After looking closely for several minutes he smiled and just shook his head in affirmation at his discovery.

"All indications confirm this is what I suspected. *It's counterfeit!* The paper, the ink and the quality of the engraving all point to the same conclusion. This man wasn't disturbed too much when he misplaced this satchel. It was probably just one of his many samples. He may have thought someone had stolen it believing the money was legit, and he did not want to arouse suspicion by inquiring about it later. Counterfeiting of Confederate bills occurred during the war by Northern printers. Initially it was distributed in the North as souvenirs. Later it was circulated by Union soldiers throughout the Confederate states to devalue their money and hurt the economy; however, the same thing occurred with U.S. currency in the North as well. The government did not encourage the practice because it feared it would backfire, which it did. That is part of my mission to root out the people in charge of this travesty and put an end to it. I have been sent south to begin there and work my way to the source. My goal is to eradicate it or put a dent in it if possible. I fear it may lead to Northern sources once I have followed the trail to the printing press. Once again I thank you on behalf of the U.S. Government."

There was a knock on the door and the riverboat pilot commanded the servant to enter. A handsome older black gentleman dressed in black trousers with a white jacket over a pressed white shirt and black bowtie stepped inside the quarters and delivered the meal to the seated men. He wished them an enjoyable dinner and excused himself.

They enjoyed the delicious dinner and good conversation. After smoking a cigar presented to him by the Captain, Matthew politely excused himself for the evening. He told the pilot he would retrieve the contents of the satchel at a later date. He did not want anyone to see him with the satchel. The pilot understood. He went directly to the cabin he had secured for him and Thomas. John and Evangeline shared another cabin with upper and lower bunks.

Matthew left his room after placing the stack of bills in a secure place. He went up on the upper deck to enjoy the sound of the water from the paddlewheels and the moonlight on the water. He watched others moving around and listened to their light conversations. He moved around until he found Evangeline and John standing along the boat's railing. He slowly moved in their direction and engaged them in light conversation at first.

"It is a beautiful evening and a great night for a stroll," spoken as a gentleman to a casual meeting of strangers.

"Yes it is!" Evangeline returned. "It reminds me of a time my family spent travelling down the mighty Mississippi on our way to Natchez."

"You must be a well travelled young lady," Matt replied.

"Yes, you might say so before the war ruined my *daddy's business!*"

John looked at them both in puzzled admiration. "I never knew you travelled so Evangeline."

"Well, of course that was all after we travelled to Europe, that is!" She laughed and smiled at him and he finally realized it was all just playacting. John smiled back at them.

Matthew inquired about Thomas' whereabouts. John said he believed he went looking for a card game on the lower deck after they had dinner. That may not have been exactly what Matt had intended by them blending in, but, it was exactly what Thomas would call normal behavior.

The trio made their way around the riverboat's bow back to the lower deck about mid ship. Seated at the table, Thomas was deep in concentration studying his cards. The game had worked down to two participants from the original six. The center of the card table had a fair stack of paper money. Across from Thomas sat a tall lean type, dressed in black suit, white shirt, string tie, a real dandy. He had dark eyes, thin black mustache, dark hair and a long scar down the right cheekbone to chin. He wasn't the type that would garner trust, more like the type you wouldn't want to meet in a dark alley. A small crowd surrounded the table to witness the drama and suspense.

Thomas broke the silence by placing five twenty dollar gold pieces in the center and looked directly at the man across from him, waiting for his response. The gambler placed one hundred dollars in currency on the table and called.

"*That, mister, is gold!* You want to call, you put up gold!" Thomas demanded.

"My money is as good as gold, you can exchange it in any Northern bank," the gambler replied. "No one questions Simon Bartlett's integrity."

"Well Mister, we *ain't* in the North and you match gold with gold or forfeit the pot!" Thomas demanded.

The gambler reached slowly in his pocket and produced a gold watch. "There, that is more than equal!"

The gambler placed his cards on the table: three kings and two jacks. He looked at Thomas with a smirk of confidence. After a long pause, Thomas laid down his cards: three aces and two queens. He looked across the table at the loser.

"*Don't touch that money, you cheat!*" exclaimed the gambler as he palmed a sleeve gun, a two shot derringer.

Thomas anticipated just such as this from the stranger and prepared himself. "*I never had to cheat. I'm just that good.* Pointed at your belly is my navy colt and that is one bluff you don't want to call. You will put down your gun, apologize for your bad manners and step away from the table; otherwise, you will be playing cards with the devil your next game! Think quickly and act slowly. The clock is ticking, *Mister!*"

Slowly the gambler placed his gun on the table in front of his cards. "I must've underestimated you, my friend. We will meet again and continue this discussion another day." He slowly rose from his seat and left the card table, pushing his way through the crowd.

A large brawler type standing behind Thomas was about to hit him over the head with his pistol. Observing this man's actions, Matt put his pistol in the man's ribs and removed the gun from his hand. "Mister, you need to use better judgment." He hit the man over the head and stepped back as the large fellow dropped to the floor.

Thomas gathered his winnings and made his way back to his cabin followed by Matt. The others milled around and watched the actions of the crowd after Thomas left. There were soldiers and civilians standing around talking and drinking at the bar.

John escorted Evangeline to their cabin and went out walking again. He indicated she should not wait up for him. John noticed Bartlett had returned to give aid to the big fellow that attempted to waylay Thomas.

John knocked on Thomas and Matt's door. Matt opened the door while John entered quietly. "I believe those two men were together. The gambler returned to assist him. I didn't see any other men that appeared associated or interested in him," John commented.

Matthew spoke, "I was given some information that involves them and may just be the starting point for our investigation. The riverboat captain told me about this man, Simon Bartlett, the same gambler Thomas played cards with tonight. It seems he left a satchel full of money on one of his trips and never returned for it his next trip south. I inspected the money and have determined it to be phony. In other words, it is counterfeit. It has all the earmarks of counterfeit currency. Here, I have a sample. Let's compare to the money you won tonight, Thomas."

Thomas gave him some bills that would have been at the top of the stack and laid out the rest on the bed to compare to the phony bill. After making comparisons of all the money, Matt determined more than half was counterfeit and probably came from Bartlett. He demonstrated the differences in the real bills and the counterfeit to John and Thomas. It became much clearer to them what their mission as agents was about. Thomas was so mad he wanted to go back and whip this man, but Matthew told him this was a good thing making the connection with the money and the man.

"Thomas, you have provided some good detective work; even though, I asked you to keep a low profile and try to act normal," Matt scolded. "But, I guess gambling and threatening a scoundrel's life is quite normal for you. We have several more days to travel on this boat before we reach Charleston and I think we should be as careful as possible and stay within each others' sight, or we may be hoodwinked and shoved overboard."

"John, we will join you and Evangeline for breakfast early in the morning; sometime around six thirty. We will still try to appear as casual strangers in order to avoid someone making a connection. Perhaps this will give us an edge in our investigative work. I believe we may yet learn some valuable information on this boat ride."

The next day was exceptionally beautiful, with a warm breeze and favorable waters for smooth traveling within the *Outer Banks*. They passed by Roanoke Island, the location of the Lost Colony; a mystery of the disappearance of the first British attempt to settle in the New World in 1587.

They also passed Bodie Island, where once stood a marvelous lighthouse, destroyed by the Confederates in 1861 to prevent the Union forces from using it against them. There was so much history along this wonderful coast. Matthew was a treasure trove of knowledge, and his traveling companions absorbed every word as would children confronted with new and interesting facts.

Evangeline was more than overwhelmed at this fantastic experience and often would stand silent as the others talked. This exceeded anything that she had ever experienced. What lay ahead for her was more than her short life could begin to dream. Sometimes she would play imaginary world with Sarah as a child. She never actually imagined these things could really happen to her. The vastness of the world was becoming more apparent by the day. It seemed even more farfetched that her mother could actually be found in such a large world, especially after so much time had passed.

This was a time to relax and take in the sights, sounds and smells of riverboat travel along America's coastline. Even traveling on a troop transport at war's end provided much excitement. They were just touching the outer layer of the underworld they sought to penetrate and destroy on their mission. Bartlett was merely the tip of the iceberg in what lay ahead, but he was the spark they needed to begin their journey into the darkness. The intrigue and excitement was felt by one and all. The awareness of danger did not escape them as they pursued this deadly game of espionage. The stakes were high indeed!

Breakfast passed without any extraordinary events, as did lunch and dinner. After dinner Matthew and Thomas were taking in the sunset as they leaned on the second deck bow railing and casually spoke about idle things. Thomas had taken the opportunity to smoke his pipe and enjoy the pleasant aroma of his tobacco. He had been able to acquire some of the best tobacco while in the Virginia countryside and North Carolina too. This he enjoyed greatly because it wasn't so readily available during the war. Matthew began to discuss some conversations that he had overheard. He also discussed strategy about future investigations to be implemented after landing in Charleston.

Thomas turned to face the aft of the boat and touched Matt on the shoulder, "You might better turn your attention this-a-way," he said as he witnessed the big ugly brawler that Matt clunked on the head and sent to sleepy town the previous night.

"Well, well! It looks like sleeping beauty has awakened!" Matt commented as the brute moved increasingly faster toward them. "Did you have a good nap, old friend?" The big ugly man bared his teeth and growled as he opened his arms in a bear hug fashion and headed directly at Matthew.

Thomas had already stepped several feet away to Matt's right. Matt took a quick step to the right and shoved his left leg out to trip the thug who had almost started to run at this point. The man's eyes got larger as he saw what was about to happen. He tripped on Matt's foot and flipped over the rail and could easily have broken his back on the lower deck if some cotton bales had not broken his fall. He landed squarely on the bales, and bounced. He landed on his back on the outer railing and wobbled there like a seesaw. He could have fallen overboard as easily as onto the deck had not a young boy walked over to pull him back onboard.

CHAPTER 16

THE LAST NIGHT ON THE BOAT WAS AN especially rough one. Darkness came earlier due to a passing squall. The wind howled as the waves kicked up causing uneasiness among the passengers, the soldiers, the livestock and the riverboat captain. It was touch and go for a while there until the storm passed. The waves had rushed across the lower deck at times cleaning off anything not tied down.

The dawn broke with a beautiful sunrise over the Outer Banks and the air was much fresher after the storm. Some of the soldiers commented that a very large man flew off the upper deck into the sea during the storm. But, they could not be sure who it was because the rain was coming down so hard. It was a dangerous storm and everyone was glad they had survived the night.

Matthew greeted his fellow travelers at breakfast to find Thomas and John bruised and battered with Evangeline sitting between them. "It looks like you two were tossed around violently during that storm last night."

John looked at Thomas and spoke for the duo, "It seems someone with a bandaged head and sore back ran his mouth too long about how ignorant Johnny Reb was; the Yankee soldiers were kind enough to step aside and let us settle our disagreements in an agreeable fashion."

"Would this disagreeable sort be among us today? I mean, is he still on the boat? Matt looked at them puzzled.

"I don't know where he is!" Thomas offered. "He may have beaten us ashore, if he knows how to swim. We gave him a head start. I think he is big enough to float. He sure had a foul mouth."

"Well, you are certainly not a good role model for Evangeline, but I am glad you have learned to function as a team. You will certainly need to watch each other's back when we get into the heat of things. Try to be somewhat more discreet when you dislodge someone from a moving craft into the deep blue sea."

Matt grimaced as he turned up his cup of bitter coffee. "I know I will be glad to start drinking Thomas' coffee once again."

The riverboat pulled into Charleston Harbor alongside others as they were docking, unloading or leaving port for other destinations. The docks were full of activity since the war was over and blockades were lifted. They were manned by blacks and whites; many former slaves were performing the tasks they had done before, but this time for pay.

The bustle of commerce was welcomed by everyone. The return to a better way of life would be years in the making; however, there were many things that the South had missed during the war and longed to have again. An import of foodstuffs from Europe and the Caribbean was definitely one of them.

The city was in terrible shape, but, not as bad as Columbia, the capital city. Sherman made sure it, along with the rest of the State, was punished for its role in the War. Charleston suffered a tremendous fire early in the War that burned a great part of the city. This was done without outside help, probably accidental. There were people milling around everywhere. There was much to be done amid the rubble to return this once opulent city to its former grandeur.

Before disembarking the riverboat, Matthew retrieved the counterfeit money from Captain Ballistae, transferred it to a less conspicuous package and thanked him for his hospitality. He also thanked Captain Wilson for his military courtesy and wished him well in his endeavors. Captain Wilson wished him safe travels as well.

Their horses and the pack mule were saddled and taken off the boat. They, man and beast alike, seemed most appreciative to leave the boat and find solid ground once again. They all gathered close to Matthew and looked to him for guidance.

They walked past a fishmonger who sold fish he recently caught in his sloop rigged keel boat. Then there was a lady wearing a bright sun bonnet and long dress, selling fresh bread from a basket. Another entrepreneur, a young man had set up business just beyond the others, selling fish he cooked over a fire and placed inside a partial loaf of bread. There were overwhelming sights, sounds and smells approaching from every direction.

"First we must ask around and search out Carson Walker's mother and sister. I was given directions by Sarah, but, it looks like much has been destroyed since she was last here. Let's go down this street," Matthew said as he turned his horse down Broad Street.

They stopped in front of St. Michael's Church on the corner of Meetings Street. A large bell from within the church was sounding the eighth hour.

An older gentleman was sweeping up the front sidewalk and turned to greet them. "Good morning, gentlemen and lady, it is a good morning the Lord had blessed us with after last night's storm. Would y'all be in need of directions this fine morning?" He laid down his brush broom against a short wall that butted up to a sidewalk filled with blooming flowers, and dusted off his frock.

John asserted himself, "Yes sir! We are in need of directions. We are traveling through Charleston on our way south and we need to find the Walker family, Elizabeth and Mrs. Walker. Carson was a friend of mine. We served together. We would like to give them some of his personal effects. Would you be familiar with them, sir?"

"Young man, you are blessed indeed, because you have reached your destination. Dismount and come inside the church and meet Elizabeth now! She volunteers, giving people food from our soup kitchen. She is in the back helping others set things up for the day. Take your horses around back where there is a watering trough under the oak tree. Pitch them some hay as well. Meet me back here. I will introduce you to her." The man appeared to be the minister or held some position with the church. He was of the kindest sort, which was quite refreshing.

"Let me introduce myself, my name is Parson Jones. I serve this parish. Follow me to the kitchen and dining area in the back and I will introduce you."

They followed him through a maze after passing through the sanctuary. It was a beautiful church and one felt a reverence walking through the voluminous building with stained glass lining both sides. There was something especially holy about this church. In the kitchen area women were busy preparing the day's meal. There were men walking in and out bringing loads of foodstuff.

Parson Jones poked his head inside the kitchen area and asked Elizabeth to step out into the dining area for a moment. She brushed back a strand of sandy blond hair from her face with her flour coated hand. She seemed a little exasperated to be distracted from her work as she exhaled a deep breath. She brushed down her apron and stepped out of the kitchen.

"Yes, Reverend, how may I help you this morning?"

"Elizabeth! There are some people here that wish to speak to you. They appeared to have travelled far to meet with you. They wish to speak to you about Carson." He spoke and moved to the side to allow the interaction to take place.

John stepped forward as he felt it was his place to make the connection. "Ma'am, my name is John Bernard. I served with your brother Carson and we were friends. I have some personal effects he asked me to deliver to you and your mom in the event of ... his death. This may not be the best place to proceed, since your mom isn't here. I also have some friends travelling with me and we could use some place to tidy up a bit after having spent the last few days on a riverboat full of foul odors."

Elizabeth stood in front of them with her eyes wide open. She was at a loss for words. She just stared for an extended moment and finally spoke as she came to her senses.

"I am sorry! I was caught off guard; this is a complete surprise." She reached out to shake John's hand and flour floated between the two.

"My name is Elizabeth and I would like to take you to meet my mom. Parson Jones, would you mind if I take off for the rest of the today?"

"Elizabeth, you are a volunteer! I can't very well fire you or dock your pay. Of course, take these fine people home." He smiled a possum-grin as he spoke.

"Let me get my horse and carriage and I will lead the way. How are you travelling?"

"We have horses behind the church. We will follow you." John and his friends proceeded to follow Elizabeth as she frantically hitched the horse and carriage.

They travelled down a street and veered off onto a lane that eventually led to a road leading out of town. Shadows danced across the street as the sunlight flowed between the trees. It was a heavenly morning and the drive was a charming event that lifted their spirits. There were forests and breaks in them where lush fields occupied the gaps. Elizabeth kept an even pace with her pony and carriage. The party followed closely in silence. The landscape was typical of a painting that one would see in the grand hallway of an estate.

After passing an abandoned farm house and its out buildings, John stopped to look across a large pasture that was overgrown from lack of care. It stood to their left. It was still covered in sagebrush from the previous year as it was no longer being used as it was intended. Everyone stopped, even Elizabeth.

No one spoke as John dismounted his horse and began to walk out into the field. He heard voices calling him. He walked out into the taller sagebrush and stood there looking in all directions. As his senses grew keener, he was able to make out shapes of young men walking around him. They appeared to be confused at best. It became clear that they were the spirits of fallen soldiers and he was in the midst of a battlefield. The battle was over, but he could still smell the acrid odor of spent gunpowder. The odor of the men was just as strong. Their clothes smelled of blood, sweat, urine and every other human odor that one could imagine occurring during such an event. It was a scene he was all too familiar with having spent much time in battle.

It was a very disturbing scene. John walked around and saw the shadowy forms of men that stood outside of their fallen bodies and wondered what was happening. Some were explaining to others that they were dead. But no matter how well they tried to explain some were never going to grasp the reality.

John was drawn to two brothers in the center of the field. They sat cross-legged playing marbles and laughing. One was wearing the tattered Confederate uniform and a blue cap while the other wore the Union blue and his brother's gray cap. It was obvious they were brothers. They could almost be twins; both had bright red hair and their faces were a maze of freckles. Their green eyes sparkled with joy and laughter. No happier boys could there be. John sat down beside them and watched. They offered him some marbles but he declined.

After a short period of time had passed, John stood up and started back in the direction of the others. He passed through the shapes of soldiers and nodded as he bid them adieu. It was a respectful acknowledgement to his fallen comrades. They returned in kind.

He stepped out of the field and into the lane to the puzzled look of his friends. He was dumbfounded and did not attempt to speak.

He mounted his horse, and turned in the direction of Elizabeth as she spoke.

"This is a *field of sorrows*! There was a battle here that happened purely by accident. I was told that the two armies did not know of the others whereabouts and walked up on each other and began to fight. Only a few soldiers survived. There was no command, just young soldiers caught out in the same field at the same time. They didn't know what to do, so they did what came natural to them and fought. The battle was over quickly. After the smoke cleared it was discovered that two brothers that had fought on opposite sides had died in the battle and they were found in each others' arms, embraced in death."

After she spoke each looked differently at John and understood. They rode on. The countryside was no less beautiful than before; however, the sentiments had changed to reverence. They knew they were moving through hallowed ground.

There has always been the struggle between men. The original inhabitants of this new country fought battles amongst themselves just to survive. Survival meant to overcome extreme changes in the elements, and to overcome wild animal attacks. Men chose strength over weakness when confronted with other men wanting to take away their gains. It was never given for men to occupy lands without the demonstration of strength. It is only human nature for strong men to assert themselves.

The hopes were that one day as people lived in closer proximity and built their lives interdependent upon each other they would learn to settle differences in a more civilized manner, and war would no longer be necessary. This was not the sentiments of all. There were still mean and angry people, men and women that still thought in vile and selfish ways. It would take years, and even generations for change to occur. Yet, troublemakers would always be with us. It is said a few bad apples will spoil the entire basket. Unfortunately, the crowd always seems to take the wrong path and follow the strongest leader instead of thinking for themselves. Wars rarely solve problems; only people working together can solve problems.

Elizabeth turned her carriage off the main road down a lane lined on each side by pecan trees putting on their new leaves. They came to a modest cottage shaded by large oaks. The lawns were neatly manicured and inviting. A very large red barn stood a short distance behind the house. Once there she directed them to take the horses to some stables to the right of the barn. They could leave them with Juan, the hired man, and he could attend to their needs.

"I want to prepare you before we go inside to meet my folks. Mom is very engaging; however, father has been very withdrawn since Carson went off to war. He got even worse when we got news of his death. There always were some underlying tensions between father and Carson.

I think he wanted a son that was more assertive, stronger and manlier. Carson was born with a deep compassion for mankind. His zest for life was different than that of the others. He was heart and soul above the rest. He was a special gift to us all."

"Father wasn't brought up to appreciate the softer, gentler things in life. He was all utilitarian. That was how he was raised."

"Mother, on the other hand, was exposed to the finer things that life has to offer. She recognized the special spirit that was Carson and she nurtured him. She accepted and encouraged his growth. Unfortunately, Carson did not live long enough to find his true calling. There is no telling what that man would have become. That is the tragedy of war, so many lives lost without knowing the fulfillment of their potential."

"Now, don't get me wrong. Carson was a fine man. All the girls desired him and the boys respected him. He wasn't someone the other boys messed with. He was rough and tumble too. It wasn't father's way to understand the refinement that Carson sought. He was a good student and he appreciated the written word. Father did not push him to go to war, neither did he discourage him. Carson must have felt he had to prove himself."

"When Carson died, father retreated within himself and his work. He cut himself off from us emotionally. The barn out back is a huge warehouse. We had a business in town selling farm implements, tools, feed, seed, tack and the like. He believed in having a large warehouse as a supply point, or back up to the business. It was forward thinking on his part because the business in town burned when the city burned. Let's go meet Mother and then I'll go get Dad."

They followed Elizabeth inside and there sat her mother with some sewing in her lap.

"Mom, I want you to meet some friends of Carson. They are travelling through and wanted to visit. Before we make the introductions let me get father here as well."

She went through the house as Mrs. Carson was seating them and offered them some tea. While she presented them with tea Elizabeth brought her dad into the room.

"Father, these are friends of Carson and they wanted to stop on their way through. Please everyone have a seat. John, why don't you introduce your friends," Elizabeth said, trying to make this a pleasant situation.

"Mr. and Mrs. Walker, my name is John Bernard. I am from Louisiana. These are my friends: Thomas Smith from Valdosta, Georgia, Matthew O'Brien from Jackson, Mississippi and Evangeline from Virginia. We are traveling to New Orleans for different reasons. Evangeline is traveling there to search for her mother. We have taken a job with the U.S. Government to restore the railroad connections with the South. It will take a lot of preparation."

"Thomas and I fought alongside Carson throughout the war. We were with him when he died. Carson was a very brave man and he was a sincere friend. He was a comfort to many with his encouraging words. He knew just what to say and just at the right time. He was given a gift that drew people to him. He often read to us from the Bible and taught us well. You cannot know how valuable those moments were to dying and frightened young men on the battlefield. Some said that he was an angel sent by God."

"He was drinking a cup of coffee and laughing with us when the Union came over the hill and surprised us. He took a bullet to the heart. I held him in my arms until his last breath. He smiled and closed his eyes. We buried him in the shade of a cottonwood and placed a marker there. He wanted me to bring some things back to you. He made me promise. Here is a journal he kept, his Bible and a few other personal items. *Oh!* And here is a gold pocket watch he carried. He put a lot of stock in it."

Mr. Walker rose up from his chair and walked over to the table where John had placed the items. He picked up the watch and held it for a moment. Then he opened the watch and read the inscription: *To Carson, from your loving Father.* With a loud wail he fell to his knees and let out a deep and loud sobbing sound. He was bent over clutching his knees. Mrs. Walker ran to him and wrapped herself around him. She held him as close as she could.

Elizabeth stood up and walked out the front door with the others close behind.

"I think he is having a reckoning with his feelings for Carson. He has bottled up so much for so long. I think it was killing him. He loved Carson, but never knew how to express himself. Let's give them some time. I will show you around the place."

An hour later Mr. Walker, accompanied by Mrs. Walker, walked outside to speak with the visitors.

"I must apologize for my actions. It has been a long time coming. Your visit has revealed my deepest feelings for Carson, feeling that I have never reconciled. You must stay on and help us celebrate Carson's life. You have opened my eyes and my heart. Elizabeth will help you get settled and freshen up. Please say you will visit with us for a few days!"

"We will be honored to visit with you, and certainly appreciate your hospitality. I want to learn more about Carson and his family as well," Matthew explained with a measured humility.

The next morning they were awaken by the sound of activity outside. Mr. and Mrs. Walker were busy making arrangements for a festive celebration. Tables were being constructed under the trees. Mrs. Walker was busy preparing foods in the kitchen with the help of Elizabeth. Juan went down to the *Low Country* to find crabs, oysters and shrimp for the party. It would truly be a celebration of Carson.

Mr. Walker had come to a reconciliation of his misplaced feelings towards his deceased son. According to Elizabeth this was a true miracle to witness. It was like her father had become *a new creature,* a transformation had occurred. One might say he was *born again.* He was just beginning to understand who Carson really was, and what others saw in him. *He was learning about life through his son.*

Evangeline assisted in the kitchen. She demonstrated amazing skills; even though, they were acquired through entirely different experiences as a child of slavery. The Walkers were surprised to discover she was the daughter of Frances, and more so that Mr. Bolling was her father. They knew the story of Frances' acquisition and her ordered sale by Mrs. Bolling.

"You are searching for your mother. Where do you start?" Elizabeth asked.

"I was told by Sarah that she was sold to a planter on the north shore of Lake Pontchartrain, across from New Orleans. He owned a sugar plantation and also maintained a home in New Orleans. That is where I will start. Sarah and I were always close as children even though her mother tried to keep us separated once she learned we were true sisters. We have some common traits and attitudes that cannot be denied. She has been very helpful in my search to find my mother." Evangeline went on to explain the circumstances behind the death of her father. She said Sarah was brave and decisive in making the decision that saved the lives of many at the expense of her father.

Thomas, Matthew and John asked how they could be of help and were politely informed that they had everything under control. They were told to relax and enjoy the peace and quiet.

Elizabeth went into town to request the presence of a select group of people at the celebration. It was impromptu as Mr. Walker had been energized and felt an immediate need to act. She would have to act quickly to get the response hoped for. She travelled throughout the town and surrounding area to seek out the people on her list. She was aglow with excitement. She had never seen this type of enthusiasm come from her father before. The event was planned for later that day and it would be difficult to reach everyone on her list. But she tried anyway.

The energy was infectious. Close friends and neighbors came together to help the Walkers make this celebration happen.

People were on the move everywhere it seemed. Matthew took the boys and rode into the city to scout around. He wanted to talk with the Union Army officer in charge and maybe get some leads on the suspected graft and black-market activity they may have witnessed or been informed of since their presence. It didn't take long for Matthew to identify the local authorities. The city was under occupation, as was the state, and military headquarters had been established in a local building near the town center. Matthew located a Colonel in command and introduced himself.

"Colonel Watts, I am Major Sean Matthew O'Brien, sir! I am travelling undercover as I am operating in the capacity of agent for the *Department of the Treasury*. Here are my credentials as witnessed by the President and Secretary of the Treasury. I seek any information you may have gleaned during your time here that may shed light on the major players operating in the black-market."

"Major O'Brien, I am sorry that I have little information for you. There are Northern operatives, commonly referred to as Carpetbaggers, and Southern collaborators that exist here, but they keep a very low profile. They wish to be inconspicuous if possible, but there are some that are brazen. They are usually dressed in the finest garb and they are usually the most obnoxious men around. You will know them when you see them. They are opportunists and have no allegiance to anyone but themselves. They are ruthless, so be careful and alert. I have little respect for them, but my interests in keeping the order is enough to occupy all of my time. I have to satisfy the townspeople while not offending the returning soldiers and looking out for the recently freed slave population, all at the same time. This is in addition to taking care of my command. I hope you understand my position. I will assist in any way I can. Will you be staying in Charleston very long?"

"No sir, I will be here less than a week before moving southwest in the direction of Jackson and on to New Orleans. I appreciate everything you are doing and wish you all the best. I hope you may return home to your family at the earliest. I will do my best not to cause you any more trouble than you already have. Thank you sir! Good day."

Matthew met with John and Thomas outside the command post. "Let's take our horses over to the church stables and walk around town. Maybe, we might pick up some local gossip or observe some suspicious activities."

"Yeah and maybe we can find some café with good food and a bottle of ale," Thomas chimed in.

"And maybe someone to brawl with, if I know you well enough," John added. They laughed, but that gave Thomas an idea.

"That's a great idea! Maybe I could sit in on a card game and root out some more counterfeiters," Thomas said as his eyes lit up with excitement.

"He may have an idea that makes sense," Matthew added.

"Please don't encourage him!" John begged.

"No, seriously, he may have a good idea. If we can go into a place where sailors or a less desirable sort hang out and gamble we may get a lead on the underworld of crime that exists here and associate it with other elements that support our investigation. We don't have to be a player here, but we can start by gathering names and faces that may consort with elements in New Orleans." Matthew's mind was moving quickly.

They moved along the docks and made note of activities. Boats were loading and unloading. There was movement everywhere. Seagulls screeched, hoping to find something to eat on the docks. Men laughed and men cussed. A young hound rested beneath some wooden crab traps stacked off to the side; it was watching and staying back far enough to avoid being stepped on by dockworkers.

It was high noon and the hot sun coupled with humidity made for a sweaty condition for the working man and those out for a stroll.

Thomas pointed out a place down the street. "*Pierre's Portside Tavern* looks like the place for us. Does anybody but me have an appetite or dry throat?"

They stepped inside and stood to the side as their eyes adjusted to the low light. They seated themselves at a table towards the rear. They placed their orders and drank a mug of refreshing beer as they waited for their food. Two big, broad shouldered seamen were talking about the card game they attended the previous night. "Let's go back tonight. There are some big players there. I would like to set in for a few hands, at least until I start to lose a day's wages. We better not forget the password at the *Port-O-Call* bar is blackjack. They surely want let us in if we don't know it."

They ate their food and left the tavern satisfied they had gained some valuable information. They rode around town a little while longer taking in the more attractive scenery beyond the parts of town that were destroyed during the fire. They talked about plans for the night as they trotted their horses back down the lane leading to the Walker's home.

The Walker's place had been transformed into an immaculate setting for a celebration of their beloved son, Carson. Tables were covered with white cloths made from bed sheets and more were built to satisfy the demand. Flower arrangements were placed on the center of the tables. Guests were beginning to arrive in carriages and on foot.

Black men and women worked alongside the family, while children played all around them. Evangeline informed them these were families of freedmen that lived on the property. They worked for Mr. Walker and were always free men. He bought their freedom and helped build their homes. He did not believe in slavery and this sometimes created a divide between him and his neighbors or business associates, but he stood his ground. He often warned the free black men to avoid confrontation at all costs because they were not accepted yet. The presence of free black men threatened the institution of slavery and the lifestyle wealthy slaveholders enjoyed, so they believed. Everyone was busy with a responsibility to prepare for the celebration.

There were pots of boiling crab and shrimp. Delicious gumbo, among other *Low Country* recipes, filled the air with their scrumptious aroma. Large bowls of rice and platters of baked oysters also tempted the salivary glands. Someone had placed a hog in the ground over a bed of coals the night before and tended it until it was complete. Yams, beans, potato salad, cornbread, okra and squash were prepared and being placed on the tables as well. It was truly a sight to behold. All had been prepared for a guest of honor that unfortunately would not be present, but in spirit.

The guests included: Mrs. Wesson, the school teacher that inspired and encouraged Carson in his quest for knowledge; the reverend, often referred to as Parson Jones, who was Carson's spiritual guide; Robert Grayson, a childhood friend that returned from the war minus his left leg; friends from school, church, work, as well as fellow soldiers like John and Thomas to name a few; and the Barnes family, a family of freedmen that lived on the property and worked alongside Carson. The Barnes family was as close to Carson as his own family. Mr. Barnes and his son Ernest felt his loss as strongly as any. Ernest and Carson were almost inseparable as boys growing up in and around Charleston. Ernest wanted to go to war with Carson, but Carson would not allow it. He maintained someone had to stay behind to watch over things and it was his place to fight.

It was about three thirty in the afternoon and the sun was still high in the blue sky above the shade of the oaks and pecan trees. Mrs. Walker called for the attention of all within the sound of her voice.

"It is time for our *celebration* to begin! We asked y'all here to recall the memories of our beloved son Carson. These friends of his are former soldiers that served with him throughout the war. They came here to present us with some of Carson's personal belongings and to share some of their memories of how he lived and how he died. We also have memories to share. This may seem a bit awkward to have something like this without the person of honor present, but we felt his life was exceptional and it should not pass without due note of his special impact on our lives."

"My husband, Oliver, whom you all know had retreated into himself upon the departure of Carson to war. He sank further down that dark tunnel of remoteness when notice of Carson's death arrived at our doorsteps. We, Elizabeth and I, thought there was little hope for him. Oliver found his *spiritual footing* when these men arrived and presented us with Carson's personal effects. I think he realized the love he had for his son and his son for him; although, it may seem too late, but it's never too late in God's eyes to change your way of thinking. Oliver will share that with you himself. I want him to speak and give the blessing before we share this feast you all have prepared. Then we can share our thoughts and memories."

Mr. Walker stood up and cleared his throat. He started to speak and stopped. He was choked up. It took him a good minute to find his voice. "I have been a stubborn man all of my life. I thought I had all the answers and there was no other way to think, but mine. Unfortunately, God had put a beautiful and intelligent creature on this Earth as my son and I was too blind to see that. He was a warm and deeply feeling man. I took his gifts as weaknesses because I didn't know better. I was ashamed of my son at times. He didn't fit my notion of a real man, but I was only being selfish and thinking what others thought of me when they saw my son. He was more of a man than I ever was. Now he is no longer with us, I understand what a beautiful soul he was. I will always be ashamed of my short-sighted approach to him but I want to shout it out that I loved him and always will. I think he knew this, but he had to be patient and understanding with me. His mother and sister loved him and they were not remiss in the display of their feelings. It was my loss. Let us all enjoy this day and share our thoughts about Carson."

"Lord, I pray your forgiveness on our shortcomings and I pray you bless this food as we celebrate one of your special children. In the name of Jesus we pray, Amen!"

Everyone enjoyed the extravaganza. The food was more than Thomas had ever seen at one time in his life. The boiled crabs and shrimp were delicious. The oysters were baked with spices and cheese on top as they were cooked on their shells. The hog was cut in many different ways and every part was consumed with the exception of the oink. Beans, corn, squash, okra and cornbread was not overlooked. Yams and sweet potato pie and fresh picked blackberry cobbler were consumed with delight. Sweet tea by the gallon washed everything down.

Friends and family began to find a comfortable place to rest after they satisfied their bellies with all the good things to eat. Old men and young men packed their pipes and enjoyed the smoke rings that floated away into the sky. Women chatted and giggled among themselves; children napped on quilts under the trees.

Elizabeth stood in the middle of everyone and called for their attention. "Everyone, I would like to start off by introducing some of Carson's friends and asking them to recall their time with him. First, I would like to introduce John Bernard from New Orleans."

John stepped forward and straightened his shirt as he stood before the folks gathered around to hear from him. *"I knew Carson from the beginning. I came around Florida on a boat and up the East coast to Charleston on my first voyage on the deep blue. It was cut short when the war started and I felt I had to join the battle and do my part.*

We met as we signed the muster rolls here in Charleston. We were destined to become friends. That was the way with Carson; most people he met were destined to be friends. He had a gentle spirit. I think that is the best way to describe him. He was not afraid to enter into the battle during a skirmish. He would fight to protect his fellow soldiers but I never heard him boast about any enemy he may have killed. He was the type to forget his own health and run out and drag a comrade to safety. He was the one to sit by a friend and give aid when he was sick or dying. I think he held the hands, wipe the brow and stayed beside more dying men on their way to paradise than any I know. He sat with young men as they cried for their mothers and drew their last breath. He cared for people. It was his Bible reading that helped more people. Men would gather round to hear him read the stories of the Old Testament and the words of Jesus. They would hang on his every word. It was like he knew the Lord personally. Often older men would stop him and they would share a prayer. He was respected by everyone. Even the prisoners would ask him for prayers. He would comfort them as well as our own. He never spoke a harsh word to anyone. I don't think it was in him. It just wasn't his nature for meanness. And he would not tolerate picking on others. He respected all men. He kept a journal and it was filled with the sweetest writings. I truly think Carson was an Angel among us. He was a fine man, a good soldier and a friend. He always spoke about his family and how much he loved them. He wanted to return home one day and work beside his father. He said he and Sarah would have a house full of children. I will always remember him." John walked over and sat down.

Matthew got up and walked to the spot where John stood. "My name is Matthew O'Brien, from Jackson, Mississippi. I had just finished West Point and was stationed in Washington D.C. at the White House when the war broke out. It was just as well because I could not fight my fellow Southerners and I wasn't a believer in slavery. I worked in the Office of the President and throughout the Capital. *I did not know Carson, but as John once said I knew many young men just like him.* I did have the opportunity to know him through his journals which

John allowed me to read. I would like to read just one specifically that touched me. It was written the day after a bloody battle with a tremendous loss of life. It reads like this:

Wednesday, 12 July

I don't think God ever wanted men to see such things as this. The Angel of Death was present with us and even he was tired and disgusted. It seems to me our politicians would not allow another day of war if they were here to witness the death and dying. These boys haven't lived long enough to know this degree of hatred. Someone has played a terrible joked on us all. Why do the poor young soldiers that claim no slaveholdings fight to the death to protect the interests of wealthy old men that want to hold the futures of every black person in bondage, in perpetuity? Who will come down to the battlefield and walk between the mangled bodies of boys and stand up and declare the merits of this righteous war? Who will walk across the yard of a burning house with women and children crying over the loss of their livestock, their home and their crops and call this victory? I know my father never taught me to hate and kill and I know this is no answer to the problems that our country faces. Until we look into the faces of young men as they take their last breath, until we stand at the stocks and allow others to draw blood from our backs with whips, until we give up our food supplies to aid the widow and orphans we will not stop this insanity. Will death be our only hope? Please, I pray, let us live long enough to change our hearts and minds from hate to love. Let me be a catalyst of change.

Matthew closed the journal of Carson, handed it to Elizabeth, and walked away.

Thomas got up and walked to the place where the others stood earlier. *"My name is Thomas Smith from South Georgia. I served with Carson too. I am not much of a talker, but I know something about him that I admired very much. Carson made people laugh; he gave people his food when he was hungry too. I remember once he left his shoes under a sleeping man's blanket whose feet were bleeding from walking with shoes that were so bad he would have been better walking barefoot. Carson was like no other man. I learned things when he read the Bible. He made me a better person. He was drinking a cup of coffee and laughing when a bullet hit him and he died. A little bit of us all died that day. I went into the bushes and cried like a baby. I never let anyone see me cry, but that was different. I wish there were more people like him."* Thomas walked back to the others and sat down. There was not a dry eye.

There were other speakers that shared their fondest memories and thoughts of Carson. His teacher spoke of his love for learning as did his minister. Elizabeth shared her fondest childhood memories of Him. Finally, his mother spoke.

"How does a mother speak of her child? No mother sees anything but greatness in their children. I have to admit I am partial as is any mother; however, Carson never belonged to me. He was shared with me. He was a child of God in the truest sense of the word. He was no trouble to raise. He was a joy and he taught me how to live. I cannot describe his passion for life. I think that sometimes he thought about life with a heavenly mind. Those who knew him understand what I am saying. I am more than pleased even with his short life. He lives on in my heart and I am sure he is skipping along in green pastures and beside the still waters as we speak."

Oliver stood up to hug his wife who stood beside him. They embraced for a very long time it seemed.

Everyone enjoyed the celebration and commented so as the evening progressed and folks made their way home. Many participated in the breaking-down of the party and cleaning-up that followed.

CHAPTER 17

MATTHEW SPOKE TO MR. WALKER AND explained how he and the others were taking a night tour of downtown Charleston, and didn't want anyone to wait up for them. He was advised to be careful of the rowdies. Matthew had acquired and distributed some smaller pistols for them to carry in a concealed fashion. It would be more appropriate while in a town setting than wearing the larger pistols in holsters.

Again, they rode their horses into town and temporarily left them at the church stables with Parson Jones' permission. They walked down along the docks and took in the scenery. A heavy fog had drifted in off the harbor and it made for an eerie setting. Oil lamps hung from poles at given intervals, but gave off very little illumination. They almost ran into people walking along the boardwalk before they could see them. Voices were heard before seeing the images of people that belonged to them.

Matthew dressed appropriately for a more formal setting. He asked John and Thomas to dress casually, which pleased them as they preferred to dress that way. They were told to search out the common places known to be frequented by the rougher sort while Matthew would explore a more genteel setting.

Matthew sought a hotel in town where many of the Union officers were staying. The lobby was very ornate with more elaborate furnishings than an ordinary hotel. He was informed that this hotel also provided some gaming options in one of the conference rooms for its guests. Upon entering he met a Union officer that was present when he spoke with Colonel Watts earlier that day. The officer extended his assistance and introduced him to the people that could allow him to view or participate in the gambling and frivolity. Without the proper introduction his presence would not have been allowed.

Matthew ordered a drink and rested his elbow on the bar while the bartender went about plying his trade. He watched the people in the large room as they moved about the tables. There were some young women that worked the room delivering drinks to the gamblers. Cigar smoke hung in the air. The room was loud and men seemed to be enjoying themselves immensely. He was watching the crowd to see who the big players were and what connections they had with upper echelon folks. He noticed some well dressed men that circulated among the officers and high rollers. They operated with efficiency, as if they occupied the higher ground among their betters. One man in particular caught his eye. This man was a taller gentleman that carried himself with an air of dignity, like he was of more importance than his present company. Others seemed to be taken with his flair and mannerisms. Matthew noted the fancy cane with heavy brass knob on the end. He waved it in the air to accentuate his point at various time. Matthew had seen his type before, up north and in Washington. He was not impressed.

The night dragged on, and Matthew gained as much information as he possibly could without drawing attention to himself. He left the hotel and made his way back to *St. Michaels* Church to rendezvous with the others. They had arranged to meet back at 1:00 A.M. and go home to the Walkers' house.

Matthew beat the others back to the church and waited for more than an hour before he left to go to the Walkers without them. He knew he would see them in the morning and hear some wild story about last night. He entered the house and quietly slipped into the bed provided him. He fell asleep immediately.

Matthew was awakened by the voices of people in the kitchen. He got up, washed his face in a basin of water, got dressed and walked into the kitchen. The women were putting the finishing touches on breakfast. Mr. Walker was seated at the table already. He was drinking coffee.

"I see you are an early riser unlike those other friends of yours," Mr. Walker commented, "and you will have a better breakfast as well."

"Has anyone seen those two this morning?" Matthew asked half looking around in a curious manner. "They did not come in with me last night!"

Evangeline dropped a stick of stove wood she was about to place in the stove and gasped.

Elizabeth grabbed her by the shoulder and asked, "What's wrong?"

Looking at Mrs. Walker, Evangeline spoke with a trembling voice, "I had a bad dream this morning and I let it pass as just that. John and Thomas were in some kind of trouble. John could see what was happening to them and could not stop them, but Thomas was unconscious. They were taken to a dark place and put in chains. They are being held captive with others. They are going to be taken away, far away where they can never return!"

"I have heard of this happening lately. Men, black and white are being taken against their will and being put to work on ships as slaves or whatever, and carried off to some port where they are traded like cattle, never to return. I think they call it *shanghaied* after an old practice that was common in Shanghai, China," Mr. Walker stated with the serious tone that this situation commanded.

Matthew was beside himself with fear and his face showed it. "What can I do? Do you know anybody that could help us find them? We have to act quickly. I know this kind of operation will be covert and I am out of my league with this type of thing."

Matthew proceeded to tell the Walkers that he was still a Union Officer attached to the *U.S. Treasury Department* by request of the President. John and Thomas were also sworn in as Special Agents; however, they were former Confederate soldiers that had sworn their allegiance to the Federal Government. He told them this in confidence that they would not reveal to anyone their secrets. They agreed.

He told them he was trained and experienced in espionage and its ways; although he had never penetrated and operated in the world of subversives like this before.

"Mr. Walker, do you have connections with the port that could give us some leads?"

"I may, but please call me Oliver."

"Father," Elizabeth spoke, "what about that parishioner Parson Jones said once was a slaver? Do you think he may be of help to us?"

"His name is O'Malley, an Irish bloke, big and dangerous, but approachable now that the Lord has done some tender work on his heart. Smitty, an old friend of mine still works the docks and could be of some help as well. We need to eat and get moving quickly. Time is of the essence. Our friends may be moved away before we reach them!"

"Evangeline, is there anything else you can tell us?" Matthew inquired.

She went over to a stool beside the stove and sat. She leaned her head back while placing her hands apart on her lap. She closed her eyes as her head slowly revolved in a counterclockwise motion. She began to speak. "I see a dark place, a basement or dungeon. They are in a place where slaves were once held and the spirits of those that died in that place are calling out for release. They seek closure for their injustice. This place was used to hold slaves, before they were sold and now is used to hold others against their will. They are not being held alone. Their place of bondage is well secured and will not be taken without a fight. It is not in town, but close to town somewhere along a river. The house has something on top like a riverboat pilothouse so the owner could view ships coming and going. I can see no more, but I can hear John's voice. He is calling to his grandmother to send help. Thomas is still not responding to John's voice. He may be dead! I cannot know for sure."

"Elizabeth, go with Matthew to see Parson Jones about O'Malley and I'll go see Smitty. Let's meet in an hour at the Anchor's Away Café. Matt, do you have a gun?"

"Yes, Mr. Walker, I mean Oliver, I have my navy colt and I have a hideout gun; how about you?"

"I will be adequately equipped as well! Now, let's get moving!"

Matthew and Elizabeth saddled and rode their horses quickly down the lane to town where they encountered the Reverend fast at work preparing his Sunday sermon under the shade of the live oak.

"Good morning young folks. I can see you are taking advantage of this beautiful morning to go for a ride," the Reverend said with a smile.

"It's not like that at all Parson Jones. We have a real problem and need your help, pronto! It seems my friends, Thomas and John, have been abducted and we need to find them quickly. Elizabeth suggests we contact a man by the name of O'Malley. How can we reach him?" Matthew asked as he stood before the man shaking with nervous energy coursing through his body.

"Come with me. I think he is helping the widow Sweeney build a new chicken coop down the street," said the little man as he dropped his sermon in his chair and started down the street at a fast clip.

Just as the Reverend said, the very big man was building the chicken coop for widow Sweeney three streets down from the church. He placed his hammer on a board on top of two saw horses and walked over to the visitors. "Howdy Parson Jones, what takes you away from the church this morning?"

"Marcus O'Malley, this is Matthew O'Brien, a friend of the Walker family and he needs your help."

"Well, I have to finish this project for the widow before I commit to another," he smiled as he offered his huge, calloused hand to Matthew. Matthew's hand was swallowed up by it. "Another Irishmen is it?"

"That is correct sir, but, I need information more than your labor. My friends and fellow veterans have been abducted during the night. I have a strong suspicion they have been shanghaied and are being held in an old slaver's stronghold in a house on a river just out of town. I was told the house could have a feature that resembled a riverboat's pilothouse on top. Does that sound like someplace you may recall?"

"You are in luck, Irishman. I know exactly where that place is, but it is a bad place to be messing around; unless you know your way around, and that I do. Let me tell the widow lady I'll be back later, and be about finding me a horse to ride."

Marcus was provided with John's horse, Belle, and he also had

John's rifle in the scabbard too. They went directly towards the pre-arranged meeting spot, the Anchor's Away Café, to meet with Oliver Walker.

Meanwhile, John had dozed off and was awaken by someone bringing in a pail of water with a dipper. It was the first sunlight he had seen that morning when the jailor opened the door. He looked around and saw men chained to the wall just as he had been. A bench had been placed so the prisoners could sit rather than stand day and night; that was a comfort, if such could be said. He saw Thomas hanging from the wall, unconscious or dead; he could not tell. The jailor walked by each one of the prisoners and offered a dipper of water. More was sloshed down John's front than he got to drink. Where he was and why he was in chains were questions he did not have answers to, but he intended to find out.

"What are we doing here? Can anyone give me an answer?" he shouted in desperation.

"You have been shanghaied my friend. You are not liked by someone and you were pointed out for a boat trip," said the haggardly looking fellow sitting next to him with his wrist in shackles too.

"You see, we will be scuttled onto a ship headed for ports unknown and may never find our way back to the states again. It is the pirates' way. We are human cargo for use wherever we are needed and to the highest bidder. You will get to know what slaves have known for years; that is, your life is only worth what someone will pay for you and how much work can be gotten from your back."

"Isn't there any way out?" John asked in desperation.

"Thomas, can you hear me; Thomas, wakeup!" John tried in vain to reach Thomas. There was no hope as far as he could see.

"Don't worry my friend, he is still alive. He was immune to whatever it was they slipped into his beer and they gave him a working over. He will have one hell of a headache when he comes around though. My name is Harry. We may be working together for some time to come, I'm afraid."

John looked around and there was nothing to be seen because it was pitch-dark. The only light was that which seeped in around the door, which was very little. He realized the dire situation they were in and wondered if Matthew knew anything about it. He could barely remember calling to his deceased grandmother for help in the night. There was no way he could get his hands loose to get to the hideout gun he had shoved into his boot before going out for the night. His mind was racing. He would have to make an attempt when they removed him from the shackles anchored in the concrete walls. He hoped somebody would find out where they were being held. Their life would be over if they ever reached that slave ship.

John sat still and prayed and then he heard a voice again, *"Use your gifts John. You have to use your gifts."* He sat quietly and probed his deeper consciousness for what seemed a long time, but it wasn't. John could see black men, nearly naked except for a small piece of cloth covering their loins. They were walking around the room looking for a way out of their condition. One older man with white hair walked over to John and asked him for help.

"What can I do to help? I am chained to this wall," John spoke to him in a voice that was not discernible to others, except for the dead.

"We can help you if you will help us," the old man said in earnest.

"What can I do?"

"We will help you escape if you will burn this place down and release our spirits from here. Will you help us?" the old man asked with a pleading voice.

"Yes, it will be done!" John told him with all the sincerity that he possessed.

The spirits gathered around John and put all their strength together and pulled the chains that held John from the wall. He was free!

"Can you do the same for all the other men here?" John asked.

The spirits one by one pulled every man free from the walls. Thomas was still unconscious. The men just stood there wondering what had happened causing them to be free. John explained to them that the spirits of dead slaves were present with them and not to be afraid.

"They freed us and in return we must burn this place to the ground to set their spirits free, forever! Will you help me?"

"Yes indeed!" the men responded

While John was working to secure his freedom Matt and Elizabeth brought Marcus O'Malley to meet with her father. Oliver had told his friend Smitty about their ordeal. Smitty gave them his full support. He had twenty dockworkers that were sitting idle and they would help mount an attack. Marcus told them where the old slaver's house was and about the defenses they would face. Together they made a plan. Some would cross on the ferry and circle around while others would come in off the river. Matthew and Elizabeth would approach on horseback as two young people out for a morning ride down the river road.

"It would be best to attack at night," Smitty explained, "but I understand they could be moved as soon as their ship arrives; so, we will need a diversion. Matt, you and the girl ride up in front of the house like you are sightseeing, and cause a ruckus if somebody starts asking you questions. This will draw more men out to see what the fuss is, while my men get in positions in the sawgrass. Marcus, get your men placed strategically behind the house, and get someone inside if possible to eliminate men with guns on the second floor. My men will have guns, spears or whatever weapons they can get. Matthew, give me your rifle and ammunition and that six-gun; they will be suspicious if you go loaded for bear. Let's split into groups and move!"

Matt and Elizabeth rode up river to the ferry to cross to the other bank. They rode casually, laughing gaily, as two young lovers out for a day of fun and excitement. As they approached the house they slowed their horses to a walk and stopped in front and started looking at the house and discussing its extraordinary features when a gruff looking man walked out to them.

"You people need to keep moving! This ain't no place for sightseers. Do you understand what I'm saying?" the man asked while visibly agitated.

Matt commented, "The owner used to keep this place better

maintained. They once had a beautiful flower garden all the way around the house. What happen to the family that used to live here?"

"I don't know and don't care either! You and the little lady need to move on before someone gets hurt."

"Well, aren't you a rude one mister. I don't think I've *ev'ah* seen worse manners!" Elizabeth said with her thick Southern accent emphasized a little more than usual.

The man grabbed the reins of her horse, pulling it closer to him; then, he grabbed her by the ankle. Elizabeth struck him across the face with her riding quirt. He recoiled and began to strike out before Matt pulled out his smaller pistol that was hidden in his waistband.

"Mister, I will put a bullet between your eyes and you will be dead before your body hits the ground between these two horses!" Matt spoke in a quiet and firm tone only the three could hear.

As they stood out front in a standoff, others came from the house to investigate what the trouble could be. The man saw the others coming out and saw his chance to act. Matt said in a very low voice, "Mister, you will die trying!" The man shoved the horse with anticipation of making a run for the house; however, that would be the last decision he ever made, and it was a poor one at that.

Matt put a slug between the gruff man's eyes just as he said he would, and the man fell between their horses, dead, as he was told.

Matt spurred his horse forward just as Elizabeth put a quirt to hers simultaneously. They bolted ahead on the road as men stood up in the sawgrass and cut down four men standing on the unkempt lawn. Others fled back to the protection of the house. One man was skewered with a pitchfork by one of the dockworkers.

O'Malley had his men positioned to overtake three men in the rear and one on each side of the house. They acted with speed and stealth, using knives and clubs to subdue their adversaries, allowing them the opportunity to enter the house from the rear. Once inside a fierce battle of hand-to-hand combat ensued.

Out on the river the slaver's ship appeared, coming around the bend as it was being alerted by a man standing in the pilothouse perch waving a red flag in one hand and a lantern in the other. Directly behind the slave ship a *U.S. Navy* sloop-of-war came in sight, turning broadside to the other ship, and sent a cannonball into the house with a loud boom. The concussion of the blast knocked most of the men standing on the banks to the ground. It also took off the top portion of the house where the man with the red flag and lantern once stood warning the slave ship.

The slaver's ship unfortunately rolled out two cannons and proceeded to point them at the Navy ship. This brought out the ire of the ship's captain and he ordered the firing on of the other ship. When the smoke cleared the ship's bow was turning skyward as the stern was diving deeper in the river's depths. Those that could were abandoning the dark ship whose evil past had finally come to a close as she settled to her watery grave.

The remaining men surrendered, having seen the sinking of their ship and the house slammed by a cannonball, and walked out of the house with their hands held high and O'Malley's men bringing up the rear.

John and the other captives were excited to hear the fighting going on outside. They had organized and placed themselves in their positions to give the jailor the impression things were normal when he entered the dungeon. Several men, including John, placed themselves to either side of the door to overtake the man as he stepped inside. They heard him coming down the stairs, rattling his keys. They jumped him as he entered the room. The man yelled and screamed when he was overtaken. They dragged the jailor across the room and placed him in shackles. They removed the bench so he had to stand. One man got his keys and en mass they left the basement to bask in the beautiful, refreshing sunlight, once again.

Sailors on the Union boat, rescuers on the grounds and prisoners just captured watched as more than thirty men walked outside the house, some for the first time in weeks. Everyone was confused to find the men coming from the dungeon still had the shackles and chains hanging from their wrists. They lined up as one man performed the task of removing their bonds with the jailor's keys. Some twirled in circles in the sun on the front lawn. Others began to find tinder and placed it at the base of the house. Two men began to empty the kerosene, found in cans out back. They completely and thoroughly soaked the house.

A primal scream could be heard coming from the dungeon. It was blood curdling and continued for several minutes before it finally ceased.

John walked around the outside of the house, setting the fire, and another man set it on the inside. Thomas was still unconscious and lying off to the side, away from the fire, at a safe distance where the other captives had laid him.

Then everyone stopped to witness something unbelievable. A large group of African slaves adorned only in breechcloth began to appear as from a fog. They came together in a circle with loud and jubilant celebration, shouting tribal war chants, as each looked skyward. They were in the middle of the front lawn of the burning house. Just like a whirlwind on a summer day lifting dust from the ground, they were all lifted in a circular fashion to ascend skyward. No one spoke, each having felt they had just witnessed a spectacular occurrence of *biblical* significance.

Matthew and Elizabeth walked up to John as he stood watching the house quickly catch up in flames.

"What happened in there? You came out with shackles still attached like they were ripped from the walls, maddening screams came from inside and everyone was intent on burning the house down without a single word passed between you!" Matt asked completely puzzled.

John looked to his side to locate Matt and looked back at the burning house. "I had some visitors in the form of spirits of deceased slaves that were stuck in this place, this dungeon, and they offered me and the boys some help if we could help them find freedom. They asked that we burn this house to the ground in return for pulling our chains from the walls. I agreed to do what I could and that was when you came along with all the help. How did you know where we were?"

"You can give the credit to Evangeline; she had a dream. How is Thomas?" they both asked in unison.

"I don't know. He hasn't spoken and someone said he wasn't affected by whatever they slipped into our beers and he was beaten pretty badly. We need to get him back to the Walker's house and put him to bed, and *pray!*" John's sense of urgency was piqued.

A troop of Union Army regulars came down the river road led by Colonel Watts. "Mr. O'Brien, I understand you have a package for me."

"Yes, I guess I do have something for you Colonel. These men are the remnants of a human smuggling ring that tried to take my friends, along with these other men, out of the country. We have put a stop to the operation, but we haven't cut off the head yet. We have to find the source to be certain it is finished. I will keep you updated. It was very opportune that you just happened to show up at this time, sir," Matt commented.

"Well, I had planned to get here earlier. You see the Parson got word to me about your dilemma and I got word to the Navy. It appears the Navy beat me here. I heard some explosions and saw the smoke starting to billow. You and your friends have done an efficient job without me, apparently. Did you have any casualties?"

"Not a one on our part, but we inflicted a number to the combatants. I have a man that hasn't recovered from the beating he took last night. I've got to get him to some help quickly, and I see Parson Jones coming with a wagon that will suffice. Thank you again, Colonel Watts. I will turn the prisoners over to you at this time."

Thomas was transported to the Walkers' house where he was put to bed and well attended to by all the women folk. He suffered a major concussion according to the local doctor, Dr. Ramey. It was possible he could have some memory loss or worse. He would have to be observed after he regained consciousness to fully evaluate any possible impairment. Everyone was very concerned and there were many prayers sent up for his full recovery.

It was late that afternoon, just before dinner, when Thomas woke up with Evangeline, John, Matt, Elizabeth and Mrs. Walker all gathered around. They were all surprised when he opened his eyes and slowly set up in the bed. He looked around at everyone, rubbing his head and said, "Man, I've got some kind of headache. And, I am starving to death! It must be some time to eat around here. What are y'all doing sitting around. Something smells bad in here, and it could be me."

They all laughed at once. Thomas wasn't sure just what he said that was so funny. The whole situation looked kind of odd to him.

John was the first to speak. "He has fully recovered! His head is harder than a pine knot and his stomach is a bottomless pit with a memory of its own."

Again they laughed, and even harder this time.

Thomas was escorted by John and Matt out back where a galvanized washtub was placed by the cistern. Water was boiling in an iron kettle for his bath. They explained all that had occurred since their abduction. John admitted he did not remember anything after his beer was spiked. He was groggy until he woke up in the dungeon. Thomas stated he could remember the faces of the men that jumped him. It was three men, two large brutes and a slender fellow. One looked like a dandy, or riverboat gambler you might see in St. Louis or New Orleans. He thought he might have marked two of their faces somewhat with a beer mug he broke on them. That might be a lead; however, Matt seemed to think they would abandon their old hangouts and move on since the house and ship were destroyed.

"Maybe we can scout around tomorrow morning and catch someone leaving town on a boat or horse or whatever means of travel they prefer. We can watch the docks and the hotels, but wherever we go Thomas will have to come along because he is the only one that can identify them. Do you think you will feel up to it in the morning Thomas?" Matt asked.

"Well, hell, I will be up to it tonight after I get some food in me. Do you think three men can take me out of the fight when the whole damn *Yankee* army couldn't," Thomas boasted. "I came from good stock, and don't you forget that. I told Mr. Lincoln I came to serve and that's what I plan on doing. Now go away so I can bathe. Go help the womenfolk set the table. I'll be along directly."

Mrs. Walker, with the help of Elizabeth and Evangeline, set a fine dinner table. Parson Jones was invited, or maybe he just invited himself; whatever the case, he was there for dinner.

He asked the blessing and everyone passed the food around the table. Elizabeth had made several pecan pies for dessert. It was a thing to watch as Thomas ate.

"Why's everybody looking at me?" Thomas inquired genuinely.

John looked at him and shook his head, "They *ain't nevah* seen a man eat like you!"

"What, am I doing something wrong?" John asked.

"No, but they are looking at you because of how much food you eat. Stray dogs couldn't eat that much."

"I'll have you know I missed at least two meals, and now that I've started eatin' regular, I don't think I can skip a meal anymore. My pappy was the one that signed me up for the army. He said he couldn't afford to feed me anymore and maybe the army could; so here I am!" Thomas just went back to eating.

"I thought you said you ran out one night and joined," John reminded him.

"I did. You see pappy signed me up and then he said I was going to plow the red field with that old cantankerous mule the very next day, but I ran off in the night and didn't look back. I think he planned it that way."

After dinner they were served pecan pie and coffee. While they were casually talking Parson Jones looked over at John and asked him how they got the shackles free from the walls.

"Well Parson, I've always been told God works in mysterious ways, and as I was calling for help a group of deceased African tribesmen that had been transported over here by slave ship appeared to me. The spirits wanted released from a form of purgatory and they agreed to help me if I would burn that satanic structure, that house where they had been held, to the ground. I must admit a peace came over me as we torched that house. I think the house itself was pleased that it no longer played such a dark role in the lives of so many," John said with a sigh of relief.

"John, you have been a blessing to many. That house was a curse on this community. I have prayed for its demise many a night. The souls of many unfortunate people found suffering and death in that chamber of horrors after living through their torturous crossing. The war's end is not the end of suffering for our nation. I believe there is not an inch on this Earth that isn't stained by the blood of innocents, and walked by spirits seeking reconciliation. There will never be enough goodwill to go around, my son," the Parson stated with a grim smile.

CHAPTER 18

THAT NIGHT THE MEN WENT OUT FOR A RIDE along the docks and down the streets in town. Their mission was to find the men that put them in bondage, get some answers and extract some satisfaction, maybe a pound of flesh as well. Weapons were carried discreetly not to attract attention. It was a shot in the dark, figuratively speaking, to find the villains and close the circle of abductions.

Everything appeared to be normal in town for a Friday night. People were strolling down the sidewalks; some were taking their sweethearts for a carriage ride. People had begun to eat at the few restaurants that were open for business. The city was taking on a new look. It would take a great deal of time for it to return to the level of grandeur it once held.

Times were changing for the better since the war had ended; although it may never regain what it lost in stature. The changes would not all be structural as in rebuilding, but just as significant would be the social changes. Time could not pass fast enough to heal the wounds that follow war or the illness that precedes it.

They walked their horses around and pretended to be typical locals out to take in the nightlife. Tying the horses outside a dockside tavern, they walked in to drink a tanker or two of beer. Sitting at a corner table, Thomas scanned the patrons coming and going with hopes of identifying the men he fought the previous night.

"This looks like a wild goose chase to me," Thomas surmised. "We might have better luck catching fish on main street than finding these jacklegs tonight ..." Thomas stopped in mid sentence and pointed at the man walking across the floor towards the archway into the courtyard. "That's one of the men!"

"Thomas, you and John follow that man when he leaves the tavern;

find out as much as you can without being noticed," Matt directed them as he got up and walked towards the courtyard.

The courtyard was bathed with low light coming from several gas lamps hanging close to the tables between the banana trees. There was a large fountain in the center with flames shooting upward through the water spouts. There was a couple drinking wine and talking at one table to his right. He turned when he caught the movement of a man out of his left eye. The man came around a stand of banana trees behind which another table stood. The man bumped into Matt, moving hurriedly from the courtyard, causing Matt to spin around. Matt attempted to offer an apology, but the man was moving very quickly. Matt stopped when he walked around to the table and discovered a man formally dressed, slumped over the table, with a knife lodged in his spine, just above his shoulder blades.

Matt stood there for a brief time before sprinting out of the court-yard, back into the tavern. "Somebody stop that man! Get a doctor, he stabbed someone in there! "Matt yelled.

John and Thomas had already jumped up and began to chase the man out into the street. Matt was close behind when they turned down an alley between two warehouses. John grabbed Thomas as someone sliced his shirt and his left arm wide open as he turned the corner.

"We don't want to follow him into that alley!" John explained. "See what happened to your arm. You are bleeding!" John pulled out his handkerchief and tied it around the cut in Thomas' arm.

Thomas and Matt followed John as he ran up the half block and then turned north to intersect the running man. They saw him as he crossed the street into another alley. They ran one more block and then stopped. "I think he is close by. I see a livery up ahead; let's go there!" John indicated.

They walked up to the livery with their pistols drawn. Matt grabbed a lantern hanging on the inside of the double door that was swung out-ward on one side and inward on the other. Quickly he struck a match on the door and lit the lantern. They didn't have to go any further to catch their man, or so they thought. There was a man lying on the livery stable floor, dead, with his throat cut from ear to ear.

John reached into the man's vest and pulled out an envelope. He searched through his other pockets looking for any identification. He had two twenty dollar gold pieces, a gold pocket watch and a business card. They looked at the card, and it read:

Horace Tolliver Marchant
Attorney at Law
New Orleans, Louisiana

The envelope contained one-thousand dollars. The man that killed him wasn't interested in the money as much as he was in silencing his partners. This was exactly the intentions of the incident in the tavern. The envelope was hotel stationary with the inscription: *The St. Charles Hotel.* That could prove to be a vital clue in our investigation. The prize must be a grand one and the incentives even greater. It was very significant that murder was used without hesitation to achieve maximum results. This could be the break they needed to launch a major investigation; although, their efforts must be covert in nature.

Upon closer inspection, the pocket watch revealed the name of Norman Booker inscribed inside the cover. It also stated it was presented by the Pinkerton Agency, for valor. This was substantial information that would need to be passed on to Washington and may be relative to their pursuits as well.

Matthew trimmed the wick to throw out more light on the livery. He told the others to look very carefully around them before they started trampling the area where the murder occurred. John commented there was no struggle by the appearance of the footprints on the ground. Thomas also commented that one of the other men must have a bum leg because it appeared he dragged his left leg somewhat rather than lifting it as high as the other. The footprints stopped in the center of the stables. They looked around to see a rope still barely swaying from one the rafters and where the carriage wheels had left the livery stable.

"I do believe he can fly!" Thomas commented. "And, the dead man's knife is still in the scabbard. He did not see this coming or he was surprised by the action of the other man. He looks like one of the men I fought that night they shanghaied us. That would account for two of the men."

John looked at Thomas and Matt and said, "I think there were two men in the livery. One was in the loft and swung down when the killer ran inside to meet Mr. Booker and knocked him down and the killer we were chasing proceeded to cut Booker's throat. The man on the rope landed in the wagon and the killer jumped in with him and they left by the back of the livery."

"Look at that man's boots. They aren't working man's boot. That is fine tooled leather, Spanish type. Those are California made boots. This man was well traveled if I am correct," Matt stated. He looked on the lapel of his coat and read the label: **Goldsmith's Fine Clothiers; Philadelphia, Pennsylvania.**

"These men are not petty hoodlums looking to roll a drunk for his money. They did not choose you two randomly. We have either ruffled the wrong feathers or they are suspicious of our intentions. I have to believe someone on that boat ride didn't like our looks or the fact that we fought on different sides of this war and now stand together, brothers-in-arms. Our enemies will be great. Our courage will be judged by the strength of our enemies." Matt walked around and made mental note of everything he saw. "Let's go back to the tavern. We will need to report what we know to the authorities."

There was a crowd inside the tavern. People had gathered around inside the courtyard to look at the dead man. A law enforcement officer, along with several Union soldiers dispatched to investigate stood close by. They questioned the man and woman sitting at the other table and they could not provide any substantial information since they were too involved in conversation to notice anything odd.

The man had died, but, he lived long enough to tell the bartender some meaningless words. He said, "To look for the snake, and the staff, and ink on ..." It was very little to go on, but, it had meant something for it to be the last words of a dying man.

They reported what they saw and also reported the dead man they had found in the livery stable. They answered all the officer's questions and then some. The soldiers had someone retrieve the body in the livery stable and bring it over to the tavern with hopes someone could identify it.

The bartender stated the dead man in the courtyard called himself Anthony Martini. Matt's head popped up as he heard that name, and he rushed over to get a better look at the man's face. He pushed his way through the crowd and asked the soldier if he could have a look at the man's face. He gave him permission to go ahead. Gently, Matt raised the dead man's head and looked at him straight on. His eyes were still open. After making certain it was an old acquaintance of his in Washington D.C., Matt closed the man's eyes and placed his head gently back on the table.

"What did you find on the man?" Matt asked the sheriff.

'Not much!" the sheriff remarked. "I did find a picture of him and maybe his wife or girlfriend. He had a watch. I didn't check for any engravings inside of it, yet. He had some coins, currency and a strange telegram from Washington D.C. It said something about keeping an eye out for an old friend, and to compare notes, maybe possible connection; signed The Eagle."

"John, give me a hand. I want to lay him across this longer table." Together they lifted him and placed his heavy body across the table.

"May I have a little privacy with this man's corpse please?" Matt asked the sheriff in charge.

"For what reason do you need some privacy with him?" the sheriff asked.

"He is my *brother-in-law*," Matt said, "and I want to say a few words to him, alone. My sister will appreciate that I handle the arrangements and have him shipped back home to Washington for burial."

Matt removed his boots and found his Secret Service badge hidden in a secret compartment that was woven there for that purpose. The badge was assigned the number 4. He also found some cryptic notes hidden there as well. He placed his boots back on his feet and checked him over for any other information. He found a room key hidden in a zippered sleeve on the inside of his pants waistband. The key was for room *212* at *The Excelsior Hotel.* After a careful search Matt stepped out and told the officer that he would make arrangements with the mortician and the army to have his body shipped home.

The other body was brought into the courtyard by some townspeople. The bartender said he recognized the man, but did not know his name. A lady stepped forward and stated his name was John Brown, which she took as an alias; however, she heard another man refer to him as Norman Booker."

"He talked with a Northern accent, like maybe someone from Boston, or Philadelphia. I overheard two men talking at a café where I work, after Mr. Brown walked out. One said he was a Pinkerton agent he once saw working around the capital in D.C. He said not to trust him." The young lady looked around and politely stated, "I wish I had more to offer. He was polite when he came into the *Blue Bird Café.* I wish more were like him; I'm truly sorry."

Thomas told Matt he did not recognize the Martini fellow. Together they walked out of the tavern. Matt lead the way and they walked three blocks to the Excelsior Hotel. They walked into the spacious lobby of the hotel where a couple was seated on a settee, patrons were walking across the lobby and the night clerk was attending to his duties behind the desk.

"Follow me and act like you've been here before and are going to our room," Matt directed.

They walked up the main staircase and turned to the left with hopes that was the right direction. They got lucky because room 212 was the third door on the right. Matt stepped up to the door and produced the key. He turned the key and hesitated for a moment, and then he thrust the door open and jumped inside. The room was vacant, to his relief. They walked inside and Thomas closed the door behind them and turned the lock.

"What are we looking for?" Thomas asked.

"Well, first let me explain," Matt offered. "This man was not my brother-in-law; however, I knew him well. We were friends at *West*

Point. He served the country with distinction in the Army. I wasn't aware that he was working with us, but I found this badge hidden in his boot. He was Agent # 4, the first assigned after us. I also found a telegraph that indicates he was to look for us and share some information he had. That might be why someone wants to kill us or worse. I will contact Washington by telegraph about his death and make arrangements for his body to be returned there as well. I knew his wife, Margaret, and will send her a letter of condolences. That will be a difficult task. The bartender said Anthony's last words were: "to look for the snake, and the staff, and ink on ..."

"That could mean a lot of things," John replied. "Doesn't a staff with a snake wrapped around it have some symbolism for medicine?"

"That is correct, and there was a political party that used a staff with a snake coiled around it as their symbol. They were referred to as the *Copperheads or Peace Democrats.* They were Northern in nature, but, they opposed the war and were sympathetic to the Southern cause," Matt indicated.

Thomas threw his suggestion in as well. "Couldn't it just mean an evil man with a cane and he could have ink on his hands because he has been printing money?"

"That would make too much sense, my budding detective! That would be too obvious and we should not overlook it as a possibility," Matt smiled at Thomas. "Let's look this room over for anything that could help us identify his killer, but don't light the lamp."

"It is my belief that the second man, Norman Booker that we found dead in the livery was working with Anthony Martini. I believe he was setup by the man that Thomas recognized when we walked into the bar. Martini's killer may have arranged to meet Booker in the livery stable and had someone hiding in the loft and swung down from above on that rope. First he surprised him, and then he cut his throat. I believe John was correct; they rode out of there in a carriage," Matt declared.

"It also makes sense that Martini or Booker balked at the shanghaiing of you two," Matthew surmised, "and were eliminated due to suspicion."

They searched Martini's room for an hour using only the light of the moon shining through the window. They went through his clothes, his suitcase and any papers he had. He left his room in such a way that nothing could incriminate him if searched. He was a very intelligent man and knew just the kind of element he was dealing with. Just about the time they were ready to give up the search, John found a loose board in the bottom of a built in closet.

"Wait! I think I've found something!" And they both walked over to look as John removed a loose board from the floor of the closet. He reached in and pulled out a large envelope. He handed it to Matt and reached back farther to be certain there was no more. He placed the board back into its place before he stood up.

Matt said, "Let's put things back in place before we leave. We don't want the next person to know someone has been searching the room."

After things were put back into place John held up his finger to his lips and motioned for the others to stand back. They moved back against the wall. John was on one side of the door and Thomas and Matthew on the other. They waited as footsteps walked up to the door and someone rattled the door. There was a brief pause and then a key slid inside the lock. The door opened and a man stepped inside. John grabbed the man as Matthew struck a match and lighted the lamp. Thomas already had his Bowie knife pulled and pointed it at the man's brisket.

They were surprised to find the night clerk staring at them in utter fear for his life. He wasn't a strong man. He almost looked like he would cry. John shoved him into the center of the room, where he stumbled and caught the edge of the bed to steady himself.

"What are you doing sneaking into this man's room after he was found dead just a little more than an hour ago?" Matthew asked him.

"Well, I might ask you the same thing Mister!" The clerk's squeaky voice lashed out.

"We are friends of the deceased and work for someone that wants answers!" Matt replied. "That is all you need to know. Give me some answers, now!"

"I don't have any answers Mister. Some man walked up to the desk and asked me to check on the man registered to this room. He said he thought he was very sick and may need help."

"Don't you usually knock when you are entering someone's room?"

"Yes, I normally do, but I go in and out of so many of these rooms I sometimes forget to knock; and I was afraid he might be dead the way the man seemed so anxious for me to check on him. He was very afraid for him."

Matt's eyes were opened to their fullest as he just realized what was about to happen. He grabbed Thomas and shoved him into John and pushed them towards the door. They rolled out onto the carpet in the hallway just as a stick of dynamite smashed through the window and hit the floor of the hotel room. It was too late to attempt a rescue of the night clerk. Each of the men scampered out of the doorway as they began to understand the danger they faced. Matthew looked as he passed the doorway and the last thing he saw was the doomed look of the clerk's face realizing death was imminent.

The blast blew the room into bits of floating splinters, bedding and what remained of the night clerk. The gore of what remained of him was sprayed throughout the room and the opposing wall across the hallway. John and Thomas stood up coughing and hacking as they looked around for Matthew. The walls were blown out of the room and boards were leaning on the far side wall across the hall. Matthew stood up and pulled a large splinter from his leg as he looked through the dust and smoke to find the others still alive and walking over to him.

"What the hell!" John exclaimed. "I never knew just how much excitement this job would be. Matt, you have very good instincts and reflexes too for a man that wasn't in combat."

"I never said I wasn't in *combat;* I just said I *never fought*! There is a difference! I said I never killed a man in anger. That doesn't mean I've never done the deed," Matt elaborated.

"Now let me tell you something! This is starting to make me mad! Somebody is going to suffer for this and everything else he has put me through lately. That little man that was in there did not deserve to die like that. Somebody is going to pay for that!" Thomas was trying to calm down because he was so mad he could not see straight. He was bleeding on his back and head and his shirt and pants were torn to shreds. Matt and John weren't much better off.

The sheriff and a handful of soldiers came running up as did dozens of other people from the hotel and off the street. Colonel Watts was standing there too. He was having dinner with some of his men when the explosion rocked the hotel. It was a gory sight to see and no one stepped forward until Matthew made his way through the debris. He greeted the sheriff and shook the hand of the Colonel.

"Good evening Colonel! How are you this evening, sir?" Matt asked as he brushed off the plaster and wall paper from his ragged clothes.

"You look horrible Mr. O'Brien. What the hell happened here?" the Colonel asked.

"If you think we look badly sir you should have a look at the night clerk inside what's left of that room. We came up to inspect the room of an old friend of mine from the Academy that was murdered tonight when the night clerk walked in. He told us someone wanted him to check on the occupant of the room, claimed he was very sick. That's when I got suspicious and shoved them out of the room. Unfortunately, I did not have time to rescue the clerk. Someone threw a stick of dynamite through the window from outside. I think there is a courtyard outside and he was waiting to attack from below. Once the night clerk entered the room and the lamp was lighted he could see our shadows or shapes in the room and knew where to throw the dynamite."

"I want to know more about this whole night. You men will need to follow me to the jailhouse. I think something is rotten here and you are at the center of it," the sheriff stated. "Weren't you also the men involved in that incident down the river earlier today?"

"Sheriff Willis, these men were a part of a joint military operation between the *U.S. Army* and the *U.S. Navy* that I personally conducted. It was brought to a conclusion today with their civilian assistance. Let them go their way tonight and I promise we will meet in your jailhouse, noon tomorrow. Is that satisfactory?" the Colonel asked.

"I guess that will be okay, but who is going to clean this up?" the sheriff asked out loud.

"I would imagine that would be the job of the night staff!" Thomas offered as he walked through the rubble on his way out.

The three men walked back to the hitching post at the tavern to retrieve their horses. The horses shied at the smell of fresh blood, but were calmed enough to allow them to mount. They rode out of town and turned down the lane to the Walkers' place.

"We just can't go strolling in the house looking like this; it might scare them all to death," John speculated.

"Where could we get clothes at this time of night?" Thomas thought out loud.

"I don't think it matters much what we think. It looks like the whole countryside is still having a get together at the Walker's house." Matthew's face was turning red. He was embarrassed to be seen in such condition.

Juan was there, along with the Barnes family that lived next door. Evangeline, Elizabeth, Mr. and Mrs. Walker, Parson Jones and even the local doctor, Doc Pritchett, were there. It seems no one had left after dinner and Mr. Walker sent Juan to fetch the Doc as a precaution. Evangeline had a premonition and Parson Jones felt a stirring also that trouble was a brewing.

"*Git your selves down off those horses and step up on this porch! I am about ready to tear your hides up!* Elizabeth, go out back along the apple orchard and cut me some limber switches, please," Mrs. Walker commanded.

"Now, Mrs. Walker, let me explain ..." Thomas pleaded.

"First thing, my name is Sue Ellen, and you can call me Mama Sue! And the second thing, I don't want to hear any excuses. I didn't give you permission to go into town and blow the place to smithereens. Do you understand me?"

"Yes ma'am, I didn't mean to cause you so much worry, Mama Sue," Thomas said with tears in his eyes and a crackle in his voice.

Sue ran over to him and threw her arms around him and they fell to the ground. They just sat there; her hugging and him crying like a little baby in her arms.

"Now get up from there Thomas! You didn't get hurt any worse than the rest of us," said John, as he stumbled and fell getting off his horse and then started walking towards the porch.

Evangeline ran over to lift him up with the aid of Oliver Walker. Parson Jones and Elizabeth followed suit and ran to the aid of Matt before he got off his horse.

They were each positioned on the porch and the Doc took a look at them. He had the women folk, including Mrs. Barnes, to cut away the tattered clothes and bring out fresh bandages along with some boiling water.

Thomas attempted to throw a fit at the notion of them removing his clothes, but there wasn't much left anyway. They promised to do all they could to maintain his dignity. The women agreed that he could not expose them to anything they hadn't already seen. He gave in and shut up.

They had more injuries than they even realized. They had multiple cuts and contusions, along with burns from the dynamite. Fortunately there were no broken bones, but there was a lot of bruising, and they would be sore for a period of time. That blast was fatal and they were alive only because of Matthew's quick thinking and quick reflexes.

Matthew proceeded to explain just what happened throughout the night. He didn't go into details about their mission, but he told them this was part of something bigger than just the events here in Charleston.

"This appears to be a concerted effort by a syndicate or organized group to carry out illegal activities against the *U.S. Government* and we are on a mission to prevent this group from succeeding. That may sound evasive; however, the less you know, the better off you are. John and Thomas have agreed to join me on this mission and they are brave men. I think they are beginning to realize how dangerous this work can be," Matt explained with a frown.

"I don't understand just what you are doing, but I know this much. If you don't slow down there won't be anything left of you to go around," Mama Sue said with her strongest motherly voice while wiping tears from her eyes with the apron.

They started to laugh, but felt it inappropriate; plus, it hurt to laugh. They surrendered and let the doctor attend to their injuries.

After all the bathing and bandaging was complete, the men were escorted off to bed and everyone else went their separate ways for a well deserved rest.

The next morning everyone was out of bed early, drinking coffee while the women were preparing breakfast. Thomas commented on how good the biscuits and bacon smelled. Quickly the table was set and Mr. Walker entered the room.

"Well, it looks like a good day for business! People are already lining up at the barn for seed and other things. I guess I better skip breakfast," Oliver said.

"*To Hell you say!*" Mama Sue piped up. "We didn't go to all of this trouble for you to work on an empty stomach."

"Mother, what has gotten into you? I've never heard you cuss before," Elizabeth remarked.

"I have never had so many stubborn and hard-headed men under my roof at one time either, and it is high time I stood up and make my feelings known. I stood idly by and watched everyone do their thing when I should have said some things, but I didn't. I watched Carson ride off to war and did not say a word; all I did was cry and stand back in the shadows. There are three young men sitting at this table that would have broken my heart if anything terrible had happened to them last night. No longer will I stand idly by, and keep my mouth shut, when I feel it is time to speak up."

"How do you want your eggs, Oliver?" Mrs. Walker asked.

"I will take them fried, honey!"

They all giggled and the boys felt a strong sense of love and belonging wash over them at the remarks of Mama Sue.

"Evangeline, how old are you?" Elizabeth asked.

"Why, I think I will be nineteen May 30; at least, that what I've been told."

"You and I are the same age! What about you boys?" she asked.

"I am twenty-three," John offered, "and I think Thomas is twelve."

"I was twenty as of last October. My Pappy signed me up when I was just sixteen," Thomas remarked. "How old are you Matthew?"

"Let's see, I was twenty-nine on December, the twenty-second. I got out of the Academy and worked two years in Washington before the War started. Time sure does fly when you are busy. One day I was just a kid, and the next day I was a grown man watching kids die all around me. It doesn't take long for *Father Time* to present his case."

"John, I wanted to ask you something about that valise you been carrying. It is stenciled with the name of **William T. Bennett**. What is the story behind that?" Oliver inquired.

"It is quite simple. After I woke up on a pile of bodies stacked for burial I ran down to the creek and jumped in to revive my senses. That's where I met Matthew. He made camp where he came upon this man that was snake bitten and later died. That suitcase, along with the horse and his clothes were given to me by Matthew," John stated. "Is there any special reason why you ask?"

"Yes, there was a man that came through in January and stayed on until April. His name was William Bennett, folks just called him Bill. He was a nice enough fellow and no one really knew his business. He kept to himself, mostly. He did attend church regularly and took most of his food at widow Mackey's boarding house. He kept a room at the Excelsior Hotel. He said he worked for the railroad and was doing preliminary work around this area. He did ride out of town often; although, there were rumors floating around that he was a Pinkerton."

Oliver scratched his head and offered, "It might be a tie-in with why there are people trying so hard to kill you young men. Someone just may have seen that bag and tied up loose ends. It may have something to do with Anthony Martini's death as well. You say you are working for the railroad and that may also create suspicion as a possible connection to the Pinkerton organization."

"Oliver, I guess it would be alright to trust you. We have been working for the Government as part of a newly established organization to search out and destroy a counterfeiting ring that operates from North to South. Mr. Bennett was probably on the same mission, as a contractor, through the *Pinkerton Agency.* Mr. Martini was also an agent of the same organization we work for. I will report his death to my Director as well as Mr. Bennett's. I am glad you brought this to my attention. Matt paused for a moment and suggested, "We should probably step away from the guise that we are employees of the railroad to deflect any further connections to the Pinkertons. It might be wise to leave that suitcase behind."

"Now we need to finish our breakfast very quickly because we have plans to meet with Colonel Watts and the Sheriff." Smiling at Thomas, Matt commented, "Some of us will need more time than others."

That drew laughter from everyone but Thomas, because he wasn't sure just what Matt intended by that remark.

CHAPTER 19

JACOB HAD JUST RIDDEN INTO THE VILLAGE OF
the Eastern Band of the Cherokee People in the hills of North Carolina.
Some called it Cherokee, North Carolina, but the Cherokees called it
Yellow Hill.

It was early morning and the rising fog from the valley, mixed
with the smoke of breakfast fires, made it hard to see too far ahead. He
walked his horse carefully to avoid a collision with men running around
in the camp. He quickly sensed something was wrong in the village.
He heard a woman scream, and saw men running about.

Jacob stopped the first man he could and asked him what had
happened. The man looked at him with suspicion, not recognizing
him. He shook the man and asked again, "What is wrong here, man?"

Then the man recognized Jacob and said, "Our Chief and his
daughter have been killed some time during the night."

Jacob hitched his horse to a nearby tree and ran in the same direction as the others. He came upon a small crowd of men and walked
up to someone he recognized. He touched Albert Longfeather on the
shoulder and asked, "What's happening here, Albert?"

Albert turned and saw Jacob, and said, "Something terrible has
happened in our village."

Together they stepped through the crowd and into the house of
their beloved Chief. There they found the desecrated bodies of the
Chief and his young daughter, Running Deer, stretched out on the floor
with pooled blood everywhere. It appeared the old chief had put up a
valiant struggle as did his daughter. Fortunately, the girl had not been
violated, but suffered a brutal death. This was a scene that made even
the grown men gasp in horror. The house was sealed off to the village
for the elders to investigate and decide their course of action.

After the investigation, the tribe elders gathered in an assembly to discuss their findings and plans for capturing the outlaws that murdered their Chief and his daughter. The young people were terribly moved by the death of one of their friends and the older people were in disbelief that a tragedy struck so close to home. They thought they could escape the horror of the white man's war. Arrangements were being made for the customary burial.

One member of the assembly spoke, giving the details of the murder as they surmised them to be. He said, "Apparently, the Chief had inflicted wounds on his attackers; as he was still a strong and capable man just barely out of his prime. It appears that three men made up the attackers by the impressions of their footprints, and one of them had on moccasins. We may be incorrect, but we think one of them was of our own people."

"Jackson Lightfoot has been spending time away from his people more frequently, and may have taken up with a group of soldier boys that recently returned home from war. Everyone else had been accounted for. One of the young girls says she saw him hanging around them and he was defensive when she asked what he was doing with them," stated the speaker.

"Buck Wilson performed some preliminary scouting and had located tracks of three horses heading due southwest," said a spokesperson.

"They were all shod ponies, but one had the mark of our blacksmith on its shoes, indicating again the possibility of one of our young men involved in this heinous crime. The motive has not been established; however, it has been mentioned to us that Jackson has been rejected by Running Deer on several occasions. The Chief did have some valuables including: gold coins, paper money, and jewelry he had given his late wife. He also had a Presidential Peace Medal and a beautiful spear point, both given to him by his grandfather. Those are the only things that appear to be missing."

"Jacob, you are a *Federal Marshal* and have been authorized by the *Indian Council* to make arrests in the *Territories*. We would appreciate it if you would bring these men to justice. Buck will accompany you.

He is young and could benefit from your guidance in the white man's world. He is a good tracker and has good woodland skills. What do you say, Jacob?" the spokesperson asked.

"I knew the Chief and considered him a dear friend," Jacob reflected. "I am honored to be chosen worthy. He would do the same for me or anyone in this community. I will bring his killers to justice, and teach Buck what I can. We will start early tomorrow morning; I need to pay my respects to the family and speak with others about official business of the *Nations.*"

The day and night passed quickly as Jacob shared food, laughter and memories of times spent hunting, fishing and living with his friends and their families. They shared their dreams and disappointments in the presence of a roaring campfire under the starry night. The next morning Jacob woke early and found breakfast waiting for him along with his traveling companion, Buck.

"My visits here are always too short. I love to walk the forest, drink from the mountain streams, stand above the clouds and listen to the thoughts of my *Creator,*" Jacob lamented.

"Please send us off in prayer, my dear friends."

Jacob and Buck mounted their horses, waved goodbye, and rode off in the direction of the tracks. Jacob trailed his pack horse close behind and his faithful dog Blue appeared from the bushes as they began their search. Buck thought they had wasted valuable time by leaving a day later; however, it would be a part of his training to find out otherwise.

"Following tracks in the dirt is only one way of tracking," Jacob commented. "Learning how to follow the tracks in an outlaw's head is just as important."

"How do you find the tracks in their head?" Buck asked, thinking this was some sort of joke.

Jacob stopped, turned in his saddle, and looked directly at Buck. "You've got to get inside his head and learn how he thinks. When the wolf hunts the deer he looks to where the deer feeds and where he beds down; he looks for his habits and his weaknesses. The owl must know when his prey is unawares. Is the fox not smarter than his subjects? You must learn to think like the predator to know how he behaves! There are many things you can learn about the hunted that will help you when the tracks play out. The wolf and the owl and the fox all have one thing in common; they are smart hunters. Does it make sense to you?"

"Yes, I see what you mean," Buck frowned. "I guess I thought keeping sight of the tracks was all one needed to know, but the trail does end when you leave the forest and go into town."

"Yes, you are correct. The better you understand him the quicker you can know how he thinks. You need to out-think him so you can get ahead of him. You need to be one step ahead of your prey," Jacob explained.

"If I am correct, they will go on into Tennessee where they can find towns and settlements. I don't believe they will go far, unless they are going to continue on a spree of violence. I doubt they will go into Mississippi, but if they do we may have to take the Natchez Trace to catch up to them. There are many renegades borne out by the war who have no plans of becoming civilized again. They have become like animals. They are the worst kind and have to be hunted down and killed in the streets like the mad dogs that they have become."

"*The Natchez Trace* is an old trading route used by the *Native Americans* before the Europeans ever arrived. It connects the great lakes of the north with the gulf to the south, where the mighty Mississippi flows out to sea."

Jacob regressed to add, "People are creatures of habits. Remember, we are not just tracking horses."

Traveling the direction the tracks had indicated led them due southwest. It was a beautiful spring morning with a cloudless sky above. Blue was the first to arrive at the killers' campsite. There had been no attempt to conceal their camp and apparently they were in no hurry. They were either arrogant or stupid. Tracking them wasn't difficult. Jacob's main concern was to catch them before they caused any more deaths. He hoped to catch them unawares.

About noon they came upon a settlement called *Bear Springs*. They watered their horses and gave them a bait of grain.

They talked with a man at the settler's store to gather information. The man told Jacob three men had been through that way the previous day. They bought some tobacco, bacon and beans. They said they were camping along the creek and would be moving along in the morning. He felt sure they were headed down Tennessee way.

"They did not seem to be in a hurry," the old man stated. "They looked haggardly; like they still had their bark-on from the war. I know it will be at least another generation before these old ills pass. We were certainly glad they moved on because they looked like trouble to us. Why are you hunting them?"

"They are killers and we aim to bring them to justice," Jacob flatly stated. "Did they mention knowing anyone in the area?"

"No, they did not. They were a salty trio. They talked big, at least the two former soldiers did. The Cherokee buck, that's what I think he was, seemed a little out of sorts with them."

"He should have been more selective when he chose his friends. Would you have a bite the boy and I could eat before we move on?"

"Yes, my wife has some beans and ham to go with her delicious biscuits! Come inside and sit."

After eating a quick meal they headed southwest in hopes of finding the men they sought.

They traveled at a faster pace than earlier. Jacob watched Buck as he exhibited good tracking skills. He was an excellent woodsman and was very observant of Jacob, and how he carried himself around others. Jacob was a statesman in the greater world. He had traveled far and met with the great men of this nation. He was an anomaly in that he appeared to be a common man, but he was much more than what the eyes beheld.

That night Jacob and Buck made camp in a picturesque mountain gap beside a fast flowing stream. Buck picketed the horses in a patch of high grass for good grazing after they had their fill of water. Jacob started a fire and put on a pot of coffee. He also placed some biscuits and ham left over from their lunch on a flat rock near the fire to warm. He gave his dog three biscuits and some ham to go with them.

After eating and drinking coffee they were resting against their saddles when Blue came back into camp. Blue ran up to Jacob and started tugging at the leg of his jeans.

"I think your dog is still hungry or has gone mad," Buck laughed.

"No, my dog is trying to tell me someone is close and wants to be quiet about it," Jacob replied.

Jacob grabbed his rifle and gun belt and motioned for Buck to move into the bushes in back of the camp. They both were hidden well enough and were so quiet the crickets began to sing again. Blue placed himself between them, watching the campsite and looking up at Jacob for direction, waiting for an opportunity to spring. They did not have to wait long for a visitor to enter the camp. It was Jackson, the young Cherokee they were hunting. He moved gently in the bush as he crouched with his knife in hand. Once he entered the campsite and saw no one there he stood up and turned around to see where everyone had gone.

Jackson quickly recognized his error and was not sure whether to run or fight. "I'm here, now where are you, cowards? Are you afraid or have you run away? I don't know who you are, but I do not intend to be followed."

Jacob stepped out into the opening and Jackson quickly turned his way to lunge before he saw the rifle in Jacob's hands.

"You are not the brave one of your ancestors. You have chosen a bad lot to travel with young man. Do you want to go back to your tribe and face the consequences of your actions or do you want to die right here and now?" Jacob offered him the choice.

"I will die here if I must die! But, I will die like a man in combat, not like a woman with a rifle!"

"Then you will die at my hand!" said Buck, the younger man of the two, as he stepped into the clearing of the camp, brandishing his knife for battle.

"You shame us and you are not a friend. You have no heart and no courage. I knew as a child you were a lowly coward and would bring bad medicine to our people if you lived long enough; and I was right! Prepare yourself to die!"

Buck leaped at Jackson, striking with his knife at his opponent's midsection. They fought apart until Buck leaped into the air grabbing Jackson's left side, throwing him to the ground and landing on top. They struggled as each tried to gain advantage. Jackson rolled Buck over and was sitting on top of him. There was a mass of energy with arms and hands filled with blade moving all about. They struggled until Jackson fell backwards, rolling off of Buck. He took a knife deep in his heart.

"I never intended to harm anyone. My only desire was to show my-self brave, but I was weak and those white men used me. Tell them I am sorry ..." Jackson relaxed as he let out his last breath and gave up the ghost.

Buck stood up and thrust his knife in the dirt to clean the blood from the blade. He placed his knife back into its scabbard. Jacob could see the blood on Buck's left shoulder. It was a deep cut and blood was flowing freely. Jacob quickly put water on to boil. He cleansed the wound and applied some healing ointment he carried for that purpose. He covered the wound with clean gauge and secured it with a strip of cloth.

"That should suffice for a while," he commented.

Jacob placed the young body of Jackson Lightfoot off to the side of their camp under a dogwood tree near the stream. He figured to give a burial later or have the body taken back to the Nations.

"We need to leave our horses here and travel by foot. The others are likely to be close by. They will be looking for him to return and we need to surprise them. Can you travel?" Jacob asked.

"Yes, I can travel. Let's go now!" Buck replied.

Jacob removed his boots and slipped on his moccasins. He kept a pair especially for these sorts of occasions. They followed Blue and kept their ears alert for any sounds. They could smell the campfire first and heard the talking next.

"Do you think that young buck will come back?" one of the former soldiers asked.

"I would think so. If he doesn't that means he is dead! Do you really care?" the man asked with indignation.

Jacob motioned for Buck to enter the camp from the rear upon his command. He waited for him to get in position before he made his move. He watched the killers closely, waiting for them to relax and drink their coffee before he made his presence known.

He jumped into the campsite directly behind the campfire to distort their vision. He said, "Make any quick moves and I will kill you!" He held his pistol on them and one man decided he would ease his hand over to his gun belt. That prompted Buck to jack a shell into his rifle camber purely for the effect. And it worked. The man stopped abruptly.

"Come into camp Buck, and you too Blue."

"You men are guilty of murder and stupidity. I want to shoot you right here and now, but you deserve much worse. I will not hand you over to the law, but I will take you to the Cherokee Council. They will measure your punishment according to your crime. What do you have to say for yourself?"

"The only thing I have to say is, I wish I killed more of those Injuns!" the young renegade confederate lashed out.

Blue jumped at the ex-soldier, growling, and the man pulled his knife from its sheath. Jacob fired a shot at the man's feet and he dropped the knife. The other renegade turned and ran towards the back of the camp, with Blue in pursuit. He jumped from a ledge overlooking a deep ravine with a river running through the bottom. Blue stopped at the edge and looked back at Jacob. Jacob stepped over to peer into the blackness and could only hear the roar of the river below.

"We will search for him tomorrow after daylight," Jacob noted.

Buck pulled out his knife with vengeance in his eyes. "Stop Buck, we will handle this properly," Jacob insisted. "These men have admitted their guilt and no court will be necessary. I believe we can administer the punishment immediately. They do not deserve to live any longer. They did not give their victims any reprieve. Find some rope or twine to bind this man's hands and feet while I contemplate the proper punishment.

After Buck bound their hands and feet, Jacob sat back and drank their coffee while he thought. He considered slicing this man up like they did the Chief and his daughter, but thought that would leave a negative impression on Buck at such a tender age. He thought about torture, but he would be no better than them if he performed such an act. He sent Buck back to get a rope from his horse.

Buck returned with the rope. Jacob formed a noose on one end and threw it over the limb of a large hickory at the edge of the ravine, securing the other end around the tree's trunk. He grabbed the former soldier and pulled him up to the edge while placing the noose over his head. The man was wobbly as this happened so quickly.

"Don't I get a last word or somethin' mister?" the frightened man asked.

"Nope, but you can talk all you want once you get to Hell." With that said Jacob put his hands on the killer's back and gave him a shove. He swung freely from the Earth kicking his way into eternity.

Coincidentally, the area where the killers found justice was called *Hanging Dog, North Carolina*, named after a *Cherokee legend*. As the legend goes a Cherokee boy was hunting when a flash flood came upon him and his dog. After the flood he returned to search for his dog and found him sitting up in the fork of a tree. Jacob thought this was an odd coincidence once he recognized the place.

After the hanging they searched the camp and found the items stolen from the Chief. They would attend to the dead man in the morning. Jacob, Buck, and his hound, Blue, went back to their camp. They got very little sleep except for Blue. He snored so loudly that it kept them awake until they finally fell asleep.

The justice meted out by them was immediate and final. There wasn't much to be said about matters as far as Jacob felt. Maybe, he could have explained his reasoning to the young man in more depth. Jacob felt he acted appropriately in civil or diplomatic matters. He was a person of deep compassion and quick action when the situations warranted it.

The next morning they went over to the outlaw's camp after

breakfast. They looked over the edge of the ravine into the river below and did not see any sign of the man's body below on the banks or the rocks. He may have survived, but that was doubtful. They put the saddles on the horses and collected the guns. They burned everything that remained. Jacob reached out and pulled the dead man hanging from the hickory tree closer to him. With a quick stroke of his sharp knife the rope was cut and the dead body plummeted down the ravine into the river below. Jacob coiled his rope for later use.

Just a short distance downriver the other killer had spent the night in a brush pile, huddled in the leaves and other flotsam to keep warm. He looked up when he heard the splash and saw his partner-in-crime floating down the river. He watched him as he floated by, facedown, with hands bound behind him. He swore he would get revenge, someday.

After breaking camp, the two said their farewells and set off for their separate destinations. Jacob set out in the same direction he had pursued the killers. He sent Buck back with the three additional horses and word of their success. He also carried the Chief's personal possessions, along with Jackson tied down across the back of his horse.

"Stay away from the settlement we passed through on your way home. They may not understand why you are leading those empty horses and want to avenge them."

"You are a fine boy. I recommend you get as much education as you can. Learn the white man's language and stay in touch with the Cherokee ways. Don't forget your heritage! Read as many books as you can; there is wisdom in the written word, it can speak to your spirit. Be careful! *Godspeed!*" Jacob spoke, as he waved goodbye.

Jacob traveled through the mountain passes and along the ridges of the beautiful eastern mountain range. He knew these trails were also traveled by his ancestors and the ancients that lived here before them. He often felt he was not alone as he picked his way through the woodlands, weaving in and out of shadows and rays of sunlight beneath the forest canopy.

After traveling for three days he became trail weary and decided a rest was in order. He had been on a very long journey and his mind was troubled. He came to a clearing that provided water and good graze for his horses. He removed their saddles and rubbed them down. Rather than staking out his horses, he just allowed them to roam free.

He fed Blue a biscuit and some jerked venison given to him by the Cherokees. He threw his canvas fly over a low hanging limb and tied it off to make a bivouac. He found himself in the midst of a natural clearing surrounded by a beautiful forest. It was a sanctuary of sorts; a green meadow carved out of the forest with no intended purpose but to provide rest for the weary traveler.

He laid his tired body down in the morning sun beneath his fly and quickly fell asleep. He awoke a few hours later and did not see his horses. He walked around the clearing and saw where his horses' tracks led into the forest. He called Blue, but he did not come. He was disturbed and began to follow the trail into the forest.

He came upon a waterfall that dropped about one hundred feet into a crystal clear pool of water. He felt thirsty. Gently he bent down on his knees and drank from the pool. The water was delicious. It was more refreshing than any he had ever drunk. He looked up at the source of the waterfalls and saw where it originated from a large granite stone recessed into the hillside.

He walked around the area and found some steps on the right side of the waterfall carved in stone, and covered with green lichen. The steps had not been used in a very long time. He decided to follow the steps and see where they led. He walked up about thirty steps where it began to circle behind the waterfall. There was a large cave behind the waterfall. He walked on inside the cave. It was very dry inside the cave, and he found tinder and some flint. He built a fire.

The fire threw out a perfect light for inspection of the cave. He found primitive drawings of hunting scenes and battles on the walls. On one side he found ancient stoneware jugs up on a rock ledge. To the other side, in a corner, he found an old spear and what was once a bow and arrows. The fletching that held the arrowheads in place had fallen away with time as had the string on the bow. But the stone and wood were in remarkable condition. He found some large earthen pots with seed corn in them, covered with lids placed there many years ago. The corn was in such good shape that it appeared usable even after many years of storage.

Jacob sat down after building up the fire. He studied the cave in more detail. He was fascinated by what he had discovered. It was the dwelling place of the ancients; however, it felt very familiar to him. After thinking about everything for a while he grew tired and leaned backwards and fell asleep. He woke up with a start, frightened. His fire had died down to embers. How long had he been here?

He got up and made his way towards the cave's entrance to find night had fallen. He walked down the steps around the waterfall and retraced his steps back to his camp. He was stumbling and ran into trees in the dark. To his surprise, his horses and dog were back in the camp. The horses lifted their ears with the sound of his return and were pleased to see him, and his dog was joyful too.

Jacob fed the horses grain and cooked pan bread over the fire. He and Blue ate, settled down, and enjoyed the comfort of the fire. Jacob drank some coffee while he considered the day's events.

His thoughts were racing with memories of tales once told by the old men of his people when he was a child. He remembered stories of people that lived in caves. They told about old people that went to the caves to sing their death song. They also told how caves gave protection from the elements and impending danger. Outlaws often used the caves to hide out.

There was a slight breeze in the forest and it tickled the flames of the fire causing them to dance from side-to-side. The flames licked at the night sky, shooting their dying arrows into the heavens. Jacob reached out into the flames and pulled back hands full of smoke towards him. He brought the smoke to bear on his face and to envelope his entire head. He did this several times to achieve a *heightened state of awareness.*

He prayed for *forgiveness and asked for spiritual guidance.* He asked that he might receive *understanding and wisdom.*

Slowly, he felt the presence of a comforting spirit wash over him. He retreated deeper within himself, letting outward concerns fall away. He wanted so very much to better understand the meaning and purpose of his life here on earth.

As he was suspended in meditation seeking spiritual guidance he began to see the outline of a man walking up to him. The image was unclear but it appeared to be someone wearing a brilliant white robe. There was a glow of bright light that surrounded him.

The bright light was blinding causing Jacob to look away and cover his eyes.

He heard a voice speak, *"My son, worry not. You path is true. You will receive the answers you need. You are not a seeker of wealth. You have been given a heart for your fellow man. Trust me! In everything trust me!"*

The man kissed him on the forehead as he knelt and placed his hand on the crown of his head. He just sat with his head bowed for a long time feeling the joy of the moment. When Jacob raised his head to look, the man was no longer there. He was gone!

Slowly Jacob regained his composure and considered the vision he had just had. He began to understand that the disappointments in his life were not really failures. They were just the necessary events that had to occur so he would become the man he was meant to be. He felt the presence of the *Great Spirit* as it convicted him of the need to trust. He would no longer stand alone in this life.

The more he surrendered the more he felt comforted. It felt very similar to that feeling he once knew when he played in the home of his father with his mother watching over him. Warmth flowed over him, through him and around him. It was a feeling he hoped never to lose. It was a feeling of being loved.

Slowly he began to draw closer to the *Truth*. He was called for a special purpose and he had to go forth and find that purpose. Jacob relaxed and felt his mind floating in a sea of calm, free of thought, cloaked in the *Spirit*. He was no longer afraid about what tomorrow would bring.

As time passed, he was awakened by the sound of birds; it was a new morning. He opened his eyes to see his dog sitting beside him and his horses grazing in the clearing. He had slept through the night or maybe he hadn't. It didn't matter which because he was fully rested; more than he had been in years.

He fed Blue from his pack and went down to the stream to bathe. He removed his clothes and walked into the water to find it was moving very fast and almost knocked him from his feet. After bathing himself he just sat in the water allowing it to flow over him. He felt refreshed and ready to go forth.

He realized this place was very different. Nothing was just as it appeared. He found it very hard to separate the dream from reality. He would have to figure this one out as he went on his way.

Jacob followed the stream up to the waterfall and Blue tagged along. He gathered some rich pine tinder, moss, and a stick to make a torch. He also gathered some more wood for a fire. He walked up the steps into the cave while Blue sat down outside at the bottom of the steps.

Once in the cave, he made a fire and assembled his torch for a closer look into the deeper recesses of the cave. He looked at the petroglyphs and studied them in more detail. He decided there was a story here someone wanted to tell, not just doodles on the wall. It appeared there was a giant man chasing the people and animals. The people were running away as were the deer and smaller animals. Then the people found a cave or some protective arch to shield them. The next scene showed the leader or father burying his family. He was saddened as he contemplated the paintings.

Jacob walked around the corner from the main room of the cave. It diverted into two smaller rooms and a larger area off to the right. He went into the larger area first and discovered a stream that flowed into a basin from a fissure in a rock above his head. The water flowed from the basin down between two large boulders. He held his torch directly over the basin and the reflection from the water was golden. He reached into the water and retrieved several large nuggets. Once he inspected them he was certain they were gold. The bottom of the basin was lined with golden nuggets. He placed the nuggets back in the water from which he found them. He did not want to disturb anything if possible.

He also found large urns where foodstuffs had been stored. He found implements of bone, wood, stone and metal used for farming and protection. He found various personal effects neatly placed in this room. He was very careful how he handled the different items. He saw their fire pit and cooking pots and utensils nearby. He felt a draft and looked up to find a downward push of air. They must have found an opening and developed a way to vent the smoke.

Jacob backtracked and walked into the first of the smaller rooms. It looked like a room for sleeping with areas padded with pine straw bedding. The material had decayed long ago.

The second room contained a ledge with a broken ladder for access. Jacob was able to reach the ledge by placing a large stone close enough to look over the top. There were human remains, bones, placed neatly in a row. He found the bodies of one adult and two children. The children were placed on each side of the woman. They were covered with an old bearskin. Time had not disturbed their placement in the slightest detail.

Jacob was very reverent in his observation and exploration of the cave. He was nervous as he walked through the different rooms; he felt as if he was intruding in someone's home. He was touched by the timeliness of everything he saw. It appeared ancient and yet it could have been placed there more recently. Why he was led to this place puzzled him. He felt he was having a dreamlike experience here also.

He walked back into the cave's main room where his fire was still ablaze. He looked up with surprise to find someone sitting beside the fire. There before him sat a man, cross-legged, next to the fire and Blue was lying beside him. It was an Indian wearing buckskin pants and shirt and moccasins. His hair was long and thrown back over his shoulders. He was stirring the fire with a branch and turned his head to face Jacob.

"You make a good fire, friend!"

"You frightened me," Jacob spoke. "I thought I was alone!"

"It isn't often I get company," the man commented. "I had been out scouting the area when you arrived. I apologize because I took your horses for a run yesterday without your permission. I haven't ridden for a long time. They are strong horses. The one you use for a pack horse is your best mount, but he doesn't protest because he is glad to serve. I believe you have met my family."

"No sir I have not met them," he answered.

Jacob could not tell the man's age. It wasn't apparent whether he was young or old. He had a calming effect about him just the same.

"Come out and meet our friend!" he commanded as he turned towards the other rooms.

Jacob was frozen with fear as he watched a beautiful young maiden accompanied by her children walk into the room and stand beside her husband. There was a boy on her right and a girl on her left, each holding her hand as they looked at Jacob.

The man spoke again, "My name is Walks-Alone, and this is my family: my wife, Little-Deer, and my children. My son is Standing-Strong, and my daughter is One-Who-Speaks! My wife adds "Often" to her name," he chuckled when he said that.

"Who might you be and what brings you to our home?"

Jacob was slow to respond. It took a moment to find his voice. "My name is Jacob, sir! I am traveling through from the Cherokee Nation and stopped to rest in the clearing." He understood the man because he spoke in the Cherokee language; yet, he was confused because he hadn't seen anybody in the cave, but the skeletons of the woman and two children.

"Don't be alarmed Jacob, we are only the spirits of those that once called this place home. We are able to reveal ourselves to you because the Creator has allowed you to walk through the walls that separate our worlds. Ours is a world where time has no bearing. This allows you to hear our voices."

Walks-Alone's speech was soft and gentle and his choice of words was deliberate. "You have travelled far and serve your people well. I am here to teach you by example. I brought my family here many years ago to protect them from the evil that exists in the world. I thought that was the best way; to hide them away so nothing could harm them. I was wrong! They needed other people like themselves, to grow and live among; whereas, while I was gone hunting they got sick and died with no one around to care for them."

"You are troubled by the world and think you should hide yourself from the White man's evil. Evil exists in all nations and it is not just the white man's war that creates evil. You have been chosen to represent our people and it means hard choices for you, but you are stronger than you realize. You must go into the world and be a beacon of light for them. *Don't be afraid, for you are not alone. You have never been alone! Go! Find rest and be on your way. You will be fine. Do not worry! All your needs have been provided.*"

Jacob sat for a long time, looking at them, and thinking of what he was told. Little-Deer walked over to him, leaned down and kissed him on the forehead. Walks-Alone retrieved his spear and handed it to Jacob.

"Here, take this as a reminder of our meeting and remember, you do not walk alone. The strength of those who came before you is always with you." Walks-Alone extended his hand and forearm to Jacob as a sign of fellowship. Slowly the man and his family began to fade away as they walked further back into the cave.

Jacob watched the fire slowly burn down to embers before he left the cave. He looked around in the dry earth where he stood and saw only his foot prints, and those of Blue.

He walked down the lichen covered steps, followed by his dog, into the fading daylight to retrace his steps back to camp.

His horses stood there waiting for him. He gave the horses some grain and found something for Blue to eat. He made a fire, boiled water for coffee and ate something himself. He was so tired that he fell asleep without removing his boots.

CHAPTER 20

THE MOCKINGBIRDS WERE SINGING A melodious tune high up in the live oaks silhouetted by blue sky, and the wondrous fragrance of magnolia blooms and sweet olive lofted through the air. It was a beautiful day to go about one's business or walk the streets and enjoy the sights and sounds of *New Orleans*. The azaleas were in full bloom before the homes on *St. Charles Avenue*. The flowers were pink, white, red and lavender in color. Lovers strolled along the sidewalk beneath the canopy of live oaks oblivious to the business transacted behind the walls of the mansions of the rich and powerful.

Frances asked her servant to bring the buggy around front so she could go downtown and have lunch with a friend. She actually intended to meet with a gentleman that was more than a friend. He was her means of support, *her master*! She was *his mistress*.

She was originally purchased by a free person of color, *gens de couleur libres*, from Mr. Walker. He later sold her, due to a strong recommendation by his wife, because Frances was even whiter, and obviously more beautiful, than she. Subsequently, she was sold to another plantation holder, and then another, until she was purchased by a French Creole, and became his mistress.

French Creoles were not persons of color, but, they used the term to differentiate themselves from more recent arrivals of *French Nationals*. They were considered colonial French, not just upstarts, in this new country; and they wanted the distinction to be duly noted.

She only knew him as Etienne. He did not want her to know his complete name for fear of being found out by his wife and friends. This could be an embarrassment that would cost him the loss of wealth, power and prestige. It wasn't uncommon to keep mistresses, but it was not appreciated in some circles. His wife was from a prominent family of Louisiana politics. For these reasons Frances had never been on the plantation proper. She was whisked away to her new home, a cottage uptown, as soon as she was purchased. Etienne was very proud of his coup.

For reasons of secrecy they never met in places where he might be recognized. She had her own residence uptown on a side street, several blocks south of Prytania Street, close to the Jefferson Plantation and within walking distance to the Mississippi River levee. He provided her with a home and everything she needed. They often met in her house, or a café, chosen by him to prevent detection.

Lincoln had declared slaves free in the rebellious states with his *Emancipation Proclamation*; however, this did not cover the occupied areas, like New Orleans, which capitulated early in the war. Slavery was abolished with the defeat of the Confederacy. Free persons of color that owned plantations suffered losses as did the white plantation owners due to the war. Union troops made no distinction between white or colored plantations when they burned and pillaged. Livestock, cotton crops and other food sources were fair game for the soldiers. Without slaves to work their lands, black plantation owners had to work their own fields as did their white counterparts, just to raise the food they needed to survive. The war left the free persons of color without distinction among the freed slaves, and they were often resented and despised by their former slaves.

Frances was a slave no longer, and being a mistress was now her choice to make. She knew she had been a kept woman and was not sure what this new status would mean to her. She wasn't certain about many things these days. She had much to consider as she made her way down Magazine Street. The rhythmic sound of her horse's hooves on the street was soothing as she moved along in a daze, thinking what this new life would mean for her. Would she establish an independent life for herself in New Orleans or go in pursuit of her daughter, Evangeline? There were so many questions that needed answers and many she hadn't even considered. She was only one of millions that would have to navigate this new life of freedom. Her situation was much more fortunate than others.

Frances was an attractive woman about thirty-six years of age. She looked even younger because of the color and texture of her skin.

The nightmare of being separated from her child was traumatic, just as it was when she and her brother were separated as children from their mother in New Orleans, which seemed like ages ago.

She was fortunate because being the mistress of a sugar plantation owner had advantages over being just a slave. Good fortune wasn't something a slave ever considered, but she knew she would have to make her own good fortune and quickly. Her situation was advantageous over that of others and she knew she held some sway over Etienne. She mustn't stumble but be surefooted in her decisions and actions too.

Over the years Frances asked questions about the whereabouts of her mother and inquired as much as she felt safe with outside contacts throughout the city. She knew slaves were watched with suspicion always and her freedoms were not without limitations.

She was allowed the liberty to conduct herself as a free person of color, but she had a housekeeper and a yardman that lived on the premises. They were also owned by Etienne, and reported back to him. They always reminded her that she was a slave too and not to get uppity or they would bring her down with just the right words to him.

She was not allowed the privilege of socializing and having friends of her own away from the house. She knew exactly when she could pass a word or question at the market or on the street in idle conversation and with whom. She hoped to gather information about her mother whom she felt would have stayed in New Orleans after Jean Lafitte sold her into slavery.

Lafitte was beside himself with anger when he was told by the voodoo priestess about the curse Frances' mother Marguerite had placed on him. He promptly had her placed on the auction block, at the St. Louis Hotel (also referred to as the *City Exchange Hotel*) along with her son. Neither he nor Marguerite knew she was pregnant with their daughter, Frances, when the curse was placed on him and his offspring.

Frances had hopes of reuniting with her mother, and her brother and daughter too. She knew exactly where Evangeline and John were and now she intended to send a letter to Virginia with hopes it would be delivered to them without prejudice. She carried the letter in her embroidered handbag given her by Etienne on her birthday. It was her desire to post the letter on her way back from their meeting. She felt their discussion would have major consequences for her future; and, she was correct.

Frances made her way down Decatur Street, watching other carriages going past and wondering what business they were conducting today. She also observed the many riverboats as they loaded cargo and people. She imagined what grand destination they would be headed. She stopped her carriage to allow a group of young folks to cross the street. They were walking to the newly opened coffee shop at the foot of The French Market.

It was obviously apparent that life was returning to normal since the war was over and people intended to get outside and enjoy the beautiful weather and make new friendships. She wondered how long it would take for her people, the colored race, to gain status and enjoy life like the white people that once traded them like cattle. Would she ever see that sort of life for the black people?

There were many questions: *First*, did she continue as Etienne's mistress, so she could have the stability of someone providing for her and a house to live in; or, *secondly*, did she move out and establish herself as an independent person that was responsible for her own upkeep; and, *thirdly*, did she feel for Etienne and did he have real feelings for her, or was this just what it appeared, an affair! If she did stand up for herself, what would she do and where would she go. She was very afraid of the questions and more afraid of the answers.

Turning north, Frances took Dumaine Street to a café suggested by Etienne. *The Magnolia Inn and Café* was a new café opened in a cottage where people were served downstairs and the café owner lived upstairs, with some additional rooms available in a detached cottage out back next to the old carriage house. The café opened up into a courtyard filled with beautiful flowers, banana and other citrus trees and a large, three-tiered Italianate fountain in the center. The fountain sat on large river stones that were laid throughout the courtyard. Blooming hibiscus plants lined the fountain and were attracting many different varieties of hummingbirds to dine on the nectar of the large red flowers. This place was obviously chosen by Etienne because just like all the other places they had dined it was off the beaten path and was less likely to be frequented by anyone that could recognize him.

There was an area to the side of the cottage for carriages. Frances positioned her carriage beneath a tree so her horse could drink from the water trough. She walked towards the front door and stopped to listen to the mockingbirds singing in the magnolia tree just to the right of the porch. It felt like a day made in heaven. The air was warm with just the slightest breeze and the humidity was very low because of the storm that passed through the day before. She stepped up on the porch and stopped again; something familiar triggered her memory. *Had she been here before?* It was an odd feeling; nonetheless, she shook her head as if to clear her mind of something that kept her from moving forward.

When Frances opened the door a slight bell rang to alert the host that a guest had arrived. She was greeted by a slender, older lady with long beautiful hair, wearing a long, attractive, floral print dress. Her face radiated happiness, but the lines also reflected hard times.

"Welcome to my home! Are you alone or are you expecting someone?" the charming lady asked, as she offered a skilled hand to guide her guest to a table.

Frances was startled. She was caught off guard at the appearance and civility of the woman that greeted her so quickly, or so she thought. She paused for a moment before she answered the woman. "I am expecting someone, a gentleman, and he should have arrived by now."

"Just make yourself at home, sweetheart! I'll bring you some cool, refreshing lemonade while you wait for your friend to arrive," the lady suggested as she moved toward the kitchen. She seated her in the courtyard just beyond the door where a breeze created the perfect atmosphere.

As Frances sat there she felt confused, like she was in a fog. What was this place and who was that woman? Something was strangely familiar here. She felt a strong tingle go up her arm and it made her jump when the woman touched her hand. Etienne walked in while she was consumed with her thoughts. He walked over to her table and seated himself beneath the overhang of a banana tree.

The hostess came over to the table with a pitcher of lemonade and two glasses before he had a chance to speak to Frances. "Welcome to our home! We are serving fried catfish today with several fresh vegetables as our main course, or would you care for other suggestions?" she asked them.

"That sounds fine with us, thank you!" Etienne replied with a smile.

"You look very nice today, Frances!" Etienne offered. "I am so glad to see you. We have a lot to discuss."

Frances was more reserved than usual. She was still affected by something about the woman that she could not explain. She ate the dinner of fish, which was delicious, while Etienne talked.

"Frances, you know you are free now, and can go anywhere and do anything you desire, within the limits of your financial means," Etienne explained.

"Yes, just like all the freed slaves! We can go anywhere and do anything, but, we have nowhere to go and nothing to go there with. Isn't that the hell of it all?" Frances stated with obvious frustration.

"That is why I wanted to meet today. I want to be completely candid as we have always been with each other. I have never treated you like a slave. That is because I respected you, and fell in love with you from the very first moment I laid eyes on you. I felt compassion for you and your plight upon learning the events of your life. You and I both know I can't marry you because I have an obligation to Amanda Sue and the children.

I have a deed, legal and recorded in the courthouse that gives the cottage to you, without any obligations to anyone. It is proper. It shows the purchase for a reasonable amount, which I do not expect from you.

It also includes the carriage house that sits on the property with the accommodations for Marcus and Lucille. I want them to have the option of staying in town or moving back to the plantation. They have been faithful and kind servants and I will offer them the same agreement offered my other servants on the plantation. They will get a plot of land there if they wish. You can also have the horse and buggy for your use; that is included in the deed. The plot of land the house sits on is small, but as you know, it will produce ample vegetables to supplement what you can get at the French Market."

Etienne reached into his jacket and pulled an envelope from the opposite side this time and handed it to Frances. She took the envelope from his hand and glanced at it before turning her eyes to look directly at him.

Etienne stated, with tears in his eyes, "I also want you to take this envelope. It contains some money I want you to have as you find your way. I hope you will come to me if there is anything I can do to help you in your search for your family. Frances, I have loved you during these years and hope you will come to understand that as you begin your new life. I would like to think you loved me too. It is my hope that your choices will provide you with the love and joy that you deserve."

Frances pondered that thought. Did she love him or not? She did not have an answer for him or herself. Fortunately for her, he did not give her time to answer before he continued. He was nervous and apparently in somewhat of a hurry.

"Please don't allow anyone to take advantage of you. I know you will stand up for yourself. You deserve great things from life. Don't forget that! With freedom comes responsibilities and I know you will measure up. My heart and prayers will always be with you. I hope you will not mind if I visit from time to time, as friends." Etienne turned away as tears flowed freely down his cheeks. He scooted his chair backwards, came around the table, and kissed her on the cheek as he walked from the courtyard through the cottage on his way out.

Frances was expecting to make hard decisions today, but apparently the decisions had been made for her. She had a lot of things to ponder and a great deal to contemplate about her future. She did have feelings for Etienne, but she wasn't sure just what those feelings really were. This new world was exciting and scary all at the same time.

The hostess walked up behind Frances and placed her hand on her shoulder. "Did you enjoy your dinner my fair one?"

"Yes, it was quite delicious! You are very pleasant and I like your café. I shall return as often as I can afford."

As she was walking out the hostess said, "Nothing could please me more, *Frances*."

With a quick spin, Frances turned to face the hostess, "And your name is?"

"*Why my name is Marguerite! I am your mother, of course!*"

CHAPTER 21

THE ABSOLUTE BEAUTY AND GRANDEUR OF the Marchant House on St. Charles Avenue stopped Albert Goldsmith in his tracks at the wrought iron gate beneath the live oak canopy. He stood in the opened gate admiring the details of the house's wraparound porch on the lower level and the balcony on the second floor. After a pause of admiration he walked across the stone walkway, up the steps and onto the porch where he lifted the iron knocker on the front door, and swung.

The butler, a black gentleman, opened the door wearing a black suit and neatly pressed white shirt, complete with bowtie. He courteously invited Albert to the library where Mr. Marchant was expecting him.

"Come in sir, Mr. Marchant is waiting in his study," he said as he walked ahead to guide the guest to the area where a gentleman sat reading a book selected from his vast collection.

The gentleman rose from his chair and placed the book he was reading on a stand beside his chair.

"Welcome to my home Mr. Goldsmith! I hope your travels have not caused you any undue sacrifices," he spoke as he allowed his right hand to sweep downward to indicate the chair for his guest.

"To the contrary, Mr. Marchant, I have found the hospitality and the accommodations exceed what I anticipated with the South in a state of occupation. Your city is well equipped to serve its visitors. I have been told by my associates of your prowess in business and feel as though I know you, or at least something about you, prior to this meeting. Frankly, I feel a kinship with you because I am a results-oriented person myself. It is with great enthusiasm that I have come to present this opportunity to you."

"Thank you for the compliments Mr. Goldsmith, but drop the

flowery speech and get to the meat of your visit. I know you have something very interesting to divulge here. Josiah, bring us a glass of Kentucky bourbon, please!"

"Mr. Marchant, you have a strategic position for the expansion of our business here in the South. Your interests in shipping, along with control and ownership of various enterprises in and around Louisiana, make you vital to our success. My associates have acquired the means to successfully produce currency that is a perfect match for the real thing. Without going into details about the means, let me state that we have acquired working plates and access to the correct paper used to produce our bills. We are not common hooligans, but respected businessmen with a viable product. We do not mean to bring down the government, but we wish to take advantage of a momentary gap of leadership that can afford us great rewards for our industry and forward vision. Do you understand what I mean, sir?"

"It appears, Mr. Goldsmith, you and your brand of Northern skunks wish to profit on the misfortunes of others on both sides of the Mason and Dixon line. Carpetbaggers have rushed down here to profit on the misfortunes of the plantation owners and their flawed labor system which led to the freeing of millions of slaves into an already fragile economy, at best. Your kind has bought up cheap land that has been abandoned or otherwise lost due to financial failures and you wish to further exploit the South. Am I correct in my assumptions, sir?"

"Well, yes, that would be one interpretation, I guess," the man stated as he looked his host directly in the eye with an honest reply. "I may be an opportunist, but not a scoundrel. Like you, I seek to make a profit. Are you interested in our venture or are you morally opposed?"

"Absolutely, I am interested, and have no opposition on any grounds whatsoever! I just wanted to get it straight what kind of man I am dealing with here. I do not like dishonest men."

"So, you want to use the riverboats that offer gambling, the shipping where foreign interests are involved and the local businesses where large amounts of currency change hands. How do you plan to insulate us from exposure?"

"Being found out could cost me a fortune and the loss of assets as well as social failure and possible imprisonment. I am not prepared to jeopardize my family for a quick gain," Marchant said with a stern and grim look at his guest. "I have word that a large amount of cash was already misplaced by one of your brilliant associates while on one of our riverboats. What do you say to that?"

"I cannot deny it! One of our operatives was careless, but it is a cost of doing business and we have assurance that it will not happen again. We employ experts in all fields, and sometimes in the process of applying one's trade, mistakes happen. Certainly, you have mishaps in your business. We will work within the framework you provide us and contact you only with the agreed upon profits from your participation. This will minimize your exposure and maximize your gains! Do we have a foundation for further talks, or should we end this discussion and part ways, Mr. Marchant?"

"We definitely have a basis for future talks! I will contact you at your hotel and indicate how and where we will meet for our next visit. Thank you, Mr. Goldsmith, have a pleasant visit in our lovely city. Good day!"

Albert placed the crystal glass filled with fine Kentucky bourbon down on the table next to him. It was with disappointment that he delivered his proposition so quickly, hardly having time to sample the delicious elixir. He made note that things do not move in the South as quickly as they did in the North, nor should they.

As Albert Goldsmith left the home of Horace Marchant and traveled back to his hotel, he felt a queer feeling of being followed or watched. He had not noticed any strange individuals but he just felt a change in the air. He wondered if Marchant was having him tailed or someone else was suspicious of him. He wasn't sure about this feeling but it was present. At no other point had he felt watchful eyes upon him. Was he correct in his assumption, or was it just paranoia affecting him?

He knew he had to say just the right things to Marchant to get his cooperation. Not too much or too little, that was how he had to conduct himself with this powerful man. Marchant was not his friend, just a business associate. He must not forget this. He knew a mistake in his current endeavor could be deadly.

Albert was a successful young business man in Philadelphia with powerful friends. He knew he was chosen as the most capable of his friends to travel south and establish this network of profiteers, along with the operatives they needed to successfully carryout the defrauding of the U.S. Government. He had to meet with and choose the people that could be trusted as capable individuals to orchestrate this operation from the top to the bottom. He was the linchpin that tied the network together. Everyone knew that, but no one more than Albert. If things got scrambled he understood they would eliminate him first to protect themselves. The greater risk was his! He wondered why he accepted this responsibility. It wasn't to prove to his wife how brave he was, or was that it precisely? Or did he need to prove to his friends he was capable?

Something registered in his mind just at that moment. How did Marchant know about the lost satchel of currency that Simon Bartlett had misplaced on the river boat? Something did not add up here. This would require a great deal of thought and inquiry.

It was an exceptionally cooler evening with lower than normal humidity that encouraged Albert to get out and walk along the streets of the French Quarter. He enjoyed a fine dinner at *The Camellia Café* and walked down Chartres Street to Royal Street where a gunsmith occupied a little shop. He was surprised to find a light on and a man working in the night with his door open. He poked his head inside *Martins' Weapon and Repairs* to which the man turned and spoke.

"Can I assist you with something, mister?" the gunsmith asked.

"No, I was just going for a stroll when I saw your light on and thought it odd to find you working so late, and your door still open for business," he replied.

"I needed to finish up some repairs and it was too nice a night to close the door. Are you interested in a firearm, Mister …?"

"Just call me Albert. I may be interested in a smaller firearm at that. One can never be too cautious these days with so many dangerous people drifting through."

"I agree with you there, Albert. Let me show you this thirty-two caliber pistol I just acquired. It is the perfect weapon for a gentleman such as you."

They spoke about ordinary things after Mr. Martin sold him the pistol with a shoulder holster and some bullets. The pistol was simple enough to operate and maintain for someone like Albert who had never held a gun before, much less owned one. His wife, Martha would be both angry and amused that he bought a gun. She might even think him manlier, thought Albert at the time of purchase; nevertheless, he felt it a wise and proper thing to do. He felt he might have made a friend with Mr. Martin and spoke of dropping by sometime, which was mutually agreeable.

Albert went down to the river and observed many people walking up and down the levee where the riverboats docked. He saw people out for a casual stroll, like himself. There were dockworkers, and fishermen throwing their lines in the fast moving river. He also saw a rowdy sort sitting by a fire made from flotsam and drinking from a shared bottle. He saw slaves wandering around not knowing where they should go next, and the downcast and defeated Confederate soldiers doing much the same.

He was glad he had the newly acquired pistol. Albert patted the gun beneath his jacket for reassurance. He prayed he would never have to use it.

Albert was not a strong man with overly masculine features, but he felt capable if needs be to protect himself. This was something totally new for him. The underworld presented a dangerous element. He had misled his wife to believe that this was just a business trip to establish clients for his export business back in Philadelphia. She was still afraid for him to travel so deep within the heart of the South. The war's end hadn't been completely recognized across the land. He was deemed the most capable by his peers to establish the network. He was probably the most adventuresome of his classmates at Harvard. His father, a shopkeeper and tailor by trade, believed Harvard was the edge he needed to be prosperous in life.

The riverboat *Natchez* was in port. He decided to make the rounds of the gaming tables. Locals knew the real Natchez had been burned in the Honey Island swamp by Confederates in 1863 to keep her out of the hands of the Union Navy; however, there had been others named Natchez prior to it and the captain wanted to name his sternwheeler after something well known and thus chose the name to garner attention. Gambling was banned on the riverboats per the rule of General Butler; but, those in the know were fully aware of where to find a back room filled with men playing cards with money to lose.

Albert boarded the boat's loading ramp under the watchful eyes of three men with a rough looking nature. They had a low growl, like mongrel dogs, as he passed them. He stared back to ascertain their intentions. His hand slid up, inside his jacket, to grip the newly acquired pistol. It was an automatic response like he had always owned the gun. He was surprised at how much safer he felt just knowing the gun was beneath his jacket. As he walked he noticed an abundance of activity that was unnoticed from the level view of the dock. There were beautiful young women sprinkled throughout, moving from group to group. They provided more whiskey, wine or beer when requested. It appeared that they kept the atmosphere livened up with their presence and their smiles. There were other women there, but men outnumbered the women.

He moved in and out of the groups as their loud speech and laughter had reached a crescendo. He walked up some stairs in the center of the boat to reach the upper deck where the air was better, away from the cigar smoke, and the din of noise. The stars were so close one could almost reach out and touch them. The moon was bright, casting its glow across the river like a beam of light to guide the path of anyone wishing to walk on the water. Lost in his thoughts about his Martha and their comfortable apartment, Albert was unaware of the young lady that had moved up next to him along the railing. She was dressed in northern fashion and very attractive. Her long hair was pulled up in a circular weave, topped with a small hat popular for the times.

"Mind if I join you in your appreciation of the celestial bodies?" she asked very politely, with a soft mannered voice.

"No! Certainly not! I mean yes! What I mean is, I don't mind, please join me. I was surprised because I didn't see or hear you approach. My name is Albert."

"My name is Cecilia. It is a beautiful night and I had to escape from that crowd so I could breathe again."

"I know exactly how you feel. I get nervous when there are so many people crowding around me. I feel like someone could yell fire and I would get trampled. Is there some kind of party downstairs?"

"Yes, my husband, John Carver, is celebrating the new agreement he signed today with a local shipping magnate. We are from New York and it will be a huge boost in national and international commerce for us and others. He is very excited and wanted to throw a party with the local dignitaries to show his appreciation and goodwill to the city. Do I detect an accent, Albert?"

"Yes, I am from Philadelphia and have come here to establish some connections for future ventures. My partners are investors that want to get a foothold in the import/export business as well. We are not as well established, as say your husband, but we feel we have to start somewhere and why not here!" Albert was nervous underneath his cool exterior, hoping his true reason for being here was never revealed.

"Yes, you are correct Albert," Cecilia commented, "it's funny I thought I heard a Boston accent in your voice. I must have been mistaken."

"No, you haven't. I went to school at Harvard and it must have rubbed off on me to some degree. My wife, Martha, is from Boston; we met while I was in school. I am starting to sound more like her every day."

"That is so odd! I am from Boston. I grew up there and met John there when he was on a business trip. I went to a local preparatory school with a girl my age named Martha McCallum; a very sweet girl she was, as best I can recall."

Albert's heart skipped a beat, "It might be the same sweet girl that I married. She has red hair and cute freckles on her cheeks and nose."

"That would be her if she has a handsome older brother by the name of Robert."

"That would be her; however, Bob died at Chickamauga during the war. It was a terrible loss for the family," Albert said with a dejected look.

"I wasn't allowed to serve because I have a game leg from childhood and couldn't march. I did what I could to support the Union effort back home raising money and helping the surviving widows whenever possible."

"I am sure you did, but I am terribly sorry to hear that about Robert. He was such a fine man and quite the handsome one, as well. All the girls thought him the best catch around. He was very smart and ambitious, too," Cecilia commented as she looked across the starlit night.

"He was several years older than myself and could have been anything his heart desired. This war destroyed a whole generation of fine men, but it had to be fought to get us back on track as a nation. Don't you agree?" he looked to her for confirmation.

"Yes, I do agree, but the loss of so many men and the destruction of so many lives and property all seems like it could have been avoided with more levelheaded men in our nation's leadership. It is terribly sad. I just wonder how the southern families will recover. And that does not address the slaves that were just turned out on the roads. How will they survive?" There was genuine and sincere remorse in her voice.

"What a small world it is! How is Martha?"

"She is well. We have two little girls, Sally and Rebecca. They are the joy of our lives. I miss them now and was thinking about them as I looked up at the stars. I usually tuck them in at night after they say their prayers. This is the first time to be away from them. Martha is a fine mother and loving wife. I am the most fortunate man I know. How about you? Do you have any children?" Albert asked.

"Yes, I have a son, five years old, his name is Jonathan. He stayed back home with his grandparents. John felt it was the best idea to leave him home. I agreed with him that things are not yet settled since the war has just ended. He is my joy, as well. Let Martha know Cecilia Harrison asks about her when you correspond. I better go now, John may have gotten worried. I hope to see you again and introduce you to John. We are staying at the Dauphine Hotel on Royal Street. Drop by and meet us for dinner some time. Good night, Albert."

"Goodnight and I will stop in soon." He watched the attractive lady turn and walk away and wondered if he would ever see her again.

It was strange, he thought, how you could be so far from home and still find people you know. No matter where you go, someone would be there to remind you just who you are. It reminded him of a saying his father had, "Whatever is done in the darkness will be found out in the light," or something like that.

Albert left the boat and was on his way back to his hotel room when he looked up from the deep thoughts that consumed him to see two men blocking his path. Quickly he reached for his pistol, but it was too late, for the man that stood behind him was quicker with the billy-club across his head; then, his world went black.

He woke up that same night in an alley on his back with an empty wallet lying open on his chest. Dizzy and disoriented, he slowly sat up. He had quite a lump on the back of his head and it was throbbing too. After regaining consciousness he began to recall that the two men had distracted him while one man jumped him from behind. To his surprise they did not take his pistol. They must have gotten the wallet first and thought that was all he had.

He got up and staggered to the brick wall and placed his right hand against it to maintain his balance. He must get back to his room and recuperate. He found his way back to the hotel and walked through the lobby. The night clerk looked at him as if he was drunk.

"Are you alright Mr. Goldsmith?" the young man asked.

"No, I was attacked and robbed! Could you help me to my room?
I must rest."

"Should I get the police?"

"No, I will contact them later after I've had some rest. Thank you
though. Just give me a hand up to my room please."

Albert poured some water into the basin and washed his face and
touched the back of his head with a wet cloth. It was as big as a goose
egg. He took off his jacket and pistol holster and sat on the bed. He
removed his shoes without untying them and leaned back onto the
bed and slept.

CHAPTER 22

MATT AND HIS FRIENDS ARRIVED AT THE
sheriff's office at the agreed upon time. After satisfying the questions
and demands of the sheriff with their testimony and the corroboration
of Colonial Watts, they were allowed to go, but, with a suggestion from
the sheriff that they leave Charleston as soon as possible. Matthew
assured him that was their intentions, exactly.

Matthew, John and Thomas rode back to the Walker home and
began preparations to restart their mission, more becoming a journey
with every new development. The goodbyes were difficult, because they
had made some true friends here. Mama Sue, as they affectionately
came to know her, made them a package of food that would feed them
for days. Oliver Walker and Juan stood in line to say their goodbyes
and longingly shook the hands of each one as they passed.

The boys could not leave without saying goodbye to Elizabeth, but
she wasn't around. "Now, where is Elizabeth?" John robustly shouted.
"She and Evangeline must be up to something!"

The sound of pounding hooves got everyone's attention. They
turned as one to see Elizabeth coming from the barn behind the warehouse on a beautiful black stallion with three white stockings, followed
by Evangeline on her horse. She was dressed in jeans like a man would
wear and had a soft case with her clothing and necessities tied behind
her bedroll that rested on top of her saddlebags, all behind her saddle.
She also wore the shiny new riding boots her father had given her for
Christmas.

"Now, where do you think you are going, *young lady*?" Mr. Walker
demanded, as he stepped forward and placed his hand on the horse's
neck.

"Before you jump out of your skin Papa, let me speak! You always promised to take me with you on a business trip to New Orleans, but you never did. Well, now I have decided the time has come, and I have excellent traveling companions. You said they needed to form a new identity as they pursued their mission. I can help them look less official," Elizabeth smiled as she stated her case.

"She is your daughter, Sue!" Mr. Walker admitted, as he stepped away and bowed to his wife in deference to her.

"Are you crazy, child? I hope you have considered the dangers out there. Is that the way I raised you?" Mrs. Walker protested.

Elizabeth knew her mother's protest was a weak one, but was made to satisfy her husband's expectations.

"Yes Mom, this is exactly how you raised me! You taught us to live each day to the fullest and always follow our hearts. Would you have stopped Carson from leaving home and denied him his *destiny?* I don't think so. I will be safe. My life is in *God's hands* and these fine men around me, plus Evangeline needs a female companion to protect her!" Elizabeth said as she stretched to her full height upon her horse.

"That settles it! My life has been reduced to spending it with this old codger I married a hundred years ago. I will become an old lady overnight. I am sure of it!" She pretended to wail and fell on Oliver's chest in mock disgust.

"I will never hear the end of it!" Oliver replied in protest.

"What about us?" Thomas shouted. "Don't we get a say?"

"You just hold your horse there, big boy!" Evangeline spoke up. "I've had to tolerate your disgusting ways for too long and I could use a woman on this journey. So close that trap of yours!"

They all laughed and it was mutually agreed upon; they would have a new traveling companion and their chemistry would evolve as they continued on their journey to New Orleans.

"What else need I say?" Matthew offered. "We must be on our way. Your daughter will be safe with us and we will post a letter along the way to reassure you."

Their departure was blocked by the carriage of Parson Jones coming down the lane. He decided to come from town to see the folks off.

"I see the hooligans are sneaking out of town early and taking the fair maiden as hostage, yes?" the Parson jested.

"And, would it be your nature to accompany this band of misfits?" Matthew interjected.

"No, my son, I have a larger flock that needs my attention, but don't fool yourself and think my age would render me unworthy. For I was the rounder in my day, before I saw the error of my ways, that is! I have come to offer my prayers and well wishes for your safety. Fare thee well, and bring them back unharmed, I pray. Good traveling my dear friends. You have left your mark on our fair city and it was a good one indeed!"

With the pack mule loaded, and the farewells all said, they moved on down the lane and out to the road. The future was uncertain and each person had different expectations. Elizabeth turned and waved to her parents as she moved along the fence line. She hoped her decision was not a foolish one. She was certain that her life would be changed forever. She could no more have forsaken this opportunity, than the rooster could stop his crowing before dawn's break.

The troupe traveled by day and camped by night, finding good water and graze for their livestock, before they retired each night. Matthew had informed them the route they would tentatively take would pass near or through towns like Savannah, Macon, Columbus, Montgomery, Meridian, Jackson and Vicksburg. From Vicksburg they would take a riverboat on to New Orleans.

They crossed the Savannah River north of the City of Savannah and from there made their way on to Macon, Georgia. They intersected with the Federal Road, a road established on land once owned by the Cherokee and Creek Nations.

The government signed an agreement to use the old trails that once were used as trade routes by the Native Americans. Later on, the same roads would facilitate the defeat of the Creek Indians by Andrew Jackson, with the aid of the Cherokee. Subsequently, President Andrew Jackson signed the Indian Removal Act to relocate all Eastern Indians to lands west of the Mississippi River.

Elizabeth Walker adjusted quickly to the demands of the road.

She had excellent riding skills and proved to have better than average wood lore. She would often point out things that were good to eat that were available just off the beaten path. She also possessed a working knowledge of herbal medicines easily gotten from the forest.

The friendship between the two girls grew stronger as they traveled together. It often riled Thomas when they laughed at him; even though, he knew down deep they really liked him.

They passed through Columbus, Georgia and saw what was typical of the destruction of the Union Army near war's end. General Wilson's troops passed through the town and destroyed the industrial sites before moving on, but not without a battle.

Upon leaving Columbus, they crossed over the Chattahoochee River into Alabama. About the noon hour, they stopped in a small community at a general store to allow themselves and the livestock a rest and a drink of water. It wasn't much of a place but probably the nearest thing for miles for people who wanted to acquire the basic necessities. It was a combination store, with post office, grist mill and blacksmith shop.

Matthew, Evangeline and Elizabeth walked onto the porch looking the community over while John and Thomas brought the horses and mule to a watering trough. The voice of a young woman could be heard pleading with the proprietor about the sale of her property. Matthew walked inside followed by the women.

"Listen to me, Annie! I know how you feel with your man in jail, but all I can offer you is fifty cents on the acre," the man standing behind the counter informed her.

"But, Mr. Leach, my man Sammie did not steal that mule. He was given to us by Massa Coates when he deeded us that place. It says so in the deed. I have it here, and if I don't get him out of jail, they will surely hang him before the circuit judge comes around. They said forty dollars will get him free and all you offer is half that!" the young woman named Annie was frantic.

Matthew stepped forward with his quick wit, assessed the situation and went into full diplomatic mode. "Young lady, did I hear you correctly that you own property along this road that is part of the old Coates holdings?"

"Yes sir, I surely do!"

"Well, today is your lucky day! I am traveling with an austere group of men on our way to Montgomery from Columbus with a mission to establish a railroad connection between the two cities. I see no reason why I shouldn't make you an offer. Would you accept an offer of five-dollars per acre?" Matthew asked.

"Mister, you are truly a blessing sent down straight from Heaven! Yes, indeed I will!"

"Now wait here just a minute, mister. The lady and I were having a conversation before you butted in. Annie, maybe I can find some money and match his offer. What do you say?" the store owner asked with obvious anger at the newcomers offer.

Just as the pause occurred, John stepped into the center of the negotiations. "Now, look-a-here Mr. O'Brien, I don't appreciate you taking advantage of my watering the livestock to acquire land without my participation. I will offer this young lady seven dollars and fifty cents an acre for that land. You know that will still bring a nice profit when the land agents come through here!"

"Annie, ten dollars an acre is my last offer!" Mr. Leach shouted as he bolted around the counter.

"Sold!" Evangeline said as she reached out and shook his hand with Annie's hand firmly gripped in hers.

"I don't have but two hundred and fifty dollars with me at the present, but I can offer the rest in trade."

"Well, you throw in that wagon out front, some flour, a bolt of cloth, some salt, bacon, coffee, dry beans and some assorted sundries along with a bait of grain for my mule and I will call it even Mr. Leach," Annie agreed with a heartfelt grin. "That is in addition to the two-hundred and fifty!"

"We have a deal, Annie!" Mr. Leach said. "Just go down to the jail and get your man and you bring him back with your mule. Here is the forty dollars you will need. I'll have the wagon loaded when you return." He was all smiles.

"Now what can I do for you fine folks?"

"We need to buy a few things from you to hold us over until we reach Montgomery," Elizabeth said.

"You are a fierce businessman, Mr. Leach," Matthew offered. "You stand to profit on that parcel of land. I wouldn't let the cat out of the bag about the railroad, because you may want to purchase other tracts of land. I believe the land agents are preparing to sweep through here very soon."

The group of travelers was about to shove off when Annie and her husband, Sammie, pulled their new wagon next to them, loaded down with their tools, personal effects, supplies and two children.

"You kind people wouldn't mind if we tag along with you for a ways. We will be moving away from here," Sammie said with a smile as he felt his burdens lifted.

"Of course not," Matthew replied, "how far are you planning to travel?"

"Maybe over to Mississippi or beyond," Annie replied, "Maybe further, just so we can get out of here before they start laying track for that railroad. Too much progress for our liking!" she smiled at her Sammie.

They all laughed, except Thomas, who had stayed outside while the negotiations were being conducted. He was confused and John promised to explain it to him when they made camp for the night.

What started out as three men travelling south had become a small caravan with the addition of two young women and a family of ex-slaves seeking a new life. Travel was easy because the sun wasn't as hot and the humidity was lower than usual. They made camp alongside the road in a community called Tuskegee. It was the site of an old cotton plantation on land that formerly belonged to the Creek Indian nation. Former slaves still worked the land, but now they were being compensated for their toil.

John rode up to the plantation house to ask permission to stay overnight. The owner said that was perfectly fine with him and wished them fair weather. Camp was set up on a creek bank where perch played in the shallows near a sandbar and lilies grew on the opposite side. Thomas gathered wood and built the fire while the women prepared dinner, with Annie's help. Matthew and John went to catch fish for dinner and bragged they were the best fishermen of the lot. It happened that Lawrence and his little sister Melissa were the better fishermen, doubling the amount caught by the men.

After dinner, in the cool of the night, the men sat around the fire smoking their pipes. They offered Sammie some tobacco for his corn-cob pipe too. They talked about places they had been and people they met during the war. Annie and her family listened as they could only share their experiences in captivity, and they wished to forget them.

Introductions had been completed when Thomas asked Sammie their last name. He said that slaves did not always have a last name and adopted that of the slaveholder; however, he has decided their last name was now Matthews in honor of the man that provided for their rescue and future days.

Matthew was speechless and offered his appreciation for their gesture. "I must admit my deceitfulness is shameful, but I felt it appropriate for the occasion. You must not hold it against me. How and when did you realize my plot was a dishonest one, Annie?"

"Well, Mr. Matthew, I think it was when I saw Elizabeth here smile and poke Evangeline in the side with her elbow. I thought the two was about to break out in laughter when Mr. John stepped into the negotiations. I just prayed Mr. Leach would not figure out he was being taken and decide to change his mind. I ran all the way down to the jail to get Sammie and I was smiling ear-to-ear. I don't think my feet touched the ground hardly at all! You don't know how much the good Lord has blessed us today. I want us to get as far away from these parts as quickly as possible. I won't feel good about things until we cross over into Mississippi, and then I want to go even farther than that," Annie commented with genuine concern.

Sammie interrupted her, "Annie, I don't feel none too good about running away from our troubles. We can't run every time someone confronts us; someday we will have to make a stand!"

"Well, if we hadn't run, we would be diggin' your grave! And I don't rightly have any good diggin' clothes and no diggin' attitude either," Annie explained. "We are much indebted to these here folks for their kindness and quick thinking."

"My dear husband, I don't like running either, but these are not the times we can afford to stand on moral high ground. It will most likely be many generations to come before we can safely stand up to the white man and speak our mind. There are those who are greedy and used us like the oxen or mule to cultivate their crops and he will not forget how he and his profits have been forever altered."

"There are also those that resent us because we are attempting to better ourselves and may get ahead of them in short fashion. No, I do not think we need to stand up on our hind legs and crow like that rooster of ours, Sir Henry. We will do ourselves a world of good to move on and find us a safe place to settle down and raise our family, Mr. Sammie," Annie explained.

Evangeline explained her plight to them and could completely agree with Annie's assessment of the matters at hand and the probability of continued oppression for many generations to come. She felt a particular advantage by being single, having no children and the fairness of her skin. She confessed it would be much easier for her to move about in the social circles, especially in New Orleans, where there was a history of mulattos of Spanish, French, Indian, black and white mixture. Some were calling them Creole in certain circles.

"I wish to help you find your mother, Evangeline," Elizabeth offered.

"And, I may be able to assist you and your family with relocating, Annie. I'm sure these gentlemen will help too."

Thomas looked around him and the camp as she spoke with surprise and dismay. "Did we have visitors while you was speaking? I was not aware of any gentlemen present."

"She was just being kind to include us in her assessment with the likes of Matthew. Try to be diplomatic and accept her kindness, Thomas," John commented, and the lady folk chuckled.

After dinner everyone settled down to rest underneath the twinkling stars and the bright half moon that watched over them. It was a much needed rest for all. It was an exciting adventure for some, a frightening escape for others, and a journey into an unknown tomorrow for everyone.

The next morning the travelers rose from their sleep to attend to their needs and pitched in to help with breakfast. They broke camp and quickly went on their way. The road was in good shape and they met with fellow travelers going to and from every direction.

There were soldiers returning home from war as the word had spread that the South was defeated. They just wanted to return home and put together the pieces of their lives. It was a bedraggled group of men that walked the roads. They were downtrodden and desperate, not much better than the former slaves that they passed along the way. Many asked for a little food as they passed. They shared all they could possibly spare. These were desperate times and would remain so for years to come.

On the third day of their journey into Alabama the weather turned ugly. It rained from the time they started in the morning throughout the day. It went from a slight drizzle to a heavy downpour at times. The road got muddier and the ruts deeper and it became harder for the mule to gain ground in the knee deep mud.

Thomas rode ahead to search out a camp site. He came back about three o'clock in the afternoon with a report. They all gathered around him in their soaked clothing and waited to hear the report he had, hoping for good news.

"It looks like we will not get over the Tallapoosa River today. The water is too high and fast for the ferryman to cross. If it rains out we may be able to cross over tomorrow or the next day depending on the condition of the river. I did find some place we could stay in a large barn and livery stable down the road a piece that is next to a tavern. It isn't much but it beats the rain!" Thomas declared.

"I almost forgot, I shot a wild hog and stashed it the bushes alongside the road. I didn't know she had piglets until after I shot her. Here they are!" Thomas reached into both saddlebags and retrieved a wet and lonely piglet from each. "Does anybody want these?"

Lawrence and Melissa jumped down from the wagon and ran through the mud puddles to Thomas with their hands held high. "We do Mr. Thomas, please!"

"You can have them if your mother and father say it's alright, but you must promise to care for them."

"Yes, that will be fine, but you will need to keep them out of trouble and clean until we get to a place where they can be properly kept. Do you understand?" Annie asked with a stern look.

"Yes, Mama, we will take care of them," Lawrence spoke for both of them.

"And," Sammie interjected, "Dey is for eating when dey get grown. Don't ever forget that!"

"We won't, Daddy!" Melissa agreed with a sad look on her face.

They arrived at the tavern and made arrangements to board their horses and themselves in the stables and barn. Sammie and Thomas worked together to prepare the hog so Annie and the girls could make a feast of it. Everyone was busy doing their part. Matthew went back into the tavern to speak with the tavern owner in hopes of learning the latest news.

John and Lawrence stabled the horses and fed them some grain and hay after they were watered. They were rubbing them down when three former confederate soldiers ambled down from the loft.

"Howdy do, mister!" one of the soldiers offered. "Not surprised to have company on such an ugly day. Where are you heading?"

"West," John offered, not looking directly into their faces.

"Coming home from the war too?" the youngest asked.

"Just like you boys, fought with Robert E. Lee, all the way to Appomattox."

"We were the last troops to stand up to Sherman in Atlanta. He broke our backs and went on through. We've been beat way before he came along though. We are half starved to death. Have you all got any food to spare? We on our way back to Texas and could use any help you got."

"We can fill your stomachs," John turned to face him eye to eye, "but we have some lady folks and a family of ex-slaves traveling with us and if I hear a cross word passed to anyone, colored or white, I will not hesitate to bring harm down on you! Do you understand me?"

"Yes sir!

Do you boys agree?" he asked his companions. They were all in agreement.

"Where can we set up a fire with all this rain?' Annie pondered.

About that time Matt came from the tavern. "There is a man across the road in that shack, in the middle of the pecan orchard; he can help us cook our hog. His name is Enoch and he is known around here as the best cook in miles. Annie, you and Thomas go over and meet him."

They walked across the road in the driving rain, stepped up on the simple porch, but the swirling wind kept soaking them in spite of the roof over the porch. Thomas knocked on the man's door.

"Come in! Get out that rain before you drown," shouted a voice from within.

Thomas and Annie opened the door and stepped in off the porch into the one-room-shack. It was clean and dry and there was a warm fire burning in the large stone fireplace to the right. A large iron cooking kettle was mounted on an iron pivot in such a way to be swung into action over the fire when needed. The cozy warmth of that place was truly inviting after the nasty day that they had endured. What looked like a shack on the outside felt like a king's castle on the inside.

There was a bed to the left and shelves lined with spices and cooking utensils to the right. Pots and pans hung from a hickory pole suspended from the rafters by ropes near the woodstove. In the center of the room sat a large table with benches on both sides that gave the appearance that he entertained guest regularly.

"What can I do for you today?" the black man asked.

"We was just wondering if you can help us cook a hog," Annie asked.

"Yeah, we have a wild hog I shot on the road today," Thomas added.

"It isn't often a black woman and a white man knocks on my door."

"Are you Enoch?" Thomas asked.

"Yes I am, and who might you be?"

"My name is Thomas and this here is Annie. We are travelling through and have a freshly slaughtered wild hog to cook, but no place to cook him. Could you be of help?"

"Yes, I can make a feast of him for you. How many are there with you?"

"We have nine, sir, plus those three starving soldiers across the street, and one more if you will join us!"

"Bring me the whole hog, innards too. We can use everything that critter has."

"We will bring him over directly, sir!"

"Will you need any help preparing it?" Annie inquired.

"No, that isn't necessary. But I could use the company. You see, I don't get out much anymore since my sweet Suzy passed away a short time ago," the man recanted with sadness in his voice.

"I'm sorry to hear about the loss of your wife, Mr. Enoch," Annie offered.

"She wasn't my wife. He was my dog. It was much easier for me when he was around. He led me around and protected me."

"I'm not sure I understand," Thomas replied with a look of confusion.

"I guess it is dark in here." Enoch walked closer to them and the light that came through the door. Annie and Thomas could see that Enoch's eyes were sightless.

"You see, the good Lord blessed me with blindness. I can see with my heart, ears, nose and hands. I also see with my spirit too. Suzy was my eyes in this world."

"I'm sorry we didn't know!" Thomas explained.

"Thomas, you and Annie have a seat at the table. I want to tell you my story. When I was born folks felt sorry for my mother because of her little blind boy. But she saw it as a blessing from God. My father was beat to death by the Massa's overseer because he didn't want my mother to have a child by no black man. She was fair-skin and quite attractive as well; and, he wanted her for himself. My parents got married in a secret wedding out in the orchard during the harvest moon. The slaves did not tell a soul because they was afraid of what would happen if the Massa found out. And it did happen! He had my pappy strung to a tree and whipped until he died, but it was too late; because my mother was already pregnant with me. He pushed her down the steps of the big house with hopes she would lose the baby. My mother was strong and she prayed to the Lord that He would save her baby."

"The Good Lord came to her in a dream before I was born and assured her that He would give her a special child, and so I was born."

"The Massa did not make me work in the fields, but he let me stay with mama while she cooked in the kitchen that was set off from the big house. She was an excellent cook and they made her cook for the White family. They would brag on her when visitors came and they tasted her good cooking, and her pies too. I learned from her many things and cooking was just one of them."

"When I was about eighteen years of age my Massa came to my mama and me and said I was free. He gave me a paper that told everyone I was a free man; but, he said I must leave that place and go out on my own, away from there. My mother screamed and threw a fit. She said that this was a death sentence for me. I sat down with her and explained how she was always telling me not to worry, but to have faith in the Lord. I told her that I would be fine! This was just a test for me to prove I was a man and was not afraid to seek out God's plan. I told her I would come for her one day and she would be free too. I don't think she believed me though."

"I got all my meager belongings, put them in a toe-sack, and sat out on the road to Montgomery. On the first day, a man in a wagon gave me a ride. He said he was a drummer, a traveling salesman, and he moved around the South selling dry goods to people that lived too far from town to get the things they needed. He was a fine man. He told me that I was not handicapped unless I chose to be. When I said goodbye and offered to shake his hand I realized he only had one arm. He explained he lost his right arm in an accident when he was a child."

"That man, Mr. Coffee, I don't think that was his real name but that was what they called him because he also sold coffee; he was the kindest man I have ever known. He told me just to call him Dave. He took me all the way into Montgomery and introduced me to Joseph Tanner. Mr. Tanner had a café in town; and, he said he could use a man with good skills in the kitchen. He got me a room down the street at the boarding house. The woman that owns that place said she would not allow a colored man to stay there, especially a blind one at that. Mr. Tanner told her to give me a room or don't come back to eat at his place again. She was ornery and difficult until I made some of mama's specialty, pecan pie, for her. That brought her around."

"I worked hard and learned my way around Mr. Tanner's kitchen. His business grew and he had to move into a bigger place. He made me a partner in the business in due time. I saved my money and asked him to go purchase my mother from Massa Gambles. Mr. Gambles did not want to sell her, but when Mr. Tanner explained to him about the danger of fires that happen in the night he had a different response."

"Mama came to live with me in a house I bought in town. She worked with me in the café until her health began to fail her. She was so glad I kept my promise to come back for her. Those were the happiest times of her life. She lived with me for twelve years. She came down with the fever and died in her sleep. She told me that last night she was very proud of me and God truly blessed her with this one special child. I buried her in the cemetery of a Black church on the edge of town."

"Things changed after her death. I trained two young men how to prepare food the way folks had come to like it. I put my money in a bank and told Mr. Tanner I wanted to hit the road for a little while. Now here I am," Enoch declared. "Bring me that sow and let me show you how it's done."

Enoch prepared a feast with that hog and had plenty left over to take with them on their journey. He also made sweet potatoes to go with their meal, and smothered them with fresh cow's butter he kept in the spring behind his house. They all ate at his house at the one long table.

John said the blessing before the meal. It was a heartfelt declaration of thanksgiving for their good fortune. Everyone was in agreement with a robust Amen. They talked and laughed as if they were old friends that had just been reunited. Enoch was overjoyed as well. He surprised them with several pecan pies he had made the day before. It was one of the ways he supported himself.

One of the young soldiers commented that he had never really been around colored folks much, but felt sorry for the bad hand they had been dealt. He wished things would be better for everyone in due time. He talked about their plans to return home to Texas. They wanted to round up abandoned cattle from the brakes and start a cattle drive to Kansas. It seemed there was a great deal of wild cattle in Texas and not much else after the war.

"Do you think we could come along and start a new life out there in Texas?" Sammie asked.

"Well, hell yes! I don't know any reason why you couldn't come. Texas is wide open country and they respect anyone that's willing to work hard to make his dreams come true. We are an independent sort of people," said Tommie, one the three soldiers.

"How do you feel about it, Annie?" Sammie asked.

"We go where you go, Father!" she replied.

"That's good," Tommie stated, "because we didn't know how we would ever get there on our own. We've almost starved to death lately. Together we will help each other. Then we can help you get your new start in Texas. Oh! By the way, my name is Tommie Houston and this is my brother Martin, we just call him Marty. Our friend here is Forrest Todd."

"Nice to meet you all!" Thomas replied.

"That leaves me," Enoch shouted. "I could tag along with you folks to New Orleans. I can pay my way and out walk any horse, they used to say. I always wanted to see what they mean when they say *Creole cooking*. What do you good folks say? Do you have room for one more?"

John looked at Matt, "I think the ladies could use a break from cooking and I could also use a break from Thomas' complaining."

"We will need another pack mule to carry your stuff, and a horse for you to ride," Matt inserted.

"You need not worry. I can buy a mule and horse from a local farmer I know. He has been dying to buy my orchard for years. By the way, I can out ride any of you. I know how to talk to horses, and *they listen well*," Enoch smiled a wide grin as he closed his eyes and let his head move from side to side in delight.

"Then we are set. We will move out as soon as this rain permits us to cross the Tallapoosa River. Matt turned to Enoch, "I need to send off a telegram when we get to Montgomery. Can you take us somewhere to get supplies when we get to town?"

"I sure 'nuff can!" Enoch offered.

Matt looked at John and said, "I had no idea when we first met that we would be tour guides for a cavalcade of characters that stretched halfway across this country. I am not certain just what our cover is now, but we look like a troupe of actors on our way to New Orleans for a theatrical production. Eureka! I think that is exactly what we are! What do you think, my fine friend?"

"I think you have gone mad, and so have I. I don't think we are equipped talent-wise or financially to mount any type of theatrical production. What else do you have in mind?"

"You are correct; however, we do have the personalities with our small core of friends, including Enoch, to pass ourselves off as a traveling group of investors seeking opportunities in a postbellum South. We need refining, naturally, and we can start by building our disguise when we get to Jackson. When we meet up with Jacob he will help us shape our plan. We are certainly building a significant group of characters," Matt proclaimed while looking out into the rainy night before them.

CHAPTER 23

THE RAINS STOPPED THE NEXT DAY; HOWEVER, the river was an angry highway looking for foolish travelers. This lull in action provided Enoch the necessary time to sell his cozy cabin in the pecan orchard and one-hundred and twenty acres of prime farm land to an anxious buyer. He also acquired a pack mule, equipped with packsaddle, and an adequate riding horse with saddle. He said his mare told him to call her Trouble, because that had been her past, up until now. That wasn't all he found. He also acquired a new friend, a young pup sired by Suzy.

"Now, wait just a minute!" Thomas declared. "How can Suzy sire a litter of pups? That is impossible!"

Enoch laughingly said, "I didn't say Suzy was a girl dog. It was not brought to my attention until several months after I named him Suzy and the name took, that someone, namely a child, pointed out to me the error of my ways. By then, it was too late to change his name! Do you understand, Thomas?"

"Yes, I do! Now, you have a girl dog. Are you going to name it Bob?"

"She told me her name is Shadow because she was the least of her litter and followed in the shadow of the other pups. I accept that as being the truth. Will that be alright with you, Thomas?"

Thomas just threw up his hands, "What can I say to a blind man that talks with the animals? I am just surprised Suzy never told you he was a boy."

"Suzy was never much for talking, but he had a big heart! There are those that believe actions speak louder than words, so they leave the talking to others," Enoch commented as he flashed his big smile.

"And another thing I would like to express to my fellow travelers before we cross the river is this; the Tallapoosa River runs north of Montgomery. We can travel due south and reach the city without crossing this river; however, we will have to cross the Alabama River directly. It is a much larger river and will have time to retreat back within its banks by the time we cross it. Flooding is vital to the rich farm lands along its banks."

"Thank you very much for your guidance on this matter, Enoch," Matthew politely offered. "It seems we were given conflicting information. One day there will be detailed maps for those that wish to travel this great land. There is always something dangerous when people have a little information. Who knows, or could even imagine, what modes of travel future generations will have. Things are starting to move at an accelerated pace. Anytime someone has valuable information, don't hesitate to share it with the group. Alright, let's look for the next road traveling due south."

"Do you think we could make it to Montgomery by nightfall if we leave now, Enoch?"

"I certainly do, and I will follow you."

"By the way, Enoch, I see you are wearing a pistol. What can you do with that gun but shoot one of us?" John asked.

"Listen! Do you hear that crow up in the pecan tree to your right?" Enoch pulled his pistol, aimed, and shot the crow dead.

Tommie's friend Forrest walked over and picked up the crow. "He blew his head clear off, he did!"

Matt looked around him and asked, "Any more questions for Enoch. If not, then let's travel!"

They travelled for the rest of the day on a road towards the city and reached there about the dinner hour. Enoch directed them to find Fletcher's livery to stable their livestock and from there to old lady Mattie's boardinghouse.

After watering, feeding and rubbing down their horses and pack mules, they staggered over to Mattie's place. She was beside herself with delight to see Enoch cross her threshold. She threw her arms around him and nearly toppled him while pulling him inside the door.

"Where have you been, my long lost friend?"

"I have come to say goodbye for a while. I am travelling to New Orleans with this fine group of people. Have you got some available room?"

"Of course I do! We may have to double up, but we will find room. Will you be eating with us?"

"No, I want to go see Mr. Tanner and have dinner with him. I need to see if those apprentices are doing as I taught them. It is good to see you again Mattie. *You know what I mean.*"

"Yes, I do and it is so good to see you too. Many people ask about you. Your absence has caused a stir, especially to your diners. They were afraid they would have to come eat at my place again! Come inside and we will get some water drawn so you all can tidy up before dinner."

After they cleaned themselves of the road grime, everyone met for dinner. Evangeline and Elizabeth looked wonderful in their dresses. Matt, John and Thomas also looked like a much better sight once they cleaned up.

They were surprised to find Enoch sitting in a chair with the rest of the group seated on the floor around him as he told them a tale he once heard around the fire where slaves would gather in the evening and share their thoughts, experiences and dreams. He was winding down the tale of how the old rabbit, named *br'er rabbit*, out foxed the wily old fox. It was amazing how the man had captivated the attention of the children as well as the young men like a magician playing the crowd.

Enoch wasn't old, but he wasn't young either. He had that distinguished look with the slight graying around his temples. He also had a way of holding an audience with his words and deeds. There was something peculiarly special about him, other than the fact that he was blind and was quite capable of handling any circumstance that presented itself. He was physically fit and quite trim, not doddering like an old man or invalid. He was not a man to be overlooked.

Once gathered, they were led by Enoch's instructions to where he remembered Tanner's Café to be. They stopped and looked at Enoch and Thomas said, "Enoch, you must have forgotten your way because this is not Tanner's Café."

Enoch smiled, "I never forget my way. This is the place where Tanner had his café!"

"Well," John said with a smile in his voice, "the sign say Enoch's Restaurant!"

They all smiled and Enoch was speechless. The door swung open and Mr. Tanner himself walked out and grabbed Enoch with a big bear hug.

"The name sounds better to me. What do you think, my friend?"

"I don't know what to think," Enoch stated.

"Well, don't think then. I had advanced word that you were coming and I put together one of your favorite meals. We are having stewed venison with potatoes, carrots and onions, and white gravy over biscuits. I also had the boys to bake blackberry cobblers. What are you waiting on? Come inside with all your friends and let's eat!"

The dinner was an event. Patrons would come over to greet Enoch and wish him well. It was obvious he was a well liked man in these parts. He was barely given enough time to shove some food down his throat with all the friends stopping by to speak to him and tell him the latest news. People were coming in off the street just to say hello, once word got out he was in town. Everyone enjoyed the clamor; even the three confederate soldiers felt at home and welcomed the elaborate meal like starving hyenas.

Annie and Sammie could not believe that they were eating in a restaurant with their children surrounded by white folks. This was not a common occurrence for that day and time. Enoch explained to them that once he had established himself as the preferred chef he made one demand, and it was that no one was turned away, no one! He would not have any person, no matter what color or what he had or didn't have in his pocket to be turned away; and, he would not have them eating in the back room either. He was taught *all God's children* deserved respect, equally. He was told *God was not a respecter of persons*, and that meant no one was treated above another.

"Joseph," Enoch spoke after the dinner, "I have enjoyed this meal and the many friends that came by to speak with me tonight. You gave me the greatest opportunity when you took me in like family. You trusted me when I was naught but a strange young man walking on the road of life. I cannot thank you enough for your kindness. You have also trained the boys well. I am glad you gave the young fellows the opportunity to better themselves. It will take many men and women with good and sincere hearts like yours to help the struggling Negro community to fend for itself. Again, I thank you!"

Good words were spoken by all in attendance and they made their way back to Mattie's boardinghouse to rest their weary bones. They would be on their way again tomorrow. They had a long road to travel to reach Jackson and to rendezvous with Jacob.

Before breakfast of the next day Matthew walked down the street to a telegraph office. He informed the agent that he wanted to send a telegram to his brother's secretary in Washington. It read: Secretary H.M. We are progressing on southern course, stop, gaining traction, stop, have already reported failures of friends, stop, will be in touch next location, stop, Number One, stop. That was sufficient to let the Secretary of the Treasure, Hugh McCullough, know his whereabouts until he established a permanent location. He planned to report back when he reached Jackson, Mississippi.

After breakfast the group replenished their stock for the long road ahead. They ferried the Alabama River on their way west. Several days later they crossed the Black Warrior River as they passed through Tuscaloosa. This was the town named after the great chieftain, Chief Tuskaloosa, whose name meant *Black Warrior*. It is stated he stood over seven feet tall and was a great leader of his people. He died as a result of battle with Hernando De Soto and his army in the year 1540. They stopped and made camp alongside a creek still in view of the town of Tuscaloosa. After camp was set up, the men went fishing along the creek bordered by longleaf pines and water oaks on one side and a pasture on the other. They took Annie's son Lawrence too. John brought a couple of bars of lye soap along so they could wash up a bit.

A little white girl, about the age of ten, walked into camp carry-ing two quart jars of peaches. The women stopped to look at her and Elizabeth walked up and said, "Hello, how are you to-day?"

"I am fine, my name is Mary and I have some peaches to sell. Would you like to buy them? We don't have much to offer since our pappy got kilt in the war. We canned them last summer. Momma is mighty weak, done taken the fever, and anything we can get will help her."

Annie walked over to the girl and took the two blue *Mason* jars of peaches and said, "Yes, Mary, we do need some fresh peaches. They look mighty good. We can buy them from you. We have money for you to give your mother. How is she, darling?"

"She is mighty poor," the little girl in the clean but tattered blue dress said with a very faint voice. "She is too weak to get up out of bed. My brother and I had to help her out to the outhouse this morning. I don't see how she is going to make it, not eating nor drinking anything. She can barely take a few sips of water."

"Will you take us to see your mother, Mary?"

"Yes ma'am."

"Evangeline, go down to the creek and call for Sammie, Enoch and John too. I'll get my medicine bag. You and Elizabeth get Thomas to help with supper."

Annie quickly got her bag that had the barest of essentials one needed to mend the broken body of the average person of those times. Home medicine was exactly that, just what someone could get their hands on to mend broken bones, cure ailments and dress the wounds that naturally occurred in the hard act of living.

Mary led Annie and the men to her house just over the rise in the pasture. There was a jersey milk cow just inside the stick fence held together by wire. The cow turned its head to make certain the intrud-ers intended no harm to her suckling. They entered the house to find Mary's mother in the bedroom to the left of the kitchen. Her son was seated beside her, wiping her forehead and face with a damp cloth and silently crying.

Annie stepped up beside him quickly and lifted the frail woman's arm, checking her pulse. There was still life, but very little to hope for. "Mary, take your brother outside please!"

Enoch stepped up next to Annie and felt for the woman's forehead. He bent over and listened to her chest. The breathing was ragged and slight. She made a noise and Enoch put his ear closer to her mouth.

"My time is nigh," she paused to gather her strength, "please help my children put in a crop or take them with you. They are good and need help to survive. Tell them to make us proud and that we love them, their pappy and me."

Sammie brought the two children back inside. "Your mother is slipping away, come inside to be with her."

They gathered beside her and told her they loved her. She opened her eyes and smiled at them, and closed them again. She took her last breath and gave up the ghost. The children openly wept and the others left the room, except Annie.

After what seemed like a long time to the others, but wasn't really that long, Annie emerged from the house with the children. "The children are going with us. Sammie tie a rope to that cow and bring along the calf too. Enoch, take Mary back to the camp with you, please. John, I want you to help the boy gather up what hay is left in the barn and pile it up around this shack."

"What are your plans?" John asked.

Annie turned to look at him and said, "Just what the woman told her kids she wanted done. She told them if they could find a place to go when she died, she wanted them to burn down this place with her in it. She told them to get away from the memories of this God forsaken place, and start a new life."

John and the boy gathered all the firewood and hay and placed it around the crumbling shack. He pulled out some matches from a dry pouch and struck one on the sole of his shoe. The fire was almost instantaneous. It went up very quickly. It sent black smoke and flames high up in the sky. Some of the neighbors came running from nearby, and others came on horseback, to find out what happened.

The boy told them that his mother had died and he was carrying out her final wish.

"Tell old man Turner he can have what's left. We won't be staying on. And, tell the old bastard, good riddance! All he cared about was his rent money. God will deal with him in his own time."

The boy walked over to the burned down remains and saw nothing inside but the metal bed frame and the potbelly stove.

"It is done!" He walked out the crude gate and stopped to knock off the dust from his bare feet. He moved out and never looked back. Together, he and John walked over the rise and back down the hill to the camp.

Matthew and Thomas came walking into camp with a long stringer of fish apiece. "We found a deep hole, full of fish, and Thomas decided to rig-up a crude seine out of those potato sacks and a couple of poles he cut down by the creek. I'm glad he did, because it looks like we've got company."

"This is Mary and her brother Curtis. They will be traveling with us. Their mother has gone on to be with the Lord. She just passed over to the other side and asks us to lend them a hand," Annie politely explained to them.

CHAPTER 24

"YES, I AM YOUR MOTHER!" MARGUERITE revealed with a calm voice, and a smile. She placed her arms around Frances and embraced the shaking, younger woman. After a long and emotional embrace, Marguerite helped Frances back into her chair.

Frances was truly speechless. After sitting in front of her mother, an event she only dreamed of, but never really expected to happen, she finally found her voice and steadied herself.

"I was so young when they took you away. I could hardly remember what you looked like, but, when you touched my arm I felt a strange feeling shoot through my shoulder and down my backbone. There was a familiarity when I stepped up on the porch. It had a smell, a fragrance, like something I used to know. I think it was the scent of you I remembered as a child. You are more beautiful than I remember. I knew you were pretty, that I do remember. I was never certain where you would be, but I knew I would find you one day, or you would find me."

"My beautiful child, I also had a dream that you would come to me and lead me to my baby boy! An angel visited me in my great time of anguish and told me that I would walk with you and my grandchildren before my time was finished on this earth. And here you are! We have so much to learn about each other. My dream has come true! I knew when I saw your face you were my child come home. God have mercy! I can't believe it either, but here you are in my house. Please let me hold you in my arms again," said Marguerite as she reached out with loving arms.

"Mother, is it alright if I call you that?"

"Yes, you are my child and the Good Lord has answered my prayers and brought you home. Do you have a home child?"

"Yes, mother, that man that I had lunch with just gave me the deed to my home located up the river a short piece. He was my owner and

I was his mistress. Now I am a free woman! And I shall never breathe another breath a slave, *Glory Hallelujah!* What a blessing to be free and find my mama on the same day! "

"Frances, let me tell the story of my life since I last saw you. I was taken to Charleston after being sold by your father, Jean Lafitte. There you were born. I was sold by that plantation owner because I would not have relations with him. He was a vain man and I resisted his vulgar attempts. He sold me about the time you were five years old. He separated me from you and John because he was a spiteful man, and hateful too."

"I was purchased by a free man of color that had emigrated from Haiti. He was an affluent businessman that lived in New Orleans. He knew my parents and recognized me. He paid a hefty sum, and his intentions were purely paternal. He brought me here to New Orleans, and granted me my freedom after several years had passed. It was he that helped me get set up as a business owner with this café. I have never forgotten the pain of having you and John torn from my arms that sorry day, and I am sure that is not a fond memory for you either. Tell me, how is my little John?"

"Mother, he is not little anymore. He is a big man with a gentle spirit. He was terribly affected when you were taken from us. For that reason he refuses to have any children for fear they will be taken from him. He had someone who desperately wanted to be his wife, but he refuses to bring children into slavery. I have not seen him in many years because we were separated too. The master was forced to sell me because we had a child together. Her name is Evangeline and she is a beautiful girl. I believe she has special gifts; however, I am not certain because it has been so long ago since our separation. I have a letter to post today in hopes it will reach her in Virginia. This sorry world has made a mess of our lives. I just hope we can find a way to bring us all together again," Frances said with a sigh.

"Mother, I must return to my home and let the two servants know just what has transpired and how it has affected their lives too. They have been given an option of living on with me or returning to the plantation to settle there. I must let them know as soon as possible.

I will return tomorrow morning and help you serve breakfast. I am excited beyond my imagination with the events of today, especially of finding you!"

Marguerite followed Frances out to her carriage. "Please be careful! I would die if anything happened to you now that we have each other again."

Frances' mind was so full with the day's events that she was surprised when she reached the house. She could barely remember how she got home. It really didn't matter now that she was home. She called the man and woman that shared the property with her. She explained that they were now free and had choices to make about their future. She told them they could stay on and live in the carriage house as they had been or move back to the plantation where they were promised a forty acre plot apiece. It would be up to them to build a cabin and improve on the land themselves. The choice was theirs to make.

"You can sleep on it, if you need the time to decide," she explained.

Her man, Marcus, said, "I don't need no spell to figure this out. I know what I'm gonna do! I'm going back and plant me the biggest and prettiest garden this side of heaven. And I'm gonna raise me some hogs and chickens; and I'm gonna marry old widow Reeshad and maybe raise us some chirren! Now that's what I'm fitin' to do!"

"What about you, Liza Jane? What do you want to do?"

"You can bet your sweet arse I ain't going back to no plantation and play in the dirt and raise no yard chirren. I done found me a man dat works on the docks and if I can get him hitched we will move into his place. If he don't have a place, we will live here until we's get our own place!"

"Well, I guess that settles that! Marcus, I will arrange for someone to give you a ride back to the old place. It has been nice having you around. Good luck with your new life!"

"Don't you fret about it! I will get my meager belongings and start walking back directly. I'll catch that ferry across the lake or just swim all de way! You take care of yourself my fair one."

Frances walked out to the center of her yard and sat down on the cast-iron bench across from the cistern. Little sun perch were swimming in a small yard pond filled with lilies, placed there by Marcus. The water from the cistern spilled over into the little pond. It was a peaceful atmosphere under the live oak canopy. She felt a calm feeling wash over her. Her life had been given back to her. Freedom was the forbidden fruit, until now. It was frightening to think there was no one looking over her shoulder. What if she went too far? How would she know when to put on the brakes? Where would her means of support come from after the funds Etienne gave her were exhausted? These were real fears and real concerns that she never had to think about. It was all so new and frightening and exciting at the same time.

Liza Jane walked outside dressed in her best Sunday attire.

"You look mighty dressed up for a Tuesday, Miss Liza! What do you have planned for the afternoon?"

"Well, if you must know Miss Frances, I am going down to the wharf along Tchoupitoulas Street to let my man know his time has come to speak for me or it may be too late!"

"Now, do you need the use of my carriage?"

"That would be mighty nice, but, I reckons I best stroll down there. I don't want him to thank I'm too uppity, now do I."

"You know what's best I think you do, and the last thing you want is for your man to think you are too highfalutin for him," Frances smiled and winked at her.

"I don't know what dat means, but you must be right! You is da one with all that book larning."

"I hope you ain't forgetting how to cooks for yourself, missy cause I may not be home for suppa."

"Do not worry for me, I can do for myself. You just shuffle along now. You can stay out as long as you want, but be careful for those river thugs if you come back late. They will overpower a pretty little thing like you." They both laughed.

While Frances had set the wheels of freedom turning for her two companions, Etienne was helping the former slaves on his sugar plantation grasp the full impact of freedom and being *property owners* instead of *property owned*. They would need time to process the change of status and all of its ramifications.

He was not as concerned about the change of the slaves from property to partners as he was the potential loss to his heart from Frances' possible choices. He realized his feelings were much stronger for her than he was ever willing to admit. To what ends would he go to have Frances' love; and, what sacrifices would he be willing to make? How strong were his obligations to family? These were the serious things he had to determine. These were the kind of things that tested a man's character and commitment.

Marguerite moved with the gentle sway of her porch swing, admiring the beauty of the wisteria vines with their lavender blooms. She closed her eyes and let the evening breeze from the river carry her away for the moment. She was intoxicated with the joy of knowing her prayers were finally answered. How else, but by the omnipotent providence of God, could her daughter have walked back into her life, from out of the blue. She was wise enough to know the difference between coincidence and the powerful will of God. She had learned ages ago that all things were possible with Him, and God's will was not accidental. The thing she had prayed for the hardest came true and she must give credit where credit was due. When her daughter, the one connection to her son, strolled back into her life, she knew this was truly an honest-to-goodness miracle. There was nothing more important to her in this life than to find her son and daughter. She felt a reverence and thanksgiving greater than she had ever felt before. Each day from here on out would be a blessing. Dark clouds passing over could not dampen the uplifted, and ever-trusting, spirit of Marguerite. She had done some bad things in her life, but her path had been changed for the better, and now she felt redemption through her current good fortune.

CHAPTER 25

JACOB WAS RETURNING FROM A MORNING RIDE with his packhorse, the sorrel mare with white stockings, he had begun to call Forgotten. He had not suspected how strong and gentle of a horse she was until it was brought to his attention by the spirit of Walks-Alone, back in the cave. Forgotten had the spirit of a champion and rose up to the calling when it was discovered she was more than just a packhorse; although, she did not shrink from the task of being the one to serve the needs of a packhorse. She rather relished the responsibility as one very proud to serve. This was an added benefit for Jacob to have two capable horses to ride, if the occasion arose.

Just south of Jacob's former camp, Blue starting barking at the scent of something along the trail. Jacob dismounted Forgotten and started looking at the ground where Blue was giving his strongest attention. There were boot prints where a man had entered the trail and left again. It appeared he was dragging his right leg or limping at times from the scraping marks with the side of the shoe in the sand. There was a distinct shoe print from the sole of the left shoe. The shoe was broken where it bent. The break ran from side-to-side. Why this should be significant escaped Jacob, because many returning soldiers had busted, broken or worn out shoes. There were many that had no shoes. But for some reason these prints should have been significant to Jacob, because they were to Blue. Blue was a smart animal and very little escaped him.

Jacob studied the situation to glean as much information as possible. It could come into play in the very near future; he was sure of that! The man had entered the road and left it apparently when a traveler came his way. He was obviously trying not to be detected. This man was hiding something. He was possibly a fugitive.

Jacob broke camp early with hopes of arriving in Chattanooga before dinner. He hoped to get the latest news and sleep on a bed rather than the hard ground. Sometime about noon Blue got his attention barking wildly up ahead of him on the road. He galloped Stonewall, and Forgotten followed close behind on a lead rope.

Blue was jumping up and down, barking madly, and demanding Jacob hurry himself along. There was something vital he wanted to reveal. It was obvious that there had been a struggle from the hoof prints, and all the footprints and dirt thrown in every direction. Jacob rubbed Blue's head to show approval, but Blue grabbed him by the sleeve and led him in the direction of some underbrush. It was there that Jacob noticed the marks of the boots where someone had been dragged.

Blue ran into the bramble of huckleberry bushes and honeysuckle vines to lead Jacob to a dead body. It was haphazardly laid in a small clearing beneath some tall pines. The man had been stripped naked except for his under garments. A dirty and ragged confederate uniform was tossed nearby. The man's shoes and identification lay close by. The shoes must have been too small to fit and the man's wallet contained only a letter addressed to John Allison and a photo of him and his wife. The wounds on the man were defensive. He had cuts to his arms and he was stabbed in the chest and shoulder. The attacker took the man's horse and rode off towards Chattanooga.

Jacob studied the scene for all the information he could gather using each of his sensory skills. He took a blanket from his gear and wrapped the dead body and placed it atop his pack horse. Forgotten did not like the smell of the man's blood, but allowed the extra weight to be added to her load anyway.

By mid-afternoon Jacob arrived in Chattanooga with his horses and gear and a dead man. Blue stayed off to the side to see how they were received before presenting himself. He never really liked towns nor people, until he was familiar with them. People started to gather and a man pushed his way through the crowd to get to Jacob.

"What ya'll got there mister?" the self-appointed spokesman said.

"I've got a dead body!" Jacob replied.

"I can see that! Who is he I mean?"

"I don't know the man, picked him up just outside of town. My dog led me to him," Jacob reported. "Hoped you could identify him, and maybe get him to his family for a proper burial. I found this wallet with his picture and a letter addressed to John Allison."

Someone in the crowd let out a muffled scream. A man walked over, opened the blanket and confirmed it was indeed John Allison.

"Someone give me a hand to get him over to the undertaker!"

A Union officer walked up to Jacob and pulled him aside. "I would like to hear all you can tell me about this situation from your perspective. I am Major Michael Thompson of the U. S. Cavalry posted here in Chattanooga. We had a sentry killed last night and I believe this may tie-in with his death."

"Sir, my name is Jacob Hewitt, an emissary of the Cherokee Nation to Washington and a Federal Marshall. I am on official business making my way down to Jackson, Mississippi and think I may have some information that is pertinent. I would like to see the murder scene first and then I can report to you and the civilian authority at the same time."

"That would certainly be appreciated, Mr. Hewitt. Let me have one of my men take your horses to be fed, watered and rubbed down. Soldier, take this gentleman's livestock and give them proper care, no expense overlooked!"

"Follow me sir and I will show you the crime scene."

They walked over to a fort and barracks set up for the temporary housing of Union soldiers after the capture of Chattanooga. He presented a soldier standing next to a wooden building where ammunition and other supplies were stored. The soldier saluted and opened the door for their inspection. Jacob was more interested in the ground outside and around the building than looking inside for clues.

"I think I can answer your questions and solve both murders at once. Do you see those boot prints?" Jacob asked, pointing down to the print with the broken sole. "I have information directly tying that man to several murders. He is a renegade Confederate soldier that killed a Cherokee Chieftain and his daughter. He was accompanied by two other men, which have been brought to justice already. Let's meet with the civilian authority in town that I may give a full accounting to you both and then I can clean up for dinner."

Together they walked back to town on a raised boardwalk to the marshal's office. As they stepped inside the marshal was informing Mrs. Allison about her husband. "There isn't any more I can offer, Mrs. Allison, but I will let you know what I can."

"Marshal Taylor, I believe this man can tell us more about the death of Mr. Allison. His name is Mr. Hewitt," the Major interjected.

"Please tell me what you know, kind sir! My husband was a gentle man and not a trouble maker," the lady offered.

"Mrs. Allison, I am truly sorry about your husband. My dog and I were traveling earlier this morning on our way here and my dog alerted me to your husband's whereabouts. I found him stowed away in the bushes just off the road wearing only his long underwear and some old confederate uniform laid nearby discarded by his attacker. He had obviously put up a fight to defend himself, but the attacker was skilled with the knife."

"From the boot print I found near the supply depot I feel confident that the man that killed your husband was also the man that murdered the night sentry. He killed your husband for his horse, and probably tied it just outside of town while he sneaked in to get some supplies. This man was the leader of two other men that killed a Cherokee Chief and his daughter. He cut them up more severely than your husband and the sentry. I was able to capture the other two; one we hanged and the other fought to his death. This man jumped from a cliff into a fast moving river below to what we thought was his death; although, the body was never found. My dog recognized the man's scent while we were traveling. And the boot print at the scene of your husband's attack and the sentry's post is a match."

"The Major told me a rifle, and some ammunition and a signifi- cant amount of dynamite were stolen. I believe this man is not only a murderer, but has plans of espionage. He may attack a fort before he is through."

"I will gather a posse and start after him tomorrow afternoon," the marshal responded.

"No, that will be too late!" The Major declared. "This is a military matter and we will handle it, with the assistance of Mr. Hewitt, if he will oblige us."

"Sir, it is my obligation to complete the mission I started. I was entrusted to track down the Chief's killers; and, it is not finished! The Chief was a very dear friend and his spirit will not rest until this man has been brought to justice."

"You have no authority to hunt down fugitives, Mr. Hewitt," the marshal said with an insolent tone. "You might have authority in the Indian Territories but not here!"

Jacob reached on the inside of his buckskin jacket and retrieved a badge. He presented the badge to the marshal and waited for a response.

"Where did you get this Federal Marshal's badge?"

"It was presented to me by President Abraham Lincoln, a friend of my father's, as well as mine." Jacob reached out to receive the out-stretched hand bearing the badge.

"I must apologize mister; I didn't know," the man said, somewhat embarrassed.

"It is a common mistake. People just assume us Injuns are a bunch of no-account, whiskey guzzlers looking for trouble," Jacob responded.

"I guess I had that coming," the marshal admitted. "I just hope you can catch that sorry excuse for an ex-confederate soldier before he does any more harm."

"I have a very good feel for how he operates now. He is more confident and will be careless. Let me get a good meal in me and a night's sleep, and we can start out in the morning. I want only one good man to travel with me; more than that and we will be ineffective. I will report to you in the morning after I have rested, Major Thompson. Good night!' Jacob walked out the door looking for a hot meal.

The early morning air was cool and a fog had floated in from the valley. Jacob was up early after a bath, and a good night's sleep. He was met by a sergeant when he was buying supplies from a mercantile.

"The major says for you to come down and eat breakfast with us."

"I'll be there shortly, after I pick up a few things," Jacob said, as he placed his purchases on the counter for the merchant to tally.

"Have some eggs and bacon and hot biscuits," the Major insisted. "Our cook hasn't learned how to mess up breakfast yet!"

"I've noticed that he still makes a good pot of field coffee," Jacob said as he eased himself down on the bench next to some soldiers.

"He makes it strong and we appreciate that, after having to drink that weak coffee we had in the field, when supplies were low. We used the same coffee grounds multiple times."

"You met Sergeant Finch already. He will accompany you on your mission. He will dress in non-military attire for the mission. You will find him quite capable, sir. He has many skills and is an extraordinary woodsman. He was raised in these mountains and can live off the land as well as any man," Major Thompson assured him.

"I am ready to go as soon as I eat these eggs. I wouldn't mind a few extra biscuits for the trail if that could be arranged," Jacob smiled.

"The sergeant is waiting with his horse and pack mule just outside the mess hall. Good luck and good travel ahead. The sergeant will report back to me on the success of your mission, Godspeed, my friend!" The Major rose from the table and shook Jacob's hand, turned and walked away.

The sun had reached its apex and the cicadas were singing their hearts out. Sergeant Finch walked his horse up to a stream so it could drink. He dismounted and suggested they build a fire and make some coffee. He also produced a sack of biscuits he procured from the cook and handed the sack to Jacob.

"The cook may be cantankerous, but he has some redeeming qualities; namely, he makes better biscuits than my grandma, and that is saying a lot," the sergeant offered his opinion. "But, I would never admit to saying as much to him!"

"What do you make of this scoundrel we are huntin', sir?"

"Well sergeant, I think he is very angry for having lost the war. He has the means now to make a point. He isn't afraid to die. He wants to take out as many men as possible. He is not going to use that dynamite to rob a bank; it's not like that at all. He wants to find a target that can give him the maximum casualties. He has no conscience and is full of hate, much like a rabid animal that is out of his head."

"Based on your assessment, we would be better off to get ahead of him and prevent any carnage before it can happen."

"Well that makes sense, but I don't think he knows just what his plans are either. I suggest we follow him and study his patterns. He appears to be heading for Huntsville, Alabama based on his direction. Do you know of anything important happening there, sergeant?"

"Nothing that I can think of at the moment; however, that is a rallying point to gather Union troops from Mississippi and the surrounding areas and load them on the train heading north. Could that be significant?"

"Well, you may be onto something there, but it is likely he doesn't know that yet. Once he does realize what is happening he may take advantage of it. Let's think as we ride on how we might approach this problem. Let's get a move on and try to put some miles behind us before we make camp!"

They were able to follow the outlaw's tracks because Jacob studied the horse's shoeprint at the point that he was stolen. He also discovered where the horse was tied on the edge of town while the same man killed and stole from the army depot in Chattanooga. The tracks were distinguishable from the many other tracks on the road traveled by a tiny star imprint on the left rear shoe. It was an identifying mark the blacksmith used to distinguish his work, a common practice among blacksmiths.

It was obvious the man stayed away from folks as much as possible. He was provisioned well enough to keep to himself; however, Jacob and the sergeant found he had stopped at a farmhouse and got some feed for his horse.

Jacob called out to the farmer from a distance. "Hello the house! Mind if we stop and have a drink of cool water from your well, mister?"

"Certainly, you may; come on in and sup with us. Mama is preparing a meal of last night's left-over homemade stew. Would you gentlemen care to join us?" the farmer offered.

"Yes sir! Let us water the horses first," explained the sergeant.

"Take those horses over to the shed attached to the barn, throw some grain in the trough, and rub them down while you are at it," the farmer suggested.

The men washed their hands and dried them at the basin provided just outside the kitchen window. Inside they found a very clean and orderly home, simple and functional.

"My name is Jacob Hewitt, and this is Sergeant Finch, how do you do, ma'am?"

"I am John and this is my wife Nancy. Welcome to our humble home. We see many travelers these days, with all the soldiers returning home and the Union soldiers leaving too."

"John, my husband, did not participate in the war. We, like many of our neighbors, did not agree with the war and tried our best not to get mixed up in the fracas. We have a son whom is very ill and do our best to make the rest of his life as comfortable as possible. He is only six and is asleep in the rear bedroom," the lady pointed out. "We are very thankful for what the Lord has provided us in our safety and all of our needs; therefore, we feel blessed whenever we can share with others."

"Make yourselves comfortable. Pull up a chair and sit," John suggested.

"John, Mr. Finch and myself are following an outlaw from Chattanooga and it appears he made have stopped here very recently. Have you had any other visitors lately?"

"Yes we have. A haggardly looking fellow riding a fine horse stopped here just this morning and asked for a little feed for his horse. He offered to pay but we told him it was our pleasure to help. He wasn't here very long. He left as soon as his horse was watered and fed. He appeared to be a troubled man with much on his mind. What are his crimes, if I may ask?"

"He was responsible for at least four murders that we are aware of and maybe more." Jacob rubbed his forehead in thought. "Is there anything else you might have noticed that can help us?"

"I noticed he walked like his right leg was kind of gimpy; maybe was injured in the war." Nancy thought, "And he held his left arm close to his body like it was of no use!"

"He asked me if he was headed in the right direction to get to Huntsville. I told him he was a good day's ride from here. I also noticed a certain look in the man's eyes. It was an empty look, much like the look of a man that had given up and didn't care about tomorrow. It was a very sad thing. Yes, he truly looked to be a troubled man."

After dinner, Jacob asked to look in on the couple's son. Sergeant Finch followed him to the room of the frail child. Jacob and the Sergeant both took a knee. Jacob said a little prayer he knew from his Cherokee upbringing. The sergeant offered an Amen and stepped back.

Jacob and Sergeant Finch thanked the man and his wife for dinner and the care of their horses. Knowing that it would be an insult to offer payment for their kindness, Jacob dropped a twenty-dollar gold piece into the farmer's jacket, hanging next to the door. They waved goodbye and the horses walked with a fresher step having been fed.

"Sergeant, my thinking is that our felon will push on into town and find a room and meal for the night. That would put him at arriving late and probably sleeping late. I am thinking we could put as much ground behind us before making camp and get an early start before daylight. That could put us in town just before noon, and we may catch this man walking to lunch at some café. I suggest you let the commanding officer of the Union garrison know what has happened and what we suspect; and then he could have some of his men on the lookout for suspicious activity. More eyes will help us catch this man much quicker. Jacob paused, "What do you think?"

"Well, it all makes sense to me, but my thinking tells me that farmer had a good point about the look in the man's eyes. I think he is a driven man on a mission. I don't think our felon will be thinking about a bed and a meal. I believe he is thinking about his last mission, or his last battle. I believe his heart is full of hatred and bent on killing as many Yankees as possible. He may push on into town and wire that dynamite to cause maximum casualties before the sun is up. What are your thoughts on that?" the sergeant queried.

"Sergeant, you may be exactly right! You think like a man that has been in a few battles. Now I understand why the Major sent you along."

"No disrespect, but I did grow up in the woods and learned to think like an animal of prey. The Indian is not the only man with a working knowledge of all things natural. Man left to his natural instincts develops a greater understanding and appreciation for his surroundings. I have been over a few roads and crossed a few streams before I joined up with this man's army. Not all of us folks that grew up watching the black man toil under the master's strong hand thought it correct. There comes a time when every man must take a stand for what he believes is right or be complicit in the crime."

The sergeant paused before he spoke again. "I guess I felt like I had something that needed saying."

"Yes you did and I'm glad you did. I could not agree more with you. The Redman learned many things from the White woodsman and adventurer, some good and some not so good. And I know many like yourself that have walked that difficult path of choosing to fight against their brother and fellow statesmen. I admire you, and am glad I asked for your thoughts. I have much to learn and there are many that have something to teach me."

"I like your idea to push on through the night. A little lost sleep may save many lives!" Jacob smiled. "Let's ride, my worthy partner."

They pushed on, sparing their horses when necessary, and as often as possible. They felt fatigue set in as the moon began to rise in the night sky, but they were on a mission and would not be deterred. Once while giving the horses a blow, Finch built a fire and made coffee. It was strong and fit the bill for what they needed to boost their morale.

The gray of dawn and the breakfast fires of soldiers camped at the town's edge brought Huntsville into view. They saw the train yard alive with activity as officials attempted to get the cavalcade of Union troops positioned for the train cars rolling into the station. They arrived in time to get set for any potential sabotage to the train or troops. Sergeant Finch quickly sought out the commanding officer and presented his credentials and their concerns for the safety of his men.

Jacob took his horses to the hostler and gave instructions for their care. He took his rifle out of the scabbard and had a pistol holstered if either were necessary. He took off in a trot to search the grounds for any suspicious activity. He was looking closely for anyone that stood out from soldiers and train personnel; and then it hit him, his killer could have taken a uniform of a soldier or even a train engineer. He began to look closer at anyone with a limp on the right leg or a damaged left arm. He had to be diligent. He saw Finch coming swiftly in his direction.

"I spoke with the commanding officer and he has more than a dozen soldiers assisting us in our search. Nothing has happened out of the ordinary as far as he knows. I spoke with the train conductor and he says all is well, with the exception of one of his more dependable assistants not showing up for duty," explained Finch.

"That's it!" Jacob shouted.

"That is what?" Finch asked.

"The killer has waylaid a train employee and taken his uniform, probably cut his throat!" Jacob twisted and turned in every direction, looking at any and all train employees.

"Finch, get the word to the army about this development and tell them to spread it around to the other observers. I'll go to the conductor and let him know."

Jacob ran to the front of the train to find the conductor and looking under each car as he went. Where could this man be? Was he hiding somewhere, and had he already set his explosives? They were going on speculation about this man's intentions; however, it was all very plausible.

The conductor gathered his men and informed them of the situation. He requested them to work in pairs until this was rectified, no exceptions. He did not want any train employee to be caught by surprise and killed. They broke the train and train yard into sectors and began a more thorough search.

Jacob convinced the train conductor and commanding officer to proceed with the loading of men onto the train. He wanted all of the noise to convince the outlaw that everything was going as planned and that they did not suspect anything out of the ordinary. They were to load each car with soldiers and then have them file out the back of the train quietly. They were to go to a place and conceal their ruse.

Jacob suspected the target was the locomotive so that the train would derail while in motion. That would require someone to be on the train to detonate the explosives while at maximum speed. This whole theory was purely speculative, but precautionary in nature. It was better to be safe than sorry!

Everyone performed their part of the charade as the locomotive was being brought to full steam. Jacob and the employees of the train, as well as the soldiers, were quite diligent in their search, hoping to find the man before someone was injured or worse, killed!

The sense of calm was shattered when the sound of a *Henry* rifle blasted from the water tank next to the railroad. All eyes looked in the direction of the shot and could see the wisp of gun-smoke curl above the top of the tank. Then a man stood up and it was Sergeant Finch holding his rifle and pointing at the man draped over the side of the tinder car. The man was clearly dead and a bundle of dynamite fell from his hand onto the ground beneath him.

"Someone check that dynamite and make sure it hasn't been lit!" Finch yelled.

One of the soldiers ran over and grabbed it and tossed it in a rain barrel. "It don't look lit but I just wanted to be sure!"

Folks ran from every direction to look at the man hanging from the train. Soldiers were gathering and train employees came running to see.

One of the train employees climbed up on the tinder car and looked down in the wood pile and saw the dead body of Jack Foster, a coworker, partially covered up with a stack of wood intended for fuel. He pulled the dead body from the wood pile and handed it over to some soldiers standing below. It was then that he shoved the dead body of the outlaw over the side to land in the hard packed ground below with a thud. It was apparent that Sergeant Finch's shot took off the upper part of the man's head.

Finch climbed down from the tank and walked through the crowd to stand beside the dead man.

"I heard some movement in that car when I walked by and decided to get to higher ground for a better look. I could see from atop the water tank and noticed a head peeping over the edge. He must have suspected something was amiss. When he rose up in a standing position, I saw the dynamite in his right hand and just drew a bead on him like I would an old turkey gobbler."

"I believe I am ready for a hot meal and a soft bed! I don't like missing my rest or my meals. Excuse me gentlemen!"

Jacob patted the sergeant on the back as he walked past. "Fine work soldier!"

CHAPTER 26

ALBERT GOLDSMITH FELT LIKE A MAN THAT had been run over by a loaded freight wagon. He could feel the pain from the working-over he received the night before much better the next day as he tried to bathe and dress himself. There was a knot on his head. It was pounding like he was inside a huge bell. He could feel the pain in his ribs and his back; there must have been something broken as a result of them putting the boot to him. It took all of his strength to move around. He wanted badly to fall back onto the bed.

He knew he shouldn't report this incident to the authorities because the last thing he needed was the sheriff questioning him; however, he was at odds about what action he needed to take, since the robbers took most of his money. He did have a little cash set aside. And he had the counterfeit money he brought as his sample to allure clients. He had plenty of it. Now he must decide whether it was wise to use it to further his operations. It would be a testament to his belief in his product to use it himself. He must be bold!

Albert would pen a letter to his wife, Martha. He wanted to excite her with the news about meeting her childhood friend. He thought she would find it astonishing how small the world really was. Hopefully, it would make her feel more comfortable with his trip south, knowing that Cecilia Harrison Carver, an old friend, felt it safe to travel south at war's end.

The bright morning sun affected Albert just like a hangover would have. He walked down to a café near the French Market for breakfast. He moved very gingerly due to the pain. He wanted to be ready and available when his first big business contact reached out to continue their discussion. He did not know how quickly Horace Marchant would respond, or, how slowly for that matter. He just wanted to be ready because this was the big test to whether he would be successful. He felt the burden was more on him than his friends, so were the risks.

John Carver was awake and dressed too early for Cecilia's taste. It was his nature to get up early and be about his business. He informed his wife that he would be busy today with clients and for her to entertain herself. He would arrive back at the hotel later in the evening and not to wait up for him.

"Oh, by the way John, I met the husband of a childhood friend of mine on the boat last evening. I was getting some air on the upper deck and I met this nice man. His name is Albert Goldsmith, and he is from Philadelphia. He is married to a girl I grew up with back in Boston, Martha McCallum!" Cecilia proclaimed with great delight.

John was surprised. "What did you say her husband's name was?"

"His name is Albert Goldsmith. Do you know him?" she asked, puzzled by his reaction.

"No! It just sounds familiar. You know how it is when you meet so many people; names start to sound familiar, just like faces start looking alike. That's all!" John felt he recovered well from his near slip.

John certainly did know Albert Goldsmith. He was the son of the tailor he used when in Philadelphia. He knew Albert as a young man prior to his education at Harvard. What was he doing here in New Orleans? John wondered if Albert would even remember him. Well, it was just a chance meeting and not likely to happen again. Just a coincidence he thought.

John Carver had breakfast with some of his operatives conveniently positioned in bars, riverboats and along the docks to act upon orders when given. He met them in an out-of-the-way café in the Irish Channel, The Shamrock Pub. The Irish Channel was home to the Irish immigrant, as well as the German, Italian and the African.

John was skilled at operating on all levels of society, from the high-society to the rough and tumble world of the New York gangs. He could be gentle or vicious, whichever side was necessary. One must never misjudge his nature. He was a product of the rough side of New York. He had a dark history that was best left well enough alone.

John Carver had set up his operation like a skilled businessman established his corporation. He left no detail overlooked. He had no intention of failure and did not allow incompetence in his ranks. Mistakes could be grave. He operated his network like a spider would work her web, controlling all facets.

"Mistakes will not be tolerated. Everyone knows his mission and needs to keep that foremost in his mind!"

John scanned the table of the men seated around him eating their breakfast and drinking their coffee. He held the eyes and attention of every single man in attendance.

"Drinking and carousing will be held to a minimum. If I hear otherwise, you will get yourself a free trip downriver, face down! Do you understand?"

They agreed in unison. No one wanted to be on Mr. Carver's bad side. There was a reason they called him *The Snake* or *Cottonmouth*. Any one that crossed him was usually found dead from a single strike and often floating in a body of water to be washed ashore after the crabs, turtles and alligators finished snacking on them. It was a point of question just what all his gentlemanly cane was capable of; some said it had a knife or sword inside, others believe it was also a gun; whatever it was, it was surely deadly!

Carver was to meet with Horace T. Marchant, the big-time lawyer, for lunch in the French Quarter. Marchant was *a mover and a shaker* in the social and political circles of New Orleans, and throughout the state. He was a *big man around town*.

Somehow, Marchant got word of the carelessness of Simon Bartlett and the lost satchel of counterfeit money on the riverboat. That could serve to unravel this nefarious counterfeiting scheme. A loss of cooperation from Marchant would not only be a major setback, but, may prove an end to southern operations and possible exposure, something Carver would not tolerate.

Bartlett was to be the gambling angle of Carver's plan. He was to quietly establish the trailhead, so to speak, gambling as a means of filtering the counterfeit money throughout the South; however, his reckless and flamboyant ways had caused the plan to go awry. To what extent Bartlett's actions had damage things was yet to be determined. Carver was not pleased in the least bit, and just might have to resolve this matter in his usual manner.

John Carver enjoyed his stroll through the Quarter. As he turned the corner to St. Louis Street a penniless Confederate soldier in tattered clothing approached him and asked with all the humility he could muster, "Can you spare some change for a meal?"

Carver tapped the man on the side of his head with a quick parry of his cane hard enough to daze the shocked and disillusioned soldier down to his feet.

"Be off with you, you beggar! You should never have taken up arms against us, you fool!" John Carver reeled with obvious delight as he berated the poor man.

It was an unjustified slight since he had never served a single day fighting for the Union. It was never his intentions to take up arms and stand in lockstep with his fellow Northerners to reunite the Country. He had better plans!

He entered the front door of Antoine's Restaurant to be greeted by the owner himself. "How are you this fine day, sir? Welcome to my restaurant! Are you dining alone today, or do you plan to meet someone?"

"I have plans to meet Mr. Marchant for the noon meal. Has he arrived yet, Monsieur Alciatore?" John spoke to impress his guest.

"Yes sir, Mr. Carver, he has indicated you would follow shortly," Antoine declared with his strong French accent. "Follow me!"

He was led down rows of engaged diners openly conversing about the delights of the day with delectable dishes in their midst. He may be one of them at this point in his life, but not too distant a time he was on the streets as was the detestable soldier, looking for his next score.

"Hello John! I am glad you could join me today. This is one of my favorite dining spots in the city. I feel I am among my element here and the food is worthy of a king. Have a seat and a glass of wine from Antoine's extensive cellar. Let's enjoy our surrounding before you tell me about your proposition." Horace Marchant was turning on the charm and flaunting his pomposity.

Antoine pulled out a chair across from Marchant and with a deft motion of his hand directed Carver to his seat. "I will have Henri' to serve you, bon appetite!" With the elegance of a skilled dancer and the diplomacy of a foreign diplomat, Antoine left the room to attend to the other guests of his popular establishment.

Henri' was at the table pouring a glass of wine for John's inspection. John accepted the glass and motioned for the server to leave the room. Marchant had ordered dinner for the two, flounder stuffed with crab-meat and covered with a Creole sauce, with a side of summer vegetables.

"Well John, I am glad you could have dinner with me today, and I would like to get down to business if that meets with your approval."

"That is exactly why I am here, of course!" John proclaimed.

"I've taken the time to think about the premise upon which you want to establish a business relationship with me and think the risk outweighs the gain. Just look at my position: first, I have a successful shipping business, secondly, I am a majority stockholder in a thriving bank, and thirdly, I have a good relationship with local planters; even though, their position is greatly diminished with the loss of slaves among other things. For what reason would I have to jeopardize all of that for a scheme?" the rotund man stated, as he leaned back in his chair and looked up at the ceiling, pondering his response.

"That would make perfect sense and logic for a successful business-man satisfied with his status in life; however, it might not appeal to a man with aspirations to be recognized as a statesman and leader of his State going forward in a new-world environment, " John smirked as he put out the bait.

"I think someone with great ambition wants to control the docks and its labor force, and maybe own the bank too. He may have his sights set on several plantations up the river!"

"And you propose all of this by the simple infusion of phony money. Before you respond, I must tell you that there is competition in your field," Marchant adjusted himself in his seat before proceeding.

"Yesterday I entertained a young gentleman from Philadelphia, by the name of Albert Goldsmith, and he proposes the same game! So, how is your pitch any different?"

"Goldsmith!" That was the second time today he was confronted with that name. He thought long and hard before he made the connection in his mind. It had to be that Simon Bartlett was conducting his own side business with the Philadelphia printer and this Goldsmith. Bartlett would definitely meet the wrath of The Snake, and very soon. His approach to young Albert was a different matter altogether.

"First Horace, let me assure you that this matter of competition will be resolved. One of my associates, the one you mentioned being reckless and misplacing a sample of our product on one of your boats, will be dealt with on short notice. I suspect he is the source of my competition and I will remedy that quickly. That will dry up Mr. Goldsmith's funds and take him out of the picture promptly."

"Secondly, I never told you the entire plan before I knew if we had a business arrangement," John paused to address Henri', the waiter, who had returned, before continuing the conversation with Horace.

"Henri', could you please bring me a glass of fine bourbon?"

"Yes, certainly," the waiter replied.

"As I was saying before we were interrupted, it will take skillful planning for you to control the docks and the bank and to acquire title to the properties along the river road. I have the means and willpower to accomplish these things; but, it will mean having me as a silent partner in these matters." John paused again, giving his potential partner in crime time to contemplate his proposal more completely. "Do we have a basis to continue this proposal?"

Horace exhaled and shifted a bit as the waiter brought out their dinner. He became aware of a gentleman seated across the aisle in a booth one position up from where they were dining. This man seemed to be overly attentive to their conversation and was beginning to lean more overtly in their direction. Why was he curious about what John Carver had to say to him? "You have an interesting way of putting things, my friend; however, it will be more appropriate that you visit my home on St. Charles Avenue where we can more fully discuss your proposal in a more discreet setting."

The gentleman across from them completed his meal quickly and thanked his waiter as he paid and made his way out the door. He appeared to be someone that had to be somewhere else in a hurry. Horace Marchant realized he wasn't the only one to notice the tall man had made an abrupt departure. John Carver was just more subtle about his observations.

"Is he an acquaintance of yours, Horace?"

"Never seen him before, but it looked like he was anxious to leave very quickly. I wonder if he heard something that interested him!" Horace pondered.

They continued to dine and agreed upon a future meeting to discuss things in more detail. Horace pulled out a Cuban cigar and offered it to John. They walked down St. Louis Street, enjoying their smoke and conversation, as Albert Goldsmith stood directly across the street gawking. He was shocked and surprised to see the two together.

Albert recognized Horace Marchant immediately and oddly enough recognized the other man, as well. He knew him as Cecilia's husband per her pointing him out in the crowd; moreover, he recognized him better as a man he once knew as a client of his father. This same man was extremely kind to him prior to entering Harvard. It was this same man that gave him the recommendation, which single-handedly tipped his application in favor of getting accepted to that prestigious institution. Could this really be the same John Carver that married Cecilia? He stood there for a long moment, without breathing.

Standing beneath an arbor of wisteria, Albert took a deep breath and exhaled. He remembered one of his friends had said that John Carver was a powerful man in New York and along the Eastern seaboard. He was not one to get crosswise with at any time. Was he in over his head? Should he pack his bags and hurry back to Philadelphia before he went too far? What was the point of no return, and did he want to cross it? These were powerful thoughts and he must be sure of his actions or he would never return to his family again.

Albert turned towards the river and found that little coffee shop that recently opened for business in the French Market. A waiter approached him as he sat at the little metal table on the patio underneath the awning.

"Welcome back to Café du Monde, Mr. Albert! It is nice that you have returned so soon. I must have regular customers if I ever hope to succeed in my new business. Thank you so much. I have some fresh beignets to go along with your coffee," the owner informed him with genuine delight at his return. It was a pleasant turn of events for the proprietor to recognize him with such enthusiasm.

Albert enjoyed the coffee and beignets, but never fully recovered from his discovery. He would return to his room and rest before contemplating recent events and how he should proceed. What a nightmare this was turning out to be!

Albert wrote a letter to Martha:

Dear Martha,

How is my little orchid? I miss you so much, each and every day. Please give a big hug to Sally and Rebecca for me. Tell them Daddy is working hard and misses them greatly. I cannot give you a specific day for my return, but trust I will stay no longer than is absolutely necessary to conduct business here. If you need anything don't hesitate to call on Dad. He will help you with anything and can call on others if necessary.

My sweet love, don't fret for I am safe and will return home directly.

Sincerely,

Your loving husband,

Albert

The days passed slowly as Albert could find no willing takers in the counterfeit money scheme he and his associates had hatched back in Philadelphia with the urging of their old and shady friend, Simon Bartlett. He fell into a depression and became more worried about his family than ever. He spent a great deal of time along the docks, day and night. He started to dress more haggardly and became worried that someone would associate him with the bums that he himself was leery of as he walked the streets.

It came to him one morning; he would take up the profession his father had taught him, the tailor's trade! That was it! It was absolutely what he should do. He wasn't a crook. He would go down to that Frenchman, Leon Godchaux that opened the department store on Canal Street and inquire about a job as a tailor.

And so he did just that. Albert got himself cleaned up and dressed in his best business attire to visit his potential future employer. The suit was one that his father had created for him after he graduated from Harvard. The proprietor was impressed with his knowledge of and skill with fabrics. He demonstrated how efficiently and artfully he could work when asked to produce a suit of clothes for Mr. Godchaux himself. He dove headfirst into his work and discovered he had not been more satisfied in all of his life's work thus far as he was working in the profession of his father.

Time passed quickly and one day Mr. Godchaux came to Albert and said there was a businessman from New York that had seen his work and wanted to meet him and have him produce some new suits for his wardrobe. The man was there and he was to meet him.

Albert stepped out onto the main floor of the department store to come directly in contact with his former benefactor, John Carver!

"Hello Mr. Goldsmith, you may not remember me, but I was once a customer of your father's back in Philadelphia when you were a young man. Your work has caught my eye and I would like to bolster your reputation as an up-and-coming man of commerce."

"Yes, Mr. Carver I do remember you and never got the opportunity to properly thank you for the kind and uplifting letter of recommendation to Harvard. I may not have gotten the chance to attend had it not been for your gracious letter. I also had the pleasure of meeting your beautiful wife one night on the riverboat."

"Mr. Goldsmith, Albert if I may, it is true I wish for you to produce several suits for me; however, there is another issue I wanted to touch on briefly today and maybe discuss in more detail as you labor to produce these suits. It has become clear to me that an associate of mine from Philadelphia may have conspired to lure you and your friends into some dark ventures. Mr. Bartlett will have a day of reckoning and he may have pulled your associates into the fire with him. It brings my heart delight to see you have chosen a nobler path of support. Am I correct in assuming you have abandoned that pursuit which was your original purpose for traveling south?"

It was the realization of his worst fear that Mr. Carver was not only aware of his endeavors into the underworld, but was an adversary of said affairs. This man was not the type to beat around the bush about things that involved him. What were his intentions and would it mean certain death to him? Albert came to the realization of what was most precious to him, and that was his family. Maybe he came to that conclusion none too soon! Now was the time to set the ship straight and back on a sound course.

"Mr. Carver, it just so happens that I have penned a letter to my friends, or associates, and have informed them that my involvement in their enterprise has reached a crossroads; furthermore, I can no longer accommodate their requests on this mission. It has come to my attention that the risks far outweigh the gains from my perspective. I once thought they chose me because of their confidence in me; however, I have since felt they may have chosen me just to insulate themselves from exposure and or prosecution. I can announce with confidence that I plan to relocate my family here as soon as I can provide safe passage for them. I have informed my father of my decision to pursue his chosen profession. He was overcome with excitement that I made that decision of my own accord."

"Albert, you can call me John. I must say it is a relief that you have made the correct decisions about your professional development. I hope your associates can chose likewise. It would be to their future advantage. Poor decisions can have grave consequences."

Changing the subject John Carver made an announcement. "My Cecilia is returning home to New York to accompany our son to New Orleans. Let me make the arrangements to have your family brought down with her. I can handle all of the accommodations for their travel to make the trip safe and pleasurable. The women can reminisce about their childhood. Would that meet with your approval, Albert?"

Albert felt he was backed into a corner and had no other choice than to accept his offer. "Well, yes that would be fine, but I must find an affordable house or cottage before they come. I wouldn't want Martha to be disappointed."

"That's settled. I will have a friend in the real estate business contact you with some suitable choices for your approval. I will also meet with you in several weeks to be fitted for those suits. We will have lunch soon. I have some great cafés you may want to try." With a feeling of satisfaction, John Carver walked down Canal Street to pursue his next order of business.

CHAPTER 27

THE THREE SECRET SERVICE AGENTS THAT began their journey in Washington D.C. were traveling at less than stellar speeds, and gathering an entourage, as they made their way south to New Orleans. There they hoped to infiltrate the growing underworld of counterfeiting espionage.

They crossed the Tombigbee River, separating Alabama and Mississippi, and moved beyond the growing town of Columbus. Columbus, Mississippi was not ravaged as many other Southern towns were because General Nathan Bedford Forrest successfully repelled the attack of the Northern Army. Many of the finer homes and structures were preserved.

The roads were well traveled. The returning Confederate soldier and the emancipated slave shared the same road; although they sought different destinations. The soldier sought to find what remained of the home that he left behind and fought to preserve. The former slave was not entirely sure what he hoped to find, but at least it would be better than what he had.

The vanquished Confederacy made a slow and painful retreat to find its homeland lay ruined by the victors. Former soldiers walked, crawled and dragged their broken and beaten bodies. They were emaciated, often minus a limb, and utterly devoid of the fighting spirit that filled them when they started off to fight for independence. The roads became littered with the weak and dying, much like a linear battlefield. Dead bodies were placed out of the way along the roadside to be dealt with at a later date. Some were buried and others left with little or no form of identification whatsoever.

Frightened and without direction, the freed slaves moved along, sharing the road and having no particular place to go, but only the dream of a life that removed the whip from their backs. They did not know what lay ahead for them; however, they were painfully aware from which they came. Their story took on biblical comparisons, as Moses led the Jews out of Egypt so was their liberator Lincoln. And like Moses, Lincoln saw the *Promised Land* but was not allowed to cross over with *his sojourners.*

The group that began as three soldiers, two *Confederate* and one *Union*, and joined by various and sundry characters moved on towards their immediate goal of reaching Jackson, Mississippi by the end of the week. Travel had been slow, provided the larger group and their needs was more demanding than just three men and two women traveling on horseback. They had expanded to a wagon with man and wife and two children, three bedraggled former soldiers, two orphaned children and an ex-slave-turned-café owner that happened to be blind and an excellent cook too. That did not include the piglets Thomas found and gave to the two black children or the puppy Enoch named Shadow.

It was mighty warm and humidity was high. Afternoon showers were very likely to occur at any given time. They were traveling a good road that had a more tolerable roll. Former slaves would stop their work in the field and watch them as they passed. There were cotton fields and pasturelands, followed by deep woodlands and occasional farms and vacated plantations. Much of the pastureland that once saw herds of cattle was mostly empty except for the few milk cows and occasional bull and heifer that had been hidden away deeper in the swamps to avoid being confiscated by one army or another. Most of the cotton fields lay fallow, with no one to harvest them. These were hard times and would be for a number of years to come.

"I hear dogs baying; maybe they done treed a coon!" Thomas declared.

"Naw, dey is chasin' a runaway!" Sammie interjected.

Off to their right, black men, women and children were in the field chopping cotton, a way of thinning the cotton plants and removing weeds. They are also singing Negro spirituals more loudly as the sound of the baying dogs grew closer.

Men on horseback were coming into view on their left, passing through a field of high sagebrush. An exhausted young black man could be seen rising up out of the sagebrush and falling back down to be bitten again by the dogs on long leashes. The men, three on horseback and two being pulled along by dogs were coming more clearly into view. The young black man was half falling and half crawling towards the road. A very large sycamore tree stood on the cotton field side of the road. Two of the men grabbed the black man and placed him against the tree, holding him out by his arms with his bare back exposed. A young woman could be heard wailing in the field as one of the men dismounted his horse and produced a coiled whip. He cracked the whip for effect.

John moved his horse in position to confront the older man on the lead horse. "What are the charges against this man?"

"It is none of your business, mister! But I will tell you anyway. He tried to run away and I am going to make an example of him, even if it kills him."

"Run away from what?" John screamed at the man.

"Mister, you are not from around here, but I am William P. Brasfield, and these are my slaves! I own this place and everything on it," the man spat his words. "Now, git out of my way or by God I will beat you too!"

Before anyone could register a complaint or move in a retaliatory fashion the man with the whip reached back and swung to strike the slave; however, from a passing cloudburst came a sudden and unexpected lightning strike to the huge sycamore. The two men who held the arms of the younger man were firmly standing on the massive root system that lay on top of the ground and were first to feel the full impact of the lightning as it struck the tree and ran through the body of the man they held in their grasp. They were lit-up and their bodies stretched out before falling dead on the ground. The whip touched the black man simultaneously as the lightning and a bolt of electricity was delivered to the arm of the overseer, knocking his shoes off as he fell dead also.

"I will finish this job so help me God if it is the last thing I ever do!" old man Brasfield roared with a string of spittle as he dismounted his horse.

Everyone, including the group of travelers and the field hands, watched in stunned fashion as the belligerent man walked over to retrieve the whip from the weeds into which it fell after the lightning struck man released it. As Brasfield reached to pick up the whip, a coiled rattlesnake launched itself and struck him in the face, attaching itself along the bridge of his nose. He apparently mistook the snake's rattler for the whip handle. He fell backwards and screamed as he rolled on the ground and tugged at the snake.

Thomas drew his pistol and shot the snake. The snake was dead, cut in half, but it still had its fangs secured in the man's nose. Thomas shot the snake not to relieve the man, but more so because of his hatred and fear of snakes.

Mr. Brasfield bellowed and cussed for a short while longer before he succumbed to the venom. The young slave, whose name was ascertained to be Toby, fell back from the tree, exhausted. Some of the people came running from the field to check on him and the other men. The three that were lightning struck were confirmed dead and so was Brasfield.

Toby was not injured by the lightning; however, the bark had been completely knocked from the sycamore tree where his body had made contact. It appeared more like the shape of a cross than the shape of his body with outstretched arms.

The last man standing walked over to Brasfield, "Father, I guess you were right, this was the last thing you'll ever do. He always said he would be damned if he had to free his slaves!"

Bill Brasfield Jr. walked to the edge of the field and called for everyone to lay down their hoes and come to him. "I believe we have all witnessed an act of God here today. That's what I interpret it to be! I can tell you it is a new day! You are free and no longer have to live in fear. Tomorrow, we will all come together at the Big House, and I will discuss the future here on the plantation and what that will mean to you. I want you all to go home and prepare your evening meals and think about things you would like to see changed for you and this place. Willis, you and some of the stronger men go back to the stable and bring a wagon out to gather up these men. Take my father back to the barn and build him a coffin. I will talk to the family about the events of the day. Build coffins for the other men too, and deliver them to their families."

Bill walked over to John and the others, "I am sorry you had to witness these events today." With that being said, he gathered the reins of his horse and walked off towards his home.

"I guess it's time to move on; we've seen all there is to see," Thomas commented.

"I didn't see anything!" Enoch replied. "What just happened here?"

"Let's get a move on before sunset. I'll explain it to you as we travel," Matthew promised.

The skies opened up and soaked everyone and everything. Travel was slowed, but the sun began drying the road very quickly. The combination of the moisture and heat made for a steamy ride.

Marty Houston, one of the Texans, rode double with Thomas as they went ahead in search of some wild game for dinner and maybe a few meals beyond.

Marty was about five feet and seven inches tall and about one-hundred and twenty-five pounds soaking wet. It was not a chore for Thomas' horse to carry the two because Thomas was a bit taller and probably no more than twenty pounds heavier. His weight was not reflected by his appetite; likewise, greater than ninety percent of all Confederate soldiers were malnourished which led to many deaths by starvation.

They both carried rifles. Thomas had his in the scabbard and Marty held his out to his side. They rode for a ways before a well-traveled game trail appeared to bear to the left of the road.

"I think we should follow it and see if we can jump-up a fat buck," Marty suggested.

"I do believe you are right about that!" Thomas agreed.

Together they merged into the thick pine forest and had to

dismount due to the low hanging limbs and underbrush. They walked ahead of the horse with Thomas holding the reins. The trail descended down a deep ravine. Marty led the way and slid down the trail covered with pine straw, almost falling, while Thomas was more cautious with his choice of steps, not wanting to spook the horse.

Once they had climbed out of the ravine and were walking along a ridge Marty put his finger to his mouth to alert Thomas he heard something. He pointed to a large buck following behind three does one-hundred yards ahead to their left. Thomas pulled his rifle and gave it to Marty because it was a newer *Henry repeater* and Marty was carrying an old muzzle loader. Marty exchanged guns and moved up closer to the game as quickly and quietly as possible. Once he was in the best position to make an accurate shot, he steadied himself against a dogwood tree. He closed his left eye and took a deep breath as he put his sights on the deer and squeezed the trigger. Boom! His aim was good! The buck leaped into the air and ran as the fur was flying from the shot. The does were out front as the buck followed until he gave up the fight.

Thomas handed Marty the reins and told him to follow the buck to see where it fell. Marty was up on the horse and off to secure his game. It was obvious to Thomas that Marty knew his way around a horse by the way he handled it through the trees and snags. He rode that horse like he was born on it.

Thomas trudged up the hill looking at the ground as the grade got tougher the further he went. Thomas stopped when he heard a shot and then another and then he began to run because they were pistol shots that he heard. Marty did not have a pistol! Thomas reached the summit to find the road again, but no sign of Marty. He looked in every direction until he saw Marty lying in a ditch beside the road. He ran to his side and gasped as he thought Marty was dead. Gingerly he rolled Marty over to find him still alive.

"Marty, are you all right?" Thomas screamed.

"Yes, I think a bullet grazed my head and I fell into this hole. Thank God that man is a poor shot. He shot at me as I was tying the buck to the horse and shot again as I hit the bottom and rolled. He thought he was finishing me off for insurance. He missed and hit beside me. I just played possum until you came along."

"Damn it!" Thomas cussed. "He stole the horse and the deer. It looks like three men and three horses by all the tracks. I think we can intercept them or get mighty close if we go back through the woods the way we came. Are you good to travel, Marty?"

"Hell yeah, let's go!" And off they ran through the woods at break-neck speed without care for the limbs and saw-briers that grabbed their clothes and skin.

The three renegades were in high spirits as they moved eastward. They were quite proud of their gain. They were malcontents that had been discharged from the Confederate Army for general purposes. They cared not the least about the man they just shot. What was he to them? Nothing!

Annie, Evangeline and Elizabeth were busy with the fire and be-ginning supper for the others. They chose a location to camp for the night that had a creek and some graze for the livestock. Sammie and Tommie Houston were picketing the horses and mules and the one cow so they could graze but not wander off. The boys Lawrence and Curtis were playing with the piglets and Enoch's young pup while the girls Mary and Melissa were helping Enoch set up his cooking gear. Forrest Todd followed Matthew and John down the creek a short distance to a deeper hole in hopes of catching some fish.

Sammie was walking back to the fire when three men on horseback came into camp leading Thomas' horse loaded down with a large buck.

"Now ain't this a purty sight! Three fine womenfolk preparing dinner for us. Ain't that sweet, fellers?" said the leader of the renegades.

"What foul wind brings this trash into our camp, pray tell?" Elizabeth barked back.

"You just watch who you are calling trash, woman! If I want any-thing out of you, I'll beat it out of you!"

"Mister, we can share our meal with you if that pleases you; how-ever, your tone will lead you to very little hospitality and possibly down a very short and dark road. Do you understand me?" Enoch boldly advised.

"I don't know who you think you are you, old blind darkie, but I'll put a bullet between your eyes if I hear another peep out of you. Do you understand me, boy?" the man asked as he pulled his pistol and pointed it at Enoch. There was a long pause while everyone stood still waiting for a reaction.

"Luther, go get us three of them horses and saddle 'em up. We are going to move out with these here womenfolk." The leader commanded.

Luther got down from his horse and proceeded to walk away in the direction of the grazing horses, not aware Tommie Houston was hiding behind the horses. Neither did they know that Thomas and Marty had walked up behind them at the edge of the tree line from the road. Marty had contacted Tommie by hand signals that they had used when in battle and even as children playing games. They would make their move and attack at the same time and with ferocity.

Marty directed Thomas to follow his lead and attack the men upon his command. Marty dropped his hand and Tommie ran out from between the horses with the loudest Rebel yell that he could muster as did Marty and Thomas running at the other two men.

Tommie caught the renegade unawares and sunk his knife deep in his throat with his first jab and retrieved the blade and sunk it up to the hilt in the man's gut for his final thrust, and twisted hard.

Enoch pulled the pistol he carried behind his back, tucked in beneath his shirt and held in place by his belt. Quickly he pointed the gun and pulled the trigger and the smart-mouth outlaw blinked once and fell dead from his horse with a bullet between his eyes.

Thomas and Marty pulled the third and final member of the gang off the horse and onto the ground before he could react. His throat was cut and scalp halfway lifted before Marty was calmed by Thomas.

"You did good! He's dead; don't want to scare the kids," Thomas assured Marty.

Matthew, John and Forrest reacted immediately, running back up the creek, scared out of their wits when they heard the Rebel yell and gunfire. By the time they reached the clearing, the fight was over and the gun smoke was beginning to clear.

"What in the hell happened here?" John yelled.

"Don't stand there; give us a hand with these bodies!" Thomas barked. "Do you want to give these kids nightmares?"

Matthew grabbed the boot-end of one man and Thomas the head and shoulders, while John assisted Marty with the removal of the other. Forrest gave Tommie help removing the third corpse across the road where Thomas directed them to just throw the bodies off the deep ravine where they would be absorbed by the honeysuckle and bramble below.

When they returned to camp Matthew requested an accounting of events.

"First, I would like some of those spirits Enoch claims he keeps just for cooking purposes," Thomas requested as he spoke in Enoch's direction.

"I think you are correct my young friend; those spirits have many purposes," Enoch smiled as he dug out a jug of corn whiskey.

"You see, it was like this," Thomas began as he sat against Annie's wagon wheel with legs crossed and drinking whiskey from a tin cup. "Marty had just shot that buck lying over there and was going to trail it. He was on the horse and I was not too far behind when shots rang out, pistol shots, and he did not have a pistol. When I reached him I thought he was dead, but they just grazed his head. We ran through the woods in hopes of cutting them off before they reached the camp with my horse and our deer. That's when we saw they were already here and had a gun pointed at Enoch. Martin, I mean Marty, alerted Tommie to go on his signal and we came a-running with the loudest Rebel yell we could muster. Tommie got one, Enoch shot the other one in the head and Marty and I got the last one. Marty would have had a scalp for his lodge pole if I hadn't stopped him."

"I heard how they were talking to the women and I thought about my mother and it just made me mad. I'm sorry about the scalp but I'd done some Injun' fightin' in my lifetime and it just came back to me," Marty explained.

"That's understandable," Matt commented. "But I want to know how you became so efficient with a gun Enoch. Have you killed many men in your lifetime?"

"No Matthew, I have not killed any men thus far, until today that is! When I bought the pecan orchard the damn crows would just sit in my trees, eating my pecans and laughing at me. So I bought this pistol and many shells and would sit on my porch and shoot at them until I got good and they got dead," Enoch smiled. "It wasn't a difficult shot to make. He wasn't five feet from me and he threatened to shoot me between the eyes; so, there you go, I had it to do! Don't you agree?"

"There was no doubt he was going to kill you Enoch," Evangeline interjected, "but, I was afraid he was going to kill Elizabeth first for calling him *white-trash*."

"Now, now, Evangeline, I just called him trash. I knew he was dangerous because I recognized Thomas' horse and felt he probably had to kill Thomas and Marty to get it." Elizabeth professed, "You can't give ground to a thief or murderer. They only understand strength. Isn't that correct Enoch?"

"From my experience, I have found that to be correct, Elizabeth. Now, can we get back to our dinner preparation," Enoch redirected the focus.

"Sammie and I will skin that deer and bring it to you, Enoch. It looks like I won't have to ride double with Thomas again and we won't have to walk all the way back to Texas either since we now have a horse apiece. We also have us a little money from the pockets of those renegades. We better check those saddlebags a little later on," Marty commented as he and Sammie dragged the buck to the nearest tree to skin.

"Those horses are fine looking horseflesh and I don't doubt they are stolen. Since they were wearing tattered Confederate uniforms just like you boys, I would suggest that we, meaning Thomas, John and myself, pitch in some of our extras and have you dressed more casually," Matthew advised. "You might as well burn what you are wearing or throw it in the gulley with those renegades. I will draw up papers for those horses giving you ownership by proxy due to the circumstances and notarize them as an officer of the law. I would not want to see you men hanged as horse thieves."

"I am not sure I understand all the words you just used, but it makes sense to me," Forrest commented. "Who is an officer of the law?"

"The three of us are!" Matthew declared, pointing at Thomas and John. "Just let it suffice that our identities need not surface at any time unless we desire it, understood?"

"Whatever you say is good with me," Forrest said with hands held out in front of him.

The buck was prepared per Enoch's instructions. Nothing would go to waste. They had an excellent dinner; fresh onions and gravy accompanied the venison, along with cooked dry beans which were soaking during the trip. They even shared two peach pies made with some of the peaches Mary had brought from home.

"I wish we had some cornbread to go with them beans," Thomas shared.

"Well, If you would go out and grow some corn, harvest it and grind it up in meal we could have some cornbread," John suggested.

"We can get us some meal when we get to Jackson, I guess," Thomas mused.

"We will be eating pretty good when we get to Jackson and down the Mississippi to New Orleans. Once we get to New Orleans you may have to take up running along the levee behind some mule to keep the weight off I reckon. It is going to be an experience for an old country boy like you Thomas. I know you will have some of the best meals you've ever eaten once we arrive in the Crescent City," John commented.

"Yes, I look forward to the experience myself," explained Enoch. "I have always wanted to know just how they prepare their food. I have always heard the white folks that travelled to New Orleans rave about the great food they have down there. I have also heard about how steamy the weather is down there. They say it is below sea level there."

"Now, how can that be? Do the people have gills to breath? I know they have a lot of French peoples there, but I just don't understand how they live under the sea," Thomas wondered.

Matthew looked at Thomas and over to John and made the suggestion that they drop Thomas off somewhere along the way as they travel down river. "He might just drown in New Orleans!"

"I will watch over him, maybe put a muzzle on him, but I believe he will be fine if we keep him out of card games and barroom fights,'" John commented.

The conversation was light and the women enjoyed the peaceful night under the stars and the crackling of the fire between them. The men smoked their pipes and shared tobacco with the Texans for their corncob pipes. The children had fallen asleep. Lawrence and Melissa were in the wagon while Mary and Curtis slept on the ground beneath the wagon.

The evening was winding down and the crickets were singing to their sweethearts a courting melody. Everyone sat around the fire watching the embers rise into the night sky as the hardwood burned and the pieces of log fell back into the glowing red coals. Their stomachs were full and they were deep in thought about the day's events and what tomorrow had in store for them.

John and Evangeline were the first to notice the faint glow over the children. It wasn't a new moon. The night was more on the dark side. Others began to notice as it grew stronger. It wasn't a bright light at first, but it illuminated the children as if to set them apart as they slept under the wagon. Even Enoch could feel the presence of something otherworldly about them. They were not frightened, but concerned and curious about the origin of the unexpected occurrence. It lasted but a short while, but it seemed a lot longer.

After the light had disappeared everyone looked around and sat in silence until Elizabeth spoke up, "Did y'all see what I just saw?"

"Yes we did," Matt replied, "but what was it?"

"Enoch spoke, "I could feel the presence of someone else in our campsite; I think we had ourselves a spiritual visitor!"

Evangeline looked at John, "I could see some people but did not hear what they were saying, could you John?"

Everyone swung their eyes from her to John and waited to hear what he had to say.

There was a long pause before John spoke. "Yeah, I heard them and I saw them too!"

"Well, what was it?" Elizabeth asked.

"I am not sure how to explain it. There were two people, but, then there were three. I believe there was a man and a woman and they were in the presence of someone else. I can't really explain it all right now. I'll have to ponder on it some. Let me think for a minute." He sat and gathered his thoughts.

"Alright, I think I saw the children's parents, Mary and Curtis' mother and father. They were pleased with the condition of their children, maybe even delighted. The larger presence, wearing a flowing robe, spoke to them about their contribution. He said that Mary would grow up to be a strong woman and loving mother. Curtis would go on to serve his fellow man and be respected by his peers. It was more than the parents could ask for; it was confirmation of success in their role as protectors. He told them that they were His children first, and would always be safe because His Spirit is with them."

"It was very odd," John spoke, "I felt His Spirit speak to me also. He said that we should not worry. He is with us always."

"It is truly odd," Annie spoke up, "but I have never really felt like a religious person, you know like all of those white folks that would beat us and tell us to put our trust in God and He would give us salvation. My mammy used to pray long and hard for the Lord's protection and deliverance, but I still wasn't sure how I felt about all of that."

Annie got up and walked to the fire where she poured herself another cup of coffee. "But, after seeing that light around those children, I can say I felt His presence too. It may sound odd, but he spoke to me also! He told me my children would live a better life than we had known. He also touched my heart and gave me a peace unlike anything I have ever felt. I still feel Him here in my heart. I knew when y'all walked into the store while I was trying everything I could to get Sammie freed that something special was going to happen. I was so scared when I realized I was praying out loud and hard too; and I am not the praying type. You is a blessing sent from heaven and I know He was listening to my prayers. I don't know what else to call it, but a blessing for certain!"

"Many odd things have happened since John walked into my camp in his long underwear looking like death. I prayed for help, knowing that I was about to be given an especially difficult assignment. I would not have thought it at first, but now I do believe he was the answer to my prayers." Matthew shared his conviction with the others around the fire.

"My auntie always said God works in mysterious ways!" Evangeline spoke up. "I was comforted by the spirit too. He told me to continue in my pursuit to find my mother; she would be waiting for me in New Orleans. He said I was to be calm and trust In Him and He would direct my path. I know who that man was, he was *Jesus*! There is no doubt in my mind but it was Him. He touched my heart and I feel a calm feeling like I ain't ever felt before!"

"Well, our mission isn't complete by any stretch of the imagination and I am a tired man. I suggest we let the fire burn down and do like these little ones and go to sleep," John directed them, knowing they were all very tired after an eventful day.

"Well it looks like Thomas has already beaten us to it!" Marty laughed and slapped his leg.

They all started laughing when they looked over to Thomas who had fallen asleep with his arms behind his head and his mouth wide open. It would disturb him deeply to realize he had slept through such an event as everyone had just experienced; however, he was often playing catch-up on many occasions.

The next morning was a beautiful event with the children rising early to swim and bathe in the nearby creek before they were again launched on their journey to somewhere they were yet to be told. The men and women broke camp after washing off the grime and memories

of the previous day's violent encounter. Each was anxious to get underway and find what life's new adventures had in store for them. It would
be something entirely different for each one.

They passed through a town that had been calling itself Kosciusko,
but was formerly referred to by its Indian name of Red Bud Springs.
They came upon a celebration of sorts on the lands of what was once
a plantation. People were preparing a celebratory feast on the grounds
under some oak trees of an old primitive church.

An older black man, bent over somewhat in his posture from obvious years of toil, approached them and offered greetings.

"Good morning folks! How are your travels? Would you like to
water your livestock and rest for a moment?"

The people in the group of travelers where just beginning to focus
on the large black man hanging from a stout limb. He looked to be
dead, definitely so; however, no one in the gathering seemed alarmed
as he swayed in the gentle breeze of spring.

"Mister," Matthew asked with a suspicious tone, "is there a problem
here that we might offer some help?"

"Oh no, this is a time of celebration! We have remedied a problem
that has plagued us for years. Get down, and set a spell while your
livestock drinks from the sweet water of the artesian well, and I will
explain what you don't understand."

They did as he suggested while Annie brought the children over
to play with the other children close to their mothers who prepared a
feast from a slaughtered hog.

"My name is Cletus, and like these other people you see here, we
were once slaves on this here plantation before Mr. Lincoln seen fit to
set us free. The master loaded up all of his family and prized possessions
and ran off before the Yankees came. He was most mad about leaving so
much behind, but we all just stayed back when he left. Now we heared
the master bought himself a new place somewhere out in east Texas
and the government man said we can have this abandoned plantation
if we file on it; so we did just that!"

"His mean overseer, Wallace, ran off with him, but after the war was over he decided to come back and pretend like he was our friend and we would not remember his bad deeds. He chased down some of our people with dogs and killed them and left them to rot in the swamp. He cut off one man's tongue for stealin' a taste of blueberry pie. Another time he destroyed a man's foot for runnin' away; smashed it with a sledge hammer on the anvil. He beat others with his whip and left them on the tree for flies and ants to pick at before he let us take them down. There are so many stories about the evil he brought down upon his own people."

"Then just yesterday he came riding in here on that beautiful white horse and proclaimed he was gonna pick out a pickaninny and take her with him, and told us there was nothing we could do about it! That's when we rose up and pulled him off that beautiful horse and proceeded to beat him. We stopped before he was dead because that was too good a way for him to die. So that was when the idea struck us. We bound his hands and feet in wet rawhide strings and stood him up under the old oak tree and tied another wet rawhide braid around his neck and threw it over the limb and tied it off. We watched and sang spirituals as the good Lord's providence tightened the noose ever-so-tightly as the rawhide dried in the hot sun. He cried and pleaded some before the rawhide cut off his wind and lifted him closer to Hell; but we ignored his cries like he ignored ours. That may not make us sound any better than him to you, but we know in God's eyes he would not be please with us if we let a mad dog go off and bite someone else."

"So, you see gentlemen how we have an occasion to celebrate the Lord's vengeance for our suffering," Cletus explained with delight.

"Yes, I do understand your dilemma and your remedy. We thank you for the hospitality but we have a long way to go before we rest. Good day!" was Matthew's farewell as they moved on towards Jackson.

They pushed on and reached the City of Jackson about mid-afternoon. It was a city destroyed by fire, more specifically by the fires set by the victorious Union Army! It looked more like Chimneyville than Jackson since all you could see of town was the standing chimneys and charred wood. The courthouse was not burned and that was where they found Jacob, sitting on the front steps.

"Well hello, old friend, we knew you were close because we have been escorted by your dog, Blue, for the last couple of miles," John shouted.

"I told him to look for three desperados weary from their travels; however, it looks like a small army travels with you. How goes it my friends?" Jacob stepped from his perch to greet his good friends.

"You look well fed Thomas! And you are a radiant as ever, Evangeline! The road has truly brought some color to your faces. I am glad to find all my friends well."

"Let's travel just south of town and we can lay over at the home of my parents and that will be a good time to introduce you to the rest of the crew. I am sure we have stories to share," and Matthew took the lead.

CHAPTER 28

MATTHEW COULD HARDLY CONTAIN HIS excitement. It had been years since he had been home. He did not realize just how much he missed his family until he saw his younger brother loading a wagon with seed and implements destined for the field. They traveled at a slow canter along the tree lined fence looking south towards a modest farm house, not exactly sure what to expect next.

Matthew had no problem distinguishing his brother, even from a distance. His brother, Benjamin Jeremiah O'Brien, was a full measure of a man. He was tall and broad like a man meant for hard work. His peers, especially the boys, thought him slow of mind because he was quiet and soft spoken; however, when he did speak it had more impact than the other children. Some would call him *gentle Ben* as he began to shoot-up in size. Others called him *idiot Ben*, but only one to his face. And he quickly learned the error of his ways. Ben was well-read. He liked the classics. His parents had collected many great books over the years for their modest library.

His parents, being teachers by trade, were quick to notice at an early age that Ben's intellect was far greater than his social skills. They allowed for that because his brother, Matthew, and sister, Angelina, were so chatty that he hardly had time to get in a word edgewise.

The Confederate militia once sent out three men to forcible recruit Benjamin for service. He returned with the soldiers on their horses, tied belly down. He said, "I told you I am not interested in that war, so leave me alone!"

Matthew bolted at the sight of the house and his brother in the yard. The others laid back to allow for the natural emotions of the re-union to take place. He brought his horse to a sliding halt, just feet from

Benjamin, and leaped from his saddle. "Benjamin Jeremiah O'Brien, haven't you grown into a force to reckon with!" exclaimed Matthew as he thrust his hand out to greet his brother.

"Well, somebody had to hang back and work the land while you were defending us. You look like you could use some meat on your bones, little brother," Benjamin commented.

"I may be smaller than you, but don't forget I am your older brother and pulled you from more than one hornet's nest in my day," Matthew laughed as he slapped his brother's beefy arm.

"Y'all tie your livestock up at the rail by the barn so they can drink. I will take care of them while you stretch your legs. Mother and father have killed the fatted calf for the return of the prodigal son. They recruited the help of friends. Go inside!"

"How did they know I was coming?" Matt asked.

"It wasn't difficult to know someone was on the road with all the trouble you've been stirring up. My old Cherokee friend, Two-Jacks rode in and said we should be expecting guests in a couple of days. He was traveling on the road and witnessed a minor skirmish between three ex-Confederates and your friends," Ben explained in brief detail.

"Cherokee Jack! Is that rascal still running the hills and hollows at his age?" Jacob chimed in.

"Sir, I wouldn't go slandering his name. He might give a young fellow like you an old fashion comeuppance," Ben smiled.

"You are referring to his father, Jack, who fought the Creek Indians at Horseshoe Bend with Old Hickory, Andrew Jackson. His son is Two-Jacks. He is all of the man his father was, and then some! Now get inside, I've said enough."

Matthew crossed the porch beneath the shade of the pecan trees and opened the screen door. He stepped inside and allowed the door to slam as the taut spring forcibly pulled it shut with a bang. He walked into the kitchen to find his mother and father half-spun around to see what fool had slammed the screendoor.

"Can't a fellow get a hug from his favorite girl?" Matthew declared to his shocked parents.

They both rushed to hug the son they had not seen in more than five years. It was more emotion than either could have imagined. To know their son had survived the war was a blessing that was not afforded everyone. So many people had died from this conflict and not all were directly related to battle.

There was an ocean of bad feelings, coming from every corner of this land. There was so much bad blood that even neighbors would be at war with each other for a hundred years or better in the South, maybe even West and North, for that matter. Many families had been separated by a great and insurmountable philosophical divide and would never speak again. This was more than a war. It was a breakdown of society and a reshuffling of moral foundations.

Matthew's mother cried so hard with tears of joy that she almost collapsed and fell to the floor. Matthew caught her and placed her in a chair in the dining room. His father finally got his voice.

"Son, you left us as a boy and returned a young man. We saw you last on a train stop in Jackson as you traveled south to New Orleans in June of 1859. Now you return to us all grownup. I must say you are a strong and handsome fellow. I want to know all about you and your plans," stated his father with pride.

"Well, Dad, there is much to tell and some which I cannot divulge. These are still difficult times and I fear the assassination of Mr. Lincoln will only bring down harsher punishment on the South than it would have had under his guidance. There are some travelers that I want you to meet. Why don't you two step out onto the porch for some introductions! Here, Mom, take my arm and I'll steady you a bit."

They stepped outside onto the porch and Matthew's mom sat down in her rocker. Everyone was stretching their legs after a long ride.

"I will not protest the killing of the fatted calf this time because you brought a host of ladies with you," Ben offered.

Matthew stepped forward and proceeded to conduct the introductions.

"Mom and Dad and my brother Benjamin, let me introduce you

to this cast of characters as briefly as possible. These two gentlemen, using great flexibility with that word, are Thomas and John. They are ex-confederate soldiers that have been recruited to work for the U.S. Government and assist me on our first mission. That is information that I wish not be circulated beyond this family."

"Jacob here is an emissary of the Cherokee Nation to Washington D.C. He is also a Federal Marshal that has chosen to keep his identity concealed, for reasons he cannot divulge either."

"This young lady is Evangeline. She is from Virginia and has requested to travel with us to New Orleans to search for her mother which she has not seen or heard from in many years. They were separated when she was only five."

"This lady is Elizabeth Walker from Charleston and she is also traveling to New Orleans for her own reasons. I think she was bored and just wanted to have an adventure of her own. We met her when we returned her brother's personal effects. John and Thomas served with her brother Carson throughout the war."

"This couple here is Annie and Sammie and their children, Lawrence and Melissa. We met them in Alabama and they are traveling through to Texas or wherever they feel led."

"These three former soldiers are Texans, Tommie, Marty and Forrest. They are on their way home and joined this traveling circus."

"These fine young folks are Mary and Curtis. Their father died in the war and we encountered them in Alabama at the event of their mother's passing. Yes, they are orphans! But they are resourceful folk."

"The last, but not the least, is probably the most distinguished of the lot," Matthew had begun when Enoch stepped forward and offered his hand in friendship to Mr. and Mrs. O'Brien.

"I am Enoch at your service. I am able to speak for myself. I have distinguished myself as a fine cook and offer my services while I am your guest. Don't let my lack of sight alarm you because my vision is better than the present company. I had to give directions when we first met to keep these folks from traveling in circles while in Alabama."

"I don't think he is blind!" Thomas volunteered. I've seen him shoot a gun and he is a better shot than most soldiers I've known."

"And I know for a fact you can out eat a horse! Does that make you a horse?" Enoch chuckled.

They all laughed and each stepped forward to meet Matthew's family. These were pleasant times indeed for a family to gather together and celebrate reunion while so many yet mourned.

Elizabeth stepped away from the group and walked over to a strange plow-like contraption with a metal seat atop of it. "What kind of thing …?"

Benjamin walked over to his new fangled plow and placed his hand on the metal seat.

"I have been contemplating this idea for quite some time. I can pull it behind two or maybe four horses. I think it will greatly aid farmers in this new day."

"I acquired some abandoned lands and have an idea to establish a small farming community. I have four sections of land, 2560 acres to be exact, and I want to resettle about fifty families, colored and white, with a general store and a schoolhouse on the premises. The schoolhouse will double as a church. The Freedmen's Bureau has offered what assistance they can to help resettle freedmen and white refugees. There will be a great deal of resistance from the planter's society and the disenfranchised that resent the former slave making any sort of progress in his new status. I have recruited several known and trusted colleagues to assist me in this endeavor. I was able to set aside money for this project by buying and selling horses and mules to the Confederate and Union armies throughout the war. I discovered folks trying to leave town before the Yankees took over were anxious to sell many of their horses and mules at bargain prices. I used the money I had been saving since I was big enough to hire out. I became a fairly good horse trader."

"I am impressed with your new plow and your plan," Elizabeth genuinely commented. "My father is in the business of buying and selling farming implements, grains, tack and other things people generally need to operate a farm. I think he would truly be interested in your new plow. Have you thought about building more of them to sell?"

"Of course I have. If it works as well as I hope, I will look for a partner to manufacture them on a bigger scale and someone to show them around to potential buyers," Ben suggested with a new sense of pride as someone noticed his business acumen.

"My father has many contacts with manufacturers and distributors that could help you reach markets up North as well as down South if you are interested."

"Well," Ben replied with a bit of humility, "we don't want to get the plow before the horse as the expression goes, do we? First, I want to be certain of its operation, and work out all of the bugs before I commit to showing it off."

"Little brother, you have grown into quite the man, physically and mentally, since I last saw you," Matt extolled. "I am very impressed with your development; not that I ever doubted you in any way. Mother always said you were the brightest of her children and I must agree. That reminds me, where is my little sister, Angelina?"

Mr. O'Brien spoke up, "She and her *husband*, William, live in Vicksburg and operate a mercantile store there. She desperately wants to see you. You had better see her before you leave this time!"

"My name is Betsy," Mrs. O'Brien offered. "You women folks, girls included, follow me into the house and you can clean that road dust off. Ben, fetch some soap and towels, take the men folk down to the creek so they can get enough dirt off of them to come inside!"

It was a great time of reunion. The weary travelers rested up and soaked in the sweet southern hospitality before the day of feast was assembled. Friends of the family and people Matthew held dear were invited over. They gathered under the trees where the shade and a cool spring-time breeze comforted all. They kept the numbers of folks invited to a bare minimum. It was in everyone's best interest not to draw attention because people knew Matthew remained loyal to the Union Army and did not take kindly to that. The last thing he wanted was to bring undue wrath to his family.

There were so many raw feelings and they were not about to declare to the community that they were staunch abolitionists, even though the war was over and the slaves were set free. It was best not to create animosity amongst the people they would have to live with for many years to come. They would never be able to publicly celebrate the victory they so truly desired. They were the real minority.

The folks were captivated by the telling of the capture and administering of justice to the killers by Jacob. He told them about the one that got away but was later dealt with in the railroad yard.

Matt, John and Thomas were just as absorbed with his telling of events as were the children and other guests. It became evident that Jacob's life was no less dangerous or less exciting than the events that surrounded his friends.

Matthew followed by relaying the events that unfolded in Charleston and beyond after Jacob parted ways to visit the Cherokees in North Carolina. His story, along with corroboration by John and Thomas, was no less fantastic than Jacob's. Matt's family was spellbound as were the others.

Mr. O'Brien could only imagine what his son's life consisted of working directly with the Heads of State. He was somewhat aware of his role in the war as an aide to the President and liaison to the top military leaders. It was not known in the community of his status with the U.S. Government. Matt knew it could put his family in danger if information about his position leaked out to Confederate sympathizers. The Confederacy itself could have used his family to gain leverage against him.

Matthew's parents were unaware that he had been in the area of Jackson and Vicksburg on different occasions delivering sensitive communications to Grant. It was Matt's influence with the President and General Grant that allowed a more favorable surrender for Vicksburg after the prolonged seize. He had played many different roles employing different disguises while crossing enemy lines.

Matthew did share with them some of the experiences he had while serving the President and his Generals. There were many he could not share. He shared his favorable opinion of Grant and told them about the days before the surrender. It was with great emotion that he relayed the events leading up to the receipt of the letter of surrender from General Lee. The atmosphere was so thick in the house provided for the meeting of the Generals that he could hardly breathe. General Robert E. Lee conducted himself as a complete gentleman regardless of the feeling that he had disappointed the Confederate Army and the South; however, his spirit must have felt the relief that not another soul would perish under his watch. Just knowing the power that these two men had over life and death for thousands of young men which they committed to battle was enough to rattle a person's nerves while standing in their presence.

The Union soldiers wanted to cheer as Lee left the meeting on his horse, Traveler, but Grant did not allow it. They saluted the fallen leader who once was considered the absolute military genius of this war. The Union Army even extended their respects to the confederate soldiers leaving the formal surrender as well. Grant made sure the fallen army was provided with rations to squelch the howling of their stomachs.

Several more days passed and Matthew felt time was starting to slip away and his mission had become his primary focus once again. The guests of the O'Brien family were enjoying a moment in their lives that they would always hold dear. Enoch had become a celebrity of sorts with his culinary skills; he always dazzled people with his personality and talents, wherever he went.

Matthew's traveling companions were getting to know him better through his family. He was really a unique individual in his own right.

Even a surprise birthday cake was presented to Evangeline. It was Thomas' and Elizabeth's idea. She was overcome with emotion because she had never had a birthday cake. It was something her half sister Sarah would get, but not her, being the illegitimate child by the same father.

Thomas said he had never had a birthday cake either, but didn't mind whose birthday it was because he liked cake so much! He said he has never eaten so well in his life until he met Matthew.

Several developments worthy of note occurred during their visit. Annie and Sammie and their children would become residents of Benjamin's planned community. They offered to pay for the plot they had decided to build on, but Benjamin explained it wasn't for sale. They got a deed to the plot, but there was a large portion of the land held communally for all of the residents to work together for the welfare and general gain of the community. Annie said she would contribute to the establishment of the store with some of their funds, which was acceptable to Ben. She convinced her husband, Sammie, that this was a good place to set down roots.

Another major development was that Benjamin decided to tag along to New Orleans with his older brother so he could make some purchases for his new settlement. He felt it was his time to step away from his home and find out just who he really was. The war was over and it was safe for him to leave his parents alone, finally.

One truly special development involved the two orphans, Mary and Curtis. The Sorensons, a childless couple in their mid-thirties offered to adopt the children if they were comfortable with such an arrangement. They were. It was an opportunity to stay together with a very loving and generous couple with a stable home and working farm. Mary and Curtis both felt it would please their mother tremendously to know they were safe and loved. Curtis cried for the first time since his mother's passing just knowing he had found a home where he and his sister would be safe. They also had to agree to take the jersey cow and her calf.

The three Texans had decided time had come for them to push on. They thanked everyone for all the help they received. Marty said they were doubtful about ever getting home before they met Matthew, Thomas and John. Now they had horses, clothes and money, not to mention hope for their safe return to Texas to find what remained of their beloved, war-torn state.

Mr. O'Brien would not allow the boys to depart before he conducted a prayer for their safety. He asked the Lord to guide and protect them, not only on their journey home but throughout their lives as well.

Matthew spoke with his parents and his brother and explained more fully what his mission was and they understood. His father told him that they would continue to pray for his safety and success, to which Matt was forever grateful.

On the following day, the Texans saddled their horses and provisioned up with a generous supply of food from the O'Briens. They were given coffee, bacon and beans along with biscuits and leftover beef from the feast. They made tracks towards Vicksburg where they would cross the Mississippi into Louisiana on their journey back to Texas. They had become good friends with everyone and were sad to say goodbye. They extended an invitation for any of them to visit if they found themselves out Texas way.

Matthew sat down with the remainder of the group and explained his plan. "Elizabeth, you will be travelling with Benjamin as buyers of farming equipment or whatever he needs for his new venture. You will pose as a couple of intendeds."

"Intended whats?" Elizabeth asked.

"I've noticed how you have been spending time with him, asking a lot of questions about his plans. It would appear you two have something in common and would make a natural fit for potential buyers for things he may need for his new community. You know your father's business well enough to help him avoid any unscrupulous merchants. Ben has never been on such a trip, and it is time for him to find his way. Plus, you can help us as we explore the lay-of-the-land by appearing to be casual buyers. It is a perfect disguise, don't you agree?"

"And, you might want to do a little shopping for china and other household items," Matthew quipped to the puzzlement of Ben and Elizabeth.

"What do you think, little brother? You and I will share a room on the riverboat and Evangeline will stay with Elizabeth. Evangeline will be my escort as we are travel about the city conducting business," Matt explained.

"I believe it will work," Ben commented; "however, I must speak with Carmichael and Stewart about things I want to happen while I am gone. They have to be vigilant and armed because there are those that will get wind of this new project and want to destroy it and everyone associated with it too. I will not have time to linger on this trip for the duration of your mission because I have other things that need my attention."

"I believe we can be convincing enough," Elizabeth concurred.

"Thomas, you and John will frequent the gambling boats, trying not to become the main attraction. Yes, you can play the tables and win some and lose some, but I don't want you to stand out as big-time players. Do you understand me, Thomas?"

"Yeah I understand, but I don't like it," Thomas said with a sulk.

"John, I want you to make contact with family and friends and find out what is happening on the docks and around the French Market now that the war is over. Renew old friendships and tell them you want to hang around for awhile before committing to anything; let them know you need to get your thoughts straight again. See if you can find any returning veterans and listen to conversations everywhere you go to gather information. I am also putting you in charge of Thomas. You need to stay together at all times. Take a room at a boarding house somewhere close in, like the Irish Channel. There are many people in that area that can give you a feel for the pulse of things in the city. We will establish two or three meeting places; maybe, a café, somewhere in the market and maybe a quiet bar somewhere away from the waterfront."

"You think I need a babysitter?" Thomas asked.

"No Thomas, but New Orleans is not like anywhere you have ever been before!" Matthew drew in a deep breath and exhaled slowly. "I don't want either of you to get hurt, and John knows his way around the city and the kind of people you will be dealing with. These are not farmers and woodsmen like the folks you knew down home. They are a vicious and conniving sort from up North, down South or from around the world coming into port and they don't give a damn about nobody or nothing. They would rather cut your throat and drop you in the canal or the river or an alley than look twice at you. When you signed on you agreed to take orders and follow my lead. Did you not?"

"Yes I did, but you have to trust me that I won't screw up!" Thomas pleaded.

"I trust you Thomas, but there is no room for error. I will not play games with your lives. This is something I have experience with and I know the consequences for failure are grave. These people are not like soldiers that line up and come straight at you like you saw in battle; they stab you in the back while patting you on the shoulder with the other hand. Do you remember the dead man in the alley and the one in the courtyard back in Charleston? Have you forgotten the bomb that was tossed into the room or the slavers that almost killed you? Those men were undercover and also operatives on the other side that did not see their demise coming. Trust me, you will never see them coming. I want to see each one of us live to talk about this mission. This is just the beginning and we will never live to see another mission if we fail this one. Am I clear?"

"Loud and clear," John replied.

"Jacob, I will trust you to follow your conscience and report anything suspicious. I sent some telegraphs via the military one day this week and reported our plan of action to Secretary McCullough. He knows you and said you will operate on the same basis as us and expect the same compensation. You have many supporters in Washington!"

"Last, but not least, Enoch, we will place you in a room or boarding house that is convenient to a café or restaurant that could use your culinary skills! You may hear about some event or person of interest while you perform your duties," Matthew informed him, having the utmost respect for Enoch and his skills.

"Don't worry about me," Enoch replied, "after folks hear about my food I will have a room in any hotel in town that I wish to reside. I will be showing Creoles how to cook Creole in just a short while. I may find the place where I can rest for a while and create a legacy for myself. I may even find myself a lady and settle down. Now what do you think about that?"

"I don't doubt you for a minute, Mr. Enoch!" John agreed.

"Now, back up for a minute!" Evangeline spoke up. "Don't I have a say about this? What am I suppose to be doing while everyone plays a part in this mission, except me?"

"Well, I thought your intended purpose on this trip was to search for your mother. I never knew you came along for any other reason than that," Matthew insinuated.

"Well yes, those are my intentions, but, seeing how everybody else has a part to play, why can't I help out too? I will be looking for my mother but I will have time on my hands and could be another set of ears and eyes for you. It would not be too farfetched for you to have a light skin companion in New Orleans. I understand the French and Spanish and Negro has been mixing in that city for generations and it is not too much out of the ordinary for me to escort a white man; you know, like a mistress or something! And us darkies are nearly invisible, or so people think, because they say things around us that they think we don't hear or understand."

"I must agree that sounds like a fine plan." Matthew looked skyward, laughed and turned to look at her. "Evangeline, you never cease to amaze me! Tomorrow morning let's get dressed for travel and leave out after breakfast. Evangeline, Benjamin, Elizabeth and I will take a carriage to Vicksburg and catch the riverboat from there. Benjamin will have one of his men take us there and our horses and mules will be pastured and cared for here at the farm. Jacob you may want to leave your packhorse here also."

"I will leave Stonewall here and ride the packhorse. Her name is Forgotten, and she is an excellent mount. Remind me to tell that story to you sometime. I'm not sure if old Blue is coming along. I think he has found a girl friend here on the farm," Jacob laughed with his friends.

"John, you and Thomas will take your horses and maintain a safe distance between us. I want to appear as though we are separate parties once we enter Vicksburg. I will make the arrangements and Jacob will communicate to you the how and where. Am I clear?" Matt asked to be certain they understood.

"Yes sir," Thomas replied.

Enoch decided to ride his mare, Trouble, and take his cooking utensils on his pack mule. He would sell the mule when they boarded the riverboat and ship his utensils on to New Orleans. He made a gift of his new puppy, Shadow, to Mary and Curtis. Lawrence and Melissa were somewhat jealous, but they already had the two piglets that Thomas had given them as pets.

The night air was on the cool side and the men sat on the porch enjoying a refreshing smoke with their pipes while the women talked and watched the stars in the night sky. The children played chase with Benjamin's dogs beneath the trees by the light of the moon.

Matthew excused himself for a walk on the old home place. It seemed like ages since he had a nice relaxing stroll on familiar ground. He remembered walking down the same path when he was troubled as a young man. Walking helped him sort things out in his mind. He remembered the smell of the pines and the wind that howled through the trees on stormy nights. It was a kind of music to him. It felt like another lifetime, but in reality it had only been a few years.

He had grown into a man overnight just as thousands of other boys like him. Childhood got passed over for a great many that jumped straight into manhood while others never reached that stage, due to the war. His thoughts ran rapidly through the years. Many people had come and gone from his life.

He would never forget the Washington years, nor would he ever forget the impression Mr. Lincoln made on his thoughts and his persona. Matthew was aware that he had been exposed to many great thinkers of his time, and that very few people would ever have an opportunity like his. Now was the time for him to grasp what he had been given and walk boldly into the future.

Walking through the fields of his childhood made him long for the youthful innocence he once knew. He wondered if he could ever return to such a place as this and be content after having experienced so much of the world beyond.

Where did his allegiances lie? What part of him did he lose when

he chose to stand with the Union? Why did he make that choice? Was
it Lincoln's power of persuasion or purely his reasoning that it was the
right thing to do? Time flew by so quickly and so many lives were lost
or changed over the past five years. Things would never be the same
from here on.

Attitudes would not change overnight; some would never change
and accept the new road ahead. His mission was to help the people
he loved accept the changing times. Just like his brother, Benjamin,
he had to break new ground for new ideas. He had to help weed-out
the old notions of how things used to be so the next generation could
prosper and move forward. His road ahead would not be an easy one,
but it must be traveled.

Matthew was not one to abandon his calling. Mr. Lincoln had
once told him that he was called to lead his people home. He had not
forgotten! Yes, he believed it was possible for him to return and help
the people of the State of Mississippi find their way through the trials
and tribulations ahead.

Matthew returned after a long and energizing walk. He surprised
the children playing hide-and-seek in the yard. They were enjoying being children for a change. He walked up when Enoch was telling how
he used a natural herb to get back at his mean master. He put something in his food that kept him running to the outhouse for twenty-four
hours straight. He was suspected, but never formally accused. Everyone
laughed. It was good to see there was still a sense of humor in spite of
all the troubles that they had encountered thus far on their journey.

"Alright folks, it is time for sleep." Matthew scanned the group,
"Ben, have you squared away your plans with your men and Annie's
family?"

"Certainly, I took care of my business well before you went for your
night stroll with the owls," Ben confirmed. "Now, I must ask; how have
you provisioned up for this trip, o' taskmaster?"

"Well, little brother," Matt replied with a grin, "we travel light
and improvise. We might acquire some refinements for the ladies in
Vicksburg, if there are any to be had; otherwise, we will acquire what

we need in New Orleans. We will cease to operate like a haphazard group of soldiers returning home and living off the land. We will assume our new roles quickly to satisfy curious observers. Therefore, I must reiterate we will travel lightly and gather as we go!"

The group broke up and made their ways to their prearranged sleeping quarters. Some slept inside and some outside. Matthew's mother and father waited to speak to him alone.

"Son," his father said, "we don't want to tell you how to conduct yourself, but we have prayed for your safety for years. We have prayed every night for you and will continue to do likewise. Now Benjamin is going with you and we are concerned for both of you. We know he is a man, and what a man he is! But, that doesn't stop us from worrying. You do understand, don't you?"

"Yes, I understand your concern," Matt said with the most reassuring voice possible. "You have been wonderful to allow me the opportunity to grow into a man in the midst of this chaotic time in our nation's history. I more than understand how you feel. Mr. Lincoln trained me well and groomed me for the eventuality that I would be in charge of leading men in a different sort of battle after the war. Now I have the responsibility of protecting my fellow agents and delving into the underworld to eradicate men with evil plans and intentions. I will not risk the health and wellbeing of Benjamin, nor will I risk the two young ladies in my care either. You can trust the young man you so willingly allowed to leave home has grown into a man of extraordinary caution and resolve."

"You are correct," his mother reassured him of their confidence in him. "We have been naïve about the life you have known since leaving home. It was safer for us not knowing what you did and how you did it. We trust you and have confidence in your judgment; however, you must realize how small our world is and how we have struggled to avoid all of the dangers in it. We have seen the best in men and the worse. Death and dying has not escaped our little corner of the world either. Now that we know you have survived the war, we don't want to lose you to the peace."

Matthew grabbed his mother by her shoulders and pulled her to him. As he hugged her, he explained, "Mom, the peace will be just as dangerous as the war! But, I do understand. Trust me just a little longer, and I will send Benjamin home shortly. If nature works its magic, he may be bringing home your first daughter-in-law! Don't let on, but I do think something is in the air."

The parents were elated to think that Ben may have found his equal. They had thought that he would be just as content to spend his life alone, roaming the woodlands with his strange assortment of friends and allies. They were more than elated with this development. Matt had successfully transferred their thoughts from imminent danger to joy.

"Enough said, now go to bed and dream of things to come." He ushered his parents to bed as he walked into the bedroom to collapse from the weight of mental exhaustion. He was the center hub of this wheel with many spokes.

CHAPTER 29

THE FRAGRANCE OF HONEYSUCKLE AND gardenia lofted through the humid morning air. There was a great deal of activity surrounding the departure of the travelers and the endeavors of Ben's crew to move forward with the planting and building phase of the new community. White men worked together with the former slaves and Indians in the building of homes and the planting of crops. Corn and cotton had already been planted. Sugar cane for molasses and peas of various varieties were growing strong in the warm Mississippi sun. Plum, pear and apple trees were also being set to go in predetermined locations. Nothing was left to chance. Individual families were responsible for the planting of their own smaller vegetable gardens.

There would be opposition from many parties to such an endeavor that would have people of different races living and working alongside each other in the same community; however, poorer Whites and Blacks had been living next to each other for years and working the same fields. In many ways this was a class struggle. Those that had wealth wanted to keep things as they were. Poor white families were not something that concerned them. The poor farmer was good enough to fight their battles but not welcomed in their circle of friends.

After breakfast everyone gathered beneath the trees to say their goodbyes. The carriage was hitched and the others had saddled their horses for the trip. By leaving in the early morning they should reach Vicksburg by evening, unless an unforeseen event caused delay. Anything could happen, nothing could be ruled out. Benjamin gave instructions of what he wanted accomplished while he was gone. Everyone said bye to the family of Annie and Sammie and the newly adopted Sorenson children.

Thomas stopped in bewilderment and asked, "Just what is your last name Annie?"

Annie spoke up as was her way to do, "We done told you Thomas. Sammie and I decided to call ourselves the Matthews family. How does that sound to y'all?"

"That sounds fine to me. My last name is Smith," Thomas said, "and I just wanted to know if you were Smiths too, 'cause we could be related! I would hate to know that I was leaving family back here in Jackson and didn't write home to tell the folks."

That brought a roar of laughter to everyone.

"Yes," Enoch replied, "they are related, Thomas, they are the Blacksmiths!"

The laughter continued.

Before the laughter ended a tall, quiet man rode up into the yard on a dapple gray gelding. He sat erect on his horse like a military man, staring ahead. He was very lean and muscular. He had strong facial features indicative of his lineage. He appeared to be a man of honor and integrity. It was Two-Jacks, son of Cherokee Jack, and a friend of Benjamin.

The noble soul spoke before anyone else took the initiative. "The hoot owl and the bear came into my camp at the same time last night. The owl said I must go on a journey to protect a friend and the bear said I must travel by water. He is my spirit guide; therefore, it is forbidden that I cross the path he travels. I watched as he walked around the camp and left the river to my back, which is the way I must go. Benjamin, I am ready, but I must cut my hair and dress like the white man for this journey. What say you?"

"That can be arranged, Jack. We can take care of that when we arrive in Vicksburg," Ben declared. "Are you ready to ride?"

"My horse is under me," Two-Jacks stated, thinking why ask a foolish question.

"I can see that!" Enoch gestured, pointing at the horse.

"I told y'all he wasn't blind!" Thomas shouted.

"Goodbye Mom and Dad! I have to get this circus started before the real clown act begins," Matt waved as the carriage pulled away.

They would travel to Vicksburg to board a riverboat. From there they would travel down the river to New Orleans, their desired destination.

Traveling was easy, and the road was still filled with ex-soldiers going this way and that, to parts unknown. They made their way to Vicksburg by late afternoon.

Jacob had become acquainted with Two-Jacks as they travelled. Two-Jacks remembered him, but pretended not to know him. Later on Jacob inquired about his parents and called them by name.

"They have moved on," was all Two-Jacks had to say, and that was all that was needed for Jacob to understand that they were no longer alive.

Jacob escorted Two-Jacks to a barber where he got a haircut and hot bath. Then he went to the same mercantile store that Matt and Ben's sister, Angelina, owned and operated with her husband, William. After all was said and done Jack was dressed in clothing that allowed him passage in the white man's world. He insisted on clothes loose enough for him to have room to perform when approached with danger. He was still an outdoorsman, but a strangely handsome one at that.

Matthew found a riverboat that could take the crew, horses and all. He had to employ the help of the Union military to secure a place on a safe boat. Many soldiers were returning home and riverboats were apt to be overloaded to the point of dangerous. In April, a steamboat by the name of *Sultana*, took on over twenty-five hundred passengers and was rated for only three hundred and seventy-six. After leaving Vicksburg a boiler exploded just north of Memphis killing over fifteen hundred men and women. That was an unnecessary loss of life due to the greed of the boat's owner.

They were scheduled on a paddle wheeler called *The Natchez Queen*. It was traveling to New Orleans with a stop in Natchez and Baton Rouge for fuel and for passengers to embark and disembark.

Angelina was so excited to see her older brother Matthew that she hardly noticed Benjamin had come along. She introduced her husband Bill and excused herself for a moment to catch up with Matt. She was brought to tears over and over at just the sight of him. She insisted on putting up Matt, Ben and the women for the night. Matt assisted the boys in finding a livery and place to sleep for the night.

Matthew and Benjamin escorted the ladies to Angelina's house while John, Thomas, Enoch, Jacob and Two-Jacks went to a café of Angelina's recommendation for dinner. She was careful to suggest a place that would be suitable for a group that included two Indians and a colored man. Most places would not entertain either as guests; however, this place was an exception. The proprietor of Riverbend Café was a hardy Irishman with a pleasant manner.

"Bobby O'Shea at your service, just call me Mac! What will it be, gentlemen? I've got a roasted kid for dinner, just butchered this morning. That will be goat I'm speaking of; don't want you to get the wrong idea. Times are hard, but not that hard."

"That sounds delicious! Would you have some roasted potatoes and mint jelly to go with that?" Enoch politely inquired.

"I do have roasted potatoes, but I'm plumb out of mint jelly. You must have a sophisticated palate, my friend," Mac suggested.

"Just get the darkie some possum Mac and a slab of mule for the Indian!" yelled a haggardly looking sort of river scum sitting at the far corner of the bar.

Thomas pushed back his chair and stood up quickly with an air of retribution about him. Enoch reached over next to him and firmly grasped his arm and guided him back to his seat.

"I'll handle his sort, Thomas."

"Sir, I use that word just as a figure of speech; however, I can prepare an opossum that will taste so good you would fight your siblings getting out the hog pen to get the first bite," Enoch said as politely as possible.

That comment served the purpose intended for Enoch. The big man shoved his chair back away from the bar hitting another patron seated behind him. He pushed his way between tables to reach the chair occupied by Enoch. With a hard slamming jolt he grabbed Enoch by the shoulders and prepared to snatch him from his chair; however, his momentum was stunted by the presentation of three guns drawn from beneath the table and aimed directly at his head. His eyes quickly adjusted and reached maximum aperture at the sound of the pistols cocking.

"Mister, you have avoided some real punishment today! Your friends have saved your life. You can believe it will be different the next time our paths cross!" said the big, filthy smelling oaf.

"Sir, you are mistaken. My friends saved your life today!" Enoch smoothly and swiftly produced a gun from beneath the table and lodged it firmly under the man's chin. It was placed in just the right place and shoved upward in the fleshy part to hold him in suspension for the desired time needed to finish his comment.

"The next time our paths should cross, you will be a dead man. I suggest you learn to use better judgment before you shoot off your mouth!" With that said, the man removed his hands from Enoch's shoulder and stomped on his way out the door.

The men re-holstered their guns and enjoyed the dinner as served. Conversation was light and carried on as if there was no incident. They thanked the proprietor, paying him for the meal as they left. There was a sigh of relief from the patrons as the group of men made their way out onto the street.

After sleeping the night in a boarding house, they dressed and went downstairs for an early breakfast. They were surprised to find Enoch coming from the kitchen with an apron wrapped around his waist. He had prepared breakfast with the owner's wife and she was delightfully pleased for his help.

"I am glad you gentlemen decided to join the living! Don't waste time, eat-up, the horses have been fed and are waiting to travel." That brought a smile to Two-Jacks who sat at the end of the table with his arms crossed and a cup of coffee before him.

The waitress brought out their breakfast. She sat platters filled with eggs, biscuits, ham and white gravy before the hungry men. As they dined, the cook walked over and announced that there was another killin' in town during the night.

"This one wasn't a shootin', but a knifin'. It looked like someone may have killed the man who was responsible for the other killin's recently. Whoever killed the man used a knife; however, he left the man's own knife jabbed directly under the big man's chin like he was making a statement, or telling us he got our killa'. He punished that man severely before he finished him off. I overheard the sheriff tell a Union officer that this man was rumored to have left the Riverbend Café earlier after getting drunk and trying to start a fight with a Colored man," I think the sheriff was right; it just saved us a heap of trouble!"

Jacob, Thomas and John looked at each other and looked over at Two-Jacks who sat with his arms crossed and still smiling.

Enoch walked into the room and removed his apron, giving it to the lady of the house. "We thank you kind madam for your hospitality. I must keep my skills fresh." Enoch cleared his throat,

"Are you men coming or do you plan to homestead here in town?"

With a rustle of chairs, and a thank you to the proprietors, they fell in line. They followed Enoch and Two-Jacks to the livery to mount up for their trip. It was a beautiful day and the sky was blue as they left the stable on their horses. They had to sidestep their horses to avoid the workers standing outside the backdoor of the livery. They were struggling to get the big man in the wagon for transport to the undertaker.

"I think that is a path you may never cross again, Enoch!" Thomas mentioned in passing.

"I can only assume there is someone nearby to which you are referring," Thomas.

"I assume you saw those men struggling to get that large dead body into that wagon!"

"Thomas, I am blind! I can't see everything that is going on around me," Enoch grimaced as he shook his head. "You worry me sometimes. I do have use of my other senses. I can smell, taste, hear and touch. I can also reason, which is a sense not everyone possesses."

"Well, if I have to spell it out, that man that tried to start trouble done went and got himself killed. They found him this morning."

"I heard that in the kitchen, Thomas."

"Alrighty then, that there was the body and it was cut up pretty darn badly. He won't be causing nobody any more trouble, especially you!" Thomas declared passionately.

"I figured there was blood, somewhere, by the way the horses shied away from it and that also means a body close by," Enoch mentioned.

"That proves you can see!"

"No, just using my sense of reasoning. You will understand one day, Thomas."

They made their way down the bluffs to the river. The boat Matthew had reserved was loading with cargo, livestock and passengers. It was once a fancy sternwheeler that catered to high rollers, gamblers and business men, traveling from New Orleans to Natchez and beyond. It was commandeered into service for the Union army's needs, whatever they were.

There was an argument next to the boarding plank. The owner of a shanty boat was threatening to shoot the riverboat pilot if he did not reimburse him for the loss of his shanty boat. Apparently, the riverboat pilot had a bad habit of swamping smaller boats on the river. It was the second such boat that he had destroyed. The pilot of the riverboat refused, until the man produced a sharp bowie knife and placed it between the legs, firmly against his crotch. Only then did he produce a wad of cash and give it to the man with the knife.

Soldiers from both armies were heading south. There was a young couple dressed in their Sunday go-to-meeting clothes waving at people on the bluffs. Two black men stood at the front of the boat to announce the ever-changing conditions as they moved down river. They had to be on watch for sandbars and snags that could impede travel or worse, sink the boat.

Matthew, Evangeline, Benjamin and Elizabeth stood on the upper deck of *The Natchez Queen* looking back at the city. They could see the caves dug in the side of the hill for soldiers and citizens alike to hide from the shelling of the Union Army during the siege of Vicksburg.

Matthew could vividly remember his intervention and conversations with Union leaders that allowed the Confederate soldiers to walk away from Vicksburg, and the Union Army to take over without the continued loss of life. He understood the Southern attitudes and was able to convey them to General Grant. Ulysses S. Grant was most gracious to allow the events to take place, without retribution.

As they were boarding the gang plank with their horses, John turned to see a dog quickly making his way down the hillside to the river. "Look Jacob, who does that look like to you?"

"I'll be damned if that isn't the spittin' image of my old dog Blue," Jacob declared. It became clearer that *it was* Blue as he got closer.

"Come on, Blue!"

The dog stopped as he got to the gangplank and looked around him several times before he lunged ahead and ran up to stand next to Jacob.

"Now, that dog has more sense than us; he thinks before getting on the boat," Two-Jacks surmised.

Jacob turned around and petted his dog and rubbed his ears. "Either you got tired of that old girl dog or just wanted to go with me to see what adventure lies in store for us down river."

Enoch laughed and looked out towards the city, "It's hard for a bachelor to settle down all at once. This old dog likes the taste of the road more than lying around under the porch with the same old tired view for the rest of his life. I think there is several in this group that will turn out just like him! I just ain't saying who."

After stabling their horses and storing their tack, they searched out a place on deck for themselves and their gear. They found a suitable place to bed down. Space was at a premium. The men did not have a problem sleeping under the stars; considering they had spent the last four years outdoors fighting the war, mosquitoes and other critters. In some cases, the outdoors suited them better than the inside of doors.

Matthew had been able to secure two berths for him and Benjamin, and the ladies. They were near midship on the starboard side of the second level. This was extremely convenient because the portion of the deck that the men chose to store their gear and sleep was adjacent to them. Matthew could open the porthole window and speak directly to them. This could not have been more perfectly planned for tactical reasons or security purposes.

The preparation of food was undertaken by a handful of men with rudimentary skills at best. Enoch was quick to find his way into the galley and offer his services. The staff consisted of five men, one white and four black. The white man, Elmo Snodgrass, considered himself top-dog and head chef of the galley. It was obvious he knew more about a bottle of rye whiskey than a bottle of fine seasoning. He spent most of his time in the kitchen stumbling around in a drunken rage, blabbering about the poor quality of help that was available to him. Enoch was better qualified to judge the kitchen staff. He made a quick assessment of the situation at hand. He told one of the kitchen helpers to go down to the bartender and fetch four bottles of whiskey and pronto. He delivered the whiskey to Enoch and asked no questions.

Enoch handed the bottles of rye to Mr. Snodgrass, stating it was a gift from the ship's Captain. He recommended some time off for his good work and not to worry about the kitchen. He would take full responsibility for everything. That was absolutely the best thing to happen on the whole trip. Enoch turned the galley, with the help of the remaining four men, into a floating restaurant. He trained the men in the culinary arts and *The Natchez Queen* became a destination for fine dining in its subsequent trips up and down the mighty Mississippi. Mr. Snodgrass was relieved of his duties and told to leave the boat once they arrived in Natchez. The Captain found him drunk and passed out in his cabin after an absence of four days, the entire distance from Vicksburg to Natchez, a result of Enoch's and the bartender's hospitality. It took him three days to sober up, and he never quite understood what had happened. The only thing he remembered was the Captain had furnished him a bottle of the ship's finest rye whiskey.

Enoch was paid handsomely for his services and for the conversion of the galley into a kitchen of fine dining. One of the kitchen workers was promoted to head chef and three new kitchen workers and four waiters were hired. In addition, Enoch gathered some valuable information that he passed on to Matthew.

Matthew and Evangeline got to know the boat's captain, Captain Barnaby Tuttle, and the Union officer on board as they floated ever nearer to their destination. He gathered information when it was deemed pertinent to their mission.

Evangeline spoke with the ex-slaves that worked as roustabouts and general laborers on the boat. It was her primary intention to gather information that might lead to the discovery of her mother's location. There was very little information to be had; however, they kept their ears and eyes open for whatever they might find. She did, however, receive a tidbit of information that could assist her. One of the laborers told her that former slaves had taken to posting their requests to locate separated loved ones on memo boards around New Orleans' market place. She became more anxious the closer she got to New Orleans.

Enoch had learned from his kitchen workers that people with large amounts of cash had been aboard their boat very recently and expected more to follow. They concluded that they were from the North by their dress, manners and accents, primarily New York and Boston. It was also concluded that the men had traveled from St. Louis by river. They most likely took the train from back East to St. Louis. Catfish, Enoch's best kitchen worker, pointed out a well dressed business man that traveled alone and always kept his satchel in his possession, even when dining.

John made contact with a former acquaintance from New Orleans. His name was Francois, an old flatboater that would ride his freight down river on a flatboat or barge to New Orleans. He would sell his goods at the end of his journey. He also sold the wood from his flatboat because he had no way of getting it back up river; whereupon, he would buy a horse to ride back to Missouri. He finally met a Creole lady in New Orleans that cared for him and married her. She became too demanding and he took a job on the riverboat to get away from her as often as possible. It wasn't a bad thing that he enjoyed traveling more than staying at home.

Francois knew some people that worked the docks back in New Orleans. He said there was a big man from up New York way that had plans of taking over the docks. He brought some big thugs with him that whipped up the place. If you didn't like the way things were run and spoke up about it they might find you floating in the river the next morning; if they found you at all! He said the Union Army was everywhere, but they did not have a handle on the events happening at the riverfront.

He also told him that his father and mother had moved back to New Orleans because things were too rough for them in Mobile. They reopened a fish market in the French Quarter near the river. Business appeared to be good because his father was advertising for help.

It was evening time when the riverboat moored in Natchez. Matthew advised against leaving the boat because the *Under the Hill District* at the landing was notorious for dangerous highwaymen and bandits. That was probably the wrong thing to tell them, because they promptly left the boat with Blue in tow. Matthew dined with his brother and the ladies and enjoyed the company of Enoch. Their evening was most pleasant.

The next morning, just before the gangplank was lifted, Jacob was walking beside the city marshal with John, Thomas and Two-Jacks in tow. They were told not to come back without prior permission.

"You boys were lucky those men you tangled with were wanted men; otherwise, you would have been thrown in jail and charged for damages. Next time I will lock you up and throw away the key," the marshal professed.

Even old Blue looked like he had been in a scrape.

Matthew looked at them and walked around them before he said anything.

It was John that spoke first. "I can vouch for them! They jumped Thomas while he was minding his own business. I will admit Thomas did escalate things when he called the woman a fella, and she did look like a man at that, and an ugly one to boot. It looked like someone beat her with an uglystick. They would have killed Thomas if Two-Jacks and

I hadn't stepped in to help. He was in a bind. Blue tore a hunk out of the big fella's leg when he grabbed Thomas. Then he kicked Blue across the barroom. That's what riled Two-Jacks. That man should not have kicked the dog! He should have left the dog well enough alone. We had things under control when the marshal came through knocking folks on the head with that big old pine noggin-knocker he had. He stopped when he got to Two-Jacks and saw that big old pig-sticker of his. It must have reminded him of Jim Bowie when he used to hang around town. Now I think we need to clean up and have breakfast," John suggested.

"I'm tired too! A little siesta would be fine with me. I mean after we eat! I could not sleep a wink on those hard cots," Thomas suggested.

"What's your side of this, Jacob?" Matt asked.

"Well, I was up in the town proper, having dinner with an old friend of the Nations, and the Mayor, when I heard someone say that a group of travelers from the boat got into it with a known outlaw, Big-Nose Bagsworth. I finished my evening, had a refreshing nap at the home of a lady friend and proceeded to gather our fellow travelers from the local jail. It appeared to me that the offending party was the recipient of the worst of the beating. The marshal is an old acquaintance and he released the boys on my recognizance," Jacob recounted.

"And how was your evening, sir?"

Matthew paused and drew in a deep breath before he spoke. "We had a charming evening with a lovely prepared meal of river catfish, fried okra and black-eyed peas; of course, there was fresh cornbread and churned buttermilk chilled in the cool spring waters. That was a delicious blackberry pie they served."

"I assume you were gathering information," Matt prodded with a searching glance at them.

Thomas spoke, "I'm not sure what all those words mean, but, I can tell you that I will never assume that anybody with a mule-face is a man, purely on face value again."

Over the next week everyone kept an eye out for anything unusual or extraordinary coming from the passengers, soldiers, or even the crewmen on the boat. These were strange times. People were focused on getting somewhere. Union and Confederate soldiers talked with each other like old friends; the old animosity, at least among the soldiers, was fading rapidly. They never really hated each other to begin with. They were just told they had to fight. They didn't know anyone of the other stripe to hate anyway. The young men that survived the war wanted to go home. The ones that had no visible scars had emotional or psychological scars that ran even deeper and were harder to heal.

The view of the river was other worldly some days, with a multitude of creatures that abounded in the marshes and the bald cypress trees: cranes, egrets, herons, eagles, ospreys, hawks, turtles, alligators, muskrats, otters, kingfishers, snakes, possums, raccoons, fish, deer, and mosquitoes by the millions. Other days were boring, monotonous, and downright suffocating with the heat and humidity.

They were constantly on the lookout for snags and floating logs. They had to slow down at some points because the river was too low. Once they sat and waited for a day while another boat dislodged itself from a sandbar before they could pass.

That was the day John saw the ghost ship pass them by. It was loaded with soldiers and sailors traveling upriver to battle. It was a Union gunboat. The men anticipated their tentative mission as they were rocked by the river's current. John heard their conversations as they discussed future plans for their lives after the war. It was the saddest thing that John could ever imagine; the sailors didn't know they were dead. The soldiers had fully anticipated death would find them on the battlefield, not in a watery grave beneath the river.

They passed so slowly that John could see the expressions on their faces. John's friends were standing on the deck watching the beautiful scenery that surrounded them when they became aware that John was experiencing something entirely different. Thomas started to speak when he noticed the tears running down John's face, but Evangeline held up her hand to stymie him. Enoch was also among the group and he started to ask what they were seeing off the boat's side, but he felt Elizabeth's embrace as to alert him that something else was happening. John was next to them, but he was somewhere else at the same time.

It seemed like a long time before anyone spoke, but maybe it wasn't that long. Shortly thereafter, John stepped away from the railing and moved backwards to sit on a bale of cotton. No one asked him about the experience. They knew he would tell them when and if he felt the need to share.

The trip down the river went well; at least they had no more incidents like the one in Natchez. They had one more stop in Baton Rouge to restock fuel and supplies on their way south. One of the galley workers went down to the river's edge to buy catfish. He met with a man from Ascension Parish named Pierre Le Monde Clarence Thibodaux, but folks called him Crawdaddy, because he always had some crawfish to sell. He would say, "Dey's good for fishing, yeah, and if you get hungry you can eat dem too, once dey is boiled."

Crawdaddy sold them a mess of river cat and had a big old loggerhead turtle that he said, "He was most proud of." He haggled with the kitchen help until they agreed on a good price for that turtle. Enoch was in store for a lesson himself on how to prepare and cook that loggerhead. It turned out to be most delicious thing he had tasted in years.

John was delighted to have turtle meat and turtle soup too. It had been years since he tasted a good Creole delicacy like cooked turtle. He wished he had bought some of those crawfish from Thibodaux; now, they would have hit the spot if prepared properly.

The river was a source of food, transportation and an overall good place to live. There were plenty of sociable people to be found. People on the river never went short of things to eat. They traded fish and such for whatever they didn't have. They knew how to eat all of the other wildlife that called the river home. There were many characters that you only knew by their handle, names like Cornbread, Catfish, Baggybritches, and Cottonmouth among dozens of other colorful names. It was often said that many people congregate on the river because it was a place to get lost and people did not inquire about your past. Others just say that trash floats downstream. No matter how you looked at it, the river provided sustenance for all God's creatures, man or beast. People on the river generally looked out for one another.

Matthew talked with John and Thomas through his porthole window one morning before breakfast. He had some good ideas about how they would approach their mission in New Orleans. He felt it vital to get close to the only connection that they had uncovered thus far along their journey south. He had a business card of Horace T. Marchant, Attorney of Law that was found on the body of the man murdered in Charleston. He believed this lawyer most likely would have a residence either in the Garden District or on St. Charles Avenue near the Jefferson Plantation. If he lived on St. Charles Avenue, then he wanted Thomas and John to find a boarding house nearby. Many people were renting out rooms to make ends meet. The war had left many widows in need.

Matt informed Thomas he could take many strolls by his house with his cane to offset the effects of his war injury.

"But, I have no leg injury!" Thomas protested.

"Yes, you will! We will fix you up with a strap around your leg and knee that will make you walk with a limp. That way you will have a reason for strolling around the neighborhood. You will be observant of the people that come and go from the Marchant residence. You may be able to slip around the house within earshot and gather valuable information while eavesdropping," Matt suggested. "Do you understand me now?"

"Yeah, I understand what you mean now you put it like that. I wasn't sure if you planned on breaking my leg or something to make me look crippled for real."

"No, you have to start thinking like a Pinkerton so you can be the most effective agent possible. I have faith in your abilities to think like an agent. You can have a future that will take you a long way in this business; however, you must take what I tell you very seriously because it can have deadly consequences. You will be placing yourself in just as much danger as you once did on the battlefield."

"There were spies operating behind enemy lines, both North and South, who gave their lives for the cause. Many were hung or shot when they were captured and it was discovered what they had done. The same results could happen with our mission. These people will not hesitate to cut your throat, stab you in the back, snap your neck, or put a bullet in your head."

"The effectiveness of your disguise will depend on your commitment. You will have to become an actor just like one on stage whose heart is one-hundred percent invested in his craft. You will have to play a role, and you cannot forget your part at any time. To protect your true identity, you may have to use an alias. I would suggest something like Tommie Jones."

"I think I am beginning to understand a little bit better what you want. Trust me I will become the best agent possible or die trying," Thomas said with a serious grin.

"You are exactly right! But I don't want you to die trying. You will develop your character as you go and become as convincing as possible, with everyone you come in contact with. You can be as simple or complex as you need be. I would suggest keeping it simple like a returning veteran that has just spent four years in hell and wants to return to the simple life again."

"John, I have been thinking, in addition to meandering around the docks and the market, I believe we should make it a regular occasion to travel uptown on the St. Charles streetcar line. You know what I mean, just riding the horse drawn streetcar along St. Charles Avenue, watching and listening to people as they go about their everyday affairs. The same will apply to Thomas. We will do what is effective for achieving our goals. John, you may want to think of another last name as well. Do you understand?" Matt asked.

"Yes, I understand fully. I also grasp the seriousness of our mission. I believe we will get a better handle on things as quickly as we get our feet back on solid ground. I am ready and anxious to start what we have set out to do. I look forward to having a successful end to report to our superiors back in Washington and then we can move on to bigger and better things," John replied. "I will use the name John Wells with people I don't know. I had an uncle once named John Wells, on my mother's side. He is deceased, but I liked him very much."

Thomas spoke up, "I will be Thomas Jones when I get to New Orleans. That almost rhymes with Smith. Don't you think?"

———◦◦◦———

Matthew had recently taken to keeping a journal of his thoughts after being inspired by the writings of the late Carson Walker. He found Carson's thoughts to be deeply insightful.

2 June, 1865

Today Confederate General Edmund Kirby Smith, commander of Confederate forces west of the Mississippi, is set to sign the necessary papers to formally end hostilities between troops under his command and the Union army. Finally, the healing can begin. It will not only take years, but it may be decades or even lifetimes. It will take generations to overcome all of the ill will that exists between North and South, brother and brother, black and white. President Lincoln often spoke of the rift that would only grow deeper and wider once the war was over. He knew it would take a force of spiritual proportions to set healing in motion. Vision of the soul is in short supply. Hate is more readily available to the masses. Hate is not limited to one group of people or another. Hate is pervasive. It is like a plague or better yet, a wildfire, whose flames are stoked by the driving winds of pride, anger, fear and greed.

This journey has enlightened me to the vast potential of my companions. They surpass the normal collection of characters found in any group. John has been given spiritual gifts that I've never known others to have. He can see beyond where our eyes take us, or our spirit can reach. I am not sure why he has this gift or where we can benefit, but I am glad he does. Thomas is a mystery at times; however, he is that which is good in all of us. He serves mankind with his subtle kindness. Jacob is a bridge for two worlds. He is unique in his skills, experience and understanding of cultures. He is another blessing dropped into this mission. Evangeline will bring a sense of renewal and hope if her mission to find her family and sustain that continuity of love to the next generation is successful.

I have been given a great commission by Mr. Lincoln to help build a bridge for our nation's revival. My contribution may be only a small part. It will take the effort of many people over many lifetimes. Each generation will have to take up the flag and bear it through many battles. I just pray that God will help us complete this mission and stop the evil forces determined to tear this nation apart forever. God help us all!

CHAPTER 30

FRANCES WAS WORKING IN HER LITTLE GARDEN behind the cottage. She was becoming more adept as a gardener since Marcus moved back to the plantation and started farming his own patch of land. She kept a bed of flowers in the front, along the edge of the porch. There were tomatoes, okra, squash, peppers and beets in her vegetable garden in the rear of the house.

She was pecking away at the pesky weeds with her hoe when a young man stopped outside her picket fence. Albert Goldsmith had begun to ride around town in a rented buggy to look at possible houses to purchase in his spare time. He wanted a home for his family when they arrived.

Frances was bent over at the waist pulling weeds when she heard a voice. She turned her head to see the billowy clouds against the bright blue sky above the live oak canopy. She was able to make out a man's head in an upside down carriage. She quickly bolted upright and had to catch herself as she had lost her balance because all of her blood had rushed to her head.

"Hello, my name is Albert and I was told that the house on the corner may be for sale. Can you tell me about the house or anything about the previous owner?"

Frances brushed the front of her skirt to knock the dirt from her apron.

"I do not know the owners, but I think they have a cotton plantation upriver and used this house when they were conducting business in town. I can only recall several times during the last few years having seen someone come or go from the house. I'm sorry I can't be of more help to you sir!"

"That is fine. I am looking for a safe place for my family when they arrive from Philadelphia. Is this a safe neighborhood?"

"I do believe so. I don't recall any mischief in the immediate neighborhood. There are strange men along the river always, but they rarely get up this far."

"Do you work here?" Albert asked.

"Yes I do, but I am the owner too. I had several servants that went off on their own after they were set free," Frances replied.

"Ma'am I hope I haven't offended you in any way. I was not implying anything in particular!" Albert struggled to regain his composure.

"No, there was no offense taken. You see I was property also, along with the two servants. I was given this property when my services where no longer required. Some white folks may not find it desirable to live so close to a *person of color*. I am very light-skin, but I have some ancestors of African descent that migrated north from the Caribbean. It is alright, we live in a new day, and there will be uncomfortable moments."

"Ma'am, I do not find fault with someone of a different extraction. I was raised in the North, in Philadelphia, Pennsylvania and I was reared with neighbors of many different ethnicities. I mean I have grown up in a multiracial neighborhood with people from all over the earth. People may find it hard to accept us Northerners moving down here. I am afraid there will be a great deal of resentment for folks coming south to stay. And I am also Jewish and we are always shunned wherever we settle," Albert explained.

"I never met any Jews, mister, but I was taught about them from the Bible. Jesus was a Jew, wasn't he?"

"Yes, he was a Jew also; however, he was persecuted by his own kind, the Jews!"

"If you don't think your wife would mind me as a neighbor, you should get down and take a look inside. The doors are not locked, and the house is large enough to raise your children. That is, if you have any!"

Albert smiled with a look of pride, "Yes, I have two lovely girls, Sally and Rebecca. I think I will walk around the place, inside and out. It has adequate shade to cool the house. I see they have a cistern for water ... that's good!"

Frances stood her hoe up against a plum tree next to the street. She sat down in an Adirondack chair Marcus had made for them. He was inspired by one he saw for sale in a store along Magazine Street while strolling one day. He also made another one to sit on the opposite side of the cast iron bench beneath the old magnolia tree.

She sat there enjoying the song birds and the squirrels as they played in the trees above. She remembered how Liza Jane, Marcus and herself would sit and talk under the trees in the evening and dream about how things would be when they were free to come and go and make decisions on their own. It was much easier when someone took care of them and decisions were made for them; however, that was not the way things were meant to be. Folks needed to be free to make their own decisions, whether they were right or wrong, she thought.

This was a good feeling for her to live as a free woman, even if she was still a woman of color. Already, the Good Lord had blessed her with a home and the discovery of her own mother. She had almost given up on ever finding her mother, but she still wanted to reunite with her daughter and brother one day. She felt anything was possible. Maybe she would find a man and have a family again, just maybe!

After a short time of inspection Albert came back around her house to the back yard. He placed his hands on the picket fence and said, "With a little fixing up she would make an excellent home. We just may be neighbors very soon. Thank you for your time and I look forward to seeing you again. Good day!"

Frances smiled and waved goodbye as he moved away in a canter with his carriage. *It is a fine house and I would make a fine neighbor. Yes I would,* she thought.

Albert rode gaily back to his hotel. He was beginning to see a brighter future now that he had moved away from the fraudulent venture that lured him to New Orleans. His letter surely had reached his old college classmates back in Philadelphia by now. They would have been disappointed that their counterfeiting scheme did not pan out;

however, they placed all of the risk on Albert and none on themselves. There was nothing they could do to harm him, unless one of them foolishly came south to make a stink. He doubted the backbone in any one of them to even think of such a thing.

He was delighted with the house. It would be perfect for his wife, Martha. She loved to plant flowers in her window boxes back home and would love the room to plant them in her new yard. The children would have a safe place to play. Martha often said how tired she got of being cold. This would be the opposite of cold for certain. There was room for his parents to stay if they decided to visit. He thanked his lucky stars that things were looking up for him. It was starting to look very bleak before he took the job for Mr. Godchaux. Albert was not a believing man as his father, who was a faithful and practicing Jew, but it did look like his attempt at prayer had paid off for him. Albert was certainly thankful for whatever it was that changed his course, because without that change, he would most certainly have died by now.

Good fortune had turned its back on Etienne. He was beyond consolation these days. His wife was fed up with his moody ways. She suggested something was wrong with him because he was not his normal self. He denied anything being out of whack with him; however, he could not lie to himself because he knew his source of irritation. He knew it was Frances, or the lack thereof, that was driving him to act irrationally.

What could he do? She was a free woman and he was a married man. It was a dilemma which he had no answer for. He thought of her day and night. She was a very complex woman unlike his wife, the mother of his children. Frances made him laugh and there was always the element of mystery about her. He may have purchased her as a slave and made her his mistress, but he never really owned her.

She was free from him, even if it was only by the spirit that set her free. He knew he could never own her heart and soul. What a farce this was to think any man could own another individual! Frances was unencumbered and free to do as her heart pleased. Etienne feared he would never have her to hold in his arms again; and he would never know her gentle touch or the depth of her love, not to mention the uplifting charm with which she conducted herself.

He was going down a bad road. He stayed in his home in the Faubourg Marigny neighborhood of New Orleans for greater lengths of time, leaving his wife and children back on the plantation, unattended. She was getting more and more fed up with his antics and threatened to move back to her father's home in Baton Rouge with the children if he didn't change his ways.

He gambled a great deal more than he should. He subdivided a piece of property across Lake Pontchartrain and sold lots to cover his debts at one point. His father was deeded the property by the King of France for his heralded service to the Crown. He left it to his son when he died. This was not something he could be proud of and played hell explaining his intent to his wife. Etienne passed it off as a noble gesture to help populate the area across the lake with people of good intentions. His friends wanted to own a piece of property away from the city for reasons of health. He only wanted to oblige them.

He knew he had to arrive at a solution for his dilemma quickly or lose everything he had. Without property and status his wife would leave him, taking his children with her. His attraction to Frances was tearing him apart. Was this love or merely infatuation? He did not have the faintest idea. It almost felt like a *curse* had been placed on him.

All the while, John Carver was building his Southern empire along the docks, and in the banking circles. He had even acquired a recently auctioned plantation property. He didn't want any minor players to chisel out a piece of the pie. He was not a man to share his wealth or his women. He wanted absolute control of everything that could affect his holdings.

It was late on a Thursday when the riverboat, *Natchez Queen*, arrived in New Orleans. It was a sultry afternoon; steam was rising from the streets after a passing thunderstorm dumped huge amounts of water everywhere. Men were jumping mud holes to avoid getting their feet wet; women hiked their dresses to avoid the same calamity.

Dockhands caught the lines thrown from the ship as the captain maneuvered safely to the docks. Matthew thanked the captain for his hospitality before they left to go ashore. The men retrieved their mounts and went ashore with them.

There was a swell of activity as always was the case when a ship docks; there are passengers looking for friends and family after a long voyage and businessmen that wish to be assured their goods have arrived safely as desired. Whatever the occasion may be, each new arrival brings news, good and bad.

Matt and Evangeline stood with Ben and Elizabeth patiently while the others walked their horses nervously across the gangplank, followed by Blue.

"Now that we are all together, I want to lay out the game plan I have in mind. It has changed a little somewhat since we last talked. Nothing is set in stone until I make contact with the other operatives and find out what they know. Ben and I will rent an apartment at the Lower Pontalba Building and rent one next door for Elizabeth and Evangeline. It may be a short term arrangement. It will suffice that we project ourselves as successful businessmen, not just folks who traveled to New Orleans for purposes of shopping."

"John, I want you to locate a boarding house for yourself, Thomas, Jacob, Enoch and Two-Jacks.

"It is three o'clock and I suggest we meet here at seven. I will take us out to eat for the first time. That building to your right is where we will be staying," Matthew pointed. "Let's meet at that little coffee shop at the end of the French Market there. Go find you a place and get washed up! See you later."

"Wait, before you check in I want to introduce you to someone I haven't seen in years," John spoke to the group.

"Follow me!"

John led his friends down the riverfront a short ways to the marketplace. There was a beautiful display of tomatoes, carrots, cucumbers, corn, squash, okra watermelons, cantaloupes, peppers and flowers too. They passed the butchers and the sellers of garden produce until they arrived at the fishmonger. They tied their horses at the hitching post and followed John over to the man and woman selling fish, oysters and shrimp.

He pulled his hat lower so that his eyes were not visible under the brim of his hat.

He walked over to the man and said, "Mista, I hear dat a man can become a much better lover if he was to eat a heap of dem raw oysters. What say you?"

"I say that they can't make a man what he ain't! Are you buying or just talking to hear yourself talk, mister?"

"Well, all that I have to say is that you are still full of it, *father!*" John lifted his hat so that his father could see his son's eyes.

Mr. Bernard ran around the counter and grabbed his son by the edges of his shirt with both hands and placed him in a bear hug. His mother was unaware of what had just happened. She looked on in surprise until John's hat fell off his head, and she recognized him. Then she ran around the corner of the display filled with fish and shrimp to grab hold of her son. They hugged for at least a full minute until his mother stopped to dry the tears from her eyes.

"Well son, I told your mother that you were too doggone hard-headed to die in that war. It sure looks like you took a bullet to the head after all. Who are your friends, John?"

This is Thomas, Matthew, Evangeline, Jacob, Two-Jacks, Ben, Elizabeth and Enoch. I will explain how we met later on, but we just got into town on a riverboat and need to find a place to stay. Do you know where four or five men can find a room and a place to board our horses, Father?" John asked.

"Yes John, the widow has a house about a mile up Magazine Street. She has been fretting about the empty house and lack of boarders. She should be able to take all of you, but I must warn you that her cooking isn't attracting diners, if you know what I mean."

"We moved into my mother's old house. She is frail but she is still full of spunk. Don't let her fool you! Widow Cassimere's house is directly behind ours. She has a stable for your livestock as well."

"When will we see you again, son?" his mother asked with a tearful smile.

"Mom, I will be over for one of your famous home cooked meals on Sunday. I warn you to have plenty to eat because I will bring the entire group; provided, you are still in the feeding business."

"You just do that! I will feed your friends and they will eat like there is no tomorrow. And furthermore, don't get sassy with me young man. I still know how to use a switch," she said, with a smile and a grin.

With another hug of his mother and a firm handshake from his father, John and his friends parted ways. Matt took the four of them to the Lower Pontalba Building. Enoch, leading his mule loaded with pots and pans followed the others. He started to sell the mule he named Trouble before they left Vicksburg, but decided otherwise. He came to the realization that he could not tote all of his kitchenware around New Orleans by himself.

Matt found there were reservations already made for him and his friends. The one apartment at the Lower Pontalba was sufficient for the four of them. It was luxurious for the day at anyone's standards, certainly theirs. He was given a note that was sealed with wax as they were issued room keys and given directions to their accommodations.

Once they got their things secured, Elizabeth and Evangeline chose which room was theirs. Matt settled down in a chair seated behind a writing desk. He opened the letter and read the contents to himself quietly.

It read:

M. O'Brien,

Please stop by for a visit as soon as you arrive, apartment # 256.

A. Friend

Matt spoke to Ben and told him he would return shortly. He could hear the giggling of the girls bouncing on the bed as he closed the door behind him.

The room numbers were clearly posted on the doors of each unit.

He didn't have to go far because their room was # 260. Matt knocked on the door and waited. Just seconds later the door was opened and a man with an alarmed look and a pistol in his right hand spoke, "May I help you, sir?"

"Matthew O'Brien per your request; and you are?"

"Step inside, Mr. O'Brien. I wasn't sure when you would arrive and I must be very cautious. My name is Henry Huggins, but for professional reasons I go by Henry Stone. The Eagle as we call him in Washington holds you in high regards. I think you have gathered some information and evidence per my last communication with Washington."

Matthew looked around at his surroundings; it was obvious that this place was well-used or better put, lived-in. "I understand you are working with another agent."

"Step into the room, Madelyn, ah Miss Cooper!" Henry suggested. From another room stepped a woman that appeared vaguely familiar to Matthew.

With a smile and recognition of Matthew, she came forward, and offered her hand. "We meet again Mr. O'Brien. I never knew you were the officer that Mr. Lincoln often spoke of. He considered you one of his closest friends and allies in the Capital. It is my pleasure and honor to make your acquaintance, again, sir!"

"It is my pleasure to meet again, Miss Cooper," Matt stated sincerely.

"It is Mrs. Stone for the moment. That is the pretense at least. We share the same apartment, but separate rooms. Strictly professional, you see! That was Secretary McCullough ... I mean the Eagle's suggestion for the cover to be most compelling," Madelyn explained.

"No explanation needed; I completely understand. I am sharing an apartment with two ladies and another man, my brother. I am using them to complete my cover as well. They are in compliance I want you to understand. They are quite trustworthy."

Matthew explained as briefly and completely as possible what they had discovered along with the evidence recovered on their journey.

He explained the death of the Pinkerton the night before he met John at the edge of the battlefield. He also spoke of the death of Anthony Martini in Charleston.

Henry also knew Martini and thought him to be the consummate soldier and professional that he was. He was shaken somewhat by that piece of information.

Matthew produced the business card of Horace T. Marchant that was found on the body of a man murdered in Charleston. He believed the same man that killed Martini killed this man. He also mentioned the file that was recovered in Martini's room just before the explosion.

Henry explained that they had not been in New Orleans very long before Matthew; however, he felt that he had received a major piece of information purely by accident while dining at a local restaurant. He recognized one of the men as John Carver, a known strong man and underworld boss from the East Coast. The other man was a business-man or maybe a lawyer. He thought he heard him called Marchant, but wasn't certain.

"They were discussing a business proposition. Carver began to explain how he would gain control of the docks, gambling, banking and real estate with his plan before the other man suggested they have further discussions at his home uptown. I believe he noticed my atten-tion was aroused at their conversation. I finished my dining and left as soon as possible. They don't know me but I don't want someone to find me floating in the river because I was careless!" Henry explained with a genuine look of fear in his expression. "The Snake is well known for his retribution."

Matt became more alert, "What did you just call him?"

"I said The Snake is widely known for his ability and willingness to settle his grudges with his adversaries swiftly and violently. He is a bad man! Why does that surprise you?" Henry inquired.

"How do you know this man and that folks call him The Snake?" Matt asked.

"If you must know, I was born Henry Huggins of East Tennessee, up in the mountains. My mother was struck and killed by a stray bullet intended for my father; that incident started a feud that eventually took my father's life as well. My sister and I were sent to live with a wealthy uncle, my mother's brother, in New York. I grew up there and came to know the Bowery District very well, and the characters that circulated there. John Carver, The Snake, was one of the toughest ones of all the bad men that operated there. Why does that grab your attention so?"

"It is odd because a dying man in a livery stable in Charleston last uttered these words: "The cane and the snake." We chased a man after the killing of Anthony Martini and there we found another dying man. What more can you tell me about him?" Matt inquired.

"Well, he is a power hungry mongrel. He goes through more people than the cavalry does horses. He is brutal! He buries his mistakes. He carries a hideout gun and uses a cane with a sword concealed inside; however, I would imagine the killer in Charleston was probably one of his operatives. He may have used a similar cane; that has become a signature piece for his closest lieutenants. He doesn't tie-up loose ends himself. It is his plan to insulate himself from exposure of detection for obvious reasons." Henry paused, "He is utterly ruthless and will be hard to take down. His absence will only suffice to slow his operation down until someone stronger steps in to take up the slack."

Matthew walked over to the window to view the riverboats docked along the river's edge and took a long moment to soak in the activity down below.

"We will have to proceed with utmost caution to avoid any loss of life. We will need a well thought-out plan to catch our prey. If he has the right connections in the judicial system, which I imagine a man of his stature does, we will probably have to kill him to end his reign. Our first goal of this mission is to identify the players in the counterfeiting espionage; secondly, to hand them over to the legal system. However, this kind of operation will not be easy to stop and it will surely continue if we can't cut it off at the roots. Are you sworn in as a part of the Treasury Department or just operatives working in conjunction with the Department?"

"We are still Pinkerton Agents assigned to work under your

direction for this operation," Madelyn offered. "It has been mentioned that if our work is satisfactory and this mission is successful that we may be offered an opportunity to join the Agency. I surely hope so!"

"I will get with you tomorrow or the next day to discuss our plan of operation. I will slide notes under your door as to when we meet. It will specify times only and they will be in code. The place of meeting will be preset. You should spend a great deal of time out and about in the city instead of your room. That will prevent someone from following you if you come and go on an irregular basis. Try not to establish regular patterns for your daily events. Do not leave any notes for me at the desk from now on, and pretend not to know me or any of my operatives either. We do not know who or what may be watching and following us; therefore, we must be casual and vigilant at all times. I will contact you for our next meeting. Have a good day folks!" Matt turned and made his way out the door, closing it behind him.

John led his crew upriver along Magazine Street to the house directly behind his Grandmother Bernard's home. He decided it was best to get everyone settled before visiting his grandmother. The widow's home was a typical two-story house similar to the architecture of the surrounding homes. It had a large wraparound porch shaded by an ancient live oak on its west corner. An old dog raised his head slightly at the guests and laid it back down directly upon inspection; that was until he saw old Blue canter up to the wrought iron gate. He stood up and began to announce who was the big dog around that neighborhood, or at least that yard.

The widow came out on the porch and greeted the men. "Good morning young fellas! Will y'all be needing a place to stay?" she asked.

"Yes ma'am, Mrs. Cassimere, we will need some long-term lodging. My papa, Mr. Bernard, said you would have some rooms available to rent. My name is John Bernard."

"Just call me Miss Ellie, and yes I do have some rooms for rent. It will be two dollars and fifty cents per week, in advance, per person, and another two dollars and fifty cents per week for meals, in advance! That is if'n you plan on eatin'. And, I don't take in coloreds!"

"Well, I'm sorry to take up your time. We have to move on," John stated politely.

"Now, wait just a minute mista, I do have five rooms and one would be empty," Miss Ellie quickly recanted.

Enoch spoke up, "Miss Ellie, my name is Enoch and you can see that I am a cook by the load of cooking utensils on the back of my mule. I will cook all the meals and you will be paying me to stay in that room before the week is over. If you have a table large enough to seat the peoples, I will have them standing in line to eat here before the week passes. We will negotiate my portion of the take at that time. This here is your lucky day. I will train you in the culinary arts so that you will never have a vacant room again. You will never need worry about your future if you let me teach you how and what to cook," Enoch declared with absolute confidence in what he was proclaiming.

"Mister Enoch, I do believe you mean what you say. You speak so highly of your talents that I will take you up on the offer. Come on in, after you take care of your horses. You will be responsible for the care and welfare of your animals and the upkeep of the stables as well. Are we in agreement?" she asked.

They were in agreement. After caring for their horses and Enoch's mule, the men brought their things inside to settle down. They helped Enoch get his cooking utensils inside as well. They cleaned up and changed into fresh clothes for dinner with Matt. John stepped next door to greet his grandmother while the others were relaxing for a wee bit.

Enoch went into the kitchen, which was detached from the main house, with Miss Ellie and inventoried her stock. He made her take down a list of items that he would need. He gave her enough money to purchase the things he suggested because she admitted not having enough funds. He just asked her to have these things before dinner tomorrow and to be sure to purchase the quantities specified. He told her that it would not spoil and to anticipate a large group of men once they smelled the aroma coming from her kitchen.

John knocked on the door of his grandmother's house and stepped right on in without an invitation. His grandmother sat in the parlor looking out the window that went from ceiling to floor, just shy of six inches, top or bottom. She couldn't see who had entered the back door but spoke as John walked into the room from her rear.

"Come on in John, I've been waiting for my little man to come home!" she said.

John walked up to her as she was seated looking out the window in the opposite direction. He leaned down and kissed the white headed lady whose long hair was coiled in a bun on the top of her head. He gently squeezed her frail shoulders. He walked around to face her, reaching down he collected her frail hands in the palms of his hands, and lifting them to his lips, he kissed them long and hard.

"How did you know it was me, Grandma?" John asked politely.

"Your Grandma Isabella told me!"

"But she is no longer with us, Grandma!"

"Yes we laid her to rest, but her spirit is still with us," his grandmother Maudie explained to him. Her voice sounded much younger as she spoke to John.

"She came to visit me a little over a month ago and told me you were hurt but you would be alright. She said you were coming home soon and would be the man, fully grown, and strong enough to embrace the gifts that you had been entrusted with as a child.

"Grandma, I had a vision that told me to come home for I had something to do! What is it that I am supposed to do?" John asked with sincere bewilderment.

"Sit down John! I want to tell you a story that you might understand now, but not before. Do you remember when you where run over by the horse, before you were old enough to attend school?"

"Yes," John proclaimed, "I wasn't yet five years old, I think! What does that have to do with anything?"

"Yes, I think you are correct." Maudie eased herself up from the chair with John's help and walked over to the window and stared out at the azaleas in the flower bed.

"You were very small, but extremely active for a child your age.

You were playing tag with the other boys in the street while the girls were playing inside the fence. A dog started nipping at old man Cain's horse and it proceeded to run with the buggy hitched behind. You were directly in its path and got kicked in the head by the horse's front hoof. A young black fellow came out of nowhere and snatched you from beneath the horse before it could trample you. He brought you inside and laid you on a bed in the front room. He quickly disappeared. We think he was one of Mr. Cain's colored boys. The children were scream-ing and your mother was there to comfort you as your father became hysterical with anger. You never lost consciousness but just laid there in your mother's arms staring at your father in his rage. The doctor arrived and sewed up the wound and applied a bandage. He said it is a miracle that you weren't killed. We looked for the boy that grabbed you so we could thank him; but he was nowhere to be found. He was seen by everyone present, but no one saw him leave."

"Your grandma Isabella was visiting New Orleans when this hap-pened. She sat with you that night as you were listless and struggled with consciousness. You would say things that made no sense to us. I came into your room about 9:00 o'clock that evening and sat with her. We were talking about how frail you looked and we held hands and prayed for your recovery. As we finished our prayer and opened our eyes we say a tall man dressed in white standing at the foot of your bed. He was an angel! He was as tall as the room. His head touched the ceiling. That's how tall he was. He spoke to us. His voice was like music. *He said we were not to worry because your life was in the Lord's hands and He would always walk with you.* Then it came! We heard another voice. It was much grander. It was the *Lord's voice.* He said, *"He will do my will and I will hold him in my bosom forever!"*

"That wasn't all that happened. The angel placed that small Bible on the nightstand and said, let him carry this with him on his journey! Do you still have it with you, my son?" she asked, as she turned and looked at John.

John was slow to speak but remembered her question, "Yes ma'am, I have it with me now. I carry it always, even into battle. I feel lost without it. I read it often and it comforts me like nothing else can. I thought I had lost it after the last battle, but Thomas had it with him when we met up afterwards."

"But that still doesn't answer the question about what I am supposed to do. What does that mean, Grandma?"

"Son, I just don't know the answer to that; however, I do know He counts you worthy and expects you to do His will. The Lord has plans for each of us, but I think He expects something extra from you, *lagniappe*! That is why He has placed His angels close. Don't trouble yourself with the where, why and what for. Just suffice it to say He is with you and expects you to do your utmost in all that you do. Don't ever give up and don't ever do less than your best!"

She walked over to him and leaned down to kiss his forehead. "Just remember this John: He loves you very much and so do I."

"Grandma, I am working for the United States Government on a very important mission. It is a secret mission and I know you won't tell anybody. I met this man on the creek bank as I was recovering from a gunshot wound to the head. He is a Union officer from Jackson, Mississippi and he asked me to join him on this special operation to set the nation on the right path, and help the South recover from the war and its deep wounds. We are traveling with an entourage of people that just came together."

"It wasn't by accident that this group was assembled, John; you were brought together by the divine hand of God for His purposes. This world is not a world of accidental mishaps; it is a world set on a perfect path. If it wasn't so, we would spin out of control into the outer reaches of the universe. The God we serve is a God of order, not chaos. We know very little, He knows everything that has been and will be! You must learn to *trust Him in everything* and not to fear Him. His will is the better will. Trust Him and He will help you to grow in *wisdom and understanding.*"

"I know your friend's name is Matthew. Don't be alarmed I saw you when you sat in the creek and he spoke to you. I had prayed very hard that night before about your wellbeing, and I was comforted in my dreams. The Lord always hears our prayers. Don't ever doubt Him!"

"Grandma, I will be staying at the widow's house next door and will be visiting you often. It is so good to see you again. I was afraid something would happen to me or you and I would not have this opportunity again."

"It is an answered prayer for my eyes to see your smile too. It reminds me of the little boy that would run inside to see his Grandma each time you would visit. It is so nice to have my little man home again! Be careful in the city John; it has a darkness hanging over it since this war began, and it is still present. There is an evil spirit running rampant. Please be careful and pray for *His will* to be done," she said with particular emphasis.

"I will Grandma, peace be with you as well!"

John gathered his friends and they traveled back into the *Vieux Carre,* the French Quarter, to meet up with the others. He found them standing outside the coffee shop, Café du Monde, waiting on them.

Matthew led them to a restaurant he had noticed as they walked down the street. He wanted the others, especially Enoch to taste the local fare. He ordered Creole gumbo as starters and shrimp etouffee over rice. French bread was served alongside the main dish; it was fresh and delicious.

Enoch was particularly quiet about the food, at least until it was complete. He asked to speak to the chef once they had finished dinner and he promptly acknowledged the request.

The chef approached the table dressed with his chef apron and tall white hat drooped over to the side. "I understand you request my audience. Is there a problem with your food?"

"No, it was very appetizing!" Enoch pushed back his chair and stood to face the chef. "My compliments to the Chef, Monsieur ...!"

"It is Monsieur Montleone, Francois! I am pleased you enjoyed your dinner, Mr.?"

"Just call me Enoch. I am also a student of the culinary arts and I would appreciate if you would allow me to visit and take note of your style of preparation. This is my first visit to your fine city and I must admit my skills are rather primitive compared to yours. I would like to understand this French and Creole style of food preparation that I might expand my talents as well. Will you permit my intrusion into your kitchen sometime?" Enoch politely asked.

"Of course, but I am confused. How can you learn when you cannot see, my friend?"

"Monsieur Montleone, I may be blind, but my nose works, my taste buds are fine, my sense of feel is good and I listen well! And most of all I know how to stay out of the way."

"Then it will be permitted; Tuesday is a slower day and you may call me Francois."

"Thank you very much sir. I will be in touch once I have settled in and am able to find my way around town better. Good day and thank you again for your delicious food, Monsieur Francois!"

Matthew paid for the dinner and they strolled outside to a slightly cooler and more agreeable temperature than the daylight hours offered. The night air was refreshing and the stroll was also comforting since they had eaten more than they had realized until they removed themselves from the table.

Matt directed them to be seated and ordered coffee for them at Café du Monde since it was outdoors with a good view of the river. Riverboats lined the river and people strolled casually down the streets as if a war had never occurred.

"How can you think of drinking more coffee after that big meal we just et?" Thomas asked.

"I am surprised that you of all people would protest more food or more coffee!" Matthew looked around and said in a lower voice, "I brought you here to share some information I have and plans for our course of action. If that meets with your approval, Thomas, then we can proceed. You do not have to drink the coffee if you don't want."

"No, I'm sure I can find more room, if I try. Don't get so snappy with me, I was just asking, that's all!" Thomas explained.

"This is a less conspicuous place to meet since we just had dinner.

There will be people watching us in all places and at all times. We are outsiders, which may present a threat to nefarious activities; that means activities that are not on the up-and-up. Here we can see and hear all that is happening around us."

Matthew paused as the waiter delivered the cups of steaming coffee and a plate of beignets compliments of the owner for their pleasure. He wanted to get their reaction to his new offering of the French doughnut pastry smothered in powdered sugar.

"I have made contact with an operative from Washington and he is working with another agent who is female." Matthew lowered his voice and looked around at the diners as he spoke.

"John, you, Thomas and Jacob should remember Madelyn Cooper, the Pinkerton agent we met in Washington. She is posing as the wife to the other agent and they are taking up quarters in the same building where we have rented for the time being. His name is Henry and that is all you need to know about him."

"He spoke to me about what he had learned since he arrived earlier. He was able to discover a vital piece of information. It appears a well known strongman out of New York is setting up a network to accomplish his goals. He plans on taking over control of the docks here in New Orleans. He wants to gain a controlling interest in banking, gambling, shipping, and he wants to facilitate a major land grab along the river with vacant plantations and various properties that can benefit his endeavors."

"This man's name is John Carver! Do not use his name; he is a vicious fiend and he will not hesitate to have you killed. He will have ears everywhere, so it is most important not to ever call his name. He is also called by his nickname, The Snake. Don't speak, Thomas; I know that is part of what the dying man said in Charleston. He also mentioned cane as well. This man uses a cane that either has a sword or knife inside that extends from the bottom. I've seen this type of contraption before. He may have other associates that use the same type of setup."

"It is my belief that the dead man in the livery was working with Anthony Martini and they both were eliminated because they learned too much about the operation. Carver was seen dining here with some-one who could have been Horace T. Marchant. At least, the agent I just met thinks it was. You will also remember that being the name on the business card we took off the dead man in Charleston. It is starting to come together. I will put together an operational plan to use the specific skills of each one of us to effect the downfall of Carver's organization along with the capture and arrest of anyone connected to it. I will estab-lish prearranged meeting places for John and myself to communicate in public. Times and places will constantly change to prevent someone from recognizing what we are doing. I will relay orders and exchange information with him to keep everyone posted."

"I would like for Jacob to find a nicer accommodation to establish himself as a businessman interested in land procurement; this will establish the need for banking connections as well. You have the back-ground and polish to pull this off without creating suspicion."

"John and Thomas, I want you to work together as much as possible for your protection. Thomas may be valuable at the gaming tables on a limited basis, but only with John watching his back and tempering his appetite for glory."

"Two-Jacks may act as backup for the two of you."

Matthew turned to Two-Jacks and said, "I would also like for you to blend in with the local Indian community and learn what you can about the changes that are happening around the city and on the docks. I understand there is a local faction of Indians that come over from the Northshore on the ferryboats to trade and sell their wares. I believe they come from an area called Lacombe. See if anyone is trying to create a big name for themselves, anyone that is from out of town or just wants to muscle in for a larger piece of the action on the docks. Do you understand what I am talking about, Two-Jacks?"

"Yes, Injun may look funny, but ain't dumb. I understand your meaning and will be successful in doing what you want and keeping my scalp at the same time. I will be Thomas' shadow because he will be good fire starter," he said while smiling in Thomas' direction. Everyone knew Two-Jacks was much smarter than he let on. He liked to tease the others.

"Alright, that should be enough for tonight," Matt indicated with the rubbing of his hands. "It has been a long day and a long journey. John, we passed a little place today just north of Decatur Street on Dumaine called The Magnolia Inn. It has a café, meet me there between seven and eight in the morning for breakfast. I will go over our plans in more detail. Have a good evening, folks."

Matthew and his crew went back to the Lower Pontalba apartments to get some rest, while John sent the others back to their boarding house. John wanted to walk around and see how things had changed since he left for the war. He hoped to look up someone he used to know or just bump into some odd characters from his past.

John walked along the river where groups of people: former slaves, Indians, stevedores and returning soldiers sat around fires here and there to shoot the breeze, in other words, to talk about whatever came to mind. There were some lanterns hanging from lamp-poles or ship moorings or carried by someone walking about. In some places the talk was boisterous and laughter in others, some were quiet, but men just seem to seek out a place, any place, to connect with others for whatever reasons. There were many like John that were just finding their way back home to something remotely familiar and wanted badly to reconnect with old ways and old faces they once knew.

John walked up to a particular fire where some older men propped up against a makeshift bench, built from a split log crudely erected with aid of several cypress stumps, and several rested their heads on a log, while others leaned against their elbows in the sand just watching the embers glow and listening to the popping of pine knots sending sparks into the air to ever increasing heights before disappearing in the night sky.

John recognized several men seated around the fire. "Hey there Blandon, who's in charge of furnishing the bottle tonight? Can't an old friend get a swig around here?"

An old fellow roll over to rise to his knees and take a look at the man approaching the center of the firelight. "Hey men, look a here what the cat done drug up! Its little Johnnie Bernard done grow'd up! Little John come on over here and let me have a look-see." Simeon Mossman, more often referred to as Old Mossyhorn, stood up and reached out to offer his hand to John.

"Old Mossyhorn, you must be a hundred and fifty years old, if a day," John spouted.

"Two hundred is more like it, and I can take the likes of you any day, hung-over or not! Hell's bells, I thought the earth done opened up and swallowed you whole, son. Where have you been?" Mossyhorn couldn't stop rocking and moving his arms up and down. He was either terrible excited to see John or just plumb unstable, or maybe both.

"Old Mossy, I've been off fighting Yanks while you've been laying around on this here riverbank tugging on that jug of corn whiskey and talking trash to all the young ladies that happened by. I don't think anything has changed around here since I left."

"Just sit down here and take a load off your feet. Butterbean, hand me that whiskey jug. Here John, take a swig; now you tell me if that ain't some of the best corn squeezins you've ever tasted."

"It so smooth it could gut a river cat from the inside out. Wow, that'll cure what ails you," John quickly passed the bottle down to the next man in line.

"John, you would be surprised how things are changin' around here just since the war's end. Old Captain Wetzel is anchored here right this minute and can't get his freight unloaded. Dem Yankee stevedores done up and drifted south and near about taken over da docks. Dem big brawlers pushing folks around won't let anybody load or unload freight unless they say so. It appears that someone is trying to take over the docks. There is going to be showdown come daylight when the Capt'n sends his boys down the plank to start unloading and dem big bullies step up to stop 'em. I don't know what will happen den!" Old Mossy just shook his head, turned and took a seat back on the ground close to the fire.

"Mossy, you get all of the old hands down here in the morning and

I will bring my friends. We will be loaded for bear! What do you say, can you do that?"

"John, you old son-of-a-fish-peddler, bring 'em on and we will be ready. Hot-diggity-dog, we are gonna have us a shindig or a rat-killin'!" Mossyhorn slapped his leg.

John went back to the boarding house and gathered up his friends. He explained what he was told and what he planned to do about it. His partners were so ready to take part that it was not likely that they got much sleep anticipating the ruckus ahead of them.

About daylight John positioned Thomas and Jacob with their rifles, if it came to that. He placed Jacob on the walkway of a water tank next to the railroad and Thomas on the schooner, Southern Cross, behind the stacks of freight intended for unloading. He strapped on his gun belt with his new revolver cleaned, holstered and ready for action.

Captain Wetzel was a salty old dog and he didn't take well to being told what he could and could not do with his freight. He agreed with John's plan and proceeded to go about his business as usual. The New York roughs were in place when the gangway was let down from the ship's hold and readied for unloading freight. They intended to stop the activity unless they were paid for the work. They didn't care who unloaded as long as they were paid. This was just one way to show they controlled the docks, by taking their cut, and doing it by force. It was blatant intimidation.

Old Mossyhorn came walking down the levee with over twenty dockworkers, hardened and ready for action. The leader of the brutes stepped up and waved over another fifteen men to augment his numbers. From a vantage point safely away from the action, John Carver watched with particular satisfaction as the events of the morning played out.

Fog was thick and still rising off the river as it floated out on the banks like a wood fire blanketing the fields. The brawny men, black and white, went about their duty and began to unload the cargo as the New Yorkers jeered and threatened bodily harm if they came off that boat with cargo in hand. As the stevedores came down the gangway,

the conspirators prepared for battle. They didn't anticipate battle hardened men, but that's what they got. It was hand-to-hand combat and
the locals gave as good as they got. There were knifings on both sides
of the fight, and bricks thrown into the crowd, and heads were busted
by thick hickory clubs whittled out just for the occasion.

Rifle shots rang out from Thomas and Jacob's position. Thomas
shot a man as he rose up from a stack of cotton bales piled high waiting to be loaded onto the boat. He was obviously intending to shoot at
the men coming off the ship. Jacob also shot a man as he stood up in
the coal bin of a freight car. He had climbed up on a load of coal and
aimed his gun down at the men below. He dropped his gun over the
side and toppled over after it.

The crowd fell back with the report of the rifles. One man was
lying on the ground next to the rail with his rifle close by and the other
flopped over backwards on the cotton bales with a flow of crimson
leaking from his chest onto the snowy white cotton.

The biggest brute of them all was standing against a large rum
barrel, bare-chested with his shirt cut to ribbons, several large X marks
cut into his skin, leaking blood down the front of his pants. Across
from him stood Two-Jacks with a very large Bowie knife in his hand,
just smiling!

John raised his pistol and shot off a round into the morning air.
"Alrightee men, you are being paid to unload this freight and no more
playing with the boys on shore! You boys on shore had better run along
home now and let these men work! Do you understand?"

John Carver scowled as a dozen Union soldiers came running
around from the north side of the French Market and down the levee
to the schooner with weapons drawn. He was certainly angry because
someone was challenging him and disrupting his plans. He would have
to put a stop to this. There would be hell to pay!

"What is this about?" the ranking officer asked no one in particular. "Who shot these men and why?"

Captain Wetzel walked down from the ship and approached the
officer. "My men were trying to unload this freight and these men

starting trouble. Two were about to shoot my men and we had to defend ourselves. You can see how they have slithered away like the vermin they are. I will have these men taken to the undertaker and dealt with accordingly. I will also report this incident to the authorities, unless you want to take care of it."

"No, that will not be necessary. I trust you will do the right thing. Now go on about your business and no more foolishness," the young officer commanded as he left the scene.

After John Carver retreated to the confines of his shadowy world, Jacob and Thomas presented themselves to the Captain and his crew. Two-Jacks was already onboard and sitting on a smaller keg next to John and the Captain as they shared a decanter of Caribbean rum.

"I thought you were asleep when we left the widow's place," Thomas inquired.

"I was asleep, but you make too much noise when you get ready. I had to follow you and make sure you didn't hurt yourself." Two-Jacks smiled, "Don't you think I was right to come along for your safety?"

"This won't be the end of it, I am afraid," Jacob inserted. "I think you men will need to form a vigilante group to patrol the docks if you plan on surviving. I got a look at the head man in charge from my vantage point. He looks like a surly cuss and somebody is going to have to pull his teeth before this is over."

Old Mossyhorn looked at John as he spoke, "Son, it is going to take a man like you with resolve and battle-tested nerve to save our livelihood and our way of life. I don't like to burden any man with such a load, but, truthfully there is none other here with the backbone to stand up to this evil force. If there was someone else, I would know, but there just isn't anyone. What do you say, Mr. Bernard?"

"I don't know what to say to you, but I did not fight for four long years to come back home and surrender to a bunch of Yankee trash that did not have the nerve to serve their country."

John stood up and looked around him at the men working hard to unload the cargo. "I will do what I can! I will certainly do *all* that I can!"

John remembered he was to meet with Matthew at a café on Dumaine Street before 8:00 A.M. He told Jacob and Thomas he would see them back at the boardinghouse as soon as he met with Matt. He mounted his horse and headed south down Decatur Street to Dumaine and turned north.

Up the street several blocks a painted white sign edged in green hung from a strong limb of a magnolia tree. It read: Magnolia Inn and Café; and, it swayed gently in a rare summer breeze. John walked his horse to the hitching post near the cistern so it could drink. He walked up on the porch and paused to look around as he felt an odd tingle run down his spine. The door was open and he walked in to find people having breakfast among the tables. He looked around and noticed there was also a courtyard for additional dining. It was beneath a large potted lemon tree that he spotted Matthew seated at a table drinking coffee and reading a newspaper.

He seated himself at the table. An attractive older lady walked over and offered him a cup and filled it with coffee. She stepped away.

"Been waiting long?" he asked.

"No, I just got here several minutes before you. You are looking kind of rough; did you get any sleep last night?"

"Not much, how about you?"

"I slept fine until just a little before dawn. I got up, washed my face and proceeded to take a walk along the river," Matt said. "Saw what looked like a run-in with some hoodlums."

"Yeah, you don't miss much. I was doing some investigation down on the river last night and I ran into some old acquaintances that needed a hand with a particular problem that involved something I am being paid to know about," John said with a little edge to his voice.

"That's correct; you are doing what you are being paid to do. Don't think I was checking on you or disapprove. I completely approve of your actions. You are thinking and acting just as I expected you to do, probably even better. You are acting like a concerned citizen and a soldier returning from war and getting involved in his old neighborhood.

Plus, you are performing in the capacity of an agent rooting out the evil that we want to drive out into the open."

"I was standing under the awning next to a vegetable stand and I got a glimpse of who I think is John Carver. Jacob saw me and indicated with the motion of his eyes to which direction I should take note."

Matthew stopped and drank some coffee while the lady returned with a plate of eggs, grits and ham for both of them.

"I ordered for both of us. I think you did more to accomplish our mission and much faster than I had expected. We will have to get this man cornered and make him come at us. It looks like he may act sooner than later. He was very angry when he walked off. I followed him as he walked down the street and now I know where he is staying. He walked into the lobby of the St. Louis Hotel and proceeded to throw a fit. He sent his flunky on an errand. He left the hotel in a hurry. I followed him down the street to The Exchange Bank. I went on from there because the bank was obviously not open until nine, and I saw what I needed to see."

CHAPTER 31

THINGS WERE PROGRESSING MORE RAPIDLY for Matthew and his investigation than he had ever anticipated. He had moved himself, Evangeline, Elizabeth and his brother Benjamin to The Royal Court Hotel on the corner of Royal and Toulouse Street.

Madelyn Cooper and Henry Stone took up residence at another hotel on Chartres Street, just a block from The St. Louis Hotel where John Carver was booked. It was a part of Matthew's strategy to keep watch on Carver and identify his contacts with as little suspicion as possible.

They took to strolling through the French Quarter and taking in the sites when possible. They visited art galleries, antique shops, coffee shops, home décor specialists, and completely enjoyed the local fare at the exquisite cafes. Matthew drank a lot of coffee while posted within eye sight of Carver's hotel. Shopping became a favorite pastime for the ladies. Elizabeth was as intrigued with the business that Ben was doing with farm implement dealers as she was the boutiques. Ben was a natural businessman and he was gaining support for his new sit-on-plow invention. He was actually getting orders for them.

It was a wise suggestion by Matthew to apply for a patent with the U.S. Patent Office. It also helped that Matthew had a personal friend in the administration of the Patent Office. He didn't want to see Benjamin's efforts be undermined as he was certain they would have been without proper protection.

Something was beginning to happen to Elizabeth as she spent more time with Benjamin strolling along the streets and the riverfront. It was starting to affect Ben too. Her mind and her heart were often lost in another world as they walked the city streets going about their business. It became natural for her to loop her arm inside Ben's big arm as they strolled down the streets. Ben couldn't understand where her mind was at times. It seemed that she was somewhere else; that was, until he was bitten by the very same bug. It was something entirely new for both of them. Matthew had seen it all before and tried not to interfere; however, he wanted them to be careful and not to rush into this new phase too quickly. He did not want to be big brother and interfere in nature's ways.

Matthew did not have to tell Evangeline what was happening because she could see for herself. Per Matthew's request, she tried to interject herself as much as possible to keep the heat of passion to a low level simmer. But, they both admitted that nature would take its course; and it was bigger than them to stifle or interfere.

Sunday dinners were taken at the Bernards' home on a regular basis, after church services naturally. Everyone enjoyed the atmosphere of a normal family dinner at home. Thomas was most insistent that they arrive early. He even attended church services regularly. They alternated between the Catholic Church and the Baptist Church because Thomas didn't understand Latin and felt more at home with the less formal Baptist setting.

Enoch began helping Mrs. Bernard after the second Sunday. He was learning the nuances of Creole cooking and wanted to learn from John's mother too. He would go to work with Monsieur Francois on Tuesdays and soak up all the things he had to teach him. He taught the Monsieur, as well. The widow was learning the culinary arts as Enoch promised and began to find her dinner table filled with hungry men and women, every day.

Two-Jacks began to bring around a young Indian girl to Sunday dinner. He asked for Mrs. Bernard's permission first. She was of the Choctaw tribe from across the lake. She gave Mrs. Bernard several cane baskets as gifts for her kitchen. They met while he was working the riverfront, talking with local Indians, gathering information about the characters that frequented the docks and marketplace. He was becoming enamored with her the more that they got to know each other. He wasn't a young buck, nor was he over-the-hill either but that did not matter to the young maiden, Dona. She could tell he was a master of the woodlands and highlands, but not as experienced socially. She appreciated his sincerity and gentleness in spite of the rough exterior he displayed. He was quite the handsome one when he got cleaned up, something he began to do more often.

The group of men and women thoroughly enjoyed John's parents and his dear grandmother, Maudie. They would sit around after dinner and talk about old times. They got to meet John's brothers and sisters as time permitted and they were available. He had a large extended family.

They especially enjoyed the stories his family told about John's early exploits. That would prompt John to insist it was time to move along. Everyone enjoyed the love that was present in their Sunday gatherings.

Thomas was beginning to get a name as an accomplished gambler, as was Jacob. They spent much time at the tables during smaller games, knowing they had to establish themselves before they could get an audience at the larger ones. They did not let on like they knew each other.

Jacob had begun to establish himself as a businessman of sorts. He opened an office on the third floor of The Exchange Bank. He had "J. Hewitt Enterprises" printed in a frosted type on the glass portion of the door entering his office. He eventually moved out of the boarding house and took a room in one of the nicer hotels in town.

Thomas spent time with Evangeline as her escort when Matthew was preoccupied with other matters. Once when Thomas and Evangeline were walking past The St. Louis Hotel, something strange and frightening happened to Evangeline. She started to tremble and broke out in a cold sweat as they walked. Someone opened the hotel door and she heard screams from a woman and two little children struggling to hold on to each other as three men were pulling them apart. She started running as fast as she could with Thomas running close behind trying to catch her. She was screaming and flailing her arms as if she was on fire. Thomas finally caught up with her in front of the St. Louis Cathedral. He held her in his arms and calmed her until she quit shaking and there they sat on the steps of the church until the sobbing subsided.

She explained what she heard and saw as the hotel door was opened. She surmised it was only a vision of events that had happened to her grandmother when her two children were taken from her during a slave auction. Those two children would have been her mother and her Uncle John. This made her quest to find her mother even more real and urgent.

That was the first event that put Evangeline on the path of finding her mother. Another happened one day while strolling in and out of shops with Elizabeth and Ben. She started talking to an old black woman sitting under an oak tree beside the square in front of the Cathedral. The old lady claimed she could tell someone's future or past by examining their hands and make suggestions for future actions with the cards. This intrigued Evangeline.

Evangeline sat down to talk with the old lady while Elizabeth expressed reservation; however, she and Ben stood and listened for what she had to reveal to them about Evangeline.

The old woman wore a sun bonnet that shaded her face from close scrutiny. She reached out and asked for Evangeline's hand. Once she felt her hand and turned the palm upwards to bring it into view, the old woman dropped her hand and jumped up and backwards, knocking over her chair. She ripped the bonnet from her head flinging it to the ground beside her. She stared at Evangeline for a while before she spoke again.

Once she had caught her breath she picked up her chair and sat down again. "You are related to someone I once knew in my past life; someone that came to me when I was a young and trusted voodoo priestess. I must admit I was inexperienced and had no idea how my actions could hurt people well into the next generation. I had reckoned what I did today would have no consequences on tomorrow. I was foolish and drunken with the power of a dark spirit. Once, a young lady came to me and asked me to place a curse on a very popular, although shady, member of the community. I was hesitant to do this initially, but she was very convincing that this was his just reward for fooling her and using her for his own personal gain. That convinced me that it was the right thing to do because I was recently hurt by a young man myself. This curse that I conjured up not only led to the death of this man, Jean Lafitte, but his son too. It affected the life of the unknown and unborn daughter also, and so on. I must ask you; do you know of someone named Marguerite?"

Now it was Evangeline's time to be startled. She moved her chair backwards a bit and looked with wide eyes at the old woman and thought for a long moment. She had to take a deep breath because she almost forgot to breathe while she thought.

"That is my grandma, Mother's mother! Her name is Marguerite. I've never met her, but my mother talked about how sweet and loving she was. Mother was separated from her just like I was separated from my mother."

"I came down from Virginia to find my mother. I believe she is here in New Orleans. My father was a plantation owner. He purchased my mom and uncle from another slaver in Charleston. He could not call me his own and had to sell my mother once I got old enough and started to favor his own flesh and blood daughter. His wife would not tolerate Mother living on the plantation, so she had us split up. He went crazy and was killed by his daughter, my half-sister."

"Do you know where my mother is?" Evangeline asked with the voice of a small child.

"My darling child, I don't reckon I have any idea where she is, but let me see your hand again," the old woman requested and received her outstretched hand. "I see many things here. You are a strong and courageous woman and will see many struggles in your lifetime; however, you will overcome and be triumphant. You will experience many changes in your life that will require your creative and physical talents to rise up. You are a pillar of strength for others. Your spirituality will become the dominant side of you, but you should not worry. You have a strong spiritual guide that will be with you and protect you for the rest of your life."

"Please," the old and withered lady spoke, "let me turn over several cards and listen to them." She flipped over the card with the Magician showing first. "You should be very careful who and what you allow into your life because it can upset your spiritual being. Always know that everything you touch has a spiritual nature to it and it can attach itself to you in positive and negative ways."

The next card displayed the Moon. "You will gain helpful information in your dreams. Dreams can guide you and protect you and very possibly lead you to where your mother can be found. But, be very careful, the Evil Spirit can also invade your dream world; for this reason, you have to draw near your good and faithful Spirit Guide. He will seek to guide you on your true journey."

She turned over the third and final card. "This card has the High Priestess and it wants you to look hard for the subtle meanings in everyday things. You must listen to that inner voice that speaks to your heart and be true to the values placed there by your Creator."

The old woman gently pushed the cards aside and looked directly into Evangeline's eyes. "I was once lost and believed in my own powers and placed an evil curse on your grandfather, Jean Lafitte, because the foolish pride of a young woman, your grandmother, led me to believe it was the right thing to do. This has caused great pain to your family. I know now that the Great Spirit which is called by many things has set this world in motion and we are given to choose which roads we want to travel. It is best for each of us to realize how little knowledge we have been given and how dangerous that can become when not used properly. We do not control the earth, moon and stars, and much less do we control the everyday events that surround us; however, what we do control is our attitude and our perspective towards the world and people that we come in contact with. You have been given a special relationship with your Spirit Guide and I recommend you seek a quiet place often and be silent before Him. Know that He is God and pray often for His mercy and to receive wisdom and understanding."

"Evangeline, you are a beautiful child growing into a more beautiful woman. Do not dwell on that fact, but concentrate on what you can give to others. This will bless you for eternity. Go and seek your mother. I believe you will find your grandmother and there your mother will be also. I will pray in hopes that the effects of this curse will be lifted. Now young maiden, go and seek and you will find," the old woman commanded as she leaned her head backwards and closed her eyes as if to say a burden had been lifted from her.

Evangeline rose from her chair and turned to face Benjamin and Elizabeth. They were speechless and startled as the look on their faces indicated. She felt weak in some respects but encouraged in others. This was so much to digest at once. They walked around the city for a while and went back to their rooms to rest before they met later for dinner. They had so much to ponder.

Several attempts had been made on John's life because he had taken a leadership role in uniting the workers along the docks. He was constantly looking over his shoulder. Two-Jacks sensed the danger and kept a watchful eye out for him.

He brought together groups of dockworkers and strengthened them to withstand the forces of The Snake, John Carver. Ship owners and captains held him in high regards for what he was doing. He prevented the loss of many shipments of cargo and the financial hardship it would have sustained. Otherwise, it would have fallen into the hands of the man that wished to destroy them and gain control of all commerce coming into and out of the port

John had taken up the habit of walking the docks and city streets at night. He would visit the places of his childhood and notice the changes that war and greed had brought about. He talked to many old acquaintances and listened to their stories about the Union occupation of New Orleans and the abuses of carpetbaggers. He also heard about the local power brokers that took the places of the former plantation owners. The plantation owners were often scattered around the country when their fiefdoms were abolished.

Something else was happening to John as he explored the night. He began to see apparitions, ghosts that appeared as clearly to him as any actual living person. They considered him as one of them and often spoke to him accordingly. Once he saw the spirit of the young man, Tony, the son of the vegetable peddler at the French Market. He had been cut down at the Battle of Shiloh in '62. The peddler and his wife could not understand why the old tomcat that used to follow Tony everywhere spent most of his day curled up in a chair purring. John noticed Tony sitting in the chair every time he went to visit his father and mother whose fish stand was next to the vegetable peddler. He was always stroking the old tomcat's fur and speaking gently to him. John never spoke to him but just smiled as their eyes made contact. Tony was as happy as a soul could be just sitting near his parents and petting the old cat. There was no need to speak; words could not convey anything more, nor were they needed.

John sat on a bench along the river and watched the world of the river men as they joked and drank the night away after a hard day of moving cargo on and off the ships. Their world was a hard one, but theirs was a brotherhood that watched over each other, black, white, red or yellow as was the case at times. Each man was held in esteem for the work shared and the camaraderie of circumstances.

Sometimes it was difficult to separate the living from the nonliving characters as they moved up and down the river. One night John was sitting on a bench when a flamboyantly dressed individual walked up and sat down next to him. He had seen him before. The moon was full, but there was a fog rolling in off the river creating an eerie feel to the night. The man removed his hat with a plume of feathers wafting about and placed it between them.

"It is a perfect night for mischief my young friend!" the man of fashion stated to John.

"I would think so stranger, if you were the mischievous sort that is!" John replied. "I didn't know we had met before to be called friend. Or do you call everyone friend?"

"I only call those that have come to my aid in the time of need friend. Anyone that contributes to my downfall I call foe and entertain with the wrath of my saber and all the hell that it holds!"

"So, you are the famous Jean Lafitte that is called pirate, villain and later hero when you came in the defense of our city in the Battle of New Orleans. You are the great ally with Old Hickory, Andy Jackson, that pushed the British back from Chalmette," John railed. It was obvious to him just who he was entertaining since he had heard his description often as a child and used to play the pirate himself while playing games with other children.

"Yes, it is I, none other than Lafitte himself!"

"Well, Mr. Lafitte, how is it that I have come to your aid when you were dead before I was born?" John asked.

"Well, it is simple to me, but I must explain it to you very slowly that you might understand. You are helping the captains and the freighters here defend their livelihood. Many of them you see are people that I knew when they were children and many of their fathers and grandfathers before them. They are friends that I still care about and advocate for them in their endeavors."

"There is also one thing more importantly that I am beholden to you for. You have been a friend and helped my granddaughter, Evangeline, as she goes about the search for her mother. I feel she must find her mother and grandmother for everyone's sake. I fear my efforts to move on have been hampered by my spirited indiscretions. Unless I can be of assistance in some way to remedy my past deeds, I will linger for a very long time. I sold her grandmother, my mistress, Marguerite, and her son to a slaver, on the auction block of all places, before our daughter was born. I was very angry with her because she caused a curse to be placed on me when she discovered I was married and housed many of my mistresses in apartments in and around New Orleans; for this, I am very sorry. I'm sorry for my indiscretion and my poor judgment. I regret many of my actions now that I have plenty of time to consider them. It is often the way, that we find our judgment is better after the fact, my young comrade."

"I hope you now understand why I call you friend," the pirate explained. "Will you continue to help Evangeline in her search?"

"Yes, certainly, and it will be because of our friendship and the deep respect I have for her; although, any help you can give would be appreciated," John replied.

"You will find me available and ready to come to your aid at all possible times of need," Lafitte declared.

John saw Jean Lafitte at various times after their first meeting. They said very little to each other at those meetings, but Lafitte expressed his approval with John's continued actions to protect the docks and assist Evangeline in any way he could.

John's new-found ability came with negative effects too. He often saw men and women that had suffered and died without resolution of personal matters. He had to concentrate his focus very tightly to keep separate that which was happening in real time and that which had already occurred.

He would spend more time than ever in his local church in prayer and meditation. His priest was pleased to see a young man so devoted to his faith. He knew he had been charged with a heavy responsibility and needed spiritual guidance.

It was most disturbing to watch the ghost of women looking for lost loved ones that had died for various reasons around and about the river. One woman wailed for her husband and small children that were shoved into the river to drown by a drunken man in a runaway carriage one night.

There was also a slave woman that was constantly searching for her husband's arms and legs because he was tied to the railroad and run over as punishment for his brashness to his overseer. His master came along after he got word of this event and shot the overseer between the eyes where he stood, more for the financial loss than for the evil the man had committed.

One day Matthew was having lunch with John, Thomas, Jacob, Enoch and Two-Jacks at the Magnolia Inn and Café. Matthew had an ulterior motive. He had overheard the lady in charge speak of the need for another cook and believed Enoch would be interested.

It didn't take an introduction for Enoch to interject himself into the conversation. He was not aware of the opening at the café, but would soon realize his eagerness had landed him a job.

"You sound like someone with prior cooking experience, my fine gentleman!" Marguerite politely inquired of Enoch.

"Yes, indeed Madame, my skills must proceed me!" Enoch lifted up his voice with pride.

"Would you like to take a stroll through my kitchen and have a look at my operations, sir?"

"Indeed I would like to stroll with you; however, I will not be able to look upon your establishment with my eyes, but my nose and ears will suffice," he alerted her.

Marguerite placed her left hand through the extended right arm of Enoch and off they went into the kitchen. There was a muffled laugh from the table as they moved away.

"Did you tell Enoch that there was a sign posted on the porch advertising for a *new cook*?" Thomas asked Matthew.

"No, there was no need to tell him. He can sniff out any situation better than Jacob's old hound, Blue. By the way, how is Blue? Has he got over that girl dog back in Jackson?"

"That Blue was sad for about one day and now he has staked out a new girl dog, a French poodle that lives next door to Miss Ellie, the widow. Blue just sits on the sidewalk for hours on end looking at that large white poodle sitting in the bay window. It is torture watching him. He is so relieved when we go somewhere. The owner, an old man, has started carrying a staff with him when he walks the poodle just in case Blue gets any ideas," Jacob laughed.

Matthew noticed Albert Goldsmith, the tailor that worked at Mr. Godchaux's department store downtown. Albert lifted his hand and waved and Matt responded.

"Someone you know?" John asked.

"Just the tailor downtown; he is a nice enough sort. He is from Boston or Philadelphia I believe. He acted a little strange when I paid the cashier for a suit I had commissioned. I know it is customary to pay for specialty work in advance, at least a significant deposit. But, that couldn't have been the reason for his concern; I don't think it was. Well, so much for that," Matt concluded.

"The real reason I wanted to meet today was to discuss how things were progressing with the agents I have been in contact with. Henry Stone and Madelyn Cooper are turning out to be excellent at what they do. They have developed a rapport with the manager of the Exchange

Bank and found him to be very cooperative. Of course he wanted written immunity from prosecution for his cooperation. The manager of the
bank reports directly to the bank's owner and board of directors. He
is aware of John Carver and reports that he has made sizable deposits
directly through one of the owners, bypassing him."

Matthew paused and looked around the room before resuming. "I
think this will be the connection we need to catch Carver and put a stop
to his empire. He is certainly not the only player in the game, but he
one of the big ones, and maybe we can glean some valuable information
when we take him down."

"Jacob, what do you and Thomas have to report on your actions at
the gaming tables?"

Jacob spoke with a quiet voice, looking at his coffee as the lady
began to bring their food out to the table. "Thomas and I have made
major inroads into the bigger games. We operate separately and rarely
speak to each other except as one gambler would to another. We win
some and lose some so as to not to be taken as cardsharps. We generally
win more than we lose to be considered for the bigger games. We both
have been invited to a big weekend of gambling to celebrate the nation's
independence on the fourth of July. It will be held on *The Creole Queen*
riverboat. I will arrange for tickets if you would like to attend. I believe
several of John Carver's cronies will be participating."

"Yeah, I've seen our old friend Simon Bartlett on board. He hasn't
been in too many games though. You remember that guy I had a run
in on the way to Charleston?" Thomas asked Matthew.

"Yeah, I remember him and his big thug that you sent for a swim!"

"Well," Thomas continued, "he looks like he had his ears pinned
back a little since last we seen him. His boy is still around. I guess he
made it ashore in Charleston. He must be a good floater. They don't
know Jacob, but they didn't forget me. It is strange, but they haven't
made any direct threat towards me; actually, they act like they are
avoiding me for some reason. I overheard one of the roughs that hang
around say that the Snake almost punched his ticket but had a change

of heart. He apparently screwed up big time and barely kept his job and his life!"

"Yes," Matthew agreed, "his actions have gotten him in hot water with the boss. Losing that money that the Captain gave us was not something that was endearing to The Snake. He is very lucky to be alive and must be needed for the overall success of John Carver's mission. You keep up with your plans and get me some tickets to the big game for that weekend. I would not want to miss the fireworks for anything. Just be careful always. Don't fool yourselves, because your lives are in danger. They will have no use for you when they get your money. Simon Bartlett knows that and does not want to cause any friction. He hopes to have satisfaction in the end."

"How goes it with you and Two-Jacks?" Matt asked John.

"It is going well! The schooner and riverboat operators have shown a great deal of appreciation for our efforts to halt the organized takeover of the docks by Carver's New York thugs. They remain vigilant to avoid infiltration by outsiders."

"Two-Jacks is valuable for more than just his skills as a fighter and woodsman. He has a good reputation with the local Indian tribe in a great part due to his girlfriend, Dona Lightfoot. They let him know when something is about to occur on the river. The Indians are much closer with the ex-slaves because they trust them more than the white man."

"They told me," Two-Jacks inserted, "that Carver plans to buy a plantation upriver and make it the center of his operations. He will stage everything out of that location. He already owns a plantation across the lake he purchased for his family. It seems a man that owned it went crazy because his Creole mistress has no interest in him once she was set free; therefore, he began to gamble away all of his holdings. His wife took their children and moved back to Baton Rouge to live with her parents; they are wealthy people with political ties to the statehouse."

Matthew interrupted, "I have heard about that plantation that lies up river. Actually it is being brought up for *sheriff's sale* due to unpaid taxes. They tried to hide the *notice of sale* in an obscure location in the *Times Picayune* newspaper. I believe it is called Hidden Oaks Plantation because the main house is surrounded by beautiful live oaks. From what I heard, the plantation owner's son was killed in battle and his daughter died two weeks later in childbirth, along with the child, leaving him no heirs. He went for an afternoon ride one sunny day and did not return. His horse arrived home later that night without its rider. His body was found downriver several days later caught in a snag; his neck was broken. The sheriff never reported to his wife that when they pulled him out of the water, his hands and feet were bound with bailing twine. They let her assume he got off the horse and must have fallen into the water. I think Benjamin and I will take a ride out to this place and meet the widow."

Jacob interjected, "I overhead some bankers talking in the hall as I was about to leave my office in the bank building yesterday afternoon. I stopped before I entered the hallway to listen because they seemed so excited about the information they had. It seems that the bank owner and John Carver have conspired with the sheriff to take over that plantation. They do not plan to relinquish the property even if the widow has the funds to redeem it. That man has to be stopped before he gains too much power. He is heavy handed and is the worst sort. This plantation must have strategic value for them to be so interested in acquiring it whatever the costs."

"I have plans to meet with the Union Commander overseeing occupation of the city. They just relieved General Nathaniel P. Banks from his command. I understand he has been incriminated in the *Credit Mobilier scandal* involving railroad collusion and trying to control the nation's railroads. It is a big mess! He will officially muster out of the army and there may be someone of sounder judgment that I can speak with," Matthew conjectured. "I have an idea! I may have some old connections with the Army that I can use to stop Carver and his cronies. I will get to work on it!"

"Thomas, I want you to escort Evangeline today on her search for her mother. Can I depend on you?" Matt asked.

"Yes, that shouldn't be a problem. I have no plans for the afternoon. I'll just follow you over to your place and we can go from there," Thomas said with a smile. He always enjoyed being around Evangeline in spite of her kidding him. She was nearly his same age and did not talk down to him. He often felt left behind in the conversation with the others at different times.

Enoch walked up to the table and stared across the way. "Don't wait on me to eat, gentlemen, 'because I've got work to do! The lady is short handed and hired me on the spot. She has a good eye for talent. I will be moving my things over here and take a room in the Inn. Don't be upset with me. It is not that I don't enjoy the company, boys, but it will be much more convenient to move in here. I hope you will understand."

"I will bring your things over along with your mule and horse," Two-Jacks offered.

"That will be much appreciated, my dear friend!"

Albert stepped over to the table and commented, "Mr. O'Brien, I have almost completed your suit, but I would like for you to stop in today if possible and take a look at the jacket. I may need for you to try it on and make a few adjustments."

"I'll do that sir! Have a good day!" Matt offered.

As Albert and his coworker were walking out Matthew commented, "That is odd! He has something on his mind more than just that suit. I wonder just what is bothering him."

The fellows enjoyed their lunch and said their goodbyes to Enoch. He was a man on a mission. It was exactly what he had hoped for when he started on this journey. He no longer felt like the young, blind Negro man thrown out on the highways and byways of life to live or die as the world saw fit. He believed he could stand on his God-given talent and nothing else. A man among men!

Albert Goldsmith approached Matthew as he and his friends and colleagues left the restaurant and walked down Dumaine Street heading in the direction of Decatur and the river.

"May I speak with you for just a moment, sir?" Albert asked with a hint of nervousness.

"Yes, it is Mr. Goldsmith, isn't it?"

"Yes, but call me Albert!"

"How may I help you Albert?" Matthew asked.

"I overhead you mention the name of John Carver. Are you a friend of his?"

"No, I am not a friend. He is someone of interest though. Do you have some connection with him, or is there something you wish to share with me about him?"

"Mr. O'Brien, I think you underestimate the depths that man is willing to go to get what he desires. I do not feel comfortable discussing this in public; therefore, I have written the directions to my home and wish to speak with you about this as I get off work at five o'clock this afternoon. Will you meet me later?" Albert appeared to be shaking with fear as he spoke to Matthew.

"Yes, I will be there in my carriage as you approach your home. Have a good day, Mr. Goldsmith, I mean Albert."

Albert spun himself around and headed in the direction of his work at *Godchaux's Department Store* on Canal Street. Matthew walked the short distance to catch up with his friends as they stood waiting for him.

He explained that he may just have gotten the break he needed on Carver. "We shall find out soon! Let's be off, gentlemen."

Thomas escorted Evangeline down to an office that the sign indicated was *The Freedmen's Bureau*. They went inside the office and took a seat and waited for someone to speak with them. There were many people there. Some were looking on pages of names pinned on a cork board with any information applicable to their whereabouts and disposition. Evangeline walked over to them and Thomas followed.

"Look for anyone with the name of Frances, please!"

"What is her last name?" Thomas asked.

"I don't know her last name. It could be the name of her last owner, and I don't know who that is, or was," Evangeline stated in a desperate voice.

An older white gentleman with gray hair wearing a gray suit came over to them and asked, "May I help you locate someone, ma'am?"

"Yes sir! I am looking for my mother; I haven't seen her in more than fifteen years. She was sold to a slaveholder down here in New Orleans. I understand she was resold and I don't know the name of either owner. I was left back in Virginia," Evangeline explained.

"That isn't much to go on. Without a name or address it would be virtually impossible to locate her."

"She was on a sugar plantation, I believe!"

"That won't help much either because most of the plantations in this part of the state are sugar plantations. I will take your name and where you can be reached and get in touch with you if we come in contact with someone by that name. Is it spelled Frances or Francis?"

"Her name is spelled *Frances* with an *e*; and another thing, I believe her mother also lives here. If she is still alive, we believed New Orleans would naturally be her home. We do not know her disposition. This is to the best recollection of my Uncle John. He was left behind to watch over me in Virginia."

"Wait! The fortune teller said my grandmother was probably here. Her name, my grandmother that is, is *Marguerite!*" Evangeline blurted out like it was the key to solving this whole mystery.

"Baby girl, I know dat name. She was given her freedom by an old friend from da Islands. She was the mistress dat once lived on Lafitte's ship and placed a curse on him when she find out dat she is not da onliest one of his mistresses." The old lady laughed and almost gained six inches in height when she leaned back and up to gain lung capacity to let out a belly laugh. "What a foolish young girl to tink dat she da only lover of dat famous pirate!"

"Does she live here in the city, ma'am?"

"Young lady, it is nearly impossible to say who knows where anybody lives dez days! For true, I hear she is alive and may be here in N' Awlins. I do hopes you find her, sweetie!" The old woman, almost bent double as she walked, disappearing into the crowd from which she came.

Thomas walked Evangeline around the city. He had hoped she would enjoy the sights and sounds of a city alive with commerce; however, his efforts seemed to be of no avail. The streets were full of people just like Evangeline; plain ordinary people walking around looking for lost loved ones and hoping to find their way again. They stopped and ate some beignets. She was stuck in her funk and it was beyond him to pull her out. It was bigger than Thomas.

"Well, I guess we best go back to your place. You are worse than a sore-tailed cat and I can't help you find your spirit again," Thomas surmised.

"It's not your fault, Thomas; I am just afraid I may never find my mother again," Evangeline explained in her sullen way.

"Now ain't you the silly one, girl! You have been here for only a few weeks and already done give up. Have you prayed about it yet?"

"Yes, I have prayed over and over and He does not seem to be listening to me!"

Thomas grabbed her by the shoulders and shook her until she was looking directly into his eyes. "Do the fish jump out of the water onto the banks when you go fishing or did you have to wait until they was ready to bite? I never know'd you to be a quitter; should I quit on you just like that, Evangeline?"

"No ... don't you ever talk like that again! With tears rolling down her cheeks, Evangeline grabbed Thomas and said, "How could I go on without you? You old redheaded, freckle face Georgia fool. You are the first real friend I ever had since my half-sister Sarah growing up. I don't know what love is, but I know that I don't want to go on without you. Do you understand what I'm saying Thomas?"

"There ain't much that I do know," Thomas sighed, "but I know you are the onliest girl I ever know'd and rightfully the prettiest and most stubborn too. I ain't going anywhere, so get out of that moodiness and let's walk around some more and laugh some too."

Matthew arrived early at the address that Albert had given him. With a gentle command to his horse, he stopped his carriage on the street beside a freshly painted picket fence. He stepped from the carriage and walked forward to stroke his horse's neck while looking around to observe the beauty beneath the canopy of oaks and blooming azaleas lining the fences and flower beds. His thoughts quickly transported him to places he had been before: Charleston, Savannah and Mobile, among a few.

He returned to reality quickly with the sound of flesh slapping flesh and the startled sound of a woman surprised and shocked. The woman quickly throttled her emotions after the shock of being struck was over. Matthew turned to find a woman sitting down on the ground gripping a swing on a large oak limb with one hand and the other placed on her cheek. There was also a man standing just a few feet from her.

Matthew walked across the street with determination. "Is there a problem here I may be of assistance to resolve?"

"Mister, no one asked for your help!"

"Yes, that is true but I am offering anyway. It is not the custom where I came from to beat on our womenfolk, mister!"

"It is not our custom to stick our heads in other people's business either. You must be a Yankee that has forgotten his place!"

"No sir, I was born and raised in Jackson, Mississippi; however, I was taught what real manners are, and they do not change north or south of the Mason-Dixon Line! You do not look much older than me sir, but I am willing to teach you some manners if needs be," Matthew emphasized as he stepped over the short picket-fence.

"This is a private matter and I have no need of help."

"Well, I am making it a public matter!" Matthew spun the man around by the shoulder and hit him hard on the chin with a right uppercut. The man went down and appeared to be out cold.

Matthew reached down and helped the woman off the ground. She looked to be in her mid-to-late thirties and very attractive. "I am sorry for intruding ma'am, but it was unavoidable."

Etienne got up and dusted himself off. "I am leaving now, Frances, and will see you *later*!"

"I am sorry you had to witness this whole affair, mister. You see that man was my former owner and I was his slave. He called me his mistress, but what is the difference? He has not been the same man since he had to set his slaves free," she explained. "He has lost all of his wealth and family by gambling. His plantation was lost too. He used to be very frugal with his money, but something has come over him since he gave us our freedom. He hoped I would still be interested in him after he set me free. I am not certain about anything these days. He can't expect me to know what I want. I am just hoping to be reunited with my family that got strewn all over the world by slavery. You do understand, don't you?"

"Yes, I do understand, and my name is Matthew. I hope you will have success in your endeavors to locate your loved ones. I am sorry if I caused any trouble, ma'am. It is not my way to stand by and watch someone hit a woman. I must be going. I have an appointment to meet with your neighbor."

Matthew stepped across the fence and walked over to meet Albert Goldsmith as he arrived. Albert had taken the streetcar down St. Charles Avenue and walked the remainder of the way.

"I see you found your way with my directions, Mr. O'Brien. Come on into my house. I must apologize there is not much here but a table and chairs. I just purchased it recently and my wife is coming down from Philadelphia with our children very soon. I am waiting on her so we can furnish the house together. That isn't something I would do without her."

"Just call me Matthew. It is a very nice house; however, you wanted to speak to me about Mr. Carver."

"Yes, Matthew, I do wish to speak to you about John Carver. I was puzzled when you placed a down payment on your suit with what I recognized as counterfeit money. Then, I could not help but to overhear your conversation with the gentlemen at lunch. You mentioned John Carver's name multiple times."

"Albert, I am interested in how you are able to recognize phony money so easily," Matt questioned.

Albert offered Matthew a drink of Irish whiskey and began to pour. "I am concerned that I may be placing myself at risk by merely discussing these matters with you."

"You do not have to worry about me because I do not operate on the same side as Mr. Carver, Albert. Explain to me your relationship to him and the counterfeit money and I will put you at ease about myself."

"It is very simple, you see. I was raised in Philadelphia and my father is a tailor. Mr. Carver was a client of my father. He was the patron that paved the way for me to attend Harvard. My old college friends had a scheme in mind to print phony money and for me to bring it down here to start a distribution system and get rich. They sent me because they knew I wanted to prove to them that I was worthy of their friendship. Now I know how foolish I was. I was skeptical of my actions and realized the danger which I placed myself when I recognized John Carver as my competition. He gave me a polite warning as he saw that I aborted my mission and turned back to being a tailor, the livelihood of my father. He is a deadly man. I heard about his exploits after I went off to college. He is known throughout the eastern seaboard. Does that answer any of your questions, Matthew?"

"Yes, I have many more, but for now that is a good start! Let me explain briefly, I represent an organization founded on protecting the legitimacy of the United States currency. The less you know of me is to your benefit. Mr. Carver is turning out to be our number one suspect. Is there anything more you can tell me?"

"There are no limits to what he will do to get what he wants. My wife and children are traveling South with his wife and their son. I fear for their safety if he believes I am conspiring against him. That's how much I fear him!"

"Albert, I will only contact you in a business capacity and would advise you not to contact me unless it was absolutely necessary. I am staying at The Royal Street Hotel if you must contact me; otherwise, I wouldn't recommend you bother."

"I will heed your advice. I just thought it was important that I warn you about him. You and your friends look like good people. I want a clear conscience, that's all!"

Matthew walked out of the house and untethered his horse from the hitching post. As he turned the carriage to return to his hotel he noticed the lady next door waving bye to him. He returned the wave and smiled as he trotted the horse down the street. He felt a strange feeling come over him as if he knew the lady from somewhere in his past. *What did she say her name was?* He thought. He shrugged it off as just an odd feeling and moved on.

CHAPTER 32

BENJAMIN TURNED THE BUGGY TO HIS RIGHT, down the lane between the groves of live oaks, in the direction away from the Mississippi River. The main house wasn't visible until you were deep inside the oaks, and it jumped out in a magnificent way. It was set back on a beautiful lawn with a massive garden of flowers to each side.

Elizabeth commented that they would never have found the place if someone hadn't the forethought to hang a little sign from the massive cedar along the river road. Hidden Oaks Plantation was gorgeously built and maintained. It was a working sugar plantation with many outbuildings and nice little cottages for its workers. Not all plantations placed importance on the living quarters of its slaves. It was the exception, not the rule.

An elderly black man, neatly dressed, approached them and offered to take their buggy. He directed them to the house. They were greeted by another black man more elegantly dressed and shown the parlor. He left them and returned with Mrs. Lafontaine.

"Hello, my name is Lucille Lafontaine, the lady of the house. You may call me Miss Luci; that's what everyone calls me. How may I be of help to you?"

"Miss Luci, my name is Matthew O'Brien, this is my brother Benjamin and the ladies are Elizabeth beside Ben and Evangeline to my right."

"It is my pleasure to meet you all!"

"We have driven out today to visit with you about a matter that must be of great concern to you. We are aware that your house is going to be sold for back taxes tomorrow at noon. You are aware of this aren't you, Miss Luci?" Matthew asked.

"Yes, I am aware that they have plans of this sort. However, I have a receipt for the payment of taxes by my late husband. They are mistaken sir!"

"Miss Luci, they do not care if they are wrong. They intend to seize your property under false pretenses. Please allow me to be candid with you. Actually, I am here in New Orleans in an official capacity of the U.S. Government. We intend to put a stop to an organization that has conspired with local officials for unlawful gain. I am concealing my official nature to aid in the capture and apprehension of all of the elements of this ring. I know that they will override any attempt to satisfy any real debts or trumped-up debts; therefore, I have made arrangements with the Union Army, garrisoned in New Orleans, to commandeer your property for official use. You should not worry because I have good connections and good intentions; likewise, they will assist me in all of my efforts to thwart the villains that wish you harm."

"Matthew, I also have a very good friend that will come to my aid," replied Miss Luci. "I place a great deal of trust in an old friend of my husband, a lawyer by the name of Horace Marchant. He is very good at what he does!"

"Marchant," Matthew declared. "He is an associate of John Carver, the very man that wants to take your home from you! He may also be the go-between that has forged the alliance with the crooked local sheriff. I have a connection with a reputable attorney in the city that I will send out in the morning to represent you. He will be by your side as the true and nefarious intentions of Marchant are revealed. His name is Walter Cunningham. I have known him since grade school when his parents would journey to Jackson, Mississippi and he would spend his summers with his grandparents there. Will that be alright with you?"

"That will be fine, Matthew; however, it is very troublesome to think Horace has ill intentions. It was he that came to me with the sad news of my husband's death and recovery. It is all very strange!" Miss Luci said with a disturbing sigh.

"Miss Luci, I want to tell you something that will be very disturbing to you. Will it be alright if I share something with you that may bother you deeply?"

"Yes, Matthew, go ahead; there isn't anything that I believe will surprise me anymore since the death of my dear Maurice. He was the light of my life! He was the most handsome man and the most thoughtful soul I have ever known. He would not harm even the least of God's creatures. He would not allow the beating of a mule, much less a slave. He fired an overseer that raised a hand to a boy once and told him to never darken the path to this house again. The facts are that there are no slaves on this plantation. He gave each slave he ever purchase his *papers of freedom* and every colored born on this plantation was born free! Now, what do you have to tell me?"

"Miss Luci, your husband, Maurice, did not die an accidental death. When his body was retrieved from the river, his hands and feet were bound with twine. Yes, he was murdered and tossed in the river."

Miss Luci, startled to the point of no response, stood up and walked to the front window and looked out into the gardens. The window was full length from the floor to just short of the ceiling. The height of the window dwarfed her small stature and she was framed like a beautiful portrait with the large emerald drapes to each side.

She turned around and faced the seated company of young folks for an extended moment before she spoke. "I am only saddened that Maurice suffered at all. He was an excellent rider. I knew he couldn't have fallen from his mount. He was the most trusting sort. I am sure his last minutes on this earth were sheer confusion, not understanding how someone intended to cause him harm. Who could have wanted him dead and why?"

"I don't know who did the deed, but the answer to why is clearly a matter of who stands to gain with him out of the picture. It is apparent to me that the property has some inherent value for its location and probably for its sheer beauty. It is also apparent that the sheriff is a tool for Mr. Carver, along with the aid of his attorney, Mr. Marchant," Matthew explained.

"I truly don't understand the ruthless nature of people. Slaveholders have sacrificed our sons to maintain their lifestyles. Satan is dancing on the graves of hundreds of thousands of Americans, North and South, and laughing his head off. I shouldn't think the killing of one dear man would cause an evil soul one moment of grief. Please send your friend, Mr. Cunningham out here at his earliest available time tomorrow."

"I would like to ask another favor of you nice young folks. Will you come outside into the garden beside the fountain and have some coffee and pralines with us?" Miss Luci requested.

"We will be honored, Miss Luci!" Elizabeth offered as she reached over and slipped her small hand inside Benjamin's much larger hand.

"Laura Belle has cooked them just this afternoon and she gets upset if we don't have some when they are fresh out of the oven," Luci professed.

They shared the afternoon with Miss Luci and they made an impression on each other. She shared with them the stories of her family and the tragedies brought on by the war. They shared their stories as well. They talked about the adventures traveling down from Virginia for Evangeline and from Charleston for Elizabeth.

Benjamin said little about himself; however, Elizabeth couldn't say enough about him. It was obvious to Luci how Elizabeth and Benjamin felt about each other. She was also very aware of how important it was to Evangeline to locate her mother.

There was much she wished to know about Matthew, but he was very reserved about himself. She was particularly drawn to him because he reminded her so much of her own son who was very handsome and smart as well.

Her son, Alexander Lafontaine, was the apple of her eye. He did not want to fight for the Confederacy because of his position on slavery. He signed up in spite of his sentiments not to bring shame to his family. Many of the wealthy landholders' sons did not fight at the request of their fathers, and possibly due to a strong fear of death.

He loved learning new things and had plans to attend the state university to learn more about farming and husbandry. She wondered just what all he would have been able to accomplish if he had survived the war. Damn that war! It took everything she ever loved.

That night, Matthew went to the Union command and spoke

with Colonel Charles F. Beauregard. He had many responsibilities and carried a great deal of sway with the upper command because he was a native New Orleanian. He knew the surrounding area and all of the turmoil caused by the defeat and occupation of his homeland.

Matthew explained in detail the situation with Hidden Oaks Plantation and found the Colonel was fully aware of the proceedings and the questionable death of Mr. Lafontaine. Matthew also revealed his command of Major in the U.S. Army to the Colonel as well as the commission of Agent for the Secret Service once he felt sure his confidence would not be revealed. He stopped short of revealing his complete mission, but the Colonel was smart enough to know there was more and did not pry for additional details.

The Colonel offered his complete cooperation and reassured Matthew his confidence in him was not misplaced. He was a man that trusted his own judgment about what was in the best interest of his city, his state and the South in general. He chose to go against his natural inclination, as did Matthew, and fight for the Union based on his better judgment. He considered himself the true patriot more so than those friends of his that went off half-cocked about whipping the Yankees before they understood the issues and the repercussions of defeat. Now it fell on his shoulders to clean up and right the ship of state, so to speak, after *the war to end Northern Aggression* proved to be disastrous.

The next morning shouted out that life was created for the living. Song filled the throats of every willing songbird. Everything was in bloom, from flowerbed to cultivated field. Butterflies and honeybees visited every nectar-filled flower available to them.

People were on the move this particular day to attend the scheduled sale of the Lafontaine plantation. They came from north and south of the Crescent City, from the east and the west banks of the Mississippi River: man, woman and child; horse, mule, wagon and carriage. Even many of the stray dogs and riff-raff of the city's back streets followed the procession to witness the theft of a plantation in broad daylight.

The sheriff arrived about the same time as John Carver and his entourage of bankers, lawyers and cut-throats, his associates, as he called them.

Matthew, Evangeline, Benjamin and Elizabeth stood to the left side of the porch, just behind the tall columns, with an excellent view of the people as they arrived and the proceedings that were about to take place.

John, Jacob, Thomas and Two-Jacks were present and placed themselves at various points on the grounds to be most effective if they had to spring into action. Each carried a pistol, but kept them concealed from view.

Horace T. Marchant stood beside the widow Mrs. Lucille Lafontaine as her legal representative.

Just when all things appeared to be in order, a company of U.S. Army Cavalry turned off the river road, down the lane between the oaks, and cantered up to the front of the plantation. It was a beautifully orchestrated arrival, with the sound of the hooves like music as they slowed to a walk on the brick patio out front.

The handsome military officer ceremoniously stepped down from his horse and walked up to Miss Luci.

"I am Colonel Charles Franklin Beauregard, at your service, Mrs. Lafontaine. I knew your husband and am sorry for your loss."

The Colonel took her gloved hand and politely kissed it; she was dressed exactly as you would expect a lady to dress. He released her hand and stepped back and to the left and moved over to stand next to Matthew.

"Soldiers, take your horses around to the north side of the gardens and return after you have secured your mounts." They saluted the officer and proceeded to carry out his orders.

It was obvious that the arrival of the military was disturbing to the sheriff and irritating to John Carver. They had planned for a quick and orderly process of taking over the property with little fanfare or notice. They had not planned on all of the witnesses or the military being present.

John and Two-Jacks had spread the word along the docks and

throughout the city that something big would be happening and was worth the trip up the river to witness the proceedings and possible fireworks. It was also observed by Jacob and Thomas that the invited guests were also carrying weapons of their own.

The big-bellied sheriff stepped up to Mrs. Lafontaine, reeking of the odor of stale, sweat stained clothes and cheap whiskey. The soldiers had returned and the crowd was getting anxious.

"I have come here today to perform my duty. It has been noted that you have neglected to pay your property taxes and I have executed the order to sell. The principal, John Carver, has satisfied the tax debt and will henceforth be named as sole owner of the Hidden Oaks Plantation, ma'am."

"Well, Sheriff Burg-ass, how can that be since I have a receipt of taxes paid for the year of Eighteen-hundred and sixty-five?" Mrs. Lafontaine asked.

"The name is Burgess, ma'am!"

"Whatever you call yourself mister, you must be mistaken," Miss Luci said.

At that point Horace T. Marchant stepped forward, "I am Mr. Lafontaine's attorney, and I will speak for Mrs. Lafontaine. Miss Luci has been under an extreme amount of stress while grieving for her husband and I believe it would be best to accept an offer from Mr. Carver. He is prepared to make a generous offer in consideration for this plantation. I advise we accept!"

"Mr. Marchant," Miss Luci proceeded, "you were my late husband's attorney, but I have my own attorney. I recommend you move aside so Mr. Cunningham can address the sheriff."

Mr. Cunningham moved forward. "Ladies and gentlemen, Mrs. Lafontaine has asked me to represent her interest in this matter, and this is what we have to disclose. Mr. Lafontaine exercised due diligence and prepaid his tax debt, to which we have a receipt. There is no tax lien and no basis to have a sale of property from that perspective."

"We anticipated an argument that Mrs. Lafontaine has diminished capacity, to which I have found no basis for such claim; and furthermore, we have drawn up the necessary paperwork to deed the entire plantation and all improvements to Benjamin J. O'Brien and his future bride, Miss Elizabeth Walker, provided they will accept this gift with a purchase price of one dollar. This will provide for Mrs. Lafontaine the use of the smaller guest manor for the remainder of her life, and a sufficient income to be decided on later, from the fruits of the land."

There was a silence over the crowd for a brief moment. "I hope you two will accept this gift. Maurice and I intended to raise our family here and later entertain our grandkids, but that has not worked as planned. This way I may live to have grand children yet! Will you accept?" Miss Luci asked.

"Yes, we will accept!" Elizabeth shouted and Ben shook his head in agreement.

"Wait just a damn minute!" John Carver shouted. "I have signed the paperwork and the money is deposited in the bank to seal the deal. What do you say sheriff?"

"Yeah, he is right, people. This place has been sold!" shouted the sheriff.

Colonel Beauregard stepped forward at the height of the yelling. "I have orders to take possession of this property for the purpose of pasturing and for livery services of our horse remuda. There will be no forfeiture of this property. I will contract for a reasonable amount to be paid the owners for their services. Do you have any questions for me, Mr. O'Brien?"

"No questions, I do accept your offer and conditions, sir," Benjamin agreed and smiled as he looked over to Elizabeth at his side.

"Then it is final and the agreement will be drawn up and signed by Mr. Cunningham as a witness and notary," Colonel Beauregard stated and reached out to shake Benjamin's hand.

John Carver swung around and signaled for his associates to come forward with guns drawn. Twenty men stepped out and drew weapons and pointed at everyone standing on the porch beneath the wrought iron balcony directly above. That was not a smart move on their part.

The soldiers drew side arms and some drew their cavalry swords to which they lowered and pointed at the men with John Carver. There were others in the crowd that did likewise. The dock workers and sailors and the friends of Benjamin also pulled some sort of weapon of their own. The assailants were surrounded and saw the error of their way. There was no chance of survival if they started a shooting match. So, quickly the men were forced to withdraw.

John Carver stepped forward and pointed his finger at Benjamin. "You will live to regret this mister, even if it is the last thing I do!"

With that said, Two-Jacks moved quickly to stand between the two men and produced his Bowie knife from a scabbard held just behind him by a piece of leather around his neck. He stuck the knife just under Carver's chin and lifted him up on his tiptoes drawing blood as he did so.

"You better hope he lives or I will have a fine scalp for my lodge pole!" Two-Jacks announced for all to hear.

Carver stepped back as Two-Jacks let off the pressure from his knife. His face was beet-red from his anger and he spun around and stormed away to where his carriage was parked. He jumped in and left the plantation without the guests that arrived with him. He pushed the horses into a fast gallop down the lane and dust was flying when he slid the back end of the carriage into the river road heading in the direction of the city.

The crowd dissipated as the events were apparently over for the day. The banker, the lawyer and the sheriff had to search for a ride back into town since Carver had left them behind.

"Benjamin, I hope you and Elizabeth don't mind that I announced your marriage plans before you got the chance to express them to your friends privately. It's just that everything happened so quickly and it all came to me yesterday, when you where visiting, that Maurice and I enjoyed the life we had here and that is over now with his death and the loss of our children," Miss Luci explained.

"Don't you agree that this is a beautiful place and it deserves someone that can love it and grow with it too?"

Benjamin opened up and spoke from the heart, "Miss Luci, this is more than anyone could ever dream of. I have always wanted a place to raise a family and help others as well. I never imagined something of this magnitude. No, I don't mind that you spoke about our plans. I had let Elizabeth do most of the talking up until now I guess, because she was saying all of the things I wanted to hear and I felt them as well as she did; however, I can see great things happening here just like I have planned in Jackson. It is more than coincidental that you and Mr. Lafontaine share the same view on slavery as my family. It is a commonly held view that everyone in the South supports the idea of slavery, but it isn't true. With your help and guidance, I believe we can continue the good work you have here and hopefully improve on it. You have cotton, sugarcane, potatoes, corn, rice and peas and many other vegetables, not to mention all of the fruit trees that are producing. You have a gristmill, a sugar mill, a blacksmith shop, people making clothes and pottery. You have dairy and beef cattle, hogs, horses, mules, chickens, ducks, sheep, hogs, goats, peacocks, guineas, dogs and cats. It seems as though the people that live on this place are very content to stay here. I have to say that the one thing which is missing is a schoolhouse. I believe highly in education because my parents are teachers!"

With a chuckle Miss Luci explained, "Ben, we have a schoolhouse here! You just can't see it. We have used the little church on the property as a schoolhouse too, but we kept it quiet because it is not accepted to educate the slaves. We have been very particular not to let on like our people are educated here. That would upset folks in the community. I would like for you and Elizabeth to open up the opportunity to all of the children, black and white, to have some level of education. I wish every one of the children could learn to read and write. You could build larger schoolhouses and hire some teachers. Of course you would have to build separate school houses and place them a safe distance apart to ever be accepted by the white community. We will need to expand our little library. It is quite limited."

"I am so excited about everything," chimed in Elizabeth. "I can't tell you how excited I am about the future here with Benjamin and you!

We will have to get my parents to travel down here from Charleston for the wedding, and Ben's parents will have to come down from Jackson. Will there be enough room?"

"Young lady, you have not seen the rest of the house. I will have to give you the tour. Why don't the four of you stay over for the night?" Miss Luci insisted.

Matthew interrupted, "That will be fine for the rest of you, but I must get back to the city. I believe we have stirred up a hornet's nest and I have work to do. Benjamin, you stay with Elizabeth and Evangeline while I go back with the others. I will see you tomorrow. Walter, I will stop by your office sometime next week. Will that be alright with you?"

"That will be fine. I will want Benjamin and Elizabeth to stop in and sign some papers after the details are finalized with the property transfer," Walter Cunningham explained.

The soldiers were coming around the house on their horses and they stopped at the command of the Colonel.

"Oh, by the way Matthew, there are several telegrams at the headquarters for you. A couple of them are from Washington D.C. and one is from a Miss Bolling in Virginia."

"Thanks, Colonel Beauregard, I will be in tomorrow for them," Matthew promised as they turned to leave.

"Do you have a horse that I can borrow, Miss Luci? It seems I have no transportation," Matt commented.

"Ask your brother, he is in charge of things around here now!" she said, and they all laughed.

—————◈—————

Thomas was getting excited about the poker championship. It was being held on one of the riverboats controlled by John Carver and his associates. He had been building up his skill at a pace not to alert others that he was better than he appeared. He won more games than he lost. Jacob pulled back from playing the tables because he was developing more recognition in the banking circles, and did not want to tarnish that image.

Thomas had started dressing nicer than usual because it was expected of a big-time gambler to have the proper attire. He also liked the reaction from Evangeline when she saw him dressed up in his finery. He never had much growing up or when he was soldiering. This gave him more confidence when he was at the poker table with the other *high rollers* and when walking around town with Evangeline.

John, Matthew and Jacob teased him so much about his high living. They said that he would have to move out and hire a buggy driver to take him around town very soon if he didn't watch himself. Well, that is just what he did; he didn't move out, but he did hire a buggy driver to pick him up and take him to the boat to play cards. He also used the driver when he wanted to escort Evangeline about town. Everyone was surprised at his metamorphosis. Who would have thought it; this rapscallion had it in him to become a gentleman. He even visited the barber on a regular basis.

John teased him, "Thomas, we have been wondering whether you will be reciting poetry down at the theatre or become a bard at the local tavern!"

"Why, Mr. Bernard, do you find jolly at my expense?" Thomas asked.

"See Matthew, what did I tell you? He is becoming so uppity that I will not be able to tolerate him in the very near future!" John proclaimed.

"Mr. Bernard, I recommend you get out more often and broaden your horizons," Thomas explained with a smile.

"Don't make me drag you outside in the yard and put a whoopin' on you, young fellow!" John commented.

The fourth of July, 1865, fell on a Tuesday and was quite subdued compared to the celebratory events that preceded the Civil War. Some bars and restaurants presented a celebration of sorts to entice their patrons; however, the local mood was not one of jubilation. There was so much hardship and resentment as a result of the war that the South did not feel a part of the United States at the present. It would take years before most of the ill feelings would be forgotten. The country was anything but united.

This did not stop the riverboat, *The Creole Queen*, from stretching a banner across its bow to commemorate the national holiday; especially since it was requested by John Carver, the power behind the *Player's Championship*. This event would draw big-time gamblers from St. Louis, Memphis and New Orleans to compete against each other. There would be a total of twenty- five gamblers. Each player would have to ante up five-thousand dollars, in gold, as an entry fee. The house would take twenty-five thousand off the top; that would leave one-hundred thousand for the winner, plus the winnings from each game. There would be five players to the table. The boat stood to make a great deal of money because it was charging admission fees and big-time prices for food and drink.

Thomas did not have more than two-hundred and twenty-seven dollars in gold. The rest of his winning was in currency, some legit and some counterfeit. Matthew had arranged with the bank for the entry fee amount in gold by way of a telegram. He had a telegram sent via the Treasury Department to the Exchange Bank president to place ten-thousand dollars in gold in Mr. Jacob Hewitt's personal account. This would not implicate or connect Matthew with the U.S. Government in any way, but it would elevate the status of Mr. Hewitt in the bank president's eyes. Jacob withdrew five-thousand and safely placed it in Thomas' possession. He was also given twenty-five hundred dollars for use in the game.

The big day had arrived, with many prominent people showing up to board the boat in their best finery. Carriages lined up along the river unloading the folks with all the regalia that would be afforded a visiting dignitary or head-of-state. Grownups and children from around the city came to witness the big show.

Matthew purchased tickets for the crew; however, Benjamin and Elizabeth had other plans and could not attend. Evangeline dressed up in her favorite dress. Two-Jacks and his girlfriend, Dona, also looked the part, while Jacob and John dressed appropriately.

The men played the part but came with their pistols concealed from others because they expected trouble. This was a day of business, not pleasure! They were there to protect Thomas while he set out to disrupt the plans of John Carver. This was just one of the ways that he planned to divert counterfeit money into the local economy and retrieve gold in exchange.

John had already crimped Carver's style by stopping him from a full takeover of the docks. This was a major plank in the scheme to bring the banks, landholdings, docks and gambling interests into a block of business that would implement the emersion of phony money back into the local economy and build up stock piles of gold and legitimate currency in his coffers.

Matthew had a special mission to accomplish here in New Orleans, but he knew his was only a small part in the grand scheme of things. Corruption was not a once and only institution. It was an ongoing proposition. The fall of the Confederacy and the reconstruction of the South was a perfect storm for the rats to come aboard and pillage in the light of day. The South was not the only victim. Crime and corruption were not obligated to any one in particular. They took advantage of every opportunity presented to them. The governmental organization to combat this injustice would not overcome and cease to exist. This would be just one of many facets of crime fighting that would be ever-growing in our nation's history. Matthew was just chipping away at the tip of the iceberg, so to speak.

Thomas entered the first round of competition, playing at table number three. He had played one of his opponents on a recent night and found him very capable. That man was from St. Louis, by way of New York. The others he did not know. The players were allowed a maximum amount of ten-thousand dollars per person. They could leave at any point that they wished or when they had exhausted their funds, but they could not introduce any more than the original amount they had started with.

The game was limited to five-card-stud or five-card-draw. The winner of each hand could choose which game he wanted. Thomas felt comfortable in his pressed white shirt with tie and black suit. He chose to remove his coat and place it on back of his chair. The rules called for no weapons, guns or otherwise. They were not checked for weapons, but were taken at their word that they were unarmed.

All of the men at Thomas' table appeared to be from somewhere else, with the exception of one man that was very anxious. He seemed to be fidgety and sweat more that the rest of them. Someone said he once owned a sizable plantation and lost it in a fixed poker game here in New Orleans. This was obviously an attempt to recover some of his losses.

Initially, winners of hands were equally distributed among the players. The local plantation owner was the first person to drop out of the game. He was not having a good day at all. He won twice, but started losing and continued to bet on bad hands. After betting on a pair of jacks against a full house, he grabbed what he had left and went out in a huff. His temperament was all wrong for this sort of thing.

The players were slowly whittling their way down to the more serious contenders. Thomas was left with the man from St. Louis, someone called Nicholas Rosales. He was an anomaly, a redheaded Latino. He was very good and did not give himself away. He was even keeled and made good decisions.

The games were halted at the noon hour and everyone was invited to the upper deck of the steamboat for fine dining. The tables and their winnings were guarded by men with rifles while the players were gone.

Thomas sat at the table with John and Jacob while Two-Jacks and Dona shared another table with Matthew and Evangeline. The food was quite delicious. There was boiled shrimp as an appetizer, prime rib for the main course. They had new potatoes boiled with the same spices as the shrimp, and Creole gumbo over rice on the side. Dessert was something new that originated in the Florida Keys. They called it key lime pie. It was the rave among the diners.

Enoch was on board as one of the chefs. He knew about the competition and had no intention of being left out of the excitement. He had Marguerite to arrange for his participation. He was escorted to the table by one of the waiters. He told the waiter to look for a beautiful, light skinned girl with a taller dark haired man.

"Hello, my name is Enoch. I am one of the chefs on board and I wished to sample our guests and find out if you enjoyed the meal. Was it to your liking?"

"Mr. Enoch, my name is Matthew and these are my guests. We enjoyed the dinner very much and thank you for your hard work!"

Enoch bumped into Matthew and dropped a fork while in the process of straightening himself. "I'm very sorry. I am clumsy at times," Enoch stated. "I knocked your fork off the table. Let me get it!"

He bent down to get it and Matthew bent over at the same time to retrieve it as well.

Enoch spoke softly, "There are two gangs of men looking to cause trouble. One will kill and take the money from the winner of tonight's game and the other gang is after Benjamin. Be careful, they are armed and dangerous!"

"Thanks!" was all Matt said.

Enoch put his arm out for the assistance of the waiter. The waiter reached for him and led him back into the kitchen. His goal was accomplished. He had done his part and more. He may have save the lives of his friends. Even without the ability of sight, he performed invaluable investigative work.

Matthew looked over at Two-Jacks, "I want you to find Benjamin and Elizabeth and warn them that they may be in danger. If they are not at the hotel, look for them at Café du Monde. They may have gone there to sit under the awning. Ben said they were going out to eat tonight, but he did not say where. Do the best you can to find them before anything happens to them. I trust you will find them and protect them, if it can be done. Hurry, we will take Dona home and God be with you!"

Matthew walked over to the table where John, Jacob and Thomas sat. "Enoch told me that there are two gangs of men that want to harm Benjamin and jump the winner of the poker tournament. I sent Two-Jacks to locate Ben and Elizabeth to warn them if possible. I will go to the Colonel and arrange for a military escort for the winner of the games. I want you and John to stay with the women. I should be back before the games are over."

"Go Matthew, we will handle the situation here," Jacob assured him.

The games had resumed. Thomas and Mr. Rosales were evenly matched. It was back and forth until Thomas won a big hand and Mr. Rosales leaned back in his chair. "Young man, you play a good hand of cards, but the day is long and I will retire before it gets much longer. I have recouped my initial deposit and then some; so, I will gather my winnings and take in the sights. I have come a long ways down from New York and my chief reason to visit this fine city was not to play cards. I have more pressing business to attend. Good day and good luck, my friend."

Rosales cashed in his chips and with a flip of his hat bid them adieu. He was a well built older man apparently with some military background and quite capable of handling matters if needs be. He was not a man of triviality, but rather a man on a mission. It surprised Thomas that the man quit the game so abruptly, but he seemed preoccupied all the while, watching people as they came and went, obviously looking to find someone in particular. Thomas thought him the better poker player.

The redheaded gentleman brushed by Thomas as he left the gaming area of the riverboat and leaned over to say in a hushed tone to him, "Watch your back friend; danger lurks!"

Along about three in the afternoon a break was called so the players could stretch their legs. All but one game had decided its winner. It wouldn't be long until the final winners were assembled at one main table for the showdown.

The main stage was set; all of the gamblers were in place to play for the main prize. Thomas, of course, was present with an old acquaintance from Charleston, Simon Bartlett, and his sidekick the thug that sailed off of the paddle wheeler into the bay, standing close by at all times. There was Morton Hardeman, a gambler and general opportunist that hailed from up Natchez way. Charlie Meraux, a local steamboat

Captain retired from his trade was a hanger-around that showed quite proficient at the game. And there was the unknown member of the game; he went by the handle of George Pemmican, but no one knew a thing about him. He wore a black suit, white shirt, bowtie, shiny black boots and a bowler hat. If one did not know better they would swear he was a Pinkerton or someone dressed like one of those types common to New York City.

The game started with each player's chips piled high on the table beside them. Several young ladies with revealing dance girl outfits came around to supply the gamblers with alcohol, or coffee or whatever they desired. But to the gamblers' better judgment, there were no takers. It was obvious that this was not their first rodeo; neither did they want to be intoxicated nor did they want someone to slip something into their drinks to cause any adverse effects.

The winners of the early hands were pretty much equally divided; however, later on the antes began to get increasingly larger. Charlie Meraux was the first person to retire. He left before he exhausted his prior winnings. It became more and more apparent, even to him that he was in over his head. In other words, his skill level was not on par with the rest. He felt his better judgment should prevail and bow out.

Morton Hardeman was known up and down the river. He was a professional gambler among other things. He was what some called a war profiteer. He saw a need and filled it, whether it was guns, horses, flour or influence. People often said that he had no loyalty, but that wasn't true, because he was very loyal. He was loyal to himself and any profit to be had.

Hardeman started losing more hands than he won. He kept playing with hopes that his luck would turn, but it did not change. He was smart enough to quit before he started going into the negative. His time was up!

"Gentlemen, I have exhausted my talents. Lady luck has packed up and hauled her trousseau to another man's chambers tonight. I bid you goodnight!"

He stood up and gathered his chips. He turned to the man that sat beside him and said, "Mister, you are not as slick as you may think. You would have already been shot in any other game!"

Simon Bartlett pushed back his chair and started to rise until the man they called George Pemmican reached over and laid his big hand on Bartlett's shoulder. "You best take his advice, mister, and leave well enough alone!"

Bartlett turned and looked at Pemmican and eased back down in his chair. He looked at Thomas to gauge his reaction and got no sympathy.

"They are right, mister; you are not playing with amateurs here. This is a gentlemen's game. So don't give us any reason to forget that," Thomas explained.

The game continued and Simon Bartlett was the next to leave. Once he knew that his cheating could not help him, but might just get him killed, he tried playing honestly and began losing badly. He threw in his hand after a bluff backfired on him. There wasn't much left in his stack, but he scooped it up and left to cash it in. He did not pause to share any pleasantries, because he had been shamed for his cheating ways. He just left the gaming area and walked outside to take in the night air.

The game continued for another hour before the strangest thing happened. Pemmican was having the better luck and winning more hands than Thomas; however, he seemed preoccupied with something other than the game. He started playing with little focus on the game like he didn't want to win anymore. The hands started to fall in Thomas' favor as if his luck had suddenly changed for the better. Pemmican was obviously distracted.

"Sir, I do believe lady luck is shining on you tonight!" George looked around at the officials and hailed them over. "I declare Mr. Smith here the winner of this competition. I am removing myself from the table. I seem to have come down with some kind of virus and will not be able to continue. Please cash in my chips. Congratulations sir, you are an outstanding card player," George Pemmican remarked, before he walked away.

The roar of cheers rose up as everyone realized what just happen. The master of ceremonies stood up on the table and announced that Mr. Thomas Smith was the winner of the big Fourth of July Poker Competition.

Thomas was stunned. He could not believe what just happened because it all happened so quickly and unexpectedly. John walked over and pushed through the crowd of well wishers and grabbed Thomas by the elbow and led him to the cashier's window. The head cashier presented Thomas the one-hundred thousand dollars in U.S. currency in a satchel to travel, along with his table winnings.

"No, I mean *hell no!*" Thomas shouted. "I want the winnings in gold, just like I gave you mister. You ain't about to pull the wool over on me! I paid gold and I want gold in return!"

Another man walked over to see what the commotion was about. He said he was the Official in Charge, overseeing the competition.

"Mister, you will take the currency or nothing at all! Do you understand me?"

John had placed a revolver under Thomas' coat, held there by his belt. Thomas knew he had just slipped the gun within his reach. He pulled out the pistol and pointed it at the man's forehead, "I want it in G-O-L-D, *gold*, do you understand me, *Mister*?"

Two men behind the cashier's cage pulled pistols and pointed them at Thomas, and John responded by pointed his pistol at the man nearest him pointing at Thomas. Five men came from different directions and drew down on John and Thomas. Jacob jumped on top of a table and pulled out two revolvers from beneath his long tuxedo coat. He had his double rigged holster strapped on the whole time. He pointed one pistol in the air and fired a shot into the crystal chandelier while he was pointing the other pistol at one of the men before him.

Just as Jacob had fired the shot, Matthew arrived on the main floor of the boat with a company of U.S. Army soldiers and the Colonel. They came into the main room as men and women were running out of the room in the other direction.

"What is the trouble here?" asked the Colonel with his soldiers directly behind him armed with rifles. There was a moment of hesitation. "Somebody better explain before I give the order to fire!"

The Official in Charge started to explain but was unable to regain his composure.

Thomas turned around to face the Colonel, "Sir, I just won the poker tournament and they offered to pay up in paper money when everyone had to ante up in gold. They collected one-hundred and twenty-five thousand in gold, of which their cut was twenty-five thousand; now, they want to give the winnings in paper money. That was not the understanding! How do you think they should pay the winner, sir?"

"Son, I know how they should, and will pay out the winnings. It will be in gold!" the Colonel proclaimed.

The Official in Charge said, "That will not fly with me!"

The Colonel gave the command for his troops, "Aim!"

The company of soldiers brought their guns up to their shoulders and aimed at the men pointing at Thomas and John. Those men dropped their weapons like they were on fire and they rattled as they hit the floor. They raised their hands as quickly as their guns fell.

"Private Stanton, get a piece of rope and get all of their guns, even those in the cashier's cage," the Colonel commanded.

"Yes sir, Colonel!"

"Sergeant MacMurphy, you and Corporal Benson get several money satchels and help that teller count out the gold in double eagles. You do have the gold here, don't you?" the Colonel asked with an air of impatience in his voice.

"Yes, we have the gold, sir!" he replied.

The gold was placed in several heavy bags and taken by the soldiers to the Army command center for safe keeping until the bank opened the following day.

The Colonel stopped to address Matthew after they had safely exited the boat ramp and stood on the top of the levee. "Was that to your satisfaction, Major O'Brien?"

"That was quite satisfactory, Colonel! You were complicit in staving off a great deal of bloodshed tonight. I thank you from the bottom of my heart, sir," Matthew replied.

"Well, I've had enough excitement for one night, gentlemen. I hope you can find your way home after this exercise, good night to all!" were the Colonel's last remarks before he turned and walked towards his home, with soldiers close behind.

Matthew stopped in the center of Decatur Street at the sight of a man running in his general direction, and was almost run over by horse and buggy by his negligence. Two-Jacks came running across the lawn in front of St. Louis Cathedral and screaming to the top of his lungs.

"Matthew, come quickly, Benjamin is hurt badly and needs your help. I'd been looking for him when I saw a crowd of people and some men on the ground. They said a big Negro was seen carrying another man to the doctor's place. It was Ben and he is hurt somethin' fierce."

CHAPTER 33

MATTHEW AND HIS FRIENDS FOLLOWED TWO-Jacks to the house of a local doctor on the corner of Toulouse and Burgundy Street. His practice was in his private residence. Dr. Alvarez walked from the examining room to speak with Matthew about Benjamin's condition.

"Excuse me for asking, but it is customary to know what relation someone is before I divulge any information about my patient; that is purely to protect the patient. I hope you understand," the doctor explained.

"I'm sorry, Doctor, but I was so caught up with events that I forgot to introduce myself. My name is Matthew and I am the young man's brother. His name is Benjamin O'Brien, and what is his condition, sir?" Matthew asked.

"I am very sorry, Matthew, but your brother has taken a terrible beating from what appears to be multiple attackers. This man standing in the corner," he pointed at a tall, barefoot, bare-chested black man with raggedy jeans held in place by a piece of twine for a belt standing off to their side with a look of fear on his face, "this Negro, as I was about to say, brought your brother here cradled in his arms and asked me to fix him. Benjamin has a bad concussion from a blow to the head with what could have been a club. He also has several broken ribs on his right side. His face is bruised as are other parts of him from what may have been kicking and stomping while he was down. His knuckles are torn and bleeding as well from fighting off his attackers."

"Will he be alright, Doctor?" Matthew asked nervously.

"When he wakes up, I can assess him more closely. His breathing is a little rough, probably from the damaged ribs. He looks as strong as a horse and I've seen men like him go through worse and come out just fine on the other side. He may have a fever over the next twenty-four to forty-eight hours and that's to be expected. I will watch him until my nurse comes in about seven in the morning."

"I will watch over him and let you rest, doctor!" Evangeline said. "I have cared for men before that have been given a beating and left tied to a tree overnight. I know what to watch for, trust me!"

The doctor looked at Evangeline as did Matthew and just nodded his head in reply.

Matthew turned and looked at the black man who stood with his palms against the wall and shook nervously. He stood about six-feet and two inches and must have weighed about two-hundred and thirty pounds.

John stepped over and placed his hand on Matthew to move him backwards because his demeanor must have caused the man to be afraid.

"I'll talk with him, Matt!" John suggested.

John walked over to the big man and held out his hand. After a moment of hesitation the big fellow slowly reached out and held John's hand in his oversized hand. John felt something extraordinary surge between him and the Negro when they touched hands. Not only did he feel the strong grip and calloused palm, but he felt an energy flow up his arm and shoulder into his chest like nothing he had ever felt before. They stood for a short time just looking at each other like they had once been friends.

"Don't I know you, mister?" John asked.

"My name is Abraham and some folks just calls me Ham, buts I prefers to be called by Abraham because that is my name! We were never introduced rightfully, but I think we met when I was much younger and you were just a boy. My master was Mr. Cain, and his horse was about to hurt you badly when I stepped in, and picked you up."

"So you are the man that saved my life; we thought it was an Angel!" John said.

"Sir, there was an Angel there. He was the one that stopped the horse from stomping you. He put his hand on the horse's chest and held him while I grabbed you from underneath. He calmed the horse too!" Abraham explained. "I was scared that I would get in trouble and ran off to hide after I carried you into the house. It was that Angel that saved you."

"Please sir, let me tell you about your friend. I was restless because I was hungry and could not sleep. There was too much noise down by the river where I had laid down for the night, so I decided to walk around the market looking for something to eat that someone might have thrown out from the restaurants. I was around the corner when I heard a woman screaming so I ran down the block and looked to see what was happening when I got to the next street. I saw some men running down the street about a block away. They must have carried the woman with them because I didn't hear any more screaming. They was running towards Esplanade Avenue."

"I saw some other men beating on your friend here and it was not a fair fight. There was about five men in all; one man was down from what I believe was a blown that Benjamin must have given him. I ran in and grabbed the biggest one because he had a club. They were just kicking him as he fell to the ground unable to defend himself. I grabbed the man from behind and squeezed hard. It must have broken his back because I heard it crack. I threw him down and grabbed the club and started in swinging at the rest of them. I got a few licks in on them when they decided to back off. I scooped up your brother, sir," he looked over at Matthew as he said that, "and I brought him here because I know'd it be where the doctor lives. I guess the other men dragged the rest of them away. And that's how it happened. Please don't take me to the law because I didn't mean no harm!"

"Don't worry Abraham, you are not in trouble, but I want you to go with John, Jacob and Thomas here. They will get you something to eat."

Matthew turned to speak to John. "They must have taken Elizabeth captive. Thomas, take Abraham down to the Magnolia Café and get Enoch to fix something for him to eat. Then meet up with John and Jacob and begin searching the riverfront and all around the quarter.

Two-Jacks, you can speak with your friends, the Indians, and see if they have anything to tell us."

"Matthew," John interjected, "I will round up some of the river-men that I know along the docks and get them involved in the search. Maybe someone will have seen something, if we are lucky."

Matthew and Evangeline took turns watching Benjamin while the other one napped.

"I am worried about Elizabeth. What will they do to her?" Matthew thought out loud.

"Please don't worry, Matthew. I have a good feeling she is going to be fine. You and your friends will have another adventure to tell your grandchildren. Ben and her will grow old together and raise many children. Don't you worry!" she said as she stroked his head and he looked up and smiled at her.

"Yeah, I guess you are right, Evangeline. They will be very happy and so will you. I've had a few thoughts myself lately. I can see you and your mother being reunited and you will be telling her about your boy-friend and how much you love him," he said with a grin from ear to ear.

"What are you talking about? Have you done lost your mind?"

"No, my mind is as strong as ever and I can see things in a different way than you and John. I may not have the gifts you two have been given, but I can tell budding romance when I see it. Experience is my gift!" he proclaimed.

"There ain't nothing between John and me; we are just friends," she said.

"Did I say John?" Matthew asked. At that time they both looked over to Benjamin who was making a groaning noise and reaching up to grab his head with his left hand.

He opened his eyes and rolled his head over to look around the room. "What happened to me? Where is Elizabeth? What is going on here?" he asked.

"Just calm down," Matt said, "you have been attacked and suffered some serious injuries. Your head was busted open and some ribs were broken. Elizabeth has been taken and we have everyone looking for her now. You need to rest!"

Ben felt his head and it was bandaged and he sat up with a loud groan as pain shot through him from the broken ribs. "I've been dealt worse when that old Brahma bull got out and came at me, head on. Now I have to get dressed and go out and bring Elizabeth back," he said as he looked around at the spinning room.

"On second thought, I better stay here for a little while."

"You just go back to sleep. The doctor will see you in the morning. I already have everyone looking for her with the exception of the U.S. Army and I will see about them joining us in the morning," Matthew informed his brother.

The next morning everyone met at the coffee shop, Café Du Monde, and had some coffee and beignets, which they had all grown to enjoy regularly. John informed them he had a network of at least one-hundred people actively searching for Elizabeth. Two-Jack shared that his network of Indians were also actively listening and looking for her. Jacob would walk the halls of the bank and listen for any talk of the abduction.

Matthew looked at Thomas before he spoke, "Thomas, I know you have been making the rounds with John, but I have another assignment for you. I got a letter that was dropped off at the desk of our hotel, The Royal Court, and I think you should get lost for the rest of the day. It says that the only way to recover Elizabeth is to deliver one-hundred thousand in gold by 12:00 o'clock midnight to a place that will be specified later. That, in my mind, makes you a target. You need to be anywhere but on the streets where someone can snatch you up. I suggest you get your horse and take a ride out to Hidden Oaks Plantation. But before you do that, I want you and Two-Jacks to take Abraham down to the mercantile and outfit him with some new clothes, several sets, and some boots that will fit him. Take him somewhere so he can have a shave and a bath; you need to knock the bark off him. Take him with you out to the plantation, more people around you the better."

"I don't need nobody to protect me. Just let those thugs come my way and I will cut them down," Thomas boasted.

"Just listen to me and follow my orders! If they follow you and Two-Jacks, then you take care of business outside of town. Both of you are better fighters in the countryside. If you capture one of them, then maybe we can find out where they are holding Elizabeth." Matthew paused before speaking again.

"I will send a courier out to get you if we locate Elizabeth and need you; so, do as I suggest and take Abraham with you. Take John's horse for Abraham. Is he still at the Magnolia Café?"

"Hell Matthew, he is probably still eating. I think Enoch fed him a dozen eggs, half of a ham, a loaf of bread, a bucket of milk and two pots of coffee." Thomas laughed and slapped his knee, "He makes me look like a man that has lost his appetite!"

Matthew was exhausted as was each one of them. He had gotten maybe several hours sleep and the rest of them probably had no sleep at all.

"I am going over to speak with Colonel Beauregard and see if he has any suggestions. It will make no sense to go to the sheriff because he may be in on the plot too. You can find me either at the doctor's home or the hotel if you get any information that we can act on. Get some rest if you can because we will be busy later today, and tonight," Matthew informed them.

They came together at the noon hour in Matthew's hotel room. Jacob said he heard some scuttlebutt about a certain kidnapping. According to him, people were talking in hushed tones, leading him to believe that there must be some connection with the bank president and Carver to the events leading up to Elizabeth's abduction. John came in a few minutes later and told them he might have some information that could be useful.

"One of the river captain's lackeys reported that a schooner was anchored behind an old warehouse that hadn't been used in years. It once was a holding pen for Caribbean slaves before they were put on the auction block. There is nothing left there but some stacks of rancid cotton bales and miscellaneous relics of the trade. The stench of human filth is still so strong that it burns your nostrils and renders the building unfit for use of any kind. There are three men with rifles posted there, one at the front and one on each side. I think it warrants further investigation after dark. I rode a borrowed horse by there and confirmed the presence of guards. They look like Carver's men alright," John declared.

"Do you have any suggestions, John?" Matthew asked.

"Yes, I have talked the situation out with one of my old friends, a riverboat captain, Captain Wetzel, and we agree on a plan that has as good a chance as any." John explained, "We can get some good men and maneuver ourselves in place with a rowboat behind the warehouse around eight o'clock and get inside to check things out. Jacob and Two-Jacks can go with me and we will bring Elizabeth out if possible. There is another important development. The schooner is loaded with kegs of gunpowder and other explosives. We can set that off after we leave the warehouse to prevent someone from pursuing us. It is all very speculative until we enter the warehouse and check things out. I think Two-Jacks will be the best one to go in and survey the situation before we run into an ambush. You can take some men and approach the front under the guise of drunken river-rats out for an evening stroll. It would be too risky to try anything before dark, in my opinion."

"I think that is as good an idea as any I can think of," Matthew surmised.

"I got another letter that was dropped off at the hotel desk and no one saw the person deliver it. It says that we are to deliver the gold by carriage down the river road just beyond Faubourg Marigny to the front yard of the abandoned Two-Sisters Plantation by midnight. At that point we will be given instructions on how to find Elizabeth. We are to do as we are told or she will be killed."

"We will never get Elizabeth back under those circumstances. She is dead already or will be once they get that gold," Jacob commented with conviction.

Matthew spoke, "I agree wholeheartedly with your assessment. If we do not find her in the warehouse, then we will not proceed with their requests. I will leave a note myself pinned to the desk for the next courier with specific instructions for them to give us proof that she is alive or nothing! Then we will go from there. John, get going with your plan for tonight, and Godspeed!"

"I will have someone approach you and bring some trusted men to play the part of drunks for your ploy; but they will be sober and capable men. They will fill you in on all of the details. Trouble not yourself, this is my town and these are my people and we will overcome."

Matthew visited Benjamin at the doctor's house and found him resting. The doctor said he should be up and about tomorrow, but he had given him a sedative to make him sleep for his own good.

Matthew had a visitor at six o'clock that evening. It was Mossyhorn and four other trusted and capable men from the docks sent by Captain Wetzel and John to assist Matthew in their plan. Old Mossy explained what they intended to do and how. He would have his men to drink some whiskey and splash enough on their clothing to create the notion that they were just drunken boys out for a stroll.

John and Two-Jacks met Captain Wetzel down at the docks and boarded the skiff with two other men in charge of rowing. It was just getting dark. It wouldn't be completely dark until about eight-thirty. They approached the back of the warehouse and positioned the boat just behind the schooner where they could climb onto the dock behind the warehouse. One of the rowers climbed onto the schooner, which appeared to be unoccupied, and prepared an explosion to be set as needed, after they had left the warehouse. It was a precaution to divert any pursuers.

Two-Jacks slid the big door open just enough to gain access into the warehouse. He slipped in and flattened himself against the wall. He waited until his eyes had adjusted to the darkness of the huge building. He moved around after hearing no noise or seeing anything to indicate there was anyone present. He saw old, moldy cotton bales lying on the warehouse floor here and there, and after looking more closely saw a dark figure that could be a person.

It appeared to be a woman tied to a chair, and her head was lying on her chest. He moved slowly towards the woman once he felt it safe to move about. She was in the center and to the rear of the building. Once he got to her, it was clear that she had a gag in her mouth. He moved in front of her and placed his finger over his mouth to indicate quiet. Her head popped up which was a good sign that she was alive. Her eyes were big and she was trying to tell him something. Two-Jacks indicated with the motion of his hands for her to be calm and they would rescue her.

John and Captain Wetzel came in the warehouse, only after Two-Jacks gave them the go-ahead signal. They could hear Matthew, Old Mossy and the boys making a ruckus outside. They overcame the guards, unlocked the front door, slid it open, and walked inside. They met up at the center of the building, once used to warehouse slave shipments, where Elizabeth was tied to the chair.

John untied Elizabeth's hands, allowing her to remove the gag from her mouth. But before she could speak, lanterns were being lit throughout the warehouse.

Men popped up from their hiding places between cotton bales. Men were also staged on the catwalk above, looking down on them. They had concealed themselves expertly. There were about twenty men standing in front and to their sides. They approached John and Matthew and their comrades-in-arms with their guns drawn.

Elizabeth spoke, "I was trying to tell you they were here!"

"Too late for that, lassie," the leader of the captors suggested, "because you all will go into the drink tonight!" He laughed a deep belly laugh just thinking of how successful he was and how he would brag to his employer tonight.

"Now, I want all you people to line up and put your weapons on the ground. You too redskin! Come out with that pig-sticker of yours," he said to Two-Jacks.

As they placed their guns on the ground a man fell from the catwalk with an extended scream before making a dead thud as he hit the ground below. Another man screamed as he fell to his death too.

"What the hell?" the leader of the captors said as that was happening.

Everyone turned their heads to the walls of the building to see the strangest and most frightening thing any of them had ever seen, with the exception of John. The people were encircled and the place was filled with the spirits of hundreds of dead slaves that had been shipped to this place from Africa, by way of the Caribbean, and died here in vain. This was the final spot on earth that they had ever drawn a breath. They came to this place, under the worst conditions possible, to die in the squalor of their own filth for reasons unknown to them. These spirits existed in an unsettled state without understanding or foreknowledge of any crimes committed by them to warrant this sort of treatment; whereas, there were no crimes committed by them, just an opportunity to profit by their captives, black and white.

The spirits of the dead slaves manifested themselves as fully as live beings in the flesh, but their strength and ferocity far exceeded the mortal man. While captor and captive alike stood in fear of what would happen next, it was John that stepped forward to parley with one of the most capable looking spirits amongst them.

There was a distinct glow about John that wasn't there prior to the appearance of the spirits. The slave, a tall and noble looking creature draped in shackle and chain, made a bowing gesture by bending down onto one knee and lowering his head. He stood up and looked John directly in the eye as he reached out his hand.

"I was told to look for you. You must be the one called John. We have been waiting in earnest!" the slave declared. "We are more than anxious to be on our way."

John reached out and accepted his hand in friendly embrace. He spoke to the man; even though, it was a language that he had never spoken before and the people around him had never heard either.

"Who told you to look for me?" John asked the spirit-man.

"It was an Angel. He said He was a messenger of God, went by the name, Gabriel. He said he would take us home. We were to look for you, sir! What do you have us do?" the spirit-man asked.

"Hold these people until we get away and do what you must with them," John explained. "There will be a loud explosion later, but you will be on your way home by then, Godspeed!"

"God-speed to you as well, for we shall meet again, my friend," the spirit-man suggested as he stepped away.

John quickly led Elizabeth, Matthew, Two-Jacks, the Captain and the other men too out the back entrance to the warehouse.

The former captors screamed as they realized that they were not coming along.

They split up and some got into the rowboat while the others got into a four-man dingy retrieved from the schooner.

"We had better make tracks and quickly!" one of the rowers announced. "I set enough explosives to go off in about five minutes that will rattle the windows of half the houses in New Orleans."

True to his word, they had just got onto the shore when the explosion ripped through the schooner, breaking it in half and sinking it in the river, and leveling the warehouse. Windows were either broken or rattled forcibly throughout the French Quarter and the rest of town.

Men and women were thrown to the ground all around the site. Only God knows what happened to those inside the warehouse. Miraculously, there were only minor injuries to anyone on the outside, with the one exception being an old man sitting on the levee with his little dog and playing his harmonica. He was struck in the chest with a splintered two-by-four. It held him upright as it lodged into the ground behind him. His dog sat beside him not quite understanding his dilemma.

The three men sent to guard the warehouse lived only because Matthew and his comrades knocked them out, tied them up and moved them away from the building into a vacant carriage house. They later reported back to their employer, who then reported back to John Carver. It wasn't like Carver to directly link himself to the commission of any crime.

Captain Wetzel offered to treat the men to beer at the Decatur Street Pub. He had plenty of takers, but Matthew and John wanted to escort Elizabeth back to her room; however, she had no intentions of going to her room because Benjamin was her first priority.

Ben was sitting up in the bed when they arrived. He was groggy from the sedative but awake enough to grasp the reality of the moment. Elizabeth hugged him about the neck and shoulders and was very careful not to disturb the bandages on his head and the rib area. She was very complimentary about how he stood up to the attackers and protected her with all of his might.

The doctor agreed with them that he was well enough to be taken over to his room at the hotel, but he would have to be transferred by carriage, he was not able to walk while still feeling the effects of the sedative.

Matthew wasn't able to sleep much because Elizabeth refused to leave Ben's bedside. After several hours of tossing and turning, he got up and got dressed. He found Evangeline sitting in the hotel lobby, fully dressed.

"What are you doing here so early, Evangeline?" Matt asked.

"I just could not sleep. I fell asleep easily enough, but I had a dream that woke me from a sound sleep and I could not shake it!" Evangeline looked at Matthew and asked, "Do you remember how I had that dream about Sarah, and so did you and John?"

"Yes, I remember very well." Matthew hesitated before he spoke again, "Did your dream tell you something about your mother?"

"Yes, it did! I was running in the forest and something or someone was chasing me, then I fell down and when I looked up there was a man on a large black horse standing over me. The man's head and shoulders were on fire. The horse was on his hind legs about to crush me when a man dressed like a pirate, with a beautiful hat, stepped between the horse and me. He picked me up and held me like a little baby," Evangeline explained her dream.

"Evangeline," Matt asked, "What did he say to you afterwards?"

"It was the strangest thing. He told me, "Go to the cupboard of darkness, and you will be fed.""

"Did he also tell you that the days are few, so hold them close?" Matthew asked.

"Yes he did, that is exactly what he said." Evangeline smiled and grasped his hand, "Did you have a similar dream?"

"Kind of similar," he said, "but it was a celebration of sorts that went along with that statement about the cupboard. I'm not sure what to make of it. It must be very significant that we both had that dream."

"I don't know what significant means, but I think it was important," she said with a smile.

They went out to walk through the streets of the French Quarter and were surprised how many people were out at the wee hours of the morning. They saw the merchants unloading the produce that the farmers had trucked in by wagon into the city from all points. They also saw the fishermen selling their night's catch of shrimp, oysters, fish and crabs to the fish mongers.

He ran into John who was helping his father set up his fish market for the day. He cleaned and sanitized the market after the day's business and before the start of each new day. It was imperative not to smell like fish if he wanted customers to buy from him.

"Hello Mr. Bernard, it's good to see John doing an honest day's work for a change," Matt commented.

Mr. Bernard smiled as he straightened his stiff back and looked at Matthew, "Yes, he has always been a hard worker, but after years of playing war and being a soldier he has gotten soft. But, it is nothing that working around the market or going out on an oyster skiff can't change."

"Hard work is in my blood! I ain't nothing like that lazy-dog scoundrel, Thomas Smith, who wouldn't hit a lick at a snake," John commented as he saw Thomas walking up out of the corner of his eye.

"Hey now, don't go slandering my good name like that!" Thomas said as he and Jacob came up with Two-Jacks in tow.

"Hey there boys, what are you doing up so early?" Matthew inquired.

"We don't waste our days sleeping like some of those people camped out in those fancy hotels!" Jacob insinuated.

"Let's all go down to the Magnolia Inn and Café for breakfast and see what Enoch has to say about anything," John suggested.

John saw Abraham, the man that rescued Benjamin standing in the shadows of the produce stand, just watching like a lost puppy that had no friends.

"Abraham," John spoke up, "what are you doing standing over there?"

"Well, Mr. John, sir, I noticed that you could not sleep and I wanted to make sure no one would cause you no harm while you was walking around with so many thoughts rolling around in your head!" Abraham explained.

"Well, that was very thoughtful of you. I had myself another powerful dream last night and I wanted to sort it out. Would you be interested in having some breakfast with us?"

"I don't see any reason why not sir!"

"Yeah, I could use a bite to eat 'cause I'm a bit hungry myself," Thomas said to no one in particular.

"Thomas," Two-Jacks stated, "I don't think I've ever seen you when you weren't hungry. I believe Jacob's dog Blue is looking kind of puny because you've been eating up all of his scraps!"

They all broke out in laughter, even Abraham who barely knew Thomas was laughing.

"I must come to Thomas' rescue," Jacob declared, "Blue is looking puny because that French poodle that sits in the bay window next to the widow's house is driving him crazy. I believe we will have to move before he starves to death."

They laughed again.

"Come on everybody, let's go down to the café," John suggested. "Dad, would you like to go too?"

"No, son, your mother made breakfast for me; and there is no one to watch the fish market while I'm away."

"Yeah, you are right, Dad!"

Enoch wasn't surprised in the least to find that his dear friends had arrived for an early breakfast. He had already rolled the biscuits and put them in the oven.

"What brings the lot of you out so early in the morning?" Enoch asked. "I haven't even heard the rooster crow!"

"You ain't heard him because you done rung his neck and put him in the pot to cook!" Thomas said with delight.

"Well, I am most surprised to see you hungry, Thomas. You are likely to dry up and fly away if you don't start eating more often," stated Enoch to the roar of laughter at the table.

"Enoch," Matthew said, "have a seat; I want to share something with everyone. I received a telegram from Sarah back in Virginia; she should be arriving here in several days. She is traveling by boat from St. Louis. She says she received a letter from Frances, Evangeline's mother, who is alive and living in New Orleans and wants so dearly to reconnect with her daughter now that the war is over. Isn't that great news, Evangeline?"

Evangeline paused for a long moment and looked up, "I had a frightening dream this morning that something bad would happen; however, I was told to look to the cupboard of darkness and I would be fed. What in the world could that mean?"

John spoke up, "I think Enoch can tell us what the cupboard of darkness means. Am I right, Enoch?"

"I do believe so! That's me; I look into the cupboard of darkness every day and find people who need to be fed." Enoch turned his head, "Let me introduce you to Marguerite, she is the owner of this establishment."

With that said, Marguerite walked out from the kitchen with a smile on her face. "Shall we bring out our new chef apprentice, Enoch?"

"I see no reason why we shouldn't, Marguerite."

Marguerite walked back to the kitchen and spoke in a hushed tone and motioned for the new apprentice to come out to the dining area. Everyone was puzzled.

A very light skin lady walked out wearing a white apron and flour on her hands and face.

"I would like to introduce you to my new apprentice, her name is Frances!" Enoch declared with a broad smile plastered on his face.

"Evangeline, do you know anyone by that name?"

Evangeline was caught off guard. The moment had overwhelmed her, as it did Frances as well.

"Frances, aren't you going to hug your daughter?" Marguerite asked.

Time stood still. Evangeline shoved her chair backwards, causing it to fall over, and ran to her mother. Frances took a second or two longer to grasp the reality of the moment and then she was swept up in the knowledge that her daughter was flying into her arms. No one spoke. They stayed back and allowed events to take their natural course. There was a great show of emotion. Both were crying tears of joy. It felt like a long time before they separated themselves from their embrace and looked at each other from an arms' distance for a moment. It was a time of reunion for a mother and a child. It had been fifteen years since they last stood in each other's presence. The last time they were together mother was being dragged off from a screaming child to be separated forever. They both realized that this moment was a miracle and how many others like themselves would not have such a happy reunion.

With the expertise of a public speaker, Enoch asked in their general direction, "Evangeline, wouldn't you like to meet your grandmother, too?"

Marguerite stepped forward and embraced her granddaughter earnestly. The event was one that could have gone the other way as easily as it went this way. No better outcome could have been wished for, or expected.

"Well, I guess that ruins breakfast," Thomas bemoaned. "We might as well go looking for somewhere else to eat. It looks like all the hired help is out for the day!"

Life for Evangeline was forever changed. She spent more time each day with her mother just getting to know her again. She began to stay at Frances' house more and more until she finally moved all of her things over there.

She also brought the fine horse that she rode down from Virginia to stable at her mother's house. It was the horse that Sarah had given her. It was also the horse that Sarah's father loved so much and often rode across the fields of his plantation. That was the very same man that had fathered her, but would not call her his daughter for fear of what consequences might arise. She couldn't leave the horse back in Jackson with the others. There was a special fondness to the horse since her father had shown it so much affection. She often imagined she was that horse and it was she that her father was showering with love. It was a fine horse.

She also spent more time working with her mother, grandmother and Enoch. Enoch delighted in teaching her the culinary arts. He once told her that she would need those skills to feed that hungry husband and all of their children in the future.

She didn't understand just what he meant by that because she had not spoken to anyone about things of the heart, especially the one person she felt the closest to. She didn't even know what others were implying. Maybe they were just guessing about things like that; but, she remembered that Matthew even spoke about her having feelings toward someone. Who were they talking about? She had no idea who! Maybe they were just giving her a hard time and didn't mean anything by it.

Frances was enjoying the lighter moments of life. Being with her daughter and mother were more than she had ever dreamed possible. She hoped to find one or maybe the other, but not expecting to find both, and so soon. One morning she paused while working in her little vegetable garden. It came to her that God had answered her two most fervent prayers and both at the same time. She fell down on her knees, getting her dress dirty as she landed between the rows of tomatoes. She bowed her head and hid it in her hands as tears flowed down her cheeks.

"God, please forgive me for ever doubting you! I believed my life had been a series of unfortunate events, but now I realize that you are working everything out to achieve the plan you had for us. It wasn't just about me.

Father, you are so wonderful and I pray that you will help me to grow my faith each day. I know I am just the created and you are the Creator and it was never meant for me to question your wisdom, but I am just a weak sister!"

Frances lifted her head and looked up at the beautiful white blossoms in the magnolia tree. Tears continued to flow as they transformed from tears of shame to tears of joy. She began to smile as she realized how much the Lord loved her.

Frances was always looking over her shoulder afraid that she would see Etienne again and he would cause harm to her or Evangeline. She had heard from others that he had lost his plantation and all of his possessions and that his wife and children had left him and moved back to Baton Rouge to live with her parents. He was a broken man, no different than a mule or a slave that did only as they were told. It had also been said by a diner at the café to another that Etienne was living like a crazy man, sleeping in neighbors' barns and eating marsh rabbits he could catch and anything he could steal from someone's gardens. The war had broken many a proud man.

CHAPTER 34

THE PURPOSE OF MATTHEW'S MISSION WAS drawing to a conclusion. He had been in contact with the Pinkertons, Henry Stone and Madelyn Cooper, as they were actively investigating the suspects that were cogs in John Carver's enterprise. The bank principals and the attorney were their prime suspects; however, the main objective was to connect the dots with other participants in the counterfeiting scheme, wherever they were found. They had people working other leads in Washington, New York and all the way down the East Coast.

Jacob had solicited the bank manager's help in a covert way. He became very friendly to many of the regulars in the bank building. He gained their confidence after renting an office there and spending time with them. He dined with them and related stories about his connections in Washington and time spent working with the Indian Bureau. They never really asked him exactly what his business was, but assumed he was a man of leisure since he dressed well and actively attended local events. He relayed information that he gathered directly to the Pinkertons. They were building the case for the government.

Apparently, Horace T. Marchant was wiser than the other suspects because he smelled a rat and backed away from Carver and his enterprise. He stood to lose more than Carver proposed to gain. There were many carpetbaggers and scalawags down from the North as well as opportunists from the South that wanted to profit from the misfortune of others while the South had fallen and would take time to get back on its feet again. He knew it was not wise to cheat his fellow friends and associates. It would only be a short term gain and would sour any future dealings with them.

It was a beautiful Tuesday morning in July and everyone wanted to be at the river landing to greet Sarah. They wanted to surprise her with the good news about Evangeline's mother as she exited the boat.

Evangeline, Frances and Marguerite had gone with Elizabeth and were fitted with very colorful dresses that she and Benjamin presented to them as a remembrance of their reunion.

Albert Goldsmith was excited as well when he helped them with their purchases. He remembered Benjamin, Elizabeth and Evangeline from previous visits they had made. He explained that his wife and two daughters would be arriving on the same day. They were traveling with his wife's childhood friend, Cecilia Carver. Everyone was radiant with excitement about the upcoming events.

Commerce was heavy and river traffic hectic with many riverboats coming from both north and south now that the war was over and there was nothing to impede the flow of goods.

John had communicated with Matthew and the others to be prepared for trouble at the river. His sources informed him that John Carver would be there with his usual entourage, including armed bodyguards. He would be there to greet his wife and son as they arrived from New York. He informed them that the Goldsmith family would arrive on the same boat. They traveled as guests of Mr. Carver.

Mr. Goldsmith and his wife had decided to escort their daughter-in-law and grandchildren to New Orleans. He wanted to surprise his son with the visit, and to inform him that he had sold his business in Philadelphia and considered moving to New Orleans to be close to them.

Mrs. Goldsmith told her husband that it was time to retire, but initially he refused. He said only lazy people and people who are not able to work retired. He was neither, and it was his responsibility to support his family; besides, he loved his work. He was blessed with a career that he enjoyed. Working with his hands and mind to create something that pleased others was a blessing. Plus, he got paid to do it! He eventually gave in to his wife's way of thinking. He missed his son and wanted to spend his time near the grandkids too.

The Mississippi's muddy water was churned by the action of the paddle wheelers as they moved up and down the river. The water was the color of brown, like chocolate milk, because of recent storms. One such storm passed through overnight toppling trees and taking off tiles from some roofs across town.

There were many people out that day, as was the case when people arrived on the boats. They wanted to be there to greet them. There were many dock workers present also. They had a great deal of freight to load and unload.

The sternwheeler, *The Buckeye State*, was a sight to see. It was full of passengers on both decks. People lined the upper deck and looked to find friends and family in the crowd. Those that were able to spot loved ones along the docks would jump up and down and wave when the connection was made.

Those on the lower deck had the economy accommodations; they slept out on the deck in between cargo and endured the elements, unlike the other passengers that could afford rooms for sleep. Disease ran rampant among the masses huddled together.

Albert Goldsmith was one of the first to locate his wife and daughters standing along the boat's railing. The girls were overwhelmed at the beauty of the city and the calamity of the crowd. The St. Louis Cathedral was spectacular in the bright morning sun. It looked like an oil painting against a bright blue canvas after the stormy night.

He waved his right hand wildly as tears of joy flowed down his cheeks. There had been moments that he honestly thought he may never see them again. He truly felt his life was in jeopardy after learning of John Carver's involvement in the same ill-advised scheme of his friends.

He grew up somewhat, realizing the danger which he had placed himself to impress his friends with his courage. Their counterfeiting scheme held little risk for anyone but him. Little did they know that their names had been linked with the overall network of ne'er-do-wells and schemers that sought to gain at the country's expense.

With information provided by Albert, the Pinkertons were able to tie his associates in with the elaborate network that ran the entire Eastern Seaboard. Matthew went to great lengths to make sure Albert's name was not associated with this scheme, although Albert would never know.

Matthew was the first person in the crowd that Sarah recognized. His dark hair and handsome face was beaming to her. He was almost aglow, causing him to stand out in the crowd. She started jumping and waving and screaming, which she promised herself she would not do.

"Matthew, Matthew, Matthew!" she screamed. Thomas saw her first and grabbed Matthew by his shirt and jerked him back and forth.

"Look Matthew, there she is along the railing towards the front of the boat in that pink and white dress!" Thomas yelled, "Can't you see her?"

"Oh, yes I see her. I can see her now!" Matthew shouted back.

Then the moment was broken with a different kind of excitement. The crowd parted to create a space between John Carver and Nicholas Rosales. Mr. Rosales had pushed Carver away from the others and had a gun pointed at him. Carver's bodyguards went for their guns, but John and Jacob had already pulled out their pistols and pointed at them.

"Stand down boys, unless you want to die!" John commanded.

"Mr. Carver, I have waited a long time for this moment," Rosales boasted, "and I have come a long way to avenge the death of my father and brother. You had them killed and thrown in the water in Manhattan to make a point. You can drop that cane. I know your tricks. You will die here today!"

"Now look here mister, I don't even know your name!" Carver insisted.

"You know my name. It is Nicholas Rosales, Jr. That's right, just like my father's name! Now, drop that cane!" Rosales commanded.

Slowly, Carver placed the cane in his left hand and let it fall to the ground, but quickly his right hand came up with a sleeve gun that he kept concealed for just this situation. Before he could bring it directly in line with Rosales and fire at him another pistol went off. It was not Nicholas Rosales' gun, but the gun of George Pemmican who stood to Rosales' right. John Carver threw the two-shot derringer into the air as he fell back from the shot that hit him in his right shoulder causing excruciating pain and rendering him no longer a threat.

George Pemmican stepped forward and seized Rosales' wrist and removed the pistol before he could accidentally shoot someone.

"My name is George McAlister, I'm a Federal Marshal, and John Carver is my prisoner. Carver, you are wanted for murder and will be taken back to New York to stand trial."

"I thought your name was Pemmican," Thomas said.

"Jacob, explain it to him," George requested.

"Do you know him, Jacob?" Thomas asked.

"Yes," Jacob replied, "I know him quite well. We were sworn in at the same time as U.S. Marshals. Pemmican means jerky, a form of dried buffalo that the Indians used for a source of food when they traveled and when other game was scarce. I knew who he was when he showed up at the card game. I didn't want to give away his disguise because I figured he was working a case. That's all!"

"Jacob, do you mind helping me escort my prisoner down to the military stockade?" George asked.

"Not at all," Jacob replied, "please tell Sarah I will see her for dinner at Monsieur Antoine's!"

The boat made its landing and the passengers disembarked. The Goldsmiths were all delighted at the reunion of their family. Sarah hugged all of her friends and was very happy for Evangeline.

But Cecilia, Mrs. Carver, was confused, frightened and angry to witness the shooting of her husband and his subsequent escorting to jail. She didn't know what to say to her son. He worshiped his father and was devastated at what he had just witnessed. He was bawling and Mrs. Carver didn't know how to comfort him.

Martha, Albert's wife, who had just travelled South with her child-hood friend, was visibly disturbed for Cecilia. She did not understand why Mr. Carver was shot and arrested. Albert told her he would explain it all later.

Albert was overjoyed to see his wife and daughters, Sally and Rebecca, and more so to discover his mother and father had traveled to be with him too. He couldn't have hoped for a more pleasant reunion. He gathered them up and took them by carriage to their new home. He had to rent a second carriage and driver to convey his parents and their luggage.

The girls were so excited that they were almost uncontrollable. This new world that their father had made for them was fantastic. It was almost unbelievable that their father bought them a house of their own. This was a life changing event.

Mr. Goldsmith was more excited than he let on. He could see the joy in his wife's face to see her son alive and healthy. Albert was glad that he purchased a home that was big enough for his entire family. It was not unusual for whole families to live together in those days.

Sarah looked at everyone and cried tears of joy. "You all look so beautiful, even you, Thomas! It is so wonderful to see you once again, Frances. It has been so long and you look so beautiful. I am so pleased to meet you, Marguerite. I've heard stories about you and would love to hear more."

"Evangeline, my sister, I never knew how much I loved you and would miss you until you rode away that day with these fine young men. I was always afraid something would happen to you. I prayed daily for your safety. I want to hear everything about your trip. And I must admit how jealous I was of your adventure too!"

Matthew walked closer to her and she turned and kissed him on the mouth, pulling their heads together with her petite hands. "I promised myself I would do that after you and Jacob saved our lives. Where is Jacob?" Sarah asked as she looked around for him.

"He went to escort a prisoner to the stockade," Matthew commented. "He will see you at dinner later."

"Let's gather your luggage and take you to the hotel. You will be sharing a room with Elizabeth. She was rooming with Evangeline who has taken up residence at her mother's house of late. You will have the room to yourself often," Matthew said, "because she is spending all of her time with Benjamin."

"My goodness, I have a lot to catch up on! And who is Benjamin and why are they together so much?" Sarah asked.

"Yes you do have a great deal to catch up on. Benjamin is my brother and they are to be wed soon." Matthew smiled, "They will live in their new plantation, Hidden Oaks, just up the river from town."

"Come, let's get you situated and we will go for a walk and I will bring you up to date as quickly as I can. You will have to meet Two-Jacks and his girlfriend, Dona. Then again, there is Abraham, but most important of all is Enoch. Enoch is the most interesting person with the most unbelievable story that you will ever meet," Matthew declared.

After getting Sarah and her things situated, Matthew walked into the courtyard, at the center of the hotel, to find Jacob, Thomas and John waiting there with their pipes and sipping Irish whiskey that John had procured from Captain Wetzel.

"Step back inside and retrieve that pipe of yours, Matthew," Jacob insisted.

Once they were all settled, Jacob passed around some pungent pipe tobacco he acquired from one of the boat captains recently.

"This is some of the most popular tobacco coming out of North Carolina these days," Jacob told them. "It has a special aroma and it is easy on the palate. I thought we would have a smoke to celebrate the conclusion of this operation."

"Henry Huggins, alias Henry Stone, informed me he has rounded up several of Carver's associates that were tied directly to the counterfeiting operation. One in particular that you will be pleased to note is Simon Bartlett. He became unbelievably cooperative when faced with a long prison sentence. It looks like he will agree to name names with the promise of a lesser sentence. That will be up to the Federals to decide, I would suppose."

"Yes," Matthew agreed, "the feds will step in and take over from here. I will write up an extensive report detailing the whole operation and all the facts that I can. I will send it to the attention of Secretary McCullough. Before we go to eat, I will send him a telegram that our mission has been successful. This is not the end, but the beginning.

We knew that counterfeiters were hard at work and we had to get a foothold into their operation. This will give us a starting point for men like Huggins and women like Madelyn Cooper to infiltrate the inner works of the organization. Once we stomp out one fire, others will pop up. Wherever there is an opportunity to make money, legally or illegally, people will jump at the chance. Carver was a big time operator and hopefully this will produce leads that will put us on the path to further arrests."

"Thomas, are you going to pour that whiskey or just look at it until it pours itself?"

"Well, yes, but I was just listening to what you were saying! Here take a glass and hold it while I pour," Thomas said as he handed him a glass.

"I think we had better take a drink before I tell you about the next item of interest." Matthew leaned back in his chair and stared up at the overhanging banana trees in their corner of the courtyard as if he expected eavesdroppers to be overhead.

Leaning forward, Matthew indicated he wanted to share something very important. Matthew spoke, "I have communicated with Secretary McCullough about the prize money for winning the poker tournament and the other table winnings too. To my surprise and shock he told me that all we were responsible for was repaying the ten thousand dollars in gold that we borrowed from the bank on a Federal I.O.U. It was money that he fully expected us to lose in the tournament."

"Oh, there was another development. The rest of the gold from the poker tournament was seized along with the other assets of the riverboat after it was established that it all was a part of the Carver operation."

"You see, they didn't expect Thomas to win. We were lucky that George McAlister and Nicholas Rosales were not in the game to win and bowed out as a courtesy to us. It became known through certain circles that some covert operation was underway to take down John Carver. It was becoming more obvious that things were unnaturally stacked against Carver when he met resistance at the docks and the land grab and then the tables. I believe he felt things were beginning to unravel for him; however, arrogance clouded his judgment."

John leaned in and spoke, "So, are you telling us that we can have that money to ourselves?"

"McCullough knows me and expects me to do the right thing." Matthew placed his left hand across his upper lip and his chin as he held his pipe in his right hand. "We are due payment for our time worked thus far. I have been taking care of expenses with money the government has provided. I am responsible for an accurate accounting of all that happens. We have used some of the counterfeit money for only those things that are directly related to the job. We haven't passed bad money for legitimate debt like lodging or food. The only phony money used was for things like gambling on the boats and to pass around to create interest from possible suspects. That was how we first got Albert Goldsmith's interest by inserting a few fake bills in with the payment for those fine clothes we bought from his department store. I have been keeping records of everything and that includes what is due us for compensation. We work on a monthly allotment and will be paid once I turn in our requests. They will most likely issue a demand note for the bank that we can cash. I believe we should put the winnings in a safe and secure place so we can have it for future operations as we deem necessary. That is what I believe would be the responsible thing to do; but, what is a secure place?"

"Wouldn't a bank be as secure as any place else, or maybe more?" Thomas asked.

"You would think that would be the case," Matt replied, "however, these are not the best of times, neither Northern or Southern banks are quite as secure as you may think. A disreputable banker could clean out the vault and take the next boat, train, or fast horse out of town."

"With that said, then who can we trust?" Jacob asked no one in general.

"It isn't money that we plan to reinvest to create wealth; however, we don't want to just hide it on some remote island like pirates of old to be lost forever. It is to be used for government purposes and it has to be accessible by each of us in the event that something was to happen to all of the others," Matthew explained.

"I do have a thought I would like to present to you and see what you think," Matthew explained with a serious expression. "I think we should take the money to a local convent, Ursuline Convent to be specific, located on Chartres Street, here in the French Quarter. I suggest we give them half of the table-winnings for charitable needs and let them store the one hundred-thousand in gold for us until we need it. It will be locked in a strongbox. We could make it necessary to have only one signature from us to release any or all of the money as needed. That would be wise since I trust each of you and all of the others could be in a desperate situation and not able to sign off for the much needed resource."

"What should we do with the other half of the table-winnings?" John asked.

"Well, that is a good question and I believe I have a good answer. There are a lot of widows, orphans, homeless people, black and white, disabled soldiers and generally people in a great deal of need. I have been hearing about this one woman, an Irish woman, from the old county that was orphaned shortly after arriving in this country at the age of nine. She married young and brought her sickly husband down here for his health and he died. Since that time she has been instrumental in helping the orphaned, the poor, the widows, the slave and the disabled soldiers. She is not an educated woman, but she has a heart of gold. She genuinely wants and cares for others. She has been instrumental in establishing orphanages and homes for widows that want to help themselves. She teaches them skills that they can use to restart their lives. What do y'all think about giving the rest to her?" Matthew asked his friends.

Jacob spoke first, "What is her name?"

"Matthew responded, "They call her by several names: *The Bread Woman, Friend of the Orphans, Mother of the Orphans, Angel of the Delta* and simply, *Our Margaret*. I think her name is Margaret Haughery. It sounds like a worthy cause, don't you fellows agree?"

"I think it is an excellent cause. If we hadn't had the good fortune to meet you in the beginning, I might not have made it home and could have easily been on the streets, cold and hungry myself! Thomas here would surely have starved!" John threw in the last comment for good measure.

"I agree with the two of you," Jacob concluded.

Matt looked at Thomas, "What say you, Thomas?"

"Well, I agree that it is a good cause, and it wasn't rightfully my money since I was using government money to enter the contest." Thomas paused and looked around, "Sounds like the right thing to do."

"There is one more thing I have to tell you," Matthew added. "Secretary McCullough said I should give each of you a bonus when the job was completed if you were still alive. It didn't go unnoticed that you risked your lives on many occasions. He left it up to me to decide how much. I think one thousand dollars for each, taken from the gold portion is sufficient; however, he has one stipulation."

"Now we get down to brass tax," Thomas shouted.

"Yes, he asked for one simple favor. He would like for you to be available for the next mission that he assigns, if your services are needed, and within reason that is." Matt looked around at each of his friends and asked, "How do you feel about that?"

After some thought John replied, "That sounds like a reasonable request. It also would depend on what other obligations we may have at that time and if you were able to get in touch with us."

"I agree with that too," Jacob indicated, "as long as I can work that within the parameters of Federal Marshal and Cherokee Liaison to Washington."

"McCullough has already gone through the proper channels and has the President's highest approval for your continued support to any and all efforts of the Treasury Department. He has begun calling our group *The Secret Service* more often in the presence of his cabinet, says Secretary McCullough," Matthew reported.

"What about me?" Thomas asked. "Who knows where I will be?"

Matt laughed, "I know where to find you. You will be wherever your wife tells you to be!"

"Now, what the devil is that suppose to mean?" Thomas demanded.

John had a reply, "Thomas, you are blinder than Enoch, I swear at times you don't have a clue!"

"Now, don't you start swearing at me, John. I don't think that man is really blind! He can see things others can't see and shoot things others can't shoot," Thomas surmised.

"I agree with them," Jacob chimed in, "I am going to take a bet on just how many kids you are going to have and how soon!"

Thomas was getting frustrated and overwhelmed, "I think y'all have lost your minds or just gone plumb crazy!"

They all laughed and Thomas just sat there confused and sulking.

Later on that afternoon, approaching the evening hour, the group was beginning to come together. Enoch and Marguerite placed a sign on the door of the café that it was closed for a special occasion and walked down to Antoine's Restaurant to dine with Mr. Antoine himself.

Elizabeth was escorted by Benjamin; it was his first time out since the attack. He was quickly regaining his strength, but it would take some time for his broken ribs to heal.

Dona had Two-Jacks escort her. She was a very attractive young woman, small in stature, but large in charm. Amazingly, she had Two-Jack's hair cut and he was dressed up like no one had ever seen him before. It was an amazing reformation for a man that spent his entire life on the edge of civilization.

Evangeline and Frances were driven in their carriage by Abraham, coming from Uptown. They picked up Thomas and John as they walked to dinner.

Matthew, Sarah and Jacob stood outside the restaurant to greet them as they arrived.

Abraham said he would be waiting for them when they came out. This was not a place where he felt comfortable. It was too soon since he was fresh out of slavery and knew little of the white man's ways or their refinements He had lived in the shadows until Matthew and his friends lifted him out.

When everyone had gathered outside the restaurant, a lady of the night approached them as she sashayed down the street. "Hey Red," speaking to Thomas in particular, "Would you like to go for a ride?"

There was a sudden commotion as someone bolted from the center of the group, like a cannonball being fired from a cannon. She stopped next to the woman of questionable intentions and grabbed her by the hair. It was Evangeline, for the entire world to see.

"I'll snatch every hair from your head if you so much as look at my man! Do you understand me, *hussy?*"

Trembling with a sudden and real fear the woman stuttered, "*Yes, yes I do, I do understand!*"

Evangeline shoved the woman and she disappeared into the night. Everyone looked at Evangeline with surprise and satisfaction, but no one more than Thomas.

Evangeline walked over to Thomas and slid her hand beneath his arm and held tightly. Thomas stood there with his mouth open.

"Are we going to eat or just stand around all night?" she asked.

"I think it is high time we go in and eat now that is finally settled," Enoch declared.

Not a word was spoken by Thomas throughout most the dinner and *even less* afterwards.

Monsieur Alciatore greeted them as they entered his restaurant, Antoine's, and seated them at a special table selected especially for them. It was almost a private room, but it was in view of diners as they congregated for the evening; it afforded them some semblance of privacy without losing the ambience of the dining experience that the restaurateur worked so hard to achieve.

"Good Evening, Madame Marguerite, it is a pleasure to finally meet the charming lady that has begun to establish a reputation for excellent dining to rival my offerings," Antoine noted as he took her hand, placing it to his lips and lightly kissing it.

"Thank you kind sir for flattering me," Marguerite replied, but any acclaim that my humble diner has garnered can only attest to the expertise of Mr. Enoch entirely. I am flattered that you are even aware of the fledgling enterprise."

"Do not fool yourself, for my own enterprise was once only a dream of a young man fresh off the boat from Paris with high hopes and lots of energy to exhaust. Your success will mirror your hard work and faith in yourself. More importantly than my speech, I want to offer you something to celebrate your family's reunion of which I have been told."

With a motion to a waiter who stood to his rear, Antoine took one of the bottles which the waiter had on his serving platter. "I would like to present this special champagne that is produced in the region of the same name in France. Please accept this as my gift to you."

They drank the champagne and enjoyed the marvelous dinner that Antoine had prepared especially for them. The evening was the most joyous that they had ever experienced. Two-Jacks and Dona enjoyed fine dining like they had never known. Two-Jacks did not partake of the alcohol and Dona followed his lead. He did not want to perpetuate the image that most people had of Indians and alcohol; however, he laughed and watched the events all the same.

Marguerite wanted to share the struggles of her life with her family. She shared with them her adventures after meeting the great pirate, Jean Lafitte and leaving her family in the Caribbean. She never believed he would have put her on the auction block. She admitted her actions were wrong. She shouldn't have placed that curse on him. She was young and naive. Only a child would have thought that she was the only woman of a famous pirate that traveled the world and visited all of the finest ports around.

Frances opened up after her mother told so candidly her misfortune and shame of thinking herself special because she was a pirate's mistress. It hurt Frances to recount how she avoided the advances of previous slavers to give in to Mr. Bolling, the father of both Sarah and Evangeline. She felt that he would be different and provide something special for them; however, he buckled to the pressure his wife applied and sold Frances just as her mother had been sold on the block at about the same age.

Evangeline felt herself more fortunate to have avoided the shame of public display and to be sold as would someone selling a prized cow at a cattle auction. She had fond memories of her father, but her feelings were never the same after he allowed her mother to be taken from her.

Growing up with Sarah was special because she never made her feel less than an equal. She was aware that things weren't equal the older they got. Beaus would come and take Sarah out for events that often occurred on the plantations, but she was never a part of that life, even though she was white enough to pass as her sister, but with dark hair.

Mr. Bolling was always nice to her and made allowances for her and her Uncle John. It was more apparent to her that her father was changing as the war went on. He was not as stable and sure-footed as he was before the war. He was more volatile than ever. He was never the same after the forced sale of Frances. It hurt him to his soul. The end of the war and the impending freedom of the slaves were the final straw. He felt his family was about to be broken up and his mind thought the best thing was to destroy them. It was obvious to Sarah that her father had gone crazy, and he could have killed her and her mother just as easily, once he had started the killing spree.

It was a brave and heroic thing that Sarah did to take her father's life. She would have nightmares for the rest of her life about that day; however, she knew there was no other choice, but to stop him from killing the slaves. Her own flesh and blood was among them. How could she have allowed Evangeline to die in a burning barn? She could not, there was no other choice, and she made it! She loved her father and wept secretly for her loss.

Right there at dinner she thanked the four men that showed up to witness and console her in that moment of need. She also thanked Matthew and Jacob for returning and saving them from the marauding Confederate and Yankee renegades that came through and would have killed them all, slave and white, to find the gold rumored to be on the plantation. Sarah explained that her father had put his gold in Northern banks for safe keeping before the war started. That did not satisfy the renegades. They were torturing John and would have surely killed him to get at what they believed was a hidden treasure, had it not been for the heroic efforts of Matthew and Jacob.

Evangeline felt the need to reveal something to Sarah. "I have a secret I must share with you Sarah."

"What is it, little sister?" Sarah asked lovingly.

"There is gold hidden on the plantation," Evangeline began to explain.

"What are you talking about? Father never said anything about any gold hidden on the plantation!" Sarah replied.

"No, he didn't tell you about it. He only told Uncle John and me about it. As a matter of fact, he had John help him bury it so no one else could tell about it. He placed a letter explaining his actions in one of his favorite books in the library. The book is called *Walden*, written by Henry D. Thoreau; he told me to remember that book. He would test John and me on the name of the book to be certain we remembered. He showed me the book once and let me hold it so I would recognize it later."

"But why did he hide the money from mother and me," Sarah asked.

"What I remember is this. He said that he put away enough money to take care of his family in the event of his death. He put it in Yankee banks so when and if the South fell you would not be destitute or lose the plantation. This gold that he buried was for John and me to start a new life after the war. He knew that John would take care of the other slaves before thinking of himself. That was what I believe he really wanted. His true motivation was to provide for the care of his beloved slaves. You know we were his family too. His parents and grandparents left us in his care and he was truly affectionate to each one of his slaves. We knew he loved us and that was why we walked into that barn and allowed him to lock the door behind us on that sad night," Evangeline spoke with tears flowing down her cheeks. "I know you love us too and

it will forever haunt you that it fell on you to take our father's life. I
have always loved you Sarah!"

"I am sorry we had to keep it a secret from you. Father told me not
to tell anyone. John did not tell anyone, and neither did I. I believe one
of those Confederate renegades must have been from the community
because folks often assumed that Mr. Bolling was hiding his gold on
the place since he did not keep it with the local banks. They were just
guessing is what I think, but I know this for certain, Uncle John would
have gone to his grave without telling them about the gold. He knew
they would've killed everyone if they got the gold. They would not have
left any witnesses." Evangeline wiped her tears.

"That is my secret and I am glad that I don't have to hide it anymore. It has been a heavy burden for Uncle John and me. He will not
do anything with it until we talk about it. So as far as I know it is still
buried where they put it."

"I am sorry that this was one of the burdens you had to carry. I
know the burden of living in the slave community and knowing your
father is white wasn't easy. I could never enjoy the privileges that I had
while knowing you existed in the shadows. I just hope and pray that
one day we will find it in our hearts to come together as a people after
slavery and the war to end it. Wars don't make friends, they tear people
apart. I believe the war has created another cancer on our country. First,
the ugly sin that slavery was allowed to exist in a country that values
freedom, and secondly, the war to bring our country together and put
an end to slavery has created a divide that may be harder to bridge."

Sarah turned and faced Frances and Marguerite and asked them,
"Will you have me as part of your family?"

Marguerite rose from her seat and walked over to Sarah. Sarah got
up and walked into Marguerite's open arms.

"Yes, my baby, today I have one daughter and two new grand-
daughters! If Thomas and Evangeline will follow nature's course, I will
have great-grandchildren too!" Marguerite smiled as she proclaimed
her joy.

Evangeline and everyone else at the table laughed, but Thomas, he did not know what to say. He just sat there with a blank stare on his face.

Enoch spoke, "Did Thomas leave the room?"

"No, Enoch, he is right over here beside Jacob. I think he has lost his voice," John replied.

"But he hasn't lost his appetite. I believe he will regain his composure in due time. It sometimes takes him a little longer to get with the program," Matt joked.

"He will be fine. Enoch is teaching me all of the cooking skills I will need. I wasn't sure what everyone was talking about either until that hussy brought me to my senses, and I understood what you all were getting at. I knew he was sweet on me that morning down by the creek when I bested him in fishing. He just hated to come in second to some old girl," Evangeline explained.

"I think you two should make it a double wedding with Benjamin and me," Elizabeth said.

"Now, just wait a minute here folks!" Thomas finally spoke up. "Yes, I am in the room, Enoch! I can hear everything you are saying, but I just can't believe you would talk about a man like he was not there. And here I am sitting right in front of you. I may not be the sharpest tack in the box but I do catch on eventually. Evangeline ..."

"Yes, dear, do you wish to speak to me?"

"Yes, that is why I called your name! Now slow down one minute. Y'all have gotten me married and are expecting children just anytime and that is just since we walked into the restaurant. I must admit I am especially fond of Evangeline and think she will make a good wife; *however*, now doggonit, look at me, I am starting to talk like Matthew. Anyway, I should at least get the chance to propose to her by myself and when I feel like it. Don't you think that is fair? Am I asking too much?" Thomas asked them as a group.

"Then are you asking me to marry you, Thomas?"

"Now, don't you go puttin' words in my mouth!"

"Well, if you aren't interested then, maybe I can find someone who is'," Evangeline remarked.

"No, you don't need to go looking around for anyone else! It's just a man likes to feel that he can make his own decisions, that's all!"

Thomas stood up and took Evangeline's hand and instructed her to stand also. "Evangeline ..."

"Yes Thomas ..."

"Will you marry me?" Thomas proposed.

"Yes, I will be glad to marry you Thomas!" she said and pulled him close to kiss him hard and long on the lips.

A roar of cheers rose up from the table drawing the attention of other diners in the restaurant.

"I do declare I haven't been kissed like that since little Sally Ketchum caught up with me in the schoolyard when we was ten!" Thomas remarked.

"I am going to tell you only once and you had better listen good, Thomas! Ain't nobody else allowed to kiss on you from here on out, except me. You better listen to what I am telling you because if you don't I will go down to that voodoo woman and put a hex on you! Am I clear?" Evangeline gave him some strong warnings.

"Yes, you are clear. And let me tell you something, sweetheart, I am the only one wearing the pants in this family, unless I give orders otherwise. Am I clear?" Thomas asked in a softer tone with his question.

"Yes, darling, you are the man in this here household. I will make sure not to forget it either. I guess we is all clear, mister!" she said.

Everyone laughed.

"See here, there you go riling me up again!" Thomas smiled and kissed her once more for good measure. "I think I could get used to this in due time."

The hot summer days passed as slowly as a snake in the shade. A rich man couldn't buy a cool breeze. The stale and humid air lingered worse than the smell of a wet dog; however, life rolled on.

Benjamin and Elizabeth mailed out invitations to friends and family. They wanted to get married on the first day of September. Benjamin's parents came down early and spent most of the month of

August with them. They still had a great deal of catching up to do with Matthew.

Mr. and Mrs. Walker followed two weeks after the O'Briens arrived. They wanted to meet Benjamin and get the lay of the land at Hidden Oaks Plantation. It was an excellent opportunity for Mr. Walker to purchase some of the latest farming implements. The war had put a damper on replenishing his inventory. He had recently acquired a new zest for business since the memorial service held that spring. Coming to terms with the death of his only son Carson gave him a new lease on life. He felt a different kind of energy just knowing that he would have a new son-in-law as an addition to his family. He was especially interested in the new fangled, sit-on plow that Benjamin had invented. He heard that Ben had applied for a patent on the implement. Both of Elizabeth's parents were interested in meeting Benjamin because she spoke so glowingly about him in her letters.

Dona and Two-Jacks went down and stood before the Justice of the Peace. They also took the *customary* vows of her tribe. In other words they got themselves *hitched*. And Two-Jacks had his name changed to Jack Jackson, making them the Jacksons. That was to satisfy his new bride. She said she would only agree to marry him if he agreed to change his name. He also agreed to never name any of his sons Jack.

His parents were deceased and he had no reason to go back to Jackson, Mississippi. He was given a section of land by Benjamin to build on and farm, if those were his intentions. He and Benjamin had been friends since Ben was old enough to go exploring and hunting with him. He wasn't as young as Benjamin or Thomas, but he must have been in his early thirties; nonetheless, he looked like the sort of man that could easily live to be a hundred. That was another reason for him to marry a younger bride.

Matthew requested time to attend his brother's wedding from his superior, Secretary of Treasury Hugh McCullough, and it was granted. He did report to the local commander of the U.S. Army garrisoned in New Orleans. He was instructed to report to Colonel Beauregard, to whom he had already built a rapport.

He made out a complete written report of the mission detailing all of the events and a record of agents and Pinkertons that had fallen in the course of their duty. He outlined a future plan of action for the course of the Secret Service in respect to combating the problem of counterfeiting. He had some good ideas and recommendations for Agency procedures in the field. He noted that a manual should be developed and would need constant updates and revisions. This he did in preparation for his report to McCullough when he arrived back in Washington.

Jacob also chose to stick around to see the wedding. He wanted to make the return trip with Matthew. They had become close friends and worked well together. He had business to take care of while in Washington, some for the Indian Bureau and the Cherokee Nation, and some for the U.S. Marshal Service, of which he was still a sworn officer of the law. In his short time in New Orleans he made new friends and acquaintances, some through the banking circles and others by happenstance. He was not bored with the extra time he had on his hands because he always had people wanting him to visit or spend time riding horses or playing cards with other friends at their homes and enjoying leisurely times with them.

Thomas' time was always occupied by Evangeline and things she wanted him to do. He was also given a section of land from Benjamin and Elizabeth's plantation. It was a gift this time from Elizabeth to her dear friends, Evangeline and Thomas. She had grown to love them as a sister and a brother. It would serve her well to have good friends close by.

Thomas picked out a spot with a beautiful stand of live oaks. There was plenty of field to cultivate and some that was excellent for raising cattle and horses. Beautiful creeks, filled with bream and perch, idled through the property from north to south. He paid a gentleman to build them a modest house and barn using the labor of returning war veterans.

He also purchased a cottage in town within walking distance from Frances. He knew that Evangeline needed time to get to know her mother better. He had enough money with the bonus paid out by Matthew and money taken from gambling; however, he and Evangeline agreed that gambling boats and gambling houses were a thing of the past. As much as he regretted having to leave that life behind, he knew it was for the best.

Thomas discussed with Evangeline the need to visit his family in South Georgia sometime in the future to let them know he was alright and to introduce his bride. They agreed that a letter would suffice until it was safer to travel. Things were still dangerous because hostilities hadn't completely vanished.

John, unlike his friends and companions, was not busy with plans for his future. He was not leaving town after the wedding was over or starting a new life with a soul mate. He was coming to terms with what he had learned about himself of late. He decided to purchase a small cottage that sat vacant in his parent's neighborhood. He recognized the potential that it had. It was well shaded to provide for cooler living in the hotter months. The winter was of no concern in New Orleans.

The message that he had received that day after the battle at Appomattox was still fresh in his memory. He was told *that it was not his time, and to go home and find his place.* He wasn't entirely certain just what this had meant for him, but he was getting closer to an answer. He realized that his new gift of communicating with spirits held in limbo was beneficial to say the least. It was odd, but it was not frightening to him to stand before the spirit of someone that lingered and wanted to be released from that undesirable state. He did not choose when, where or who to communicate with, but it seemed that they sought him out.

His dreams were just as vivid. He had dreamed about imminent danger and his friends. He was a receptacle for things much bigger than him. Maybe that was what was meant by *go home and take your place.* There was so much that needed to be done in his world, but he knew he could not cure all of life's ills. But he could do his part in protecting the people that he loved. What more could one ask for, but to be a positive force in the lives of those near and dear to him. It was given for him to understand that God had a purpose for his life and he must search out God's plan each and every day.

Enoch was quickly establishing himself as a man of great skill. He was no longer that Negro that could cook, but he had become a chef that just happened to be a *man of color*. He helped turn the Magnolia Café and Inn into a destination for the palate; but not without Marguerite's charm and Frances' burgeoning skill in the kitchen. People of notoriety often stayed in the inn when they visited New Orleans. It was becoming more than just a diner.

Abraham had also found a purpose in that environment as well. His skills at procuring the best fruits, vegetables, meats and seafood made him invaluable. He was the perfect man to take care of many needs around the café. He found a permanent residence at the Inn.

The growth of Abraham from the beaten-down former slave with very little self confidence to a man of many talents was largely due to the insight of Enoch. He had a vision of what the man could become, not of what others saw in him. He looked into the man's soul and saw a brighter light and lifted the bushel that covered it. He understood that the freedom that was afforded them was not given, but was fought for by the blood of others, and they would have to continue to fight for it continually or lose it forever.

Frances was enjoying her life; a new world that she could hardly imagine. She woke each day and had to remind herself that this was real, but she wasn't sure it would stay that way. Any person that lived in the bondage of slavery never assumed that a life of freedom was permanent, or guaranteed. She hoped and prayed that things would never go back to the way they were. She wanted her children and grandchildren to live as free people.

There was always the threat of Etienne returning and getting his revenge. He was always controlled by his lust and need for Frances' inner strength. According to word on the street and throughout the French Market he was living life as a wildman. He would not leave her alone until he was dead. This wasn't what she wanted, but it might be the only thing that could stop a man like him that had lost everything including his pride. This was her burden of fear. He was now living in a kind of mental bondage.

The day of the wedding had finally arrived. With a great deal of pushing and cajoling, Elizabeth and Benjamin convinced Thomas and Evangeline to hold their wedding on the same day and have a double wedding on the grounds of Hidden Oaks.

Sarah was a staunch advocate for the idea of them being married on the same day. She didn't know what she would do after the wedding. She knew that her mother was well looked after because John, Evangeline's uncle, had taken special interest in her wellbeing. There was a loyalty there stronger than blood. She did not understand the depths of John's devotion to her mother and all things concerning the plantation. It was true that her father went first to John to resolve issues concerning the slaves and the welfare of the business of managing the plantation.

Sarah got to spend much more time with Matthew while in New Orleans. She thought she felt a kinship with him when they were back in Virginia; although, who wouldn't feel a strong attraction to a bright, handsome, and resourceful young man passing through. All semblance of stability had been destroyed along with the futures of all of the brightest young men that returned maimed, or had died on the battlefield.

Sarah and Matthew spent countless hours walking through New Orleans, or riding a riverboat, or taking a streetcar uptown or riding horses out to Benjamin's place. They laughed and shared many great meals and sat in the courtyards enjoying a glass of wine in the moonlight; however, they did not talk about the future until one day when Sarah reached over and gave him a kiss in a playful moment. It was a surprise to both of them. They stopped and looked at each other and Matthew leaned in to kiss her. It was a beautiful moment.

Matthew explained how he had felt that same connection during those days in Virginia. He was impressed with the strength that she exhibited when she took the life of her father to save the lives of so many others. He had not forgotten her strength, or her beauty.

"I am torn in my thoughts and feelings," Matthew explained. "I have been living a life of service for so long that it doesn't require me to think about the future and then you came along. What kind of life do I have to offer someone like you?"

"That is a question neither of us have an answer for, Matthew," she replied. "What kind of life do I have to offer you, a man that has seen it all? I feel like my life's experience has so little appeal to attract a worldly person as you. I know this about myself; I don't want to return to Virginia and the life that I left behind. It was the life my parents chose to live. Maybe they did not have a choice, but I do. I would love to continue on here in New Orleans for the time being. It isn't because of the attraction of this exciting and lively city, and it is all of that, but I think it is because I have friends here and I want to be near them. You and your friends have made me one of you."

"Matt, I don't need your money. My father left me with more money than I could spend in my lifetime if I take care to manage it correctly."

Sarah took a moment to gather her thoughts. "I felt that same attraction when you rode up and saw the barn burning and me standing there holding the rifle that just killed my father. I saw a strong man that I could be proud to call my mate and my husband."

"I didn't know just what I was going to do after the wedding, go home or what! Now, in this very moment I have decided what I want to do. I will send a wire for funds to be transferred down here to a bank and buy myself a cottage in town. I don't know what tomorrow will bring but I have a plantation in Virginia and I will have a place here as well. It doesn't have to be much, just a place to call home. If you think you want to spend time getting to know me better after you make your trip to Washington then just send a telegram that you are on your way back. My friends will know where I live and get it to me. What do you think about them apples, *Yankee boy?*"

Matthew grabbed her and hugged her close and put her at arm's length. "I do not have any better proposals than that and it will give me a mite to consider on my way to Washington."

"Now," Matthew said, "let's get ready for a wedding. We can ride out together in my carriage."

"I never intended to go without you, Mr. O'Brien!" Sarah said, with a smile.

What a beautiful day for a wedding. Birds were singing songs of joy and flowers were in bloom. People gathered for this joyous event, coming from miles away to join in this celebration of love. Evangeline and Elizabeth's beauty was breathtaking. Benjamin and Thomas had never been so handsome in all of their lives, in spite of the grumbling and discomfort.

Carriages formed a line down the lane out to the river road. Abraham, dressed up like he had never been before, helped the others take the carriages out under the oaks and put them in order after the horses were given water to drink. Numbers were written on a piece of paper and given to the passengers to keep so they could reclaim their carriages later. Colonel Beauregard attended with his wife and so did the Goldsmiths and their children.

Mrs. Lucille Lafontaine was dressed up so lovely you would have thought she was one of the brides. It was the best thing that could happen for her since losing her dear and loving husband so recently. She was the life of the party. She had a family once again to share her life.

To the surprise of everyone but Elizabeth, who wasn't aware of his presence, Parson Jones had traveled down from Charleston and kept hidden until the day of the wedding.

"You didn't think I would miss this event, did you?" he asked Matthew and John. "I was the one to baptize the wee child you see! You should never doubt the fortitude of the shepherd for his flock," Parson Jones declared.

The wedding went off without a hitch. Someone went so far as to bring the piano out onto the lawn to play the wedding hymns. There were some chuckles in the crowd when Thomas almost lost his voice when he was asked to recite the vows, but he overcame. They were now and forever married in the eyes of God and man.

Tables with white linen were set up on the lawn for the wedding cakes and the food served afterwards. Enoch had the event catered by his good friend, Monsieur Antoine Alciatore. People were seated and standing outside under the trees, enjoying the late afternoon breeze that preceded the cooler dusk air, that flowed off the river. Drinks were served by the bartender and punch was made especially for the younger guests and the nondrinkers that attended.

Thomas and Evangeline were standing next to Marguerite. Frances and Enoch were seated while they shared a toast to the bride and groom. Frances turned her head to catch a glimpse of a man on a dark horse charging down the lane from the river road. She could not speak because she was so startled once she recognized the rider to be Etienne.

He pulled back on the reins of his horse as he slid to a stop just in front of Frances. She was frozen with fear. Here was the man that once carried himself in such control covered in filth, bearded and wearing tattered clothes.

"Yes, I know I can never have you and everything I ever held dear is lost to me. I will take that which you hold dear. If I can't have you, I will take your daughter!" He pulled out his pistol and aimed at Evangeline and fired.

As Etienne leveled his gun to fire Thomas screamed, "No ..." and threw himself in front of Evangeline and stopped the bullet as he leaped up in the air with his arms spread skyward. He fell to the ground in front of Evangeline, having taken the bullet meant for her.

A man, but not just any man appeared from thin air; it was an apparition of Jean Lafitte in full regalia. He pulled his pirate's sword and flashed it at the stallion. The horse reared at the sight of a spirit standing before him. When the horse reared, Etienne lost his balance and fell. It was immediately obvious that he had broken his neck when he fell by the awkward position of the body.

Now Frances screamed, but not at the sight of Etienne, but to see the husband of her daughter lying on the ground with his white shirt covered in blood.

"Wake up, wake up! Don't you die on me Thomas!" Evangeline was shouting and shaking him with all of her strength.

John, Matthew and Jacob had rushed to Thomas' aid.

"He is opening his eyes!" John screamed.

"Please, please!" Thomas asked.

"What is it my dear, Thomas?" Evangeline asked.

"Please get off of my chest with your knee!" Thomas asked in a strain voice. "I can't breathe."

Evangeline pulled Thomas to her and hugged him very tightly, "I thought I had lost you my dear husband!"

"Will somebody please do me a favor and get this bullet out of my shoulder before she squeezes me to death," Thomas asked his friends as they gathered around him.

The pirate, the man, Jean Lafitte walked over to Marguerite and said, *"My lady, all curses are absolved,"* as he bowed before her. *"Long may you and our lovely daughter live!"*

He moved his head in John's direction and touched the brim of his hat to acknowledge his friend before he turned and walked away beneath the oaks as if to evaporate into thin air.

THE END

JOEL TERRY MAY writes and paints as he seeks the voice of God in all things. His writing exemplifies his relationship with God and his willingness to obey. He is also the author of *Harvest of the Soul*.